RESOLVED

ALSO BY ROBERT K. TANENBAUM

FICTION

Absolute Rage
Enemy Within
True Justice
Act of Revenge
Reckless Endangerment
Irresistible Impulse
Falsely Accused
Corruption of Blood
Justice Denied
Material Witness
Reversible Error
Immoral Certainty
Depraved Indifference
No Lesser Plea

NONFICTION

The Piano Teacher:
The True Story of a Psychotic Killer
Badge of the Assassin

ROBERT K. TANENBAUM

RESOLVED

ATRIA BOOKS

New York   London   Toronto   Sydney   Singapore

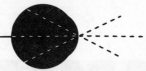

**This Large Print Book carries the
Seal of Approval of N.A.V.H.**

ATRIA BOOKS

1230 Avenue of the Americas
New York, NY 10020

ISBN: 0-7434-6762-0

First Atria Books hardcover edition August 2003

10   9   8   7   6   5   4   3   2   1

ATRIA BOOKS is a trademark of Simon & Schuster, Inc.

Designed by Melissa Isriprashad

For information regarding special discounts for bulk purchases, please contact Simon & Schuster Special Sales at 1-800-456-6798 or business@simonandschuster.com

Manufactured in the United States of America

To those most special,
Patti, Rachael, Roger, and Billy
and to the memories of my legendary mentors,
District Attorney Frank S. Hogan
and Henry Robbins

Acknowledgment

Again, and yet again, all praise belongs to Michael Gruber, whose genius and scholarship flow throughout and who is primarily and solely responsible for the excellence of this manuscript and whose contribution cannot be overstated.

—————— Now

The governor was late. No governor, no ceremony; the distinguished people gathered in the private office of the district attorney muttered to themselves and to their pals. They brought out their cell phones and their Date Minders and juggled their schedules. The office buzzed with talk, quiet or annoyingly loud, directed at people not physically present, so that the place took on the appearance of a day room in a mental institution. The DA himself, John X. Keegan, did not talk on either a cell or a regular phone, but simply relaxed, smiling, a drink in his big fist, and chatted quietly to a small group of men who were too big to bother about their own schedules. Keegan wore a wide white smile on his broad red face. It had hardly been off that face (not even in slumber) since he had gotten the news of his appointment some months ago. Today was his last day as district attorney after nearly a decade on the job. He was going to become a federal judge, a lifetime's ambition, or rather an important step toward his real ambition. It had never escaped Jack Keegan's notice that Chief Justice Earl Warren had started as a DA.

One other person in the room, now slouched against a corner of the long conference table in the center of the office, was equally unconcerned with schedules. His own smile was thin and a little false, because he disliked events of this kind. Even slouching, he was the tallest person in the room (at six-five), well-knit, and still athletic in these, his middle years. He had a peculiar flat, sallow face, close-cropped brown hair just starting to show gray on the sides, and eyes set slightly aslant over strong cheekbones. These eyes were his signal feature apart from his hugeness: bright, inquisitive, don't-███-with-me eyes, gray in color, shot with flecks of gold. An ethnologist observing the room as if it contained a herd of beasts would have noted that this tall man, like the DA, occupied the center of a circulation, a node of power. People came up to him, said a few words, smiled harder at him than he did at them, and were gently pressed away by others. The man's name was Roger Karp, called Butch by everyone, and he was the chief assistant district attorney, the operational leader of the six hundred or so lawyers who prosecuted criminal cases in the County of New York.

Taking advantage of an interval in which no one was in his face, Karp walked over to a window and peered out into the gathering gloom. It was snowing harder. Fat white flakes descended from the dust bunny—colored sky, obscuring the dun buildings across the street. This was why the governor was late.

Karp checked his watch. Clearly the ▓▓ damn thing would not begin at two, as scheduled. As if answering his unspoken desire to know when it would start, someone dinged on a glass. The governor's advance person, a thin redhead in a bright red suit, announced that both Teterboro and La Guardia Airports were socked, JFK was iffy, and so the governor's plane had been cleared for MacArthur Field, farther out on the island. He'd be landing shortly and would then come into the city by car. Regrets. The weather. If you'd all reassemble at four . . .

Murmurs and sighs from the crowd,

which began to move toward the door, the juniors swiftly, the elders with more stately pace.

"He'd better use the Batmobile," said a voice at Karp's elbow: Murrow, his special assistant. "Can you imagine what the expressway's going to be like in this weather?"

"He's the governor, he'll find a way," said Karp, casting an eye over the man's outfit and frowning. "What is that you're wearing, Murrow?"

"This? A Harris tweed jacket, whipcord slacks, a Brooks shirt and tie. Why?"

"I mean that," said Karp, pointing.

"Oh, you mean this plum-colored velvet waistcoat, with gilt buttons. It's seasonal."

"So is a Santa suit, but we don't usually wear them in the courthouse."

"I could rush home through the freezing snow and change into something more funereal. Have I made you ashamed of me? Again?"

"A little. Look, I'm going to go hide in my office. Spread the word that I'm out of the building. Tell Flynn to hold the calls, too. Except from my family."

Karp glowered in a friendly way and vanished more easily than you would have thought possible for someone that large.

His office was across the hall from the DA's, and its door had a jolly wreath on it, like all the others in the suite. Karp frowned at the wreath, went in, took off his sufficiently funereal navy pin-striped jacket, and sat down in his big black judge's chair. He swiveled and faced the window.

For a while he amused himself by seeing how long he could keep a single snowflake in focus. The burble of voices outside declined in volume. Karp knew that there would be a coven of old pols gathered around Keegan, sipping discreetly at his scotch, glad of the unscheduled demiholiday. They would be stroking or stinging one another in the ancient old-pol way. When pressed, Karp knew he could slip into that style and stroke and sting with the best of them, establishing himself as an in-guy, as he would clearly have to do now that Keegan was going. The difference was that, unlike Jack Keegan, he didn't love it. He sucked no nectar from the schmoozefests. They left him drained and irritable, as now. If he were a little more paranoid than he was (which was more paranoid than most people not actually on lithium), he would have imagined that Jack had done it for just that reason: to make him writhe. He leaned forward and pressed his nose against the glass. The streetlights were already on, made into haloes by the snow. The glass was cold. A chill ran across his shoulders, and he got up to put on his jacket. It was colder in his office than it had been this morning, and he recalled something, a memo, about the building's boilers being replaced over the Christmas break. They must have already started the work.

A sharp rap on the door. "Go away!" he said, too low to be heard. Murrow appeared. He whipped neatly through the doorway and pulled it closed in one motion, like a character in a farce. He was holding an irregularly shaped object draped in a bar towel. This he deposited on Karp's credenza, and drew away the draping with a flourish, revealing a plastic tray with a bottle and two snifter glasses on it.

"What's that?"

"It's cognac," said Murrow. "It's a kind of liquor made from wine."

"I know what cognac is. You know I don't drink."

"You can learn how. In exchange for everything you've taught me over the years. It's only fair." He shivered. "My God, it's freezing in here! Can't you turn up the heat?"

"They're fixing the boilers."

"Well, we'll certainly be perfectly Dickensian by the time the gov gets here." He uncorked the cognac and poured a generous slug into each glass. "Aren't you sorry now you don't have a cozy plum-colored waistcoat?"

Murrow sat on the worn leather couch across from Karp's desk and raised his glass. "To the future, or at least to an end to this horrible year!"

"Oh, I'll drink to that," said Karp, sipping. A surprise: the liquor was stingingly warm, and seemed to expand like a gas into his sinuses. He held the glass balloon up to the light. "This isn't bad. It doesn't have that boozy taste."

"No. Mr. Hennessy has it removed when he puts the XO on the bottle. It's the beverage of the ruling class. You should get used to it."

"I can live without it," said Karp, taking another small sip. His face became warm. The roiling in his gut, which had begun with his awakening that morning, diminished.

"Again?" asked Murrow, holding out the bottle, grinning.

"Sure. Why not? Jack and his pals are hitting the scotch in there. We might as well all get loaded. When the governor gets here we can all lean against each other and sway."

"I notice you're not in there."

"No. I'm not one of the boys. I'd cramp their style, and Jack deserves a couple of hours of fun. It's a big day for him, too."

"Why aren't you?" asked Murrow. "One of the boys. I always wondered about that. You're a boy and you've been here since the year one."

"It's a long story."

"We have time."

"It's longer than that. Let's just say they don't really trust me. Let's just say . . ."

The office door burst open and a woman walked in. Murrow stared up at her, higher up than he ever had at a woman before, for she was over six feet tall, even without the thick-heeled knee boots she wore. She also had on a knee-length dark leather coat lined with grayish fleece and a flat gray wool hat, dotted with melting snow.

"So, here's where you're hiding!" she exclaimed. "I should have known. And a secret drinker, too, I see. Who's your friend, and will he pour me a shot of . . . what is that, cognac?"

"You'll have to ask him," said Karp. "Murrow, this is Ariadne Stupenagel, a friend of my wife's. A reporter." His tone on this last word was what he might have used saying "pedophile."

Murrow stood up and shook hands with the woman. A man of moderate size, he felt as if he were back in third grade. He tried not to stare, but this was difficult; she seemed to invite staring: the bottle green eyes, heavily made up with mascara, shadow, and cynicism; the big beak; the enormous, ravenous-looking mouth slashed with orange-pink lip gloss. She whipped off her hat and flung it onto a filing cabinet, spraying droplets.

"I'm sorry, we only have two glasses," Murrow said.

"Oh, that's not a problem," replied Stupenagel, reaching into the capacious canvas sack she carried and coming out with a heavy cut-glass Old-Fashioned tumbler. As he poured, Murrow noticed that the bag was stenciled with Cyrillic lettering and was extremely dirty.

"Absent friends," said Stupenagel, raising her glass. She drank deeply, sighed. "Oh, this is good. I should come here more often." She plopped herself down on the couch and stretched out her legs, which were draped in a full shin-length skirt of black wool. Murrow estimated that these legs were very nearly as long as he was.

"I thought you were in Afghanistan," said Karp.

"Oh, I was, I was, but it's winter and the facilities are not all one might wish. They should only stage wars in warm climates. Plus the men won't talk to you, and how many stories can you read about the plight of Afghan women? So I'm back in what I think I now have to call my homeland. How's Marlene?"

The abrupt change of subject was a reporter's trick, but it was a prosecutor's trick, too, and Karp was not discommoded. "She's fine. You should go see her."

"She's still with that kennel business out on the ass end of the island?"

"The dog farm, yes. Business is booming, I hear. Security dogs are a hot item nowadays."

"I'm not a dog person myself. I hear you're breaking up."

"Where did you hear that?"

"Around. I'm a reporter. Is it true? Because if it is, I want to get on the Karp short list."

"You're supposed to be her friend, Stupenagel."

"I am! Ciampi is my dearest pal in the whole wide world, but do you know how few men on the planet there are that I don't have to look down at their bald spot? Of those, eliminate the brainless, the evil, the smelly, the faggots, the needle dicks, what have you got left? You and Bill Bradley, and Bill turned me down already. Ciampi's only five-four. It's not fair."

"No, it's not, and as flattering as it is, I have to tell you I'm not on the market." An image of what it would be like to be in bed with Ariadne Stupenagel crossed unbidden across Karp's interior TV. He had to look away from her then, and his eyes fell on Murrow, who was staring at them, as if at a show.

"I believe Murrow is single," said Karp. "You could fit him with lifts."

"Stilts," said Stupenagel. "But he certainly is cute," she said, turning her gaze full upon him. Murrow felt warmth rising on his neck. She added, "Mm, yes. A lickable item. Maybe you'd like to sit on my lap, Murrow?"

"Yes, I would," said Murrow, "but my Mummy said I mustn't."

A booming man's laugh from Stupenagel, in which, after a pause, the men joined. Karp recalled Marlene once saying that Stupe was the most infuriating and also the most uninfuriating person she knew, someone who would both steal your shoes and give you the shirt off her back.

"In that case, you can pour me another

drink," she said. "Oh, now, this is cozy. A blizzard outside, great changes in the DA, and the death of the year. You know where I was when the story of the century broke a couple of blocks away? In Havana. They wanted me to check if Fidel was actually still alive."

"Did you ▓▓ him?" asked Karp.

"Puh-lease! He could barely get it up in eighty-five. I never worked so hard for a story in my life."

"Yes, Murrow," said Karp, "if you succumb to Stupenagel's charms, you'll be able to share STDs with some of the world's great leaders, past and present."

"That was unkind," she pouted. "See, that's what happens to nice men when they're not getting it regular, they become unkind. Fill him up again, Murrow. Anyway, when Nine Eleven hit I realized there was no point in coming to the city, because everyone was here, so I hopped a flight to London and then to Pakistan, because it was obvious the story was going to be there. I heard you had quite a summer, by the way. Escaped maniacs . . . ?"

"Felix Tighe."

She said, "Yeah, Tighe. I remember the original case. I was in Guat at the time, but I read what the wire services had on it. I recall thinking that it was hard getting all excited about a couple or three people getting killed in New York when we had them in windrows along every road in the country. That was the guy that snatched Marlene, or was that his brother?"

"The brother," said Karp. "And the mom. She was running a Satanic pedophile ring out of a fancy day-care center. The brother was a feeb, and she'd trained him to pick up stray little girls off the streets, like a Labrador retriever. She was aiming to make Felix the next prince of darkness, or whatever, but he liked freelance evil instead. Go have children."

"I thought that whole Satanic ritual in the day-care center was a load of horseshit. Like an urban legend."

"It is," said Karp. "But there's always the exception. One giant alligator really does live down in the sewers, and one poodle really did go into the microwave. This one was it for the Satanic day cares. We never tried the case. The old lady killed herself in custody and the brother died, too, and the only other witnesses were the kids, and I wasn't going anywhere near that."

"Marlene plugged him, didn't she?" asked Stupenagel. "Now it's coming back. God, how the years fly! This was when you were still a rug rat, Murrow. I might have dandled you on my knee. I might still, if you're lucky. Yeah, now that I think about it, that was Marlene's first hit, wasn't it?"

Karp was silent.

"Yeah, it was. But not anywhere near the last. What's the count now, or don't you keep track? No comment? Oh, right, this is talking rope in the house of the hanged, isn't it?" She slapped her cheek. "Naughty, naughty Stupenagel—again! Murrow, this is why I so infrequently get invited back, except regrettably, by horny short men. There was something else about the mother, too, wasn't there? Didn't get a lot of play?"

"Felix was screwing her," said Karp. "They used to meet in a hotel, I understand, her in disguise, him in some kind of trance. It came up in pretrial, the defense feeling out how we would sit with an insanity plea, but Felix put the kibosh on it. 'It never happened,' says Felix, 'my mom was a saint.' I think Ray Guma has to get credit for the best line: 'And here I thought that "mean motherfucker" was just a figure of speech.'"

She laughed. "Dear old Guma. But that's interesting. I wonder if it happens a lot or rarely. Mother-on-son incest. The other kind we know all about, girls blabbing about what bad old Daddy did every time you switch on the ██████ing TV. But the boys don't blab. Does that mean there's nothing there? Silence arouses my journalistic instinct. What about it, boys? Anyone want to confess. Off the record, of course. I'm not on duty."

"Rare, but not unknown," said Murrow after a pause. "A lot of fantasy around it, which is suggestive. Just check out the Internet. As a matter of fact, about ten percent of child sex abuse vics are boys, but that includes dad as the perp, of course. Then there's art. Luna by Bertolucci, Le Souffle au Coeur by Louis Malle."

"My God, he talks!" crowed Stupenagel. "It's a pity you're not up for adoption, Murrow. Or doesn't that hold any interest? I'd wear a housedress and you could be in diapers. No? Then you can refresh my drink."

She drank, and said to Karp, "So, do you think it was Mom who warped him and sent him on a life of crime?"

"I try never to speculate on causation. It's irrelevant, although there's practically never a case where the defense doesn't try to bring up their boy's sad life. A mutt is a mutt."

"Even when he's a cop?"

"Especially then."

"I could never figure out what happened in that thing last summer," she said. "I mean, even after all the shit that's been going down about bad shootings and police brutality, why a cop would even take the chance . . . what did you make of it?"

"Are you back on duty?"

"No. But as a victim of police brutality in four countries, including this one, I have an interest."

"It wasn't a police brutality thing," said Karp. "Not really. It was a police stupidity thing. A hell of a lot more common, to tell you the truth."

"So there must have been a lot of pressure on that case," said the reporter. "White cops, black victim. How come you took the case?"

Karp explained the situation and added, "Even so, I didn't think Jack would let me take it. They usually keep me away from cases with racial overtones, as you know."

"But I don't know. I was out of the country at the time. I'm a foreign correspondent."

"Then what are you doing here?" Karp said, not quite keeping the snarl from his voice. I'm getting drunk, he thought. Am I going to be a mean drunk?

She appeared not to notice. He imagined

people snarled at her all the time, given her personality. She said, "Every place is foreign from the standpoint of someplace else. Pretend I'm reporting on the strange customs of American jurisprudence for a Canadian paper. No, really, all I know is the gossip. You punched out a black reporter is what I heard."

"I didn't punch him out," said Karp. "He got in my face in a hallway and I pushed past him and he tripped on some TV cables. Then a guy fell on him with a TV camera and his face got bruised. There was some tape with me scowling and this little guy with blood streaming down his face. The press made a big thing of it. And it was the case I was working on at the time, that had a lot to do with it."

"Okay, now it's coming back. That was that wacko who was after black grannies. You lost that one, if memory serves. Another racial thing?"

"Not really. It was a good jury. I just got beat. The guy, Rohbling, was a weedy white boy with a lot of money. His family hired the best lawyer in the country and the rest is history. He's in Matteawan now, until the shrinks decide he's not a danger to the community. It happens. The African-American sector was not pleased."

"Was that when they started calling you KKKarp?"

"Around then. They thought I was being insufficiently aggressive. They thought it was funny that a prosecutor who'd won over a hundred straight homicide convictions, mainly, if you want to know, where the defendants were what they call people of color, just couldn't hack it when it came to nailing a rich white guy."

"Did they have a point?" she asked slyly.

Before

1

THE INTERIOR OF NEW YORK STATE GETS
surprisingly hot in the summer, and this was a hot-
ter than usual week, even for the last of August.
The guards at the Auburn Prison, located nearly
in the center of this region, were more than usually interested in the weather reports, for hot
weather does not play well in the cell blocks.
Auburn is a maximum security joint, like Attica,
its more famous sister. Most people have forgotten that in 1929, in a similar hot spell, the prisoners had rebelled and burned the whole place
down. But the guards remember. Prison cell
blocks are not air-conditioned. Air-conditioning
would be coddling convicts and the legislature
will not countenance it, although if it were up to
the guards, they would chill the whole place down
so low that frost would form on the bars.

The fight started on a Monday, which is the
worst day in prison, because Sunday is visiting

day. Those who have received visits from loved ones are pissed off because they can't actually make love with their wives or hug their kids, and the ones who haven't are pissed off because they haven't, and the air is stale and stinking that monkey-house stink, and in the shadeless yard the sun boils the brain. Twelve hundred men, not one of whom has particularly good impulse control, all with little to lose, most with grudges against the world, mingle on that barren plain in the wilting heat. There are gangs. Half the prisoners are black, a third Hispanic, the rest white, and the gangs track this assortment. Someone makes a remark, and if the ethnicity of the remarker and the remarkee differ, that's all it takes. The guard in his tower sees a rapid movement, a coalescence of men's bodies around a center, like dirty gray water sucking down a drain. He goes for his radio and picks up his shotgun. The guards rush out with clubs swinging. They disappear into the mass.

Felix Tighe woke up in the prison infirmary with an aching head and a dull pain in his side. It took him a little while to recall where he was and what had put him there. It was hot, he remembered that, and he was on the bench in the yard, doing bench presses, 380-pound presses, with some Aryan Nation cons around him, also working out, ignoring the niggers at their weights, as usual, and then one of the niggers had said something about the sweet little white-boy ass of Kopman's punk, Lulu, which was bad enough, but then—it was Marvelle, the Crimp, he now recalled—Marvelle had actually grabbed Lulu and started dry-humping him right there in front of everyone, and all the white guys had dropped their weights and gone after him.

Felix had picked up a weight bar and gone in, too. After that it got blurry. He remembers cracking some heads with it, before the screws came in and started whacking everyone they could reach. He touched his side, moved his left arm. It stung, but didn't feel that bad. Someone had shanked him. He'd have to find out who and get even. Felix always got even and everyone knew it. It was one of his two main things, which was why no one had ████ with him after the first week, and now it was going on nineteen years here in Auburn. He was nearly forty-two.

A face swam into his field of view. A thin, pale brown face, the color of a sandy dirt road, shaven-headed, beak-nosed over a cropped gray beard, with prison glasses glinting in front of wide-set intelligent eyes. The Arab.

"How do you feel?" the Arab asked. He had a soft voice, only slightly accented. The Arab had been the chief trustee attendant at the infirmary for at least ten years. The Arab wasn't in a gang, not even in the Muslim Brothers, although he was an actual Muslim. Everyone left him alone for two reasons: one, you never could tell when you might have to go into the infirmary and hence find yourself in his power, and two, he provided dope for the whole prison. The doc was a junkie, and nodded off half the time. The Arab ran the place. Actually, three reasons. There was something about him, a look. The toughest cons, the yard bulls, could read it, and they treated the Arab with respect, and so, accordingly, did everyone else, including Felix. The prison records gave his name as Feisal Abdel Ridwan, which was somewhat true, and the crimes for which he had been sentenced as felony murder and armed robbery were also somewhat true. His actual identity and his actual crimes were kept secret, even from the prison authorities. This was part of the deal his lawyers had negotiated, to keep him safe, and to keep the information in his head on tap, should any of a number of U.S. government agencies wish to tap it.

"Okay, I guess," said Felix. "My head hurts. What the ▆▆▆ happened?"

"You were knocked out, a concussion. Also you were stabbed, but the blade twisted against a rib and did not penetrate far. Would you like some pills for the pain?"

"▆▆▆ yes."

The pills were produced, two tabs of Percocet. After swallowing them, Felix asked, "So I'm okay? No permanent damage, huh?"

"Not to your body. Your legal situation is not so good, I am afraid."

"My legal . . . ?"

"Yes. The guard Daniels is dead. They are saying you killed him."

"The▬▬ they are! That's bullshit! Who's saying I killed him, the niggers?"

"No, you were seen by several guards, apparently. Daniels was killed by a blow to the side of the neck, a blow from a naked hand. There are not many men who could deliver such a blow."

Without thinking, Felix looked at his hands. A heavy rind of callous ran along the edge of each. The knuckles barely rose above the thick hornlike skin that encased them. Felix had been a karate black belt before coming to the prison, and he had been scrupulous about practicing during his time here. That was his other main thing—his body and its effectiveness as a weapon. Had he killed Daniels? He wasn't sure, although some details were returning now, as the drug relaxed him. The iron bar had been torn from his hands, and then he'd felt the jab of the knife. There were angry black faces all around him and he'd kicked and struck out at them. Someone had tried to grab him from behind and he'd whirled and chopped at a neck. Then nothing. That could have been Daniels. By then everything was a blur, the red haze of rage, sweat in his eyes. They couldn't hold him responsible for that. It was

Marvelle who'd started the whole thing anyway.

"It was Marvelle started the ███ing thing. Whyn't they ███ with **him** for a change?"

The Arab ignored this. "I think you are in a lot of trouble, Felix, you know? A great deal of big trouble. Killing a guard is murder in the first degree. They have the death penalty now. I think they intend to pin you for this murder."

"Let them ███ing try," said Felix, "I didn't kill anyone. Not on purpose anyway."

Later that same day, however, two state police detectives arrived at Felix's bedside, to interview him and to confront him with the evidence against him. The whole thing had been captured by the video cameras perpetually trained on the yard, they said, and it was perfectly clear who had killed the guard. They desired a confession, which Felix did not give them. It was an essential part of his psychology never to confess to anything, not for strategic reasons, but because, in his own mind, he was incapable of wrongdoing of any kind. That any act of his was justified, correct, blameless was, in a sense, the core of his being. Felix Tighe was a psychopath.

He asked for a lawyer then, which meant that they had to stop questioning him. It did not mean, however, that they had to stop talking to him, and one of the state detectives did that, describing in some detail what would happen to him after he was convicted of first-degree murder. New York had never executed anyone under the new statute, but it was the detective's belief that the state was merely waiting for someone just like Felix: white, a convicted murderer of a woman and a child, who had killed an officer in the line of duty. "A poster boy for capital punishment" was the phrase he used more than once.

The next day, a lawyer appeared, a court-appointed local, bored and irritably earning his twenty-five dollars per, who explained to Felix the legal doctrine of intent. It did not matter, he said, that Felix had not arisen that Monday morning planning to murder Officer Phillip K. Daniels. He had directed a blow against the victim's neck, knowing his own power and skill, knowing that it was potentially deadly. It was precisely the same as shooting a cop in the commission of a crime. "I didn't mean it" was not exculpatory under law. The lawyer advised Felix to take the plea, and he'd try to work out something that did not involve lethal injection. Felix refused. The lawyer explained what a refusal meant: that he would be tried locally, in Cuyahoga County, before a jury composed of people having zero sympathy for New York City bad boys, who all knew someone who knew someone who worked as a corrections officer at the prison. Felix then cursed out the lawyer so violently that the man got up and left.

After that Felix napped, untroubled by the future. Like many of his fellow psychopaths, he had the imagination and foresight of a newt. It was the Arab who brought him to his senses. He was sympathetic, to start with, and Felix was a great consumer of sympathy. In the long quiet night hours of the infirmary, the Arab sat in a chair by Felix's bedside, listening to the sad story of how Felix had been shafted, screwed, betrayed by everyone with whom he had come in contact (especially women), how all his plans had been undone by bad luck, how his reasonable efforts to seek justice had been misconstrued, how he had been so many times unjustly accused of crimes, as now. To all this, the Arab listened calmly, silent except for little clucks of concern. This made Felix happy, not because he thought he was becoming friends with the man—friendship was a category void of meaning for Felix—but because the jerk seemed to be swallowing the story whole, which meant he could be manipulated to Felix's advantage. Which he already was: he was a willing source of drugs, and a faker of medical reports, so that Felix got to hang out in bed all day instead of having to hump laundry baskets or slave away in the roasting stamping shop, making license plates. The infirmary was air-conditioned.

On one of these pleasant nights, Felix was expatiating on one of his favorite themes, how the niggers got all the breaks, because the hebes wanted it that way, so that real Americans got kept down. Felix did not actually believe all this.

Sympathizing with the downtrodden, even the class of which he was a member, was quite alien to him. All of it was in service of manipulation— he figured the Arab would have a thing about Jews. And indeed, the man spoke for the first time after Felix said this, but not about the Jews.

"They are going to execute you, you know," said the Arab. "It is inevitable. And that will be the end of your sad story. A pity, really. You are clearly a man capable of larger things."

Felix stared at him.

The Arab's eyes were sad as he resumed. "Yes, you see I have many contacts in the administration. And outside. It is amazing how much information one can buy if one has an endless supply of painkillers and soporifics and diet pills. Everyone is looking for the drugs smuggled into the prison; it never occurs to anyone that drugs can be smuggled out, as well. In any case, my informants tell me that the indictment is already prepared. It will be for first-degree murder, and the state has absolutely no incentive to ask for anything other than death."

The word brought Felix back from a reverie in which he blackmailed the Arab into letting him into the drug supply business in the prison, running it, in fact. He'd be the ████ing king of the yard if he could get his hands on . . .

"Death?"

"Yes. Inevitable. The trial will be a slam dunk.

That is correct, yes, a slam dunk? As I say, a pity. Unless you were able to escape."

"What're you talking about?"

"It could be arranged. I could arrange it, in fact."

"How?"

An elegant shrug. "You could go into a decline. Dr. McMartin is not punctilious and we have an unusual number of patients because of the riot. Your wound becomes infected. I start an IV, for antibiotics. Unfortunately it is of no use. You slip into a coma. You die. You have no close relations, do you?"

"No," said Felix, and had the strange, if fleeting, notion that the Arab already knew this fact. "What do you mean, I die?"

"Just that. I will give you a substantial dose of morphine, enough to make it appear to a casual observer that you are deceased. In the early morning hours, I will move you into the morgue cooler. There are drugs I have that can slow your breathing so that it is almost imperceptible, and also your heart rate. Dr. McMartin is not a skillful physician. He will examine you briefly, with a stethoscope that I will have altered so that it would not detect a jet engine. Your skin will be quite cold. The picture will be a sick man who has passed away in the night. He will sign the death certificate with no qualms. Then I will autopsy you."

"You'll what?"

"It is required. I do it all the time, although it is not authorized for me to do it alone. However, the doctor does not care for autopsies and he is glad of my skill."

"You're not a doctor, how the ████ can you fake—"

"I am, in fact, a physician, in all but the details of licensure. I had four years of medical training in Cairo before I was arrested by the regime. I will make shallow cuts in a y shape on your chest and sew them up again, as if I have removed your organs. I have put aside organs from a real autopsy, which I will present as yours, if anyone asks. Which I doubt that they will. Everyone, in fact, will be delighted that you are dead. Then your body will be shipped to your cousin in New York City."

"I don't have a cousin in New York."

"Oh, but you do," said the Arab. "It is all arranged."

Felix felt irritation grow in him, for though he certainly wanted to get out of prison, he wanted even more the feeling of being in control of things. Nor did he enjoy being in the debt of some sand nigger.

"What do you mean, it's all arranged. How the hell did you know I'd be in here?"

Another little shrug. A smile. "If not you, then someone like you. You see what I look like. On the outside I have . . . colleagues, who look the same. People who look like us are now restricted in their movements because of the recent events in New York. I have need of someone who does not look like that, an American, for certain tasks."

Now Felix smiled. "You're a ████ng terrorist?"

"Why use such a meaningless word?" said the Arab, not smiling at all now. "The rulers of the world, the rich, the powerful, the Jews and their agents, the same people who have spoiled your own life, as you have told me, they will always call terrorists those who refuse to be crushed. Like us. Also, I thought you would be a good choice because we have several interests in common, you and I."

"Yeah? Such as?"

"A desire to exact revenge on people who have hurt us. To achieve what we are meant to achieve despite the conspiracies against us. As I said, I have friends in administration. I know about you, your records."

"Oh, yeah?" Felix didn't like this, but he kept his face friendly.

"Yes. Do you know that we were both convicted by the same man? And not just the man. He has a wife who was involved in both of our cases. Isn't that strange? He is a Jew, of course."

"Karp?"

"Yes, Karp. Wouldn't you like to pay him back?"

"Yeah, him and a lot of other people," said

Felix. "So what's the plan? You got people on the outside?"

"Yes, many. People who have been here for many years, very secure. But Arabs, unfortunately. They may be watched, do you see? Because of these events of last year. You, on the other hand, will not be looked for. You will be the invisible man."

"The hell I will! Nobody they're looking for more than an escaped con . . ." Felix stopped short, as the thought hit him, and his face broke into one of its rare genuine smiles. "No, they won't. I'll be dead."

The two men shared a laugh. "Yes," said the Arab, "you will be dead, a ghost. Like a ghost you will strike fear. Karp is a senior prosecutor, an important man, but they will not be able to protect him. Or his family. The wife, of course, and they have three children. One by one they will fall, and him last. I want him to know fear and despair and helplessness."

"So, that's your end of this deal? You want me to whack Karp and his bitch and the three kids. That's it?"

"Yes. Precisely."

"What's the catch?"

Felix had to explain the joke. After that, the two men laughed louder than before.

The plan proceeded smoothly. No one in the prison system likes trials involving the murder of a corrections officer. Such an event speaks to incompetence, to carelessness in handling violence. It also clouds the future recruitment of guards. Thus, no one in the hierarchy of the prison was greatly put out by the news that Felix Tighe was ailing. As he approached death's door, no one insisted on heroic measures to save him. Dr. McMartin stumbled over to the bedside a few times and observed what seemed to be a dying man. When Feisal announced the death, the doctor inspected the corpse and signed the papers without demur.

The Arab was well pleased. He had worked with men like Felix many times, and considered that he was a good example of his type. Brutal, with a grudge, intelligent enough to carry out a plan, not intelligent enough to see that once his mission had been accomplished he could under no circumstances be allowed to live, since his very existence compromised the Arab's own position at the prison. On autopsy day, then, he looked down at the faux corpse with something approaching affection.

Two days later, a man from the State Department of Corrections called the office of the chief assistant district attorney for New York County. The chief ADA had a short list of convicts about whose status he wished to be notified whenever the status changed in any way. These were all people sentenced to long prison terms, whom

Karp never wanted to see let out on the street, or given new trials, or shifted to lower levels of security than maximum. Felix Tighe was on that list, so the corrections guy called Karp to tell him that the man's status had changed permanently. Karp called his wife to tell her the news.

"Can we spit on his corpse?" she asked.

"Not officially. I guess I could find out where he's buried and dance on his grave."

"We could hire a band. God, that was a long time ago! I was pregnant with Lucy and we didn't know. That horrible woman. His dear old mom. I had nightmares about that for years."

"But not anymore."

"No, now I have nightmares about me. How are you?"

"Keeping up. It's hot. I thought I'd come out with the boys this weekend, hit the beach."

A long silence. "I don't know if that's such a great idea. You could go to Jones Beach."

"Oh, ████ Jones and ████ his beach! Marlene, you can't hide out there forever. You have a family. We miss you."

"Do you? My warm maternal ways. I need some more time, Butch, you know?"

"It's been almost a year."

"I'll come in."

"When?"

"I'll call you," she said.

2

IT WAS THE KIND OF CASE THAT KARP WOULD have liked to try, if they still let him try cases. Failing that, he thought Terrell Collins was doing a pretty good job for the People on this, the first day of trial. Collins was a tall, graceful man nearly the same color as the victim in the case, one Moussa Onabajo, late of Nigeria. On the stand was one of the several witnesses to the killing, a man named Touri. As Collins took him through the warm-up—who he was, how he knew the victim, what if anything he saw on the night of— Karp turned his eye on the defendants, Eric Gerber, detective third grade, NYPD, and Frank Nixon, detective second.

Only the backs of their heads were visible from the rear of the courtroom where Karp stood; Nixon had a full head of dark yellow hair, Gerber's skull was a thick blocklike object covered with short red bristles. Gerber should have picked different genes had he set out to be the defendant in this sort of case. He looked like the Nazi trooper in a dozen war movies. Nixon had a more intelligent look, but he could have played the SS officer, the one who lifts the heroine's chin with the riding crop. There was no evidence in either man's record of racism in action, but in their minds, who knew?

Collins and the People's case had nothing to say on the subject. Karp had made that decision early on, in the face of Keegan's broad hints and the rage of what seemed like a good two fifths of the city's population. Karp caught some eyes upon him, including some hard ones. He had the rep as someone insensitive to racial issues, a rep he shared with a recent mayor of the city. Karp had every right to be in the courtroom, to sit at the prosecution table if he wanted to, but he was turning heads now and he wanted all the heads to be turned toward Collins and the witness. He slipped out.

He knew what Touri was going to say anyway. That on a certain night six months ago, while standing outside the Club Balou on Greenwich Street, he had observed his friend, Moussa, being accosted by two men, the present defendants. That he had heard the two men try to buy dope from Moussa. That Moussa had grown angry, because Moussa was a good Muslim and didn't even use dope, much less sell it. That Moussa had pushed that man there, the defendant Nixon, and shouted abusive words and had engaged in a shoving scuffle with Nixon, and struck Nixon in the face with his fist. That the two men had then pulled pistols and shot Moussa dead. Thus the testimony of Bradley and three others was essentially the same. Against this was the defense's story, which was that the two undercover cops had identified themselves to Moussa as police officers and he had attacked Nixon physically. In the ensuing scuffle, Moussa had tried to grab Nixon's pistol, and that was when the shooting had begun.

None of the witnesses had seen or heard anything resembling this series of events. What Karp surmised was that the cops had made a simple mistake and compounded it into tragedy. They had picked the wrong guy, neither Gerber nor Nixon being experts at distinguishing among several Nigerians on darkened street corners, and when it had become perfectly clear that it was the wrong guy, since the right guy would have sold them dope if he hadn't made them or would have been cool if he had made them and been holding, neither of the two cops had possessed the sense to disengage, to stay in their tourist personae and drift off. Certainly there were plenty of actual dope deals going down along Greenwich Street that night. Instead, they had responded to the victim's outrage with outrage of their own, abandoned the rules of engagement set down in elaborate detail in the NYPD Patrol Guide, and blew the fellow away, using seven bullets from two guns to do it.

A stupid tragedy: that was what it actually **was,** Karp believed, but the law, that Great Ass, had no slot for stupid tragedy. Its only concern was culpability. Was the act criminous? The grand jury had determined that it was. Were the defendants culpable? That was what Collins and all of them were doing in there. Yes, they were, said the People. No, they weren't, said the counsel for the defense. Now, now, boys, said the judge, when necessary. It is as dignified and noble as a schoolyard punch-out, or the scuffle outside a mean little nightclub that had cost Moussa Onabajo his life.

Karp shook his head violently to clear it of these thoughts, unseemly ones for someone in his position, and drew a startled look from a passing clerk typist. Oh, great, he thought, now I'm twitching like a maniac in the courthouse halls. I'm going crazy, too. And this "too" his mind tossed up made him think of she to whom it referred, the one already crazy. This recollection hit him with the force of a blow, as it did several times in each day, and he paused at the door to his office and leaned heavily upon the doorknob to keep himself upright, to keep from falling to the floor and writhing in pain, howling. The spasm passed as always, leaving the perpetual dull ache, tinctured with resentment. **Why** did she have to be like that?

The monster in her lair. It is close, dank, fetid with the bones of her victims. In reality it is large, sunny, white-painted, a bedroom on the upper floor of a farmhouse near the shore on the north fork of Long Island. But what is reality? Marlene no longer knows. She lives alone now with a varying number of large fierce dogs and a dog trainer named Billy Ireland, with whom she is strenuously not having an affair, although she often wants to. Marlene has strong sexual desires, and a likely relief for them nearby and willing, but she denies herself this, and she denies herself also the solace of her children and her home. It's part of the punishment. Marlene is clever enough to organize a mass assassination and escape the grip of the law, but not clever enough to escape the guilt. She organized this crime to avenge an attack on her son Giancarlo. Giancarlo is blind as the result, or perhaps he is not blind at all. His vision tends to flick on and off, like an old bar sign. Her favorite child, the artist, blind: this was her thinking, and his brother, the twin, probably had murder down to his name at age eleven, although you couldn't tell what was going on inside him at all, you were lucky if you got three words a day out of him, Giancarlo does all the talking the two of them need. Maybe he's twisted inside there, that's her big fear, like Mom, thinks of nothing but guns, shooting, maybe we'll see him up on the tower one day, a sniper, one of those beautiful, smooth, deadly American boys. "The mother's fault" is what they always say, although in this case definitely true.

So, the deal is she has to stay away from the bunch of them, the boys to protect them from the Monster Mom, and far from Butch, to protect herself from that look he gives her without meaning to, a look of revulsion. No, she could take revulsion, it was her desert, after all; but he mixes it with the still-warm embers of love into an emotional slurry that she can't endure seeing. She doesn't have to avoid her daughter, because her daughter has removed herself from the maternal orbit. Or has she? She doesn't run away, she talks on the phone, but like a stranger, which is fine with Marlene, one less thing to strip off, although one would think that Lucy, of all people, would understand why she did it. Lucy has that rage, too, when the family is threatened, some kind of gene from Sicily? Although she has succeeded in keeping it under better control than her mother has. A real Catholic, Lucy, of the Saint Teresa rather than the Torquemada type. Marlene is pretty sure that Lucy has not actually killed anyone. Accessory, maybe, but not actually the trigger person yet, for which the mother is truly thankful.

She drags herself out of bed and steps over a huge black dog into the bathroom. Minimal ablutions, only a blurred look in the mirror. She has cut off her hair. Dressing is no problem. She has slept in her underwear and a faded Take Back the Night T-shirt. She pulls on greasy overalls and socks and goes down the stairs, the dog like a thumping shadow behind her. In the sink the evidence of her dinner, a can of soup eaten directly from the pot. Marlene lives now on soup, bread, cheese, and wine. She looks at the bottle she opened last night and its companion juice glass, sticky with red remains. A little aching here, ruthlessly suppressed. She will have a large glass of wine with lunch, which is European and permitted and then not a drop more until suppertime. She is not a lush. Drinking to oblivion after a good day's work is what a lush does. She can't have a family, but she can run a business, and she does. The dogs love her. Breakfast is black espresso made in an hourglass stove-top pot and a chunk of bread and sliced tomato from Giancarlo's old garden. She tries to keep the garden up, but the weeds are gaining on it. Symbolic.

After pulling on green Wellingtons, Marlene goes out the back door. She sees a large, sagging barn, white-painted and peeling, with the sun

just rising over its roofline, and several outbuild-
ings. The yard is covered with tanbark. This place
used to be a dairy farm, but now it is a kennel and
dog training establishment. She can hear the
barks and howls as she steps out into the Sound-
scented morning and lights her first cigarette.
Wingfield Farms Registered Neapolitan Mastiffs
is a non-no-smoking facility. She enters the barn
and flicks on the lights. There is louder barking,
panting, and whining, and the sound of many
claws against stone. She checks the stock in
leisurely fashion, caressing or admonishing as
required, accompanied by her own private dog,
Gog the mastiff, who is silent amid the barking as
befits his exalted status. There are six Neapolitan
mastiffs, several dobes and shepherds, and a
bunch of smaller dogs, mixed curs and beagles, in
training as dope and bomb sniffers. Business is
good in that area.

Steps on the stairs as Billy Ireland comes
down from the apartment he occupies in the former hayloft. He is a small, well-knit man, of the
type Marlene particularly likes, brass-haired,
with pool green eyes and a cocky manner. (Of
course, being Marlene, she married a completely
different style of man.) He is an ex-junkie and a
Mozart among dog trainers. They desire each
other, but they play at being perfect lady and
gentleman, while enjoying the pleasures of flirta-
tion. Having him around enhances her self-

disgust—a barely controllable slut after all—
which is all to the good, a bonus in fact. They
inquire as to each other's sleep, trade earthy
innuendos, and discuss the day's program.
Ireland is sleeping with Marjorie, one of the dog
agitators; Marlene knows it, but he is careful not
to flaunt it. The charade requires that he be smitten with Marlene, and he obliges, this being the
best job he has ever had.

They work the dogs through the brief cool of
the morning. Marlene does basic training, lead
work, and the standard commands. Ireland works
with Marjorie and Russell, the agitators. They are
people who are skilled in annoying big dogs, and
who don't mind being mauled and knocked
down. Ireland does Kohler training, turning the
mastiffs into guard dogs. It is simple, hard work,
requiring concentration. The dogs know if you
mean it, unlike most humans. Marlene sinks
gratefully into the doggy world; she thinks these
are her only purely honest relationships.

They work until one, when it becomes too hot
to work out of doors. It is Marlene's turn to get
lunch at the snack bar on the beach road. She
drives there in her battered red Ford pickup. In
years past, Marlene often spent a few summer
hours lying at the beach while her sons played.
No longer. She avoids the beach now. Her bikini
tan has faded. Now she has a workingman's tan,
face, neck, and forearms. She looks piebald and

ridiculous, but what does it matter? No one is going to look at her body.

At lunch, the conversation among the four dog people is lively and mainly about dogs, although they tell junkie stories with self-deprecatory laughter and Narcotics Anonymous stories with simple sympathy. She thinks they are decent, damaged people and is happy to spend her life among them, in that she has a life.

After lunch they work the sniffer dogs inside the barn. Marlene has been supplied with baits by the law enforcement authorities with whom she has contracts: eau de coke, eau de smack, eau de Semtex, C-4, dynamite, black powder. This is even more concentrated work than the guard training. A dog is brought out, it finds the hidden bait, gets its lavish praise. Or else it becomes confused, and wanders sniffing around the barn, and signals at the wrong thing. He's a pet, says Russell after Morris the schnauzer has failed three times to find the hidden dope. "Pet" is not a compliment at Wingfield Farms. Some dogs get it right away, others never do. Part of the art is telling which is which, whether a little extra effort will create a working dog or whether the beast is doomed to chase the Frisbee in the 'burbs. Dog training is a profession that inspires a deep respect for the inexplicable differences between one beagle and a seemingly identical beagle. Marlene reflects that none of her five siblings is a rage-maddened criminal like her. Bloodlines or training, she can't figure it out. She worries about her children. Bad seed? Evil training? It doesn't matter anymore. She's out of all that.

Around four, Marlene goes into her office and does business, pays bills, talks to officials, takes orders for dogs, pitches dogs to prospective owners. In the late afternoon and through the early twilight hours they work the dogs outside again. The agitators menace, the dogs attack, the dogs always win. At dusk they leave. Marlene has her first drink and her second, from a bottle of wine identified only as being a product of California and being red. Billy Ireland goes off somewhere. Marlene makes herself a can of something, she who once could barely tolerate any canned food in the house, she the maker of sauce from scratch, the roaster of veal shanks for stock. Wine with dinner and wine after dinner, too. Ireland comes in around nine. Unbidden, he stands behind her chair and massages her neck and shoulders. He has good hands, he is skillful with the animal body, regardless of species. They have come close a time or two, when she was deep in the wine fog, but have never actually done it. The world's longest first date, Ireland calls it. He is slightly afraid of her, she knows, and he will not press it.

Tottering a little, she climbs the stairs and falls into bed. Another day, barely distinguishable from the day before. Gog the mastiff licks her face and thumps his two hundred pounds down in the doorway, rattling the windows. She weeps briefly, clutching a photograph of her children, and falls asleep.

Karp left the courtroom and climbed down the stairs to his office, one at a time now, where once he had taken flights in three bounds. Karp always used the stairs, up and down, and never the elevator. He hated being trapped in conversation during the painfully slow rides. He had nightmares about being trapped on a slow elevator that, when its door opened, revealed that it was on the same floor from which it had departed so long ago. Too much like his life.

In the office, he disposed of some bureaucratic details swiftly and efficiently and then turned to the pile of case reports he had selected for review. Karp thought that this was the most important part of his job and the one he enjoyed the most. He could review only a small fraction of the cases that the various bureau chiefs thought worthy of trial, but the fact that Karp was looking over their shoulders kept them honest and kept standards from sliding too far. Or so Karp believed. He picked up the case file from the homicide bureau. Husband kills wife, a nobrainer. What was interesting was why the guy wouldn't deal, since he had clearly done it and would go down for it. Middle-class guy, a furrier. Everyone thinks they're O.J., they can walk with a good lawyer. Not today, not in New York County. He made some notes and moved on. Narcotics. Why did he bother? He didn't know the heroin was in his apartment, the cops planted it. Another race thing, the defendant's lawyer was one of the ones who figured if he stacked the jury with enough black faces, they'd walk his guy to piss off the Man. Maybe he would. Karp spotted a flaw in the chain of evidence record and made a note. Check it out.

Next, the rape bureau. More interesting: a doctor was the D, the victim a patient, the charge sexual abuse, first degree. Not completely unusual that, but unusual to try it. Usually, their main interest was in getting past it as quickly as possible, cop a plea to misdemeanor and try to smooth things over with the state medical board and the hospitals. A little public penitence, too: yes, a terrible problem, I'm in therapy, my wife supports me, ask for the forgiveness of God and the victims, etc. An actual trial would do the opposite, keeping the case in the public eye for a week at least, and revealing all the juicy details to the press. Kevin Hirsch, M.D., was the guy, a gastroenterologist. No priors. The alleged crime had taken place at the Aurora Community Health Center, located in a semidecrepit zone of upper Manhattan, where

Dr. Hirsch volunteered. The alleged victim was one Leona Coleman, forty-four. According to her statement, on January 12 of the current year she had gone to the clinic to have a colonoscopy. She suffered from bowel problems and chronic diarrhea. The accused had sedated her and begun the procedure, in the midst of which she had suddenly become aware that the physician had his head between her legs and was tonguing her vagina.

Karp read through the file and then thumbed back through it again, thinking he had missed something, but he hadn't. The rape bureau was apparently going to try this fellow on the completely unsupported word of the alleged victim. According to the police report, the alleged assault had taken place on an examination table shielded from a busy ward only by curtains. Was this at all likely? And the act itself, a colonoscopy in progress, diarrhea, the smell . . . Karp was not at this stage capable of surprise at any of the acts that people chose to relieve the sexual itch, but this still seemed extreme.

There was a pattern of abuse alleged in support of the state's case. The rape bureau had put out an 800 number: call if Dr. Hirsch diddled you or worse. He paged through the testimony. Four women had responded. Two thought something had happened during deep anesthesia but weren't sure what. One felt she'd had her breast touched inappropriately. The last claimed that

Dr. Hirsch had seduced her in his office and they'd had a wild affair for six months and that he'd promised he'd leave his wife for her and then didn't. No tonguing of vaginas during colonoscopies. A dozen years back, Karp's wife had been the founding chief of the sex crimes bureau and so Karp knew more than most about the particular difficulties of prosecuting such cases. If this guy had done it, why hadn't he copped to a lesser? Why did he want a trial? Why, come to that, did sex crimes want a trial? Little bells were going off. Karp put the file to the side and reached for his phone.

Laura Rachman, chief of the sex crimes bureau, was a big blonde who dressed in colors more flamboyant than were usually seen in the courthouse, the colors of national flags. Today she was wearing a crisp linen suit of an eye-challenging green with a white blouse. Her hair was arranged in sprayed waves around her wide oval face, which she had carefully painted in matte fleshtones to resemble human skin. Karp did not like Rachman particularly and was unfailingly polite to her as a result.

"You wanted to see me?" she asked. **Wonted**. Rachman's vowels were artificial, like her face. She had escaped Queens and did not wish to be mistaken for an outer-borough person.

"Yeah, have a seat." He gestured, she sat, crossing her legs. The short skirt of the suit rode up over her nylon-covered thighs. Karp focused his eyes on her face. "It's this Hirsch thing. What's the story there?"

"What do you mean, story? It's pretty clear. He's a serial sexual abuser and we're going to hit him with the max. You have a problem with that?"

"Yeah, I do. What did you offer him?"

"Sex abuse two and six months. He spit in our eye. He says he didn't do it."

"Uh-huh. Well the thing is, I don't see that you've got a trial here. That's my problem."

Little patches of natural color appeared under the blusher. "You're questioning my judgment?"

"It's my job, Laura. I question everyone's judgment. Basically, the whole thing rests on Coleman's testimony, with no corroborating evidence or witnesses . . ."

"It's a sex case. There's never corroborating testimony in sex cases."

"Not often, right, but here you've got a doc doing an unlikely act in a place where it'd be easy for him to get caught. You've got nothing solid that he's not a Boy Scout . . ."

"That's not true. We've got three other women."

Karp waved a hand. "You've got two women who think something happened when they were under anesthesia. The third woman says she had an affair with him, he seduced her, but I don't see any background on her. Is she cool?"

"She's fine. She'll stand up."

"Great, but I want to see it in writing that someone checked that she's not a fruitcake who also had passionate affairs with the mayor, the pope, and Warren Beatty. Also, your defendant, the guy's done nine thousand colonoscopies, according to his statement. And he's never indulged his taste for fecally flavored cunnilingus until now? Until your victim came along? What's she like, the victim?"

"Wait a minute, we're blaming the victim now? I'm sorry, when did the middle ages come back?"

Karp suppressed a sigh. "Laura, the defense is going to attack the character of the complainant because that's your entire case. The woman has to be squeaky, and I don't see from this file that you've made a significant effort to determine that. Does she have a grudge against the doc? Is she trying to muscle him on something? Is she a flake? Does she have any pattern of complaints against docs for this kind of thing?"

But Rachman was not listening. "I can't **believe** I'm hearing this crap. I'll tell you what the problem is. The problem is the D is a nice Jewish doctor and the victim is black."

"No. The problem is that the case is not prepped for trial, and I'm not going to sign off on a trial slot until it is."

She stood up and yanked her skirt down. "Fine. I'm going to Jack on this."

"Go ahead," said Karp, "and I'll tell him the same thing I told you: The case isn't ready."

After she was gone, Karp spent a few moments predicting what would happen if Rachman took the wretched thing to Keegan. She would get on his calendar, Keegan would call him and ask what it was about, Karp would tell him, and Keegan would yell at Karp for not handling it at his level, meaning that Keegan wanted to be protected from having to make decisions on cases that would rile either the blacks or the liberal bleeders, the two squishiest elements of his political support. And Karp would therefore need something else, something that wasn't in the case file, to give the DA.

"Murrow!"

In a moment the man appeared. Karp understood that Murrow was out and about much of the day on his master's business, but it seemed that whenever Karp called him, he materialized, like a djinn. Karp thrust the Hirsch file at him.

"Look this over," said Karp and explained his problems with the case. "There could be something fishy about the vic here. Ask around."

Felix opened his eyes upon blackness. He was stiff and crampy and didn't know where he was.

It took a few seconds for him to recall even **who** he was. He tried to sit up and bumped his head. His exploring hands told him he was in a box, his ears said he was in a vehicle of some kind. He pushed upward against a slightly yielding stiffness slick against his palms. Waxed cardboard?

Memories arose now, like the ghost images on photo paper rising to sharpness in the developer bath. The Arab. Injections. He touched his chest and felt the hardness of staples in the Y-shaped pattern made by an autopsy. But his own organs were intact. He was alive; it had worked; he was out.

The vehicle slowed, turned, and came to a halt. Felix felt himself lifted, carried, heard the grunts of men and short bursts of a foreign tongue. There were clicking sounds. The cover of the cardboard coffin rose up. He blinked in the sudden light. A face came into view, tan, with a short beard and thick hornrims over dark eyes.

"Are you all right?" The voice was soft and slightly accented.

Felix sat up, wincing a little at the pull of the staples. There were two other men in the room. The smell of gas, gray concrete walls—it was some kind of garage. The other two men were darker than the first one, with close-cropped heads and hard features, one meaty, the other a whippet. The muscle, Felix thought, and wondered briefly if he could take them. One at a time, maybe. The two hard men grabbed his arms and helped him out of the coffin. The third man brought a striped cotton robe for him to wear. Felix felt rubbery and weak. "I got to piss," he said. His voice sounded strange to him, shaky and hollow. They had to almost carry him to the bathroom.

It took Felix three days to get back on his feet. It was the drugs, Rashid said. Rashid was the one with the beard and the glasses. The others were Carlos (big) and Felípe (thin). Felix didn't figure that an Arab would hang with a pair of greasers, and they were definitely that, because he heard them jabbering away in Spanish. Felix knew enough jailhouse Spanish to deliver an insult or make a demand, and so he knew they were for real. They were out of the house all day working, Rashid said. Rashid had a little home business, something to do with computers. He had a couple of machines in a room on the top floor of the house, at which he sat and tapped when he wasn't hanging around Felix, making sure he was all right and bringing him food and smokes. Felix figured him for some kind of faggot butler, not a real player.

On the fourth day, Rashid let him out in the yard, a patch of ragged grass surrounded by a chain-link fence and equipped with a picnic table and a couple of aluminum lawn chairs. The house was a three-story structure sheathed in gray asphalt shingles, one of a row of identical houses, with alleys leading back to small yards and detached garages. He could see the backs of another, similar row through the trees and foliage of the adjacent backyard. It was, he learned, in Astoria, Queens.

Felix sat in one of the chairs, and basked in the afternoon sun. They had supplied him with jeans and T-shirts, in the right sizes, and socks and sneakers, as well. Rashid sat on the edge of the other chair and handed him a beer.

"I thought Arabs didn't drink," Felix said. "I thought that was a big Muslim no-no."

"It is as you say. But here we are obliged to fit in and act like Americans. We drink, we eat swine, we look at women's bodies."

"I'd like to look at some of that. What about throwing a little party?"

"Perhaps later. When our work is done."

"What kind of work is that?"

"We are going to blow some things up. Our friend believes you would not object to this kind of work."

"Our friend? You mean the Arab?"

"Ibn-Salemeh, yes. Was he correct in this?"

"Hey, if there's any money in it I don't have a problem. What're you going to blow?"

"We'll tell you when the time comes. We have a number of targets. Some will be of interest to you personally."

"Meaning Karp."

"Yes, him," said Rashid. "But first his family, one by one."

"Uh-huh," said Felix. "And what's the story with you? You're what, the butler?"

"I have a number of functions."

"Yeah, bring the beer, cook the food, make the beds. What about the money. You got it here, right?"

"It is where I can get it, Felix. And you cannot." Rashid stared into his eyes. "So you must put out of your mind any thought that you can, ah, get what you want and disappear. Rip us off, as you say. We require an American to travel around and go places where someone who looks like me would draw suspicion. That's why you are here and not rotting in that prison. There will be eyes on you all the time, Felix. And I would keep in mind if I were you the fact that you are already a dead man. And that you can be easily replaced. There is no shortage of Americans. Am I making myself perfectly clear now?"

Felix shrugged. "Whatever," he said, and pulled his eyes away. Not a butler, Rashid, that was a mistake, but the fucker had no call to talk to him like one of his niggers. Felix added him to the long list of people he would get if the opportunity presented.

3

"WHAT DO YOU DO ALL DAY UP IN THAT room, Rashid?" Felix asked, smiling. They were at lunch at the picnic table in the backyard of the Queens house.

"I work with the computers," said the Arab. "I have a computer business."

"Yeah? What kind of business?" Felix had the con man's art of feigning interest, but in this case he was genuinely interested. He had been in the joint while the computer revolution unfolded and was anxious to catch up. Felix had always been a reader of magazines, and the constant association in them of the words "computer" and "fraud" had piqued his interest.

Rashid, for his part, was not reluctant to expound. His weakness, which Felix had not been long in ferreting out, was that he felt unappreciated. The glory of derring-do, of planting bombs and carrying out midnight strikes was not for him. Rather, he was an arranger, a mover of paper and electrons and funds, vital but never to be a star. Even the Spaniards, who could barely read or speak English, had the gall to condescend to him. He thought Felix respected him. He thought Felix had been properly cowed.

He was therefore inclined to be expansive. "It is a very simple business. Now, you understand e-mail, yes? Very well, then, you see it is possible to send out an extremely large number of e-mail messages for no cost at all. Ten, twenty million messages, all around the world. So, even if only a few respond, there you have a business."

"What, you're selling something?"

"Of course. A number of things. Stock tips. Pills for various energy-type things. Special interest videos."

"What d'you mean, like fuck videos?"

"I don't see them, I just take the orders," said Rashid delicately. "Mainly, it is books, a program. You pay up front, and you get material showing how to run an on-line business, so you recruit others in the same way. Everyone pays a little up the line. It grows automatically."

"Yeah? You doing okay, then?"

"Well enough for my modest needs."

"Man, I'd like to get into that. I used to sell credit furniture. What a pain in the butt that was! Going into a million shitty apartments, putting on the fucking charm for a bunch of old bitches. No more, man. Was it hard to learn?"

"It requires concentration, of course." Rashid looked carefully at Felix. "I could teach you, if you like to."

Bingo, thought Felix. "Yeah," he said, "that would be cool."

Concentration was not Felix's strongest point; when difficulties presented themselves in his life, his instinct was to smash something or someone, or blame someone, or both. But he also had the ability to suspend this instinct in a good cause. He had learned karate in this way, and a variety of swindling tricks, and in this way also he learned how to operate a computer, and was soon cruising the Web and sending out millions of e-mail messages, and ordering useless or obscene junk for the remarkable numbers of suckers who responded. He was delighted with the sorts of things you could find on the Web nowadays, and amazed that they were allowed. You could spend all day viewing videos of very young girls being raped, for example, if you had stolen credit card numbers, and Felix spent many happy hours thus enriching his fantasy life. Even more valuable, however, was the ability of the Web to locate people. If you had a social security number, it was no trick to find an address. Felix had one and found the address he needed, which was, remarkably, only a few miles away, in Forest Hills, Queens.

Rashid was a pedantic and exhausting teacher, always offering more than his student wanted to know, or really needed to know about the mysteries of Windows and the Internet. He also ran a thick sidebar of editorial comment on the decadence of the West and the contempt he had for the pornography available on the Web. His own tastes were not quite as exotic as Felix's in this, running more to fat, older women in degrading poses and lovely young men in copulation. Of course, they both spied on each other's movements across the electronic prairie. Rashid had password-protected files and Felix devoted a considerable amount of time trying to crack these, but with no success.

Three weeks after Felix's "death" in prison, Rashid called him over to a monitor and showed him a color photograph of a young girl. She was talking, it seemed, to a man dressed in layered rags with a strange hat on his head. The photo had been taken from the side, and showed the girl's generous curved nose and strong jaw. She was very thin, with prominent cheekbones.

A dog, was Felix's thought. "Who's that?" he asked.

"Karp's daughter. Her name is Lucy. She volunteers in a soup kitchen. It's where I took this picture. At great risk to myself," he added importantly. "My face is known to the authorities. Here is another one, with the zoom lens, from the street." She was wearing shorts in this one, baggy ones, and a loose black T-shirt. No body, decent legs. Put a bag over the face and she'd be halfway fuckable, Felix thought. He said, "You want me to whack her?"

"Eventually, but first we need that she gives us some information. There is a man we need to settle with first, a Vietnamese, a friend of hers. He's disappeared. We believe she knows where he can be found. First you find out that, and then you can dispose of the girl."

"Why do you want the guy?"

"That's not your concern," said Rashid quickly, and then, unable to resist demonstrating the confidence placed in him by those higher in the organization, he added, "He was instrumental in the capture of ibn-Salemeh. A traitor to the oppressed peoples."

"Well, we can't let him get away with that shit," said Felix. "So, what's the plan—I grab the girl and we make her talk?" Felix looked at the photo of the screen again and imagined this procedure. He felt a pleasant tightening in his belly.

"No, of course not! Can you imagine the uproar if we kidnapped the child of a senior prosecutor? Not only would our major operations be entirely compromised, but the Vietnamese would surely hear of it and go deeper into hiding."

"What major operation?"

Rashid shook his head. "Need-to-know, need-to-know basis entirely. It does not concern you at this point in time. No, what you must do is to befriend the girl, get close to her, tell her a story, perhaps she will tell you a story, as well. Patience is the thing here. She is a kind girl, this work with the charities. She should not be hard to approach. And you are charming, I understand. It should not be difficult for a man like you."

It was not. Felix held it as a matter of deep faith that all cunts were essentially stupid and that they would believe any line of bullshit you threw at them. Also that they secretly wanted to be hurt. It had worked that way throughout his life. The few exceptions required special treatment, after which the dogma re-established itself, since the exceptions were no longer among us.

The next morning, Felix had his photograph taken with a digital camera, and watched, fascinated as Rashid reduced it in size and printed it out, and then delaminated a New York State driver's license, substituted Felix's picture, and relaminated it. Felix was now Larry Larsen. He was somewhat disappointed to learn that no car went along with the license. Rashid explained that the less the cell interacted with the authorities the better. No credit cards, no cars to get into accidents with or collect tickets. Felix would take the subway. He was given a hundred dollars for what Rashid called operating expenses.

"I'm not going to do much fucking operating

with a hundred bucks," said Felix, eyeing the sheaf of old twenties that Rashid extended.

"It is for subway and meals," said Rashid. "An occasional taxi. Buy flowers for the young lady. No drugs and no drinking."

"Never touch the stuff," said Felix. Except for speed and downers that was entirely true, but speed and downers weren't really drugs as far as Felix was concerned. They were medication; doctors prescribed them to millions of squares.

In any case, it felt good to be out of the house. Felix thought he could get to like being a terrorist. He walked over to Broadway in Astoria and entered a large hardware store, where he purchased a set of painter's gear—white coveralls, cap, and booties—plus some rubber gloves, an Ace Hardware ball cap, a masonry hammer, a roll of duct tape, and an eight-inch butcher knife. At a CVS nearby he bought a package of condoms, and made a phone call. Then he stopped at a coffee shop, where he had coffee and a Danish, and used the men's room to change into the coveralls and cap. Carrying his clothes and the hardware in the store bag, he walked down to the Steinway Street subway station, a working stiff on his way to a job.

The house was a solid middle-class dwelling in the lower-priced north end of Forest Hills, a two-story red-brick detached, set back from the street behind a small front yard deeply shaded by a maple. Felix went up the front walk and rang the bell, although he was pretty sure no one was home. That was why he had called. There was a neat label below the doorbell that read CHALFONTE.

He walked down the side alley to the back door. He found it locked by a solid dead bolt, but this was no problem because the lady of the house had conveniently left a key under a flowerpot at the edge of the back stoop. He let himself into the kitchen after replacing the key under the flowerpot, but then cursed softly, reversed direction, and retrieved the key. He wiped it off, slipped on rubber gloves, and replaced it again. Leave no trace. Felix had once left a good many traces at a murder he'd committed, which was what had nailed him. But he had been young and foolish then, and not dead. Leave no traces. He had learned a lot in prison.

Felix slipped on the painter's booties, removed the butcher knife from its cardboard sheath, and slipped it into the thin leg pocket of the coveralls. He ripped a number of strips off the roll of duct tape and stuck them on the edge of the kitchen counter. He would use the kitchen. The one small window faced a hedge, and the door led to the heavy foliage of the backyard. He didn't figure that there'd be much noise in any case. He strolled through the house while he waited. Mary had done all right for herself, he concluded. There was a picture over the mantelpiece in the living room, an oil portrait made from a photograph. The new husband looked like a banker, a middle manager—a three-piece suit, bald dome, a little moustache, a pleasant sheeplike benignity in his expression. Mary looked like a church lady standing next to him. There was a teenage boy, probably his, and a little girl, four or five, who had Mary's round face and blue eyes. Theirs. Felix felt a pleasant glow of anticipation.

A car rumbled down the driveway. Felix grabbed his hammer and took up a position behind the door that led to the basement, leaving the door open just a crack. His ex-wife had gained a little weight since he had last seen her, which was not surprising since the last time he had seen her she had been tied hand and foot to a bed, and had not been eating all that well. She was wearing a sleeveless white top and blue Bermudas and was carrying two grocery bags. She'd let her hair go back to its natural color, which was brown. He'd always insisted that she wear it blonde.

He let her place the bags on the kitchen table before he stepped out from behind the door. He said, "Hi, honey, I'm home." She whirled around. He had thought a good deal about this moment, about what the expression on her face was going to be, and he was not disappointed. He didn't even have to grab her or sock her one with the hammer, because she crumpled to the floor in a faint.

It was a quiet neighborhood and no one disturbed Felix for the three hours the business took. The phone rang a couple of times, but he let the answering machine take it. An unexpected bonus was that her little girl came home and let herself in through the back door. The portrait over the mantel must have been done a while ago, because the girl was about nine, just old enough to be interesting. He had Mary in the chair and the girl, Sharon, taped facedown on the table, so Mary could watch the whole thing. He could have kept it going on for a lot longer if he'd wanted to, but he was worried about hubby coming home. He changed out of the painter's stuff, jammed it and the tools in the hardware store bag—it was plastic and wouldn't drip—and went out the back with the ball cap jammed on his head. The tricky part was how long to hold on to the stuff. The farther away he got, the less likely that the cops would find it and associate it with the scene, but the longer he held onto it the more chance there was of some dumb-ass lucky cop spotting him and wondering why a guy in his forties was wandering through a residential neighborhood on a workday, carrying a shopping bag.

But he got to the subway station all right and here he caught a break. A crew was just emptying the station trashcans. He knotted the top of his bag and thrust it into one that had not been emptied yet. The stuff would be on a barge by the end of the day. He took it as an omen of good fortune. He felt ready for anything now. All he needed was a little notebook. He liked to write stuff down in a notebook, and today would make a terrific entry. People started looking at him in the subway going from Queens to the city because he was grinning. He switched to a scowl and changed cars.

A jailbird was her first thought when he came down the line, not a homeless. The overdeveloped arms and neck said prison, as did the new suntan. They were always in a rush to lose the prison pallor so they stayed out in the sun too long, or under the lamp, leaving telltale redness along the rims of the ears. Clean clothes that looked new; he might have a place to stay. A halfway house? Probably. A number of guys from St. Dismas took their meals here at Holy Redeemer. She ladled out his stew and he smiled at her. She smiled back, a formal one, because she couldn't see his eyes behind his dark glasses, and she felt uncomfortable about smiling without meeting the eyes of the person. That's what the social work ladies did, the professional smile. No one looked these guys in the eye from one week to the next, except her. Guys had told her this, that they felt invisible on the streets.

She had a real smile for the next man in line, a smelly bundle of rags with no front teeth. "How's it going, Ramon?"

"Doin' g'ate, Rucy, g'ate."

"Your ship come in yet, man?"

"Not ret, but I got a numbu doday. You p'ay for my numbu, huh, Rucy?"

"Sure thing, Ramon."

Dollop of thick stew, slice of homemade bread. Same smile for the next one and the next, the same kind of chatter. Now one of her favorites, Hey Hey, born Jeffrey Elman. Despite the heat, Hey Hey was wearing a red doorman's coat with gold braid over a T-shirt with the planet depicted on it and bearing the legend "Love Your Mother." On his head he wore what must have once been a fedora, but which was now a vast tangle of monofilament line, tinfoil, brown plastic packing tape, fish hooks, and electronic components. Hey Hey said the rig was necessary to keep his thoughts from escaping his head.

"Hey, hey, hey, hey, Lu, hey, hey, Lu, hey, Lucy," said Hey Hey.

"Good afternoon, Jeffrey," said Lucy, with the big smile. She thought that the peaceful kind of schizophrenic was in many ways preferable to the majority of the sane.

"How's it going today?"

"Oh, hey, hey, you know, hey, okay. Hey, hey, I got hey, something to hey, show you after lunch, hey?"

She smiled her agreement, and turned to the next one. They didn't just come for the chow, according to the Catholic Workers who ran the place, but for the civility. There were paper tablecloths on the tables and flowers in vases, and real crockery and cutlery and napkins. Men would carefully tuck napkins in at their waists to protect clothing that had not been washed in years.

Felix took a table in the rear of the church hall, back to the wall, ignored his stew and bread, and watched the girl. The pictures told the truth: a skinny little bitch, no tits, a big nose, hair cut short like a boy's. Probably a lesbo, probably because she was shit-ugly and never had a real man. Getting close to her ought to be a cinch, she'd probably come in her pants the first time he hit on her. He was not interested in eating charity soup with fucking piss bums. Besides, it reminded him of prison, although there were a bunch of women here, too. He checked them out: none of them were worth looking at, old bags mostly, and niggers. That might be one reason the bitch worked here, she was a dog but at least she had a set of teeth. It probably gave her a charge to be the best-looking piece in a room for once.

The diners finished their meal and drifted out. Felix hung out by the door and watched Lucy Karp and a couple of old cunts in aprons and headscarves strip the tablecloths and the few abandoned utensils from the tables and wash the tables down. Lucy and one of the women began to sweep the floor. Felix removed his sunglasses, strolled over to the girl, and said, "You need a hand with that?" He put his smile on maximum charm.

She looked at him, their eyes met. He saw that hers were pale brown, almost the color of cigarette tobacco, with gold flecks, and he also saw that her face was not, as he had previously thought, simply that of an ugly girl. It did not have the beaten look of the unbeautiful, but instead challenged his previous concepts of what beautiful was. But beyond the discomfort this caused (for Felix did not like having any of his concepts challenged) was his sense that the girl could see into him, past his array of masks, down to a place he had nearly forgotten himself. He felt fear, and for an instant he thought it was because she recognized him, that something had gone wrong with the plan, that the cops were wise. He stood there like a dummy, the smile congealing on his face, until she broke the spell by saying, "Yeah, thanks, you can hold the dust pan."

He held the dust pan. In the next few minutes he told himself a plausible story that explained in a way more suitable to his self-image the feeling he had just had. She had confused him with someone else, some other guy she knew. He was spooked a little, this was dangerous, this bitch was the daughter of a big prosecutor, who knows what she really knew? It was incredibly brave of Felix to expose himself like this, like something you could see in the movies, heroic.

They swept the floor together. When they were done, she held out her hand. "I'm Lucy Karp." He took it, and shook it like he would a man's hand, which being a dyke she probably liked. Some deep protective instinct told him that hitting on this one would not be a good idea. Another scam, then, not sex.

"And you are . . . ?"

She wanted his name. "Fel . . . Fellini," he stammered. "Joe Fellini." He felt a flush and sweat broke across his brow. He'd forgotten the name on his new ID. Uncool, but nothing major. He'd recover.

"Italian?" She gave him the real smile now, which, had he still been capable of human feeling, would have flooded his heart with gladness. "I'm half Italian myself. You from the city?"

"No, Buffalo. I'm here trying to get my kid back. I'm a little short, so I figured I'd save on lunch." He smiled in self-deprecation. Good, the story was flowing into his head. It would work; women were suckers for kids.

"When did you get out of the can?" she asked.

Always tell a little truth to cover a big lie. Some con had told him that and it was good advice. He hung his head. "You can tell, huh?"

"A guy's got weight-bench arms, no color on his neck, a fresh sunburn, and he sits in the back of the hall, too nervous to eat and watching everyone who walks in, I figure he's just out."

"Well, yeah, okay, what can I say? I did a three-year jolt in Elmira, out this past Thursday. A guy paid me five hundred to pick up a package at one of those private mailboxes. They had the place staked out. It was full of dope."

"What did you think was in the five hundred-dollar package, Joe? Stuffed bunnies?"

He shrugged, easing into the part—a working stiff nailed for a stupid mistake. "Yeah, it was dumb, but it was Christmas, I got laid off just before Thanksgiving, and I wanted to, you know, for my little girl . . ."

"It happens. What's her name?"

"Who?"

"Your little girl."

"Oh," a laugh, "it's Sharon. She's nine. She's with a foster family in the Bronx, nice people and all, but we really want to get back together."

"Her mother isn't . . . ?"

"Oh, man, that's a long, long story and I got a

job interview to go to. Listen, would it be okay if I got a meal here once in a while? I'm not really homeless and I don't want to like deprive . . ."

"No, it's fine—whenever you want. We get some really high-class people in here, because the food's so delicious."

"You're kidding."

"Our motto—Nothing's too good for the poor."

Felix felt a laugh was called for, so he laughed. "I'll see you around then."

"No doubt," she said, and watched him walk away down the street.

Lucy went back into the church hall. Sister Mac was mopping the floor. Lucy got another mop and joined her. Sister Mac was in her late sixties, with jaw and hair of iron, and a grudge against His Holiness the Pope. She'd spent twenty-three years in the Republic of the Congo and was working fourteen hours a day for the Catholic Workers as a form of rest cure.

"Who's the boyfriend?" she asked over the bucket.

"Just another con."

"Which kind?"

"Oh, definitely the behind the bars kind. Maybe the other kind, too. He's got a kid. A plausible villain, if a villain."

"Nice bod, in any case," said Sister Mac.

"I didn't notice," said Lucy airily. "Unlike you

nuns, I only focus on the spiritual elements of men."

"Uh-huh. How's the real boyfriend? Daniel."

"Went back to Boston. He wouldn't focus exclusively on the spiritual elements."

"You give that boy a hard time."

"He gives **me** a hard time. He won't take no."

"He wants to marry you."

"No, the opposite. We're twenty and twenty-one. We're still in college. We're too young to get married. But he'd like a down payment on nuptial bliss while we wait."

"My sister Kate was married at eighteen. Five kids and married to Jim for twenty-nine years. Happy as clams, according to her."

"Try to tell him that, though. People don't get married young anymore, by which he means professional people with careers. I honestly don't see why he stays with me, unless he's like one of those 1890s guys who just wants to deflower virgins, me being the only one in the Boswash region not actually in a religious order. Maybe I should just, I don't know, **do** it, like everyone else and then he'd be happy and leave me alone. We could be normal cohabiting lustbuckets, for God's sake."

"Would that make you happy?"

"Oh, don't try to be therapeutic, Mac," Lucy snapped. "I'm not in the mood."

"I'm just mopping the floor," said the nun

cheerfully. "I'm not a spiritual advisor." This was said in a tone that implied that certain people perhaps needed to check in with **their** spiritual advisors, instead of mooning, and complaining, and biting other people's heads off. They mopped: Lucy morosely, the nun with the same efficient cheerfulness with which she addressed the tasks that came her way, from making soup to assembling the remains of murdered children. In fact, Lucy had not seen her spiritual advisor in some time. She was avoiding him because she knew he would ask her about her mother, and she didn't want to talk about her mother to anyone, although she knew very well that this was the reason she drove her boyfriend away and snarled at nuns. Although she was perfectly at ease with thugs like Fellini, or whatever his real name was. The bad boys were no problem; in this she was also her mother's daughter.

Outside the church, she saw that Hey Hey was waiting. He beckoned and moved off in his dancing way, his hat pulled low to protect his thoughts, his red coat swirling. She followed, sighing. She did not want to follow a lunatic halfway across the city just now. She wanted to go home and shower the grease smell and the summer sweat off her body. But the man had once led her in this way to a pile of rags that turned out to be a man dying of hepatitis, and a life had been saved. So she followed.

Hey Hey always took the indirect route to any-where he was going, sometimes risking his life in traffic, to avoid dangerous nodes where his thoughts had been sucked out, despite all his pre-cautions. They ended up in an alley behind a pizza joint, where Hey Hey showed her a cat that had just had kittens.

Felix watched her emerge from the alley with the wacko. Why did she follow him in there? Sex? Dope? He couldn't figure any other reason, and the inability made him irritable. Still, he thought the first approach had gone pretty well. The dumb bitch had bought the story, and being a do-gooder like she was, she was obviously inclined to be sympathetic. He didn't like the way she had made him as a con, but that couldn't be helped—probably just luck, a lucky guess. And the thing with the name, which didn't matter that much. He thought it was pretty cool the way he had recovered with the little girl story, and how he had come up with her name. Sharon. That was the name his ex-wife had been yelling while he was working on her brat. Sharon! Mommy! Sharon! Mommy! It was a sketch, before it got on his nerves and he'd taped their mouths shut. When the time came to do Lucy Karp, he hoped it would be in a place where he could let her yell a little. He thought about this off and on, all the way back to Queens.

● ● ●

"What kind of sick fuck . . . ?" asked Detective Lieutenant James Raney of the room at large, the room being the kitchen of the Chalfonte home, but received no answer. The people in the room—detectives and crime scene technicians and a woman from the medical examiner's office—were naturally dying to know exactly what kind of sick fuck, and his name and address, but just now they could only look at the unbearable scene in silence. They'd seen everything, they had thought, but they hadn't seen many like this one. Detective lieutenants do not ordinarily visit crime scenes, but Raney had come because Rick Chalfonte had been a cop, a detective. He had been retired on a disability for some years now, and Raney wasn't exactly a friend, but they had friends in common, they'd had drinks together, and in the NYPD it was expected that a little extra would be forthcoming when a cop had this kind of trouble.

Raney made himself look at the bodies. This was also part of his job. He felt the bile rise in his throat. He coughed to hide this discomfort and turned to Detective Second Grade Rafael Beale, who had caught this case. Beale's cordovan-colored skin looked muddy, almost greenish, like a shoe left for a long time in a lake.

"We got anything yet?"

"Not much. ME says they died around mid-day, maybe a little earlier. It's hot, so they didn't cool much. No obvious prints; he probably wore gloves and some kind of wrapping around his feet. You can see where he stood, there"—he indicated smear marks in the pools of stiffened blood on the kitchen floor—"and there, probably when he was doing the girl. Both of them were penetrated vaginally and anally by an object, we don't know what yet. Maybe raped, too, but the autopsy will show it either way. Tore them up pretty bad internally, especially the girl. He left, um, produce in the orifices, bananas in the girl, carrot and celery in Mrs. Chalfonte."

"Rick came home and found them like that?"

"Yeah. Fuck! I'll tell you, Loo, we find this scumbag, it's gonna be hard to get him to a court-room."

"I don't want to hear shit like that, Beale, okay?" Raney snapped, and added in a calmer tone, "How did they die?"

"After he had his fun, it looks from the spat-ters, he cut the girl's throat. Sprayed blood all over the mother. That was after he cut the breasts off her, you can see there . . ."

"Yeah, I get it," said Raney quickly, "and then he smashed her head."

"Yeah. Some kind of hammer or steel bar to do that kind of damage. We haven't found the murder weapon or anything he left. He was real careful."

"Uh-huh. You'll run this through the bureau?"

"Oh yeah, VICAP, the works. Looks like he

had practice, maybe he did it before. And also the posing, the sexual shit. Could be. You ever work a serial, Loo?"

"Once. A pair of wack jobs was snatching little girls, a mother and her son. Satanic rituals. But nothing like this. This is fucking off the charts. Anything back on the canvass?"

"Not a whole helluva lot. Of the four closest houses, two were unoccupied at the time of, one neighbor had the TV on, didn't hear shit, the other's an old lady, heard screaming at about the right time, but she thought it was from a TV."

"Then he must have had the tape off their mouths for some of it."

"Yeah, the sick piece of shit. He wanted to hear them scream; that, or else he was torturing them for some information, or whatever."

"What kind of information?"

Beale shrugged. "You know, where's the money or the dope?"

"What, you think Chalfonte's a **guapo** drug lord?"

"No, but, you know, it's something to think about. Why he didn't leave the tape on them."

"Yeah, you're right. Okay, check that aspect out, but low-key it, you know? So it doesn't get back to him. I mean the guy was on the job, he works for Radionics, all that police communications gear . . . there's probably not a lot of money in his life. Anything else?"

"The across the street neighbor, old retired guy, saw a white male exit the house around maybe eleven, give or take. Blue ball cap, white T-shirt, chinos, sneakers. Odds are it was our perp. Couldn't see the face, average height, husky build. Walked off."

"That's interesting. No car?"

"Not that our guy could see. You're thinking a bad license? He's afraid to drive?"

"Or he doesn't own a car. Or he parked around the block. You'll check that out. Expand the canvass. I'm not sure we've ever had a serial killer who didn't have wheels . . . except . . ."

Beale waited, but Raney was chewing on his lower lip and staring up at a corner of the ceiling.

"You got something, Loo?" Beale asked.

"Maybe. That serial I worked on, the perp used the subway. He was some kind of feeb, probably he couldn't drive at all, but thinking about it just now . . . it hit me that Mary Chalfonte was married to his brother. Do you know this story?"

"No, what story?"

"No, right, it's twenty years now; you were in junior high. This nut, this satanic sacrifice woman had two sons. One of them did the kidnappings of the victims, and the other one wasn't involved in that. He was just a regular lowlife murderer. I arrested him, as a matter of fact, with my old partner Pete Balducci. Completely unconnected crime. He killed a woman and her little boy, slashed them to pieces. A real con man, too. Felix Tighe. The fuckhead kept Mary locked up and chained to a bed. Beat her with a hanger, among other bad stuff. Anyway, around this time, when Felix was on the run, she managed to escape and go to the cops, and the main cop she wound up with was Rick Chalfonte. He helped her through all the horseshit, and after Felix went up for life, she divorced him and her and Rick got together. And now this."

"So . . . what, you like this Felix for this one? He can't be on the street?"

"Beale, I would fucking **love** Felix Tighe for this one. Unfortunately, or fortunately, however you want to say it, he's dead. Died in prison just recently. But let me tell you, it's still a fucking weird coincidence. It gives me the chills."

4

"So, did you make your contact?" asked Rashid.

"Sure, no problem," said Felix. He'd scored some meth after leaving Lucy and was feeling pretty good. "No prob-bob-lemo. She was eating out of my hand."

"Very good. Our friend contacted us today. I will tell him this when I return the message. He will be pleased. This operation is of great importance to him."

Felix looked at Rashid blankly, but smiling.

"Our friend in prison."

"Oh, yeah. What, he called you?"

"No, of course not. All our communication is through the lawyer Bascomb. The message is to launch the other operation now. Here you will help us."

"The other operation?"

"Yes. Come with me, I will show you."

Felix followed Rashid into the kitchen of the house and down the stairs to the basement. Barring the way was a heavy door closed by a large hasp and a combination padlock. Rashid opened it, holding the lock closely as he dialed so that Felix could not see the combination. When the door was opened, Rashid flipped a light switch and ushered Felix inside, closing the door behind him and throwing a bolt to lock it.

A long hanging fluorescent fixture cast its industrial glare over a substantial cement-walled basement room. Shop tables lined one wall, with pegboards on which hung a variety of tools, and there were racks of cardboard part bins neatly arranged below these. Industrial shelving lined the other walls, stocked with cardboard boxes, cans, and lengths of pipe. There was a pipe-cutting vise on a tripod and a complex-looking electrical meter on the shop table. Rashid picked up a length of three-inch pipe capped on both ends, rusty black except for a small toggle switch emerging from a hole drilled in one of the caps.

"Do you know what this is?" Rashid asked.

Felix looked around the shop and then at the cylinder. What else could it be? "A pipe bomb," he said.

"But sophisticated, a sophisticated bomb," said Rashid. "I will explain. You see this small switch? This is the arming switch. Pushed down, like now, the bomb is harmless. Up? I will show you." Rashid moved to the work bench, laid the bomb gently on it, and picked from one of the bins a j-shaped plastic tube, white, as thick as a ballpoint's barrel. It had a squarish lump on one end from which two wires emerged and another pair coming from the belly of the j. He shook it; a tiny rattle.

"That is a ball bearing in there. When the device is on safe, this electromagnet holds the ball bearing in a little shallow cup. When the arming switch is thrown, the magnet shuts off and the firing circuit turns on. Any movement then knocks the ball out of its cup. It slides down the tube and comes to rest between these two contacts, which connect to the firing circuit. The ball closes the circuit and the bomb goes off. This is for cars, you understand, or lean it against a door where the target will come in. Or leave it in a bag at a shop. It can't be moved, do you see?" He jiggled the little tube again.

Felix saw, and struggled to keep his face neutral and interested. Rashid's pedantic manner was getting on his nerves. He thought about hog-tying Rashid and ramming the bomb up his ass and flicking the switch. He played with the thought for a while as Rashid droned on about the other types of detonating devices he had at hand: radio-controlled, timers, spring detonators for package bombs. And the explosives: homemade RDX, ammonium nitrate, and acetone peroxide.

"The explosives are the hardest to get," Rashid explained. "With the recent events, the authorities are being very cautious. We have enough for small demonstrations, but we are still assembling material for our larger project. Here you will come in."

"Me? How?"

"Fertilizer purchases. Small lots in garden and farm supply stores in the area, not enough at one time to be suspicious. Someone who looks like you, an American, would not be suspected. Despite that their own people bomb very often, the Americans are crazy looking for Arabs. It is very amusing, do you not think?"

"Yeah, I'm laughing my ass. What's your larger project?"

Rashid smiled in that annoying smug way he had. "Need to know, need to know. You will be told at the proper time. Now we are ordered to plant one device. The target is a judge. Evan Horowitz."

"What did he do?"

"He condemned our friend to life imprisonment without the possibility of parole, on the testimony of a lying traitor. It is impossible in any case for someone like ibn-Salemeh, an Arab patriot, to get a fair trial in New York with the Jews in control, but I think this action will demonstrate that we are not sheep to be slaughtered at their wish. So, here is what you will do: Horowitz keeps his car in an open lot behind the courthouse. You walk through the lot with several newspapers under your arm. You drop one, you stoop to pick it up."

Rashid retrieved the black pipe bomb. "In another newspaper you have one like this. You slip it out and attach it, under the car. It will have a magnet on it so it will stay. You throw the little switch and walk away. Do you think you can do this?"

"Uh, let me see if I get it," said Felix. "Do I throw the switch before or after I put it on the car?"

"After! After! It is the trembler detonation I showed you. If you throw the switch before . . ."

"Calm down, Rashid. I was joking, okay?"

Rashid frowned. Was it possible he was being made fun of? "This is not time for joking, Felix. I mean it."

"Sor-reee. So when do I blow the judge?"

"Tomorrow morning. I will give you further instructions then. Now, I have more work to do. You will leave now."

Felix made no move to follow this order, but wandered around the room poking into the various bins.

"Do not touch those things, please! I ask you to leave. Now!"

Felix had found what he was looking for. "Okay, okay, don't get all bent out of shape. I'm going."

He went out of the room. Rashid shut the door and threw the bolt. Felix took a moment to study the combination lock hanging open on its hasp. The sense of confidence and brilliance from the methamphetamine was still strong in him, and the idea that popped into his mind at that moment seemed like a stroke of genius. He left the house and walked with a spring in his step along Broadway to the hardware store he had visited that morning. There he purchased a Master combination lock exactly similar in appearance to the one on the cellar door hasp. He went back to the house and down the basement stairs. The door was still shut, and the lock was still hanging open. He switched locks and crept up the stairs.

When the Spaniards came home, Felix was in the living room watching television. He had been surprised to find that the house had cable, something new since he left for upstate. He was watching MTV with the sound off. He liked watching the girls but thought the music was shit. Carlos picked up the remote and switched the channels rapidly until he found a soccer game. Felix didn't object. He had scored some downers, too, and was working on his mix, just the right combination of prescription drugs for the feeling he wanted, strong and confident, but relaxed, too, so that he wouldn't get into one of his rages. Later maybe, but not now. He had to find the money, find out where the little Arab fuck stashed it. There had to be money. Everyone knew terrorism was a cash business. Then all these fuckers would get theirs.

The little Arab fuck came up from the basement and started jabbering in Arabic to the two Spaniards. They spoke Arabic, too, which didn't make much sense, since they were spics. Maybe part of Spain was Arab now. A lot of things had changed while he'd been in—cable, computers, all this terrorist shit, the weird people on the streets, women in fucking veils, niggers from Africa. He didn't like it, but what could you do? The main thing was the money. Keep calm, get the money, that was the plan. And revenge, that was important, too. That girl.

Rashid went out and drove off in his green Toyota station wagon. Of course, **he** got to drive a car. Felix waited until the sound of the car had faded. The Spaniards were glued to soccer. He went down to the basement, opened his lock, and went in. The completed bombs were racked neatly in a cardboard box, seven of them, separated by bubble wrap. He took one and adjusted the wrap to mask the loss. He replaced the original lock, went up to his room, and stashed the bomb under his mattress.

"What the hell was that?" said Karp to no one in particular. The sound had been loud and sharp, and seemed close, quite different from the muffled roar that he and everyone else in lower Manhattan had heard on September 11. Karp was in the fifth floor hallway of the courthouse proper. For a moment after the sound, everyone froze and let out an exclamation similar to Karp's, exclamations of astonishment, curses, a few prayers. Then the small crowd moved as one down to the end of the hallway by the elevator banks, to where tall windows gave views of the street. Karp could see nothing except wisps of dark smoke. The word "bomb" was much heard. And "terrorists." This was New York in the zero years of the new century.

Karp crossed through the security door to the DA's side of the building and climbed the three flights to his office floor.

"Did you hear it?" he asked Flynn, the secretary.

She had. She thought it sounded like a bomb, too.

"Murrow!"

Murrow came out of his cubbyhole. "It was a bomb, apparently," he said without being asked. "One of the judges' cars."

"Anyone hurt?"

"Yes, one killed. A court officer, Bedloe. You know, the one who tells you you can't park in the judges' lot. He was moving one of the cars like he does when the lot's jammed and it blew up."

"Christ! Where did you find this out?"

"When I heard the explosion, I called Jerry in the ground-floor snack bar. He always knows what's going on before anyone else. What do you think? More terrorists?"

"Doubtful. I was under the impression that the terror community was into clipping federal judges, not lowly state ones. Do you know whose car it was?"

"A brown Lincoln is all I heard. I could find out."

"Do so. Oh, and Murrow? Did you get anywhere on that other thing? I'm booked in with Jack and Rachman later."

"Yeah, Dr. Hirsch and the lovely Leona. Memo's on your desk."

Karp found that Murrow had done his usual thorough job, a page and a half of pure fact, which the sex crimes bureau should have discovered, but did not. He absorbed the details and turned to other things.

At lunchtime, Karp went down the street and walked around Foley Square to the special lot where the judges and other court officials kept their cars. Crime scene tape was up and the area was thronged with police and media wagons. Also present were the small band of demonstrators, with placards and bullhorn, demanding justice for Mr. Onabajo. They had been there since the trial started, local Nigerians, the women in loud prints, the men in African caps, together with the usual representatives of the African-American community. The wrecked car had been towed away, but a police tow truck was lifting another car damaged by the blast. Karp approached a detective he recognized from another case.

"What's the story, Sam?" he asked.

Sam Moscow looked around with a hard cop expression on his round face, which softened when he saw who it was. In response to Karp's questions, he said, "Oh, this here? We like it as an attempted assassination of a judge. Unless someone had a hard-on for old Bedloe. He gave out one ticket too many."

"Who owned the car?"

"Judge Horowitz. Nice Lincoln Towncar. There's frag all over the lot. No question it's high explosive, not any cheap-ass black powder jobbie."

"That doesn't sound good."

"Tell me about it!" said Moscow, turning a hard eye on a couple walking past, the man bearded with a turban, the woman in a sari, and also taking in the Onabajo people.

"Fuckin' city these days."

Karp let this pass. "You on the case?"

"Me? Nah, our loo sent a bunch of us from the Five down here to help out with the canvass. A red-ball obviously, with a judge being a probable target. The bomb squad will get most of the action. We're trying to see if anyone saw the perp."

"Did anyone?"

"Not yet. What's this Horowitz like? A hard ass?"

"Not particularly," said Karp. "He's been in Supreme Court about twelve years. I don't recall anyone shaking their fist at sentencing—'I'll get you if it's the last thing I do, you bastard.' But you never can tell. Or it might have nothing to do with his courtroom life. He might not even be the target. You recall those scumbags who were whacking cops at random, back in the day."

"Oh, yeah, them," said Moscow, morosely. "That's all we fuckin' need. Anyway, we'll find out which. Or not, as the case may be. I gotta go."

Karp watched the detective walk over to a group of uniforms. He thought about bombs, and bomb cases, of which there had been more than might be expected in his career, and Judge Horowitz. Out of his vast memory for cases the connection floated up: Evan Horowitz had been the judge who sentenced Feisal ibn-Salemeh to life imprisonment without parole for several murders and for plotting to bomb the offices of B'nai Brith, what was it? ten or so years back. That was a connection, thin but real, between terrorism, bombs, and the judge. He thought briefly of going over and telling Moscow this, but dismissed the idea. They'd find it out in short order. As the man had said, people who tried to assassinate judges got the full attention of the police.

At 4:30, Karp slid Murrow's memorandum into one of the green accountancy ledgers he used as notebooks, and went into the DA's office.

Laura Rachman was there already, today in an insistent violet costume. She was talking animatedly at the DA, who was studying the never-smoked Bering claro he used as a prop. He seemed happy to see Karp, if only to terminate Rachman's spiel.

"I hear you're interfering with the course of justice again," Keegan growled.

Karp sat down and nodded to Rachman. "Just a difference of opinion on **People versus Hirsch**. I don't think it's ready, Laura does."

"He wants a corroborating witness," said Rachman. "For crying out loud, it's a rape case."

"Actually, I didn't say that. What I said was I wanted something else besides the completely unsupported testimony of a woman against a doctor where we don't have a breath of anything else against him."

"Also untrue," said Rachman. "We have enough other stuff. Jack, this is a critical issue for me, I mean if I don't have your confidence . . ." She left it hanging.

Keegan said, waving the cigar dismissively, "No, no, come on, Laura, you know that's not the issue. What **is** the issue, Butch?"

"Well, I always thought that if your whole case depended on uncorroborated testimony from the victim, with no forensics at all, with the victim not reporting until five days later, like we have here, then the quality of the witness was pretty important. So is this the case with Ms. Coleman? You'll judge for yourself. It appears that Ms. Coleman got herself evicted from her apartment late last year, for nonpayment. She eventually came up with the rent and they let her move back in. She subsequently sued her landlord, claiming the stress and whatever of the eviction had caused her severe digestive upset, so severe that she had to quit work. She's suing for two million."

"What relevance does all this have—" began Rachman, but Keegan stopped her with a gesture.

Karp resumed. "A week after she mounted her lawsuit, she became a patient of Dr. Hirsch, who's a specialist in gastroenterology. She complained of severe stomach pains. Hirsch examined her and found no organic cause for her pain, but being a careful man, he arranged for this colonoscopy. Five days after said procedure Ms. Coleman reported the alleged assault to the police. Five days."

"She couldn't find a precinct with an African-American policewoman," said Rachman.

"So she says. Although she doesn't seem to have any trouble finding Albert B. Pearson, her lawyer in the civil suit she's been preparing against Hirsch. A litigious person, Ms. Coleman."

"She has every right to sue," said Rachman. Little spots of color had appeared on her cheeks.

"It's every citizen's right," Karp agreed blandly. "And her case will be a lot better if Hirsch is convicted. Moving on, we have the curious incident of the post-traumatic visit. The colonoscopy occurred on a Monday, the fifth of March. On Wednesday, Ms. Coleman arrived at Dr. Hirsch's office, without an appointment, and insisted on seeing him. He agreed. In the office, Ms. Coleman asked the doctor to be a witness in her lawsuit against the landlord, to testify that her putative intestinal ailments were a direct result of the stress caused by her eviction the previous year. This Dr. Hirsch refused to do. He said he could find nothing organic wrong with her at present, and even if he had made such a finding, since she hadn't been his patient before the eviction happened, there was no way in good conscience that he could testify to any physical debility attendant upon that event. At that, Ms. Coleman became angry and, for the first time, accused him of the assault. He vigorously denied it, and continues to deny it. Two days later, she reported it to the police. Now, none of what I've just said was included in the sex crime bureau's presentation of the case. But it was easy enough to get."

"Yeah, from Hirsch," Rachman said. "Of course, he's going to deny it and tell stories."

"Did you know all this, Laura?" Keegan asked.

"Of course we did. As I said before, it's irrelevant to the crime. The fact is, Ms. Coleman was abused. And we can prove it."

"Can you?" asked Karp. "Really? I mean, you

don't think all of this material rises to the level of reasonable doubt? The unlikelihood of the event given the medical situation, the exposed locale, the prior reputation of the accused, the lack of credible supporting witnesses, the failure to report, the return visit, during which no mention was made of the assault until after Hirsch refused to testify, the financial benefit of a conviction to the supposed victim . . ."

"I told you, it's irrelevant. And we'll make sure none of that is allowed at trial. With a halfway decent judge . . ."

Karp felt his jaw drop and his belly tighten. "Laura! For God's sake, what the fuck does it matter what you can get suppressed? It's fucking exculpatory evidence."

"Don't yell at me! Don't you dare yell at me!"

"Guys, guys, calm down," said the DA, who despised histrionics in his office that he did not himself initiate. "Maybe we can avoid trial in the first place. What would Hirsch say to a deal? The charge is sexual abuse first—we drop it to third, it's a misdemeanor, he might not even lose his license."

"We tried that," said Rachman, "Terry tried that and Hirsch told us to get lost. He says it never happened."

"Terry?"

"Teresa Palmisano, the ADA, very competent, very thorough."

Karp could not suppress a sniff here, and got a furious glare from Rachman. They were silent for a moment, while the DA cogitated. Karp thought he could almost see the wheels whirring in the man's head. Another racial case, black vic, white defendant, how would it look to the black vote, Rachman with connections to the liberals, to the women, percentage of votes that represented, plus the black, weak there in the first place, Karp a liability because of the racial thing, the doctor ought to deal, he wouldn't so he gets it in the neck, go ahead with the trial, the low-risk solution . . .

"Well, I'm inclined," said Keegan, "absent any other information, to let the case go forward. Let the jury sort it out. That's what juries are for. And next time, Laura, let's put everything, good and bad, in the pretrial package, so that Butch doesn't have to get bent out of shape off of this kind of crap."

Karp couldn't meet his boss' eye. He nodded his head and made a note in his ledger. A little forced chitchat to show that they were all still good friends, and Karp was out in the corridor with Laura Rachman. She turned to him and said, "No hard feelings, Butch, huh?"

"No, of course not," said Karp stiffly. "It's all part of the day's work. But, I admit it's still a little bit of a shock to see him do it."

"Do what?"

"Pervert the law for political purposes. I don't have a sister, but I guess that if I did, and she turned into a whore and I had to drive past her stroll every day, after a while I'd get used to seeing her in her little hot pants with her tits hanging out. But I bet it'd take a while, and I guess I haven't gotten to that point with Jack Keegan."

Her face wrinkled in distaste. "You know, Karp, you really are an offensive son of a bitch."

"So I've often been told," he said, turning away down the little dogleg corridor that led to his office.

"We're going to win this case," she called after him.

Karp stopped, turned to face her. "Yes, you might. There are enough asshole judges in this building, and one of them might actually allow you to suppress all the material about that woman's history and actions. That's not the point. Winning isn't the fucking **point**. We're not playing girls' soccer here, Laura. The point is that you know and I know and even Terry what's-her-name probably knows how incredibly, extremely unlikely it is that Hirsch actually stuck his tongue into the alleged victim's shit-smeared vagina in the way the alleged victim described it. The woman is a fraud, and the case is a fraud, and nobody seems to give a shit."

"Girls' soccer?" cried Rachman, her voice rising.

"And furthermore, whatever happens here,

you're going to get creamed on appeal even if you get your suppression. Appeals Court judges tend to take a dim view of the state junking exculpatory evidence."

"How **dare** you talk to me like that!" cried Rachman. Her face had gone pale and blotchy under her makeup, giving it an unfortunate clown-mask appearance. He turned again, and went into his office, slamming the door behind him.

Karp heard her shouting at him, heard himself called a misogynist as well as a racist, heard threats of formal complaint. Rachman had a famously aggressive tongue when aroused.

Terrell Collins was sitting in his office. Karp felt a flush of embarrassment rise to his face.

"You heard all that?"

Collins nodded. "Uh-huh. What's going on?"

Karp sat in his chair and put his feet up on the desk. "Don't ask. Yet another case flavored by racial overtones, into which I inserted myself with totally predictable results."

"I hear you're a misogynist, too. That line about girls' soccer was probably not wise."

"No, it wasn't. I lost my temper and Satan made the phrase swim into my mind."

"Will that be your case when she brings you up on a sex harassment complaint?"

"It might be. It might even work. It's more plausible than the case against Dr. Kevin Hirsch."

Karp took from his desk a baseball signed by

Mickey Mantle and threw it hard against an opposite wall a number of times, catching it one-handed on the rebound, enjoying the sting in his palm.

"Ah, fuck 'em all! Let them fire me. It'd be a mercy at this point." Karp tossed the ball into his out-basket, shifted his chair, and stared out the window for a moment, thinking about what his life would be like if he didn't have this job. A descent into the bowels of the profession, chasing ambulances, wills, and closings? Or in a gilded penitentiary, doing civil litigation for Wall Street? He snapped out of the brief, unpleasant reverie and said briskly, "So. What's new with the Gerber and Nixon case? Any sense that they'll deal?"

"Not a whisper. Both Gerber and Nixon claim they did nothing wrong, it was a clean shooting. The victim was grabbing for the gun, et cetera. Unfortunately we don't have criminal stupidity as a charge, because it would be a slam dunk to nail this particular pair on it. They're consistent, I'll say that for them."

"Yeah, like Hirsch," said Karp. "Well, Terry, look at the bright side: Even if you lose, they won't accuse you of letting them off because you're a racist."

"No, only an Uncle Tom."

"We all have our cross to bear, son," said Karp, in his faux paternal mode. "Meanwhile, I think I'll go home."

• • •

Felix loved it when the bomb went off. Rashid
had warned him not to hang around the area of
the courthouse, but he'd wanted to see it go up.
He had gone east of the courthouse, into
Columbus Park, and there sat with a newspaper,
pretending to read, and keeping an eye on the
parking lot. It was a lot louder and more gaudy
than he had expected, and he experienced an
almost methlike wave of pleasure when the
sound and the tail of shock wave reached him in a
little line of blown dust and scattered trash. He
loved, too, the expressions on the faces of the
people in the park. For the first time he understood suicide bombers; to have that kind of effect
on people was almost worth dying for. His pleasure was hardly diminished when he learned, a
few hours later, that the victim had been a parking attendant and not the judge. It was actually
better in a way, because if they still wanted him
to clip the judge, they would have to give him
another bomb. As the sirens began to wail, he
started uptown to the Holy Redeemer soup
kitchen to find Lucy.

5

KARP WENT HOME. HE LIVED IN A HIGHLY
gentrified loft at Crosby Street and Grand, a short
walk from the courthouse. It had not been gentrified at all twenty years ago, when his wife had
lived there, but over the years and through many
adventures involving the earning and expenditure
of large sums, they now owned it and it was now
all that a tony SoHo loft should be. Karp had been
offered truly nauseating sums of money for it,
which his wife had always refused to consider.
Karp would have considered even somewhat
smaller sums. He liked being able to walk to work,
but a loft had never figured in his dreams of what
adult life ought to be. Left to himself, he would
have chosen a large sprawling home in the nearer
suburbs, set back under old trees, with a basketball hoop over the garage. That was a proper envi-
ronment in which to raise children: good schools,
fresh air, no dangerous people. He imagined him-

self coming home from a day at the office, driving
an old car from the station to his broad driveway.
Inside his wife would be waiting for him or, not to
be a complete neanderthal, she would have just
arrived from her decent, lucrative work in a suburban law firm. . . .

Walking through the hot summer streets, he
often thought along these lines, especially when,
as now, he had to step around some passed-out
derelict, or the garbage generated by the
Chinese grocery that was his nearest neighbor,
but this sort of thinking had become a mere tic,
or something like an itch from an old amputation.
Even though he was at present literally left to
himself. When his interior tape got to this point,
it always escaped from its little rollers and tangled. He switched to more immediate concerns.
Lucy had not called him, so he didn't know
whether she'd be having supper at home tonight.
That was annoying.

He concentrated on the annoyance as he
worked the key for the elevator. That was new,
installed since the building had gone expensively
condo. He used to have to walk up four flights,
often carrying one or more children. That had
been the peak point of his desire for a suburban
homestead. In fact, he would have liked to have
reproduced his father's establishment in leafy
New Rochelle, with a happy family in residence.
He had not been able to manage either the house

or the happy family, it seemed. Was that Marlene's fault, or his? People whose professional lives are devoted to a fine assessment of blame often apply this art to their personal lives, with unhelpful result, and Karp was no exception. He thought bad thoughts about his wife as he walked into the loft.

As always, it was clean, smelling of floor wax and furniture polish. Lucy kept it so. A little pang of guilt here for Karp. His daughter had taken a leave of absence from Boston College so she could help out at home. Definitely Marlene's fault that, not the catastrophe per se, but the aftermath, her withdrawal, her refusal to face the toxic elements of her personality and . . .

He turned these thoughts off, a mental switch he used not less than fifty times a day. He went to the gigantic Sub-Zero refrigerator and pulled out a can of soda. Now he noticed that except for the purr of this machine, the loft was utterly silent, too silent to contain a pair of eleven-year-old twins. He checked. Gone.

Not unusual, actually. Lucy could have taken them out, or they could be down at the basketball courts, or at a friend's house. But they were supposed to leave notes on the refrigerator in the case of the former, or call in the case of the latter. More annoyance. He called Lucy's cell phone, found it turned off, and left a message. Karp changed clothes—a cutoff sweatshirt, chinos, and sneakers—grabbed his own cell phone, and went out, intending to do a quick check of the usual places before starting to call the friend list. He walked north on Centre Street. As he passed the cigar and magazine shop at Spring Street, he heard singing, a high pure voice backed up by a button accordion: "Rose of Tralee," with plenty of vibrato. People were coming in clumps out of the nearby subway station, and a small group had gathered around the singer. The boy singer was wearing black glasses, and he sat on a folding stool, in front of which his accordion box lay open with a sign affixed to it that read, BLIND BOY PLEASE HELP. Crouching against the wall behind him lay his guide dog, a large black lab. A drift of bills and silver lay in the case, and as the boy finished the song, more rained down from the listeners. Karp waited until the people moved on, went up to the boy, and asked, "What do you think you're doing?"

"Oh, hi, Dad," said the boy. "Pretty neat, huh? We made almost forty dollars since rush hour started."

"Giancarlo, why are you begging in the street?"

"I'm not begging. I'm providing music for weary travelers. It's part of the service economy."

"Uh-huh. What about the sign?"

"Oh, that was Zak's idea. He thought it was more authentic."

"It would be more authentic if it was scrawled in crayon on a piece of dirty cardboard and not printed on glossy paper using a two thousand-dollar computer."

"You think so? Maybe we should change it."

"Maybe you should lose the sign and the soliciting money on the streets routine. Unfortunately, some people have to earn their living this way and you don't. It doesn't strike me as fair for you to scarf up charitable contributions that should go to them."

The boy took off his dark glasses. His eyes were perfect, huge and glossy brown, and rimmed with lashes thick as mink. He could see out of them only intermittently and imperfectly, owing to a shotgun pellet lodged in his visual cortex. The rest of his face was in the style that fifteenth-century Florentines liked to cast in bronze or paint to suggest heavenly beings. Karp was always a little stunned to find he had fathered a child (two of them actually) who looked like that, especially after the girl had turned out so plain. When Giancarlo and his brother walked down the street, they stopped traffic. Just now the divine features were cramped into an expression of shock.

"Da-ad! We don't **keep** the money," the boy exclaimed. "We give it to Lucy and she gives it to the poor. I mean, **duuuh!**"

"I beg your pardon, then," said Karp. "This was Lucy's idea?"

"It was all of us's actually. We never have any money and she said we could do good and do well at the same time and I like singing and playing and it's kind of a goof. In Muslim countries, all the people have to give alms so they think people who beg are really doing poor people a favor, because they can, like, give a penny and then they're cool."

"Well, we're not a Muslim country **yet,** are we?" said Karp a little testily. He felt he had been caught wrong by his kid, never a pleasant experience of fatherhood, and he was also aware that it was his embarrassment and not the boy's that was now driving his bad mood. "And what's this about no money? You both get an allowance."

"When you remember. And it's tacky for us to have to nag for it. And it's not the same as when you earn it."

"I thought it was for the poor."

"We take a small administrative fee," said Giancarlo blandly.

"Oh ho."

"No, Dad, real charities do it, too. Lucy says. Even Mom's charity does."

"I'm sure. By the way, where **are** Lucy and Zak?"

"They went up Broadway to get some new sneakers."

"How about you? Don't you need new ones, too?"

"Da-ad." The long-suffering diphthong. "Obviously, if they fit Zak they'll fit me."

"Oh, you mean . . . you're twins?" said Karp, and Giancarlo laughed, a glory in itself. Which did not much improve Karp's unease. Lucy had slotted into the space Marlene had occupied so smoothly that it was only in moments like this that Karp understood how little he knew about the domestic arrangements necessary to raise two boys. Marlene had done it all—shopping, school, church, feeding, doctor, dentist. Like most men of a certain stamp, Karp had restricted his parenting largely to the fun stuff: sports, excursions, roughhousing, giving valuable advice. He realized that dads were supposed to be different nowadays, to be more domestic, but . . . he would think about that later, maybe have a talk with Lucy. Other charges accumulated on the rap sheet he kept in his head for Marlene.

"Well, I'm hungry," said Karp. "Why don't we see about gathering the clan and getting something to eat?"

"Could we go to Mercerama?"

This was perhaps Karp's least favorite place to consume calories: a large echoing chamber on Mercer Street full of video games, pinball machines, boys between eight and fourteen, guilty parents, and electronic cacophony. It served greasy pizzas and burgers. The guilty parent said, "Sure. That'll be fun."

• • •

"You really know how to show a girl a good time, Dad," said Lucy, rolling her eyes. "Why did you agree to eat here? You hate this place."

Karp was looking through the mob of juvenile males, trying to spot his sons. Zak was at a video game, killing pixels. A couple of younger kids were sneaking looks at his scores, which were, as usual, spectacular. And an even more interested group was observing Giancarlo, who was playing Skee-Ball.

"How the hell does he do that?" Karp asked, rather than answer her question. "He can't see."

"It's called blind sight," she said. "There's nothing wrong with his eyes; he just has a problem processing the image. But he can make an association between what his eyes take in and the sound of the ball, so he gets better at hitting the holes. I asked at the lab and it was explained to me in tedious detail."

"What do they say about the prognosis?"

"Guarded hopeful. It could get better, but it could get worse, too. Neurons tend to deteriorate if they're not used." With a sigh she added, "There's no treatment and no point in talking about it. Wait and pray is all we can do. He seems pretty happy, though, considering. How was your day? Bad, right?"

"Oh, you know. The usual crapola. I had a run-in with Laura Rachman in which Jack decided to hang some poor schmuck to make a point. How could you tell I had a bad day?"

"Your eyes get all pouchy and you snap at the boys more than usual. As you used to continually tell me, don't take the blame for every damn thing that goes wrong in the world."

Karp let out a short rueful laugh. "And aren't I sorry now! How about you? How were the poor today?"

"Always with us. But I've picked up an admirer."

Karp felt a small chill. "Oh?"

"Yes. Larry. Yesterday he was Joe Fellini, but today he's Larry Larsen. He even showed me a driver's license. He said he was embarrassed about giving out his real name because of having to eat at a soup kitchen. But now he trusts me. We're pals, now."

"This is, um, not a guy like the last guy, I hope."

"Meaning David Grale?"

"Yeah, him."

"No. But also the dangerous type. Or likes to think he is. He's an ex-con. Very handsome in a movie star way, square jaw, thick dark hair, lying blue eyes. He's got that terrific body-builder shape they all come out of the can with. A lot of magnetism."

"Oy vey. When's the wedding?"

"Yeah, right. No, Dad, this is an old guy, over forty probably."

"Oh, that's a relief. Because most guys give up thinking about sex when they're thirty-nine or so."

"I meant, it's not that kind of thing, not a kid-crush thing like I had with Grale . . . what's wrong?"

"Nothing."

"Yes, there is. You just sucked all the air out of this booth."

What was wrong. Karp had just processed the observation that well over three quarters of the adults in the place were middle-aged professional men like himself, casually dressed, with stunned expressions and false smiles. Were they all like him, currying favor with their kids by taking them to this hideous place, feeding them empty calories, supplying game tokens? Was he in divorced dad hell?

He became aware of his daughter looking at him peculiarly, waiting for him to speak. He dismissed the idea of sliding by with a polite fiction about just being tired. The girl had a bullshit detector equal to his own. He thought to himself: But I'm **not** divorced. I'm at home and my kids are home, too. What was it, then?

"I don't know, hon," he said. "This place gets on my nerves. It symbolizes . . . I don't know, barbarism: noise, hypnotic lights, children practicing reckless driving and killing. And it just made me think, when you mentioned Grale, like, Oh God, my daughter has a close relationship with a serial killer, and her nanny was a Vietcong assassin, and my wife arranged to have a couple of dozen people killed and got away with it, and she's hiding from me and her family, and one of my sons is blind and the other one is deep into violence and hardly ever talks ... . it's a little too much, you know? I didn't want this. And somehow, despite what you say, I feel it's my fault."

"Because you're the dad."

"Right. I'm the dad."

"Mom says the same thing. It's all her fault, too. Honestly, I get so tired of the two of you."

"Then who's to blame?"

"Oh, God give me strength! **Nobody's** to blame. This family's been immersed in crime and violence since day one. The pair of you are crusaders against the dark forces, and a good thing, too. You run the DA and Mom is an unindicted felon, but what the hell, to each their own. And it can't help spilling over. If you were doctors in a plague city, you'd bring disease home, if you were shrinks you'd bring craziness home, if you were Martha Stewart you'd bring stupid table decorations home. It's our fate. Do you see any of us whining for things to be different? Or blaming? Look at Giancarlo. He's a great little artist, he loses his sight through no fault of his own, and what does he do? He picks up music. Six months after inheriting Nono's old accordion, he's playing practically like a pro. Zak is perfectly happy as long as he's got his brother to protect from all enemies foreign and domestic. If the marines took recruits at eleven he'd be in paradise. I'm fine as a lab rat and little sister of the poor, it suits me to a T."

A trace of bitterness here, but Karp chose to let it by. "And your mother?"

"Oh, her. Well she's a special case. She's got it into her head that she's poison, that she's some kind of curse on the family. But she's really a very religious person who's pissed off at God because He won't be bullied like she bullies everyone else. She knows she has to repent and forgive and be forgiven, but she'd rather drink and be a noble hermit. It's pride, is all. It's the deadliest sin."

"I thought the problem was she wasn't really religious. I thought you thought her stuff with the Church was all for show."

Lucy rolled her eyes. "Dad, please! Where do you think **I** get it from? Not from **you**." She saw his face fall and was instantly sorry. "Oh, I didn't mean it like that. You're religious, too, only you don't know it."

"How do you figure that?"

"Because you love the truth," said Lucy, as if stating the obvious. "It's the basis of all real religion. Don't you think you're closer to God than some Vatican cardinal all rotten with lies and cover-ups and evasions?"

"Oh, good, you mean I might avoid the eternal

fires? To be honest, as long as you brought it up, I always hoped that they'd put me in a somewhat cooler corner because of you being a saint."

"Did you really think that?" She laughed, an act that transformed her face. Light seemed to shoot from her eyes. "Good Lord, I'm not anything like a saint. I just have a religious gift, which isn't at all the same thing. There's only one saint in the family." Here she turned in her seat and looked through the crowd to where Giancarlo was blindly tossing a skeeball. It made a short, graceful arc and landed in the smallest hole, right in the center.

Somewhat to Felix's surprise, Rashid was not particularly disturbed about the miss on Judge Horowitz. More important, he had not discovered the missing bomb.

"Actually, now that I think of it," Rashid said that evening, "it has a greater effect if he is killed while being guarded. First we demonstrate that we blow up a car right in front of the courthouse. They are thinking, Is this random, is this against the policeman who was killed? Or against the judge? They don't know, they are in confusion. Then we strike again."

"You mean **I** strike again. You're sitting here, right?"

Rashid gave him one of his hard looks. Felix

had to suppress the insolent grin that clawed at his mouth. "We are together, all together. Teamwork. Do you think it is easy making bombs? It's dangerous, highly dangerous tasks. One mistake . . ." He lifted both hands in the air and made a throaty noise. "Anyhow, we wait a day or two, until their guard is a little down. We are in no rush. Tell me about the girl."

Felix shrugged. "Hey, we're making friends. I figure the way she looks, nobody ever gave her the time of day. But . . . you know, if I'm really going to get close to her, like **close** close, I need a place."

"A place?"

"Yeah. Where am I supposed to take her? The fucking park? I got to get her in the rack, get her wanting it so bad that she'll do anything I want. You want her to talk about this guy Tran? That's what it's gonna take. I need an apartment in the city, not a shithole either, and more money, too."

Rashid stared at him. Felix met the stare. The Arab smiled. "Well, you are the expert. This can be arranged. I will see to it. Anything else?"

"Yeah, I need a kid, a little girl. Eight or nine."

A look of distaste crossed Rashid's face. "For what purpose?"

"It's my hook into her. I told her I had a little girl and I can't get together with her because of my bad record. She wants to help. She keeps asking where she is, who's watching her. I promised her next time I'd bring some pictures."

Rashid nodded. "This can be arranged, too. Also, you will be happy to learn, we have provided you with a car."

"Yeah? What kind?"

"It doesn't matter what kind—a car that goes is all. You will need it to transport devices here and there around the city."

"When is this happening?"

"Soon. Timing is everything in this kind of campaign. We desire the maximum of fear, and this is obtained through timing—terror, terror, then a pause, enough to bring life back to normal, and then terror again. The confidence of the people in the authorities must be gradually destroyed, until they will do anything to obtain safety. This is his doctrine."

"You mean ibn whatever—behind bars?"

"Yes. My leader. He is a very great man."

"Then what's he doing in the slammer?"

"He was betrayed," replied Rashid with heat. "By a source that could not have been predicted. But he will be free. Or I will bring this city down around their ears."

Jim Raney sat with all the other detective lieutenants and captains in the five boroughs of New York, in a large auditorium on one of the higher floors of One Police Plaza, the headquarters of the

NYPD, and listened to the man from the FBI talk. He took notes, as did all his peers, because they were under the eye of practically the whole of the department brass and wished to look engaged. They already knew most of what the FBI man had to say, having received a thick wad of paper earlier that morning. It was the third week of what the media were calling the Summer of the Bomb.

Raney had not been professionally affected by the bombings, which had hit only in Manhattan so far. Crime was down in the city these past years, especially in north Queens, and his squad, although reasonably busy, was not stressed. His major concern at present was the murders of Mary and Sharon Chalfonte, and his mind kept drifting back to it as the FBI man spoke on about the person they were calling the Manbomber, after the location of all but one of his attacks. Raney knew that the bureaucratic purpose of this meeting was to prepare the detective squad leaders for a diminution of their troops. A major task force was being formed, ran the grapevine's message, and everyone was going to have to kick in. Raney had every spare man-hour devoted to the Chalfonte case, and that would suffer if he lost guys. He was thinking about who to send to the Manbomber task force when they asked. Or maybe they would just pick them, which meant he would lose his best people.

The FBI man was describing the Unsub now,

the "unknown subject" in their queer parlance. A white male, over forty, it seemed, strongly built. This was conjecture, based on the report of witnesses who had survived the explosion that destroyed a Madison Avenue bus. Apparently, the Unsub had boarded the bus at Thirty-fourth Street just before rush hour, shoved a time bomb under his seat, and exited at Fortieth Street. The bus had been crowded, and, of course, all the people who had sat next to him were dead, but an exhaustive canvass of everyone who had been at the Fortieth Street stop at around the right time, together with interviews of the survivors of the bus blast, had produced the sketch now projected on the screen in front of the detectives: a white everyman with a thickish neck, a ball cap, and sunglasses, essentially useless for identification but all they had.

A map of Manhattan next appeared on the screen, marked with the location of the six Manhattan bombs: the courthouse parking lot; Baxter Street; the midtown bus; a subway car at Eighty-Sixth Street; a bakery truck on Greenwich Avenue in the Village; and a movie theater on Lexington and Thirty-Fifth. There did not seem to be a pattern in the targets, the timing of the explosions, or their location. The terror was as random as the weather, its author of no discernable political or religious persuasion.

They had done a psychological profile of him,

too. A loner, they thought, not political, a grudge against society, a careful worker, probably college-educated, an American, may have been institutionalized at some point, either between jobs or a nightshift worker. They didn't think this series of bombing was the work of a foreign terrorist cell. Next, the FBI man talked about the Horowitz connection. Judge Horowitz's car had been blown up in the courthouse parking lot, killing an officer. Nine days later, the judge had been killed by a large bomb placed underneath a truck on Baxter Street and detonated by radio control as he drove by it in his brand new Lincoln. Theory: Horowitz was the target, and the other explosions were distractions. The judge's cases had been examined all the way back to his service in municipal court. Any convict he had ever sent to jail and was presently at large had been interviewed. His personal life had been minutely examined. The only halfway interesting suspect was Feisal ibn-Salemeh, presently incarcerated at Auburn, whom Horowitz had sentenced. But ibn-Salemeh seemed to have no contacts outside the prison. An exemplary prisoner, according to the prison, and a useful source of information about terror far from Manhattan. For a number of reasons, the American intelligence community did not wish to put the screws to Mr. ibn-Salemeh, and so the word came down from the highest levels that he was not to be unduly disturbed.

➤ Another chart flashed on the screen. This displayed the names of the fifty-three people who had died in the six explosions, with lines showing how they were connected. There were a lot of lines, unfortunately; there always were. Raney stared at the reproduction of the slide provided with his handout. If six degrees of separation connected any two inhabitants of the planet, it was likely that fifty-six out of the city's nearly eight million would be connected in some way. It didn't necessarily mean much, although it had to be checked out. For example, two partners in a jewelry business had been killed in two separate blasts; a man killed in the bakery truck, Hassan Daoud, had once appeared as a witness before Judge Horowitz in a case involving that same ibn-Salemeh. Raney remembered that one—he had been the detective on the case. A minor drug dealer, Jongo S. Wallace, had also been killed in the bakery truck explosion, just walking by on the street. He had also once appeared as a prosecution witness before Horowitz.

The bus and the movie theater had yielded a total of sixteen victims with some connection to the criminal justice system. Raney scanned the names. A couple seemed familiar. Steve Lutz, for one, a lowlife and a part-time snitch. Raney recalled Lutz, a minor character in the drama of the late Felix Tighe, a reluctant prosecution wit-

ness. That got him thinking about Mary
Chalfonte again. The case was cooling already.
All they had was a few white cotton fibers and
some could-be-anybody descriptions. Chalfonte
seemed clean, no girlfriends they could find, no
money troubles, the man seemed both devoted
and destroyed by what had happened. So a wandering serial killer had caught up with Mary; she
who'd escaped the clutches of one maniac had,
through the mysterious workings of chance, been
picked by another. Like the people killed in the
bombings, bad luck was the only real connection.

The FBI man finished and was replaced by a
colleague, who had diagrams of bombs to show.
Apparently Manbomber was something of a
genius in this line. The devices were all powered
by RDX, a military explosive, mixed with plasti-
cizing wax at nine to one, a combination known
as Composition A3 that was normally used in
artillery shells. Where did it come from was the
question. The obvious place to get it was scav-
enging from military stores, but small quantities
could be manufactured in a kitchen, if you knew
what you were doing or were very lucky. This guy
knew what he was doing. The FBI man guessed
that the stuff had been homemade. Acetone peroxide had been used as a booster. This was a dangerous and unstable substance much favored by
terrorists the world over. The bombs had been
detonated by standard blasting caps, triggered by

either timers, radio receivers, or trembler switches. They thought that the devices used had been carefully homemade from parts recovered from junk appliances, and hence untraceable.

The head of the FBI's terrorism task force, a rock-jawed, graying man named Earl Brannock, now took the podium to sum up. The Unsub was a white American, middle-aged, unemployed or a night-shift worker, probably unmarried. He may have spent time in mental institutions, but was probably quite intelligent, maybe college-educated. He had a high level of technical skill and may have trained in the armed services. The bombings were random and seemed to express nothing more than a general rage at the people and places of Manhattan. He may have had some contact with the criminal justice system. All these leads were being checked out. He wanted the detectives to keep alert, to report any suspicions no matter how far out. We're going to catch this guy.

After that, the chief of detectives made a brief statement: thank you, thank you, all work together, total commitment by NYPD, spirit of cooperation, know you have a lot to do, but details will be drawn from all detective squads in the city, notifications already on their way. We're going to catch this guy.

The meeting broke up. On his way out, waiting for the elevator, Raney fell in with Roy

Arnolf, a detective he'd worked with in the old days at the Five in lower Manhattan. He remembered that Arnolf had been with the joint FBI-NYPD Antiterrorism Task Force for a couple of years.

"So, Roy, we gonna catch this guy?" he asked.

Arnolf snorted. "Yeah, if someone drops a dime on him or we get real lucky. He tries to rob a bodega with a bomb in his pocket."

"That's it?"

"Hey, how else? The explosives are untraceable. Like he said, you can make RDX from common chemicals or smuggle it in. What're we gonna do, inventory every shell and mine in every military in the world? He's making the detonators from scratch, just like the Unabomber used to do, and **he** never would've been nailed if he hadn't sent in that letter to the papers and if his brother hadn't recognized his particular brand of looney tunes. George Metesky, the Mad Bomber—he wrote letters, and he had a hard-on for Con Ed, so they caught him through employee records. The original Arabs on the World Trade Center were a bunch of amateurs. We traced them through the truck they used. So it's the usual thing, we get him with snitches or some bonehead mistake. Anyway, all this," he gestured broadly at the milling detectives, "is for popular consumption, so the bosses can say we've got two hundred of our best men on it."

"So basically you're saying an arrest is expected soon."

This raised a sour laugh from Arnolf. The elevator came and they got in and talked about other things for the ride down.

Felix liked the work. He especially liked having a place of his own and spending money and no fixed hours. It was practically the best deal he had ever had since he left his mother's house. The apartment Rashid had found for him was on Thirty-Sixth and Tenth, a fourth-floor walk-up in what started out as a Hell's Kitchen tenement, but was now a **Clinton studio, mod. kit. strt. vw**. He had plenty of new clothes, in a variety of styles—work clothes, business dress, tourist get-ups. He fancied himself now a master of disguise. He had a blond wig and a false beard, and a number of distinctive hats. Fooling the schmucks of the world had always been one of his prime delights, and now he was being paid to do it, and blow some of them up in the bargain. It was a boy's dream come true. Why Rashid was employing him in this way he never asked, nor did he care. He thought it had something to do with religion, that Arab shit, although Rashid did not seem to pray or perform any rituals, like the Muslims in the joint did. But who knew what the miserable little fuck got up to? Felix himself had no use for religion, which he conceived as mere lists of things you couldn't do. His mother had been religious in a way, a devout Satanist, but there they had lists of things that no one else was allowed to do, which you **had** to do, which sucked, too, as far as Felix was concerned. He had never found an object of worship more worthy than himself.

Rashid was a pain in the ass and would get his when Felix was good and ready, but he had to admit that the bastard knew what he was doing. He had provided Felix with a phony job, at Haskell's, a heating and cooling contractor where the two Spanish guys worked, which was some kind of front operation. So Felix had pay stubs, and a fake SSN, with which he got his gas, power, and phone turned on. Also, Rashid let him make his own decisions about where and when to bomb, only specifying general targets—a bus, a train. This was to cover the actual revenge targets, Horowitz and some Arab guy who needed to be clipped for some Arab reason. Felix didn't much care, and he'd applied the method of settling some scores of his own. It was no problem following a particular guy until he boarded a bus or a train, and leaving a package under a nearby seat.

One thing Rashid had taught him that was useful: always use unidentifiable components. He'd found the stout cardboard box behind a liquor store, a long thin one that had held expensive scotch. The stolen bomb slipped neatly into it, and he'd wrapped it with brown paper from grocery bags and strapping tape. There was a tiny hole in one side, through which one could stick a stiff wire and flick the arming switch. He checked his new watch—almost 2:30. He left the apartment with the thing in an athletic bag. He was dressed in green coveralls, a green ball cap with a company logo stitched to it, and work boots—a dumbass on the way to or from some night shift. His car was around the block, a dark blue Crown Vic six years old, but in good shape. Another Rashid purchase, anonymous and efficient. He turned it on and checked the taillights and brakelights. He definitely did not want to give a bored cop some excuse to stop him, even though he was white.

He took the tunnel to Queens, nearly deserted at this hour, and drove at a little under the posted speed limit, making a full stop at every stop sign, to an address in Rego Park, a two-story brick bungalow with a fig tree in the front yard and a statue of the Virgin glowing under the sodium lights. He went through the chain-link gate, propped his package up against the door, armed it, and left. The guy would come out in the morning to get his paper and good night, Irene. Felix wished that he could be there to see it, to see the expression on the cop's face before it melted off his skull, but he figured you couldn't have everything.

6

LIEUTENANT JIM RANEY PICKED UP THE call on his police radio on his way to work the next morning. They gave the address and said there was one man dead. Raney felt his stomach knot; he knew the address well and could figure out who the dead person was. With siren and lights he made it to Sixty-Sixth Avenue in Rego Park, Queens, in eight minutes, and found fire trucks, an EMS vehicle, blue-and-whites blocking either end of the street, and a couple of unmarked police vehicles. The firefighters were finishing up, coiling their hoses, watched by knots of people from the neighborhood, staring from behind hastily stretched tape lines. There was smoke in the heavy air, a stench of burnt wood and asphalt shingle. Raney parked, clipped his shield to his jacket, and walked toward the house, crunching on broken glass. He noticed that nearly every window on the block had been blown out, giving the rows of modest brick homes the blank-eyed look of tragic masks.

The target house had lost its façade and almost the entire front room. A scorched upright piano sagged over a dark void, from which thin smoke emerged. Most of the ground floor had collapsed into the basement. Raney saw a carpet he recognized, impaled on floorboards. The statue of the Virgin that had stood in the little front yard was lying in scorched pieces. Also in the front yard: a paramedic picking red globs up with tongs and placing them carefully in a yellow rubber body bag. Raney's gorge heaved and he had to look away and take deep breaths.

"Pretty bad, huh?" said a voice behind him. It was Rafael Beale. Of course! Raney now realized, with something of a shock, that the crime had taken place in his own bailiwick.

"Hell of a blast. Lucky there's only one vic, but he's **really** dead. There isn't a piece of him wouldn't go through a one-inch hole. Guy's name was . . ." He looked at his notebook.

But Raney had the name: "Pete Balducci."

"Yeah," said Beale, surprised. "How did you know?"

"He was my first partner, right after I got my detective shield. In the Five, downtown in the city. He retired like twelve years ago. Christ,

I've been in that house a thousand times. Shit!"

Randy kicked at a piece of debris.

"Sorry about that, Loo. And the remarks, I didn't know—"

"That's okay, Beale. We have anything so far?"

"Not much. I talked to the arson guy from the FD. He's scrambling around down there in the scene. The special unit from the bomber task force is on route."

"They think it's the guy?"

"Well, it's early yet, but the FD says it was definitely a big, high-explosive-type bomb, like the six we got over in the city. Anything new on all that the other day? At One PP?"

"We're looking for a white guy, forties, muscular. He might have a hard-on for the criminal justice system, the feds think, but really, bottom line, who the fuck knows? Anything come back on the canvass yet?"

"Nobody saw shit," replied Beale, "which figures, a neighborhood like this goes to bed early. It looks like the perp came by at night, left the thing by the front door. A motion detector on it . . ."

Raney cut him off. "Yeah, well, we might as well get back to the house. This case is going over to the task force."

Beale said something else, but Raney didn't hear him. The word "random" was buzzing in his mind, a word that Special Agent Bannock had used often in his presentation. Terror was random by definition: that's what made it terrifying. The universal goal of any terrorist was that no one in the target population be able to predict who might be the next victim. The task force had analyzed the connections among the victims and came up blank. Raney had seen the charts. So it had to be random that Felix Tighe's ex-wife, and a witness who had testified against him, and the cop who had arrested him had all been killed. Just a coincidence . . .

"Loo, are you okay?"

Raney snapped out of his reverie. "What?"

"I been talking at you for five minutes and you were someplace else."

"Sorry, Beale, I was just thinking about Pete. I need to call some people, get with the family and all. He's got two daughters, grandchildren."

His eyes drifted over the scene: the crime scene technicians, the firemen, the medics, all picking at the ruin. It seemed mindless and far too weak a response, as measured against the enormity of what had happened. September 11 again, in miniature. At some level he understood that this is what you did because it was all you could do—put things in little labeled bags, a pathetic attempt to reorder chaos. He saw an unmarked van pull up at the head of the street. Three men and a woman emerged, and Raney felt relief, tinged a little with shame.

He said, "Meanwhile, there's the task force guys. Let's turn this over and get out of here."

Marlene is selling a dog to an airport security man from New England. Selling dogs is not something she likes to do particularly, but it's necessary and she's good at it. She briefly reflects on how much of her life has been consumed (often she uses the word "ruined" to herself) by tasks where these three things are true. Also, Billy Ireland is impossible at sales. His chief sales tactic is "take it or leave it, asshole"; often they leave it. He regards any criticism of his trainees—real, implied, or imagined—as a personal affront. So Marlene does the selling. It's not hard, since there is something of a seller's market in this kind of dog nowadays.

The customer is a big, middle-aged white man with a wary look, and the dog is a medium-sized brown dog, with a black muzzle, floppy ears, and an eager expression. Marlene has noticed this before: the dogs know they are being talked about.

"Well, I don't know," says the man. "I was expecting a pure-bred, you know. Five thousand dollars . . . that seems steep for a dog that . . . well, it looks like a mutt."

"That's because she is a mutt, Mr. Willowes," says Marlene. "She's also a talented bomb sniffer, trained right here. She has a good disposition, she's only three years old, and she's a good worker. Aren't you, Violet?"

Violet agrees with this assessment by wagging her tail. Marlene goes to a wooden filing cabinet and takes from it a waxy red cylinder. "This is commercial dynamite," she says, "but she'll find all the conventional military and industrial explosives. I'll give you a demo." She takes a tissue from a box on her desk and wipes the dynamite stick, as if polishing it for the Terrorists' Ball. Then she hands the tissue to Willowes. "There's a flagstone path outside and a drystone wall on the other side of the yard. Go hide this, and give me a yell."

Bemused, the man does so. Marlene clips Violet to a short lead and, when she hears the man's shout, walks the dog outside into the warm afternoon. Bark. Whine. Scratch. Violet finds the bait under a stone. The man is impressed and wonders why the dog is not given a reward for finding. Marlene explains that the finding is its own reward; a little praise is enough. "They're better people than we are, you know," says Marlene sadly.

The phone in the house rings. Marlene tells Violet to lie down, excuses herself, and trots into the house. Mr. Willowes is making calculations, figuring out how many Violets he will need, how many handlers, to keep his airport safe, and whether he would be better off with expensive sniffing machines and min-wage staff to work them, when he hears a great shout from inside the house. A shout of dismay, he thinks. More shouting. A few minutes later Marlene emerges, dabbing at her face with a tissue, perhaps the same one.

"Something wrong?" he inquires politely.

"A friend of mine was killed this morning," she explained. "In the city. Another bomb."

They go back into the house, where Marlene sells him four bomb dogs: Violet, Peaches, Trampette, and Lola.

During the noon recess of the fourteenth day of **People v. Gerber & Nixon,** Karp invited Terrell Collins into his office to discuss the trial. The prosecution had concluded its case in chief that morning. Karp had the transcripts strewn in piles on his desk. Collins threw his lanky frame into a chair and puffed out air.

"What do you think?" he asked, indicating the transcripts.

"What do **you** think," countered Karp. "You're in the courtroom. I can only derive so much from reading transcripts. How did your case play with the jury?"

"They were polite. They listened. No one dozed off."

"That's not what I mean," said Karp.

"Yeah, I know. I guess . . . look, the whole point of our case is do you believe our witnesses or do you believe the two cops. Just now, with Nine Eleven and the dead heroes in the background, people in this city are inclined to believe the cops. It doesn't matter how many civilian witnesses I drag in there, and it doesn't matter if they all confirm one another and contradict what the cops say. Klopper stands up on cross and asks each of them if the DA went over their testimony with them, which they say yes to, of course, and he has a way of implying, without actually coming out and saying so, that we made it all up. I've called him on it when he actually claimed we made it all up and the judge backed me, but you know how that goes. The seed is planted." He sighed. "Frankly, I think we're gonna get creamed."

"Yeah, and as long as that's your attitude, you **will** get creamed," Karp snapped. "What the fuck, Terrell—don't say shit like that in the middle of a trial!"

Bridling, Collins replied, "Hey, you think you can do better, boss, be my guest!"

Karp felt the blood flowing into his cheeks and made a conscious effort to calm himself. In fact, he **did** think he could do better, although Collins was a perfectly competent, even a brilliant young lawyer. He had not, however, won over one hundred straight homicide cases like Karp had. He had not met Hank Klopper on two separate occasions and ground him into the courtroom floor. That made a difference.

"All right, Terry," he said soothingly, "let's not get in each other's face. This is still winnable. It's civil service, you're not going to be fired. Cheer up!" He moved his face into an expression of confidence and bonhomie. The glower on Collins's face broke into a thin smile.

"Let's talk about the defense case," said Karp. "Today is what?"

"He's leading with a Marlo Burns, a homeboy who's got a different story on the shooting. I think I can bring out that Mr. Burns has a thing against Nigerians. Then Hugo Selwyn, guy's a defense-hack forensic expert. I presume he's going to cast doubt on the trajectory data we presented, the fact that the victim took four rounds while he was lying flat on the ground. It argues against pure self-defense."

"Good. Exploit the hack aspects. Challenge his credentials. You up for that?"

"Yeah. I know the guy's whole life story. He was fired from a crime lab in Jersey for incompetence. Since then he's been a defense witness in cop shootings all around the country. Aside from that, all they have is the defendants."

"You think he'll call them? Hank never calls defendants."

"Ordinarily, yes, but this is a special case. My

sense is that these guys don't just want acquittal, they want total exoneration. They may be pushing him to call them."

"What're they like?"

"Nixon's the brains, Gerber's the brawn. Not that either of them is a rocket scientist. I'm guessing that after it went down, Nixon came up with the story and got the partner to go along."

"Okay, so their story is—tell me if I got this right—the victim tried to sell them dope, they identified themselves as cops and tried to arrest him, he grappled Nixon and tried to grab his gun. In this struggle the gun fires twice and the vic takes a round through the flank. The vic's still grabbing for the Nixon pistol, and Gerber draws his gun, yells 'hands up' or 'get down,' whatever. Nixon has control of his gun now and shoots again, and hits Onabajo's arm, but the victim of steel keeps holding on. Gerber shoots him five times and he finally falls."

"You got it. The sequence we have from the witnesses and ballistics is that Onabajo slugs Nixon because Nixon is trying to make him out to be a dope dealer, which he isn't, and Nixon shoots two bullets into him. Flank and arm, but both flesh wounds, nothing mortal. He staggers away. Gerber shoots him, he falls, and Gerber shoots him four more times while he's out flat, making seven wounds in all. That's our murder case, as you know. Gerber shot a helpless man."

"Yes. But Nixon didn't."

"Yeah, right, and you'll recall we offered him a deal. He wouldn't move off the story. Like I said, they think they can beat us clean, go back on the cops, collect the pension."

Karp grunted, turned away, and looked out his window. Something was struggling to emerge from deep storage, something about this case. It wouldn't come, and he knew better than to try and force it. It was like Giancarlo's blind sight: he could see it, but he couldn't process it. That was the trouble with coaching a dozen trials and attempting to keep an eye on the whole range of cases running through the system: stuff got tangled and lost and confused, the facts blended, going spongy and vague, not standing out sharply like gems in a bracelet, as they did when he was actually running a single trial. Something about Nixon's story, maybe from the grand jury? Collins should have come up with anything real, of course, so maybe it was just the old war horse smelling gunpowder, somewhat pathetic, really. . . . He turned back to Collins, who was staring at him with interest.

"Well, we can't let them do that, can we?" Karp said.

"No brilliant ideas?" Collins asked hopefully. "I thought I saw the mighty brain at work just then."

A derisive snort. "No, I'm clean out of brilliance nowadays. But there's something . . . I can't quite come up with it. In the grand jury testimony, or the ballistics . . . what you just said set me off, but I'm drawing a blank. You should look into the grand jury transcripts and the ballistics reports again, see if anything pops up."

"If there was anything pop-upable, don't you think it would've popped up by now," said Collins peevishly. "Jesus, I've been over this case until it's coming out of my ears."

"Do it again."

"Okay, right, but we're running a little short on time here," said Collins, rising. "The damn trial'll be over in a week or so." He rose. "I got to get back."

Collins left, drawing with him the sourness of defeat. Karp knew he had hoped that the old magician would pull a last-minute trick out of the bag, but Karp had not. He didn't believe in last-minute tricks anyway. Perfect prep and perfect delivery equaled a conviction: so he had been taught and so he had always taught. Maybe that had changed, too, though: everything else had.

He shook off the cloud enough to pursue his routine work of reviewing cases, signing papers, hosting meetings. A man delivered a sandwich and a soda and he ate it at his desk. After lunch there was a particularly rancorous and irritating meeting about the budget. Laura Rachman was there, being chief among the irritators. Karp wondered

whether it was about her, or him. He detected in
her manner toward him an assertiveness that bor-
dered on the rude. He didn't think he was a cave-
man where professional women were concerned,
but she seemed to treat him as if he were—furs,
club, sloping forehead and all—and he found that
this actually brought out the residual Neanderthal
in him. He snarled at her, she snarled back, and
seemed almost glad to have her paranoia thus confirmed. Marvelous!

Next in was Arno Nowacki, the superinten-
dent of the courthouse, a bulky, florid man in a
plaid shortsleeved shirt and a tie covered with
little pictures of hard hats. He had on his face
the fixed and humorless grin of a man whose
every customer is dissatisfied. Karp was not in
his chain of command, but still a figure to be
reckoned with around the courthouse, so
Nowacki's grin was a little broader and sadder
than usual. After the usual guy-sports talk, Karp
said, "Arno, the heat. Jurisprudence is a product
of the cooler northern climes. Do you want us to
descend into the lawlessness of the benighted
tropics?"

"What can I say, Butch? I didn't make the
decision to fix the AC system in the middle of a
heat wave. We got the money late in the fiscal
year and we have to spend it before the year ends
in October. You know what it is: you got a state
building, under city codes, and a project funded

sixty percent with federal money. It's a wonder we get anything done."

Karp had to laugh. "But you can guarantee that the system will be up and running by the time the cool weather hits, right?"

Nowacki's grin became nearly genuine at this. "Almost guarantee it, and another thing I can guarantee is that we'll get to the heating system in the middle of a fucking blizzard. I got eight sub-contractors on that job, including a couple of low-bid pissant outfits I never heard of. Two new boilers, installing natural gas lines, ripping out the old oil system. The boilers alone, Jesus talk about a job and a half. . . ."

"I don't want to hear the word 'boilers' today, Arno," said Karp. "Can you get me more fans?"

"After this meeting, he left his office, telling his secretary that he might be found for the next hour in Part 39. This was the courtroom where they were trying **People v. Hirsch**. Karp slipped in as quietly as he could and took a seat in the spectators' area. There were plenty of empty seats, in contrast to the **Gerber & Nixon** case's courtroom, which had been packed from the first day.

An athletic woman with short dark hair and wearing a short dark suit was standing in the well of the court questioning a witness. This was the ADA, Terry Palmisano. She was an active pacer and whirler. Karp had noticed recently that with the plethora of law shows on television, the younger attorneys had begun to model their behavior on fictive representations of lawyers, much as the actual Mafia had done after the success of the **Godfather** films. This woman, he noted, was wearing a skirt right out of **Ally McBeal,** descending a good three inches below the curve of her buttock. Karp checked the jury: there were two youngish women on it, and ten rapt men. Karp wondered whether she had used her preemptory challenges to bump frumps who might be jealous. Or maybe the jury also failed to distinguish between truth and fiction, just as, during the immediate aftermath of 9-11, Karp had heard a number of people say, as if guaranteeing the veracity of their eyewitness, "It was just like the movies!"

Karp watched the Terry Palmisano Show with some interest, therefore, to find out how people were now supposed to behave in a courtroom. The witness was a distracted-looking woman, somewhere north of forty, a vaguely bohemian mien. She had on a flowered dress and a fringed shawl and a crystal pendant with which she toyed. Her graying blonde hair was worn in a three-foot braid, also toyed with alternately with the crystals. The woman, a Ms. Winograd, was describing the complex of digestive symptoms that had caused her to visit the defendant some sixteen months ago. Palmisano let her ramble on about her dietary theories and her reluctance to seek help from what she called "the medical model." The defendant's lawyer objected on the grounds of relevance. The judge waved this away: she seemed fascinated by the Oprah-like spiel from the witness.

On the bench was Her Honor Margaret Anne Fogarty, or Mad Meg as she was affectionately called around the courthouse. Mad Meg had attained to the Supreme Court of the State of New York (which is what that state somewhat idiosyncratically calls its felony trial courts) on the basis of her professional qualifications, which (as with all judges) were two in number: she had a law degree and she knew a politician. In Karp's opinion, Mad Meg Fogarty was not only unfit to rule a courtroom but barely competent to mop one, yet there she sat, robed and majestic, dumb as a sack of hammers, massively prejudiced, and destined to be overruled on appeal. Karp wondered if Laura Rachman had arranged to get this particular judge. It was against the rules, of course, but not unheard of.

So the witness was allowed to tell her story in detail: how she was drugged and seduced by Dr. Hirsch in his clinic, how he pursued her, how he subjected her to degrading sexual practices, how he finally abandoned her when she threatened to go to the authorities. Karp looked at the jury: Were they buying this lunacy? Yes, they were, it seemed. It was just like on TV.

The defense counsel was Lew Waldbaum, a well-known courthouse bull, bald and aggressive and (outside court) genially profane. But he was gentle, almost courtly, with Ms. Winograd, which is how Karp would have handled the woman, too. On cross, Ms. Winograd added some details that Palmisano had not chosen to bring out, such as that Dr. Hirsch often appeared at Ms. Winograd's apartment wearing an animal suit. What sort of animal? Here Palmisano objected as to relevance, and was sustained. Waldbaum changed tack. You testified that Dr. Hirsch supplied you with drugs? What sort of drugs. All kinds, I don't recall exactly. Um-hm. And you're no longer taking any medication? No, except for the Clozaril. I have to take that for my condition. What condition is that, Ms. Winograd? I was diagnosed with schizophrenia, but it's in remission.

Objection, of course. Ms. W is not on trial. The fact that she's a fucking lunatic dragged up here to besmirch a man's reputation, to support a piece-of-shit case based on the testimony of a known liar should not be made known to the jury, Your Honor. Palmisano did not really say that, but if she had, Karp imagined, Judge Fogarty would have sustained the objection. The jury was instructed to disregard the testimony about the medication and the witness' medical history.

That was all Karp could take for the day. Outside the courtroom he spotted Laura Rachman.

She gave him a nod and an empty smile, which
Karp did not return. He watched her enter Part
39, to observe the work of her protegée, he
imagined.

Karp knew that if he stayed in the office,
steamed as he was from his visit to the Hirsch
lynching, he would make errors and enemies, neither of which he could afford. He decided to go
home. The boys would be glad to see him earlier
than usual; maybe he'd take them somewhere—
not the video game place, someplace quiet—for a
civilized meal, and Lucy, too. Lucy was always
calming. He would tell her about his sad life and
she would say something gnomic about the moral
order that would make him feel not utterly abandoned. He wondered whether this was entirely
healthy; a man was supposed to share this kind of
stuff with his wife, not his daughter. Was he warp-
ing her? Clearly not: of all the people in his life,
she seemed to be the one that most demonstrated
the quality of straightness, like a steel rule against
which everything else might be tried. But maybe
he shouldn't burden her anymore. He should
suck it in and drive on.

On the sidewalk in front of his door Karp
threaded his way through cartons of obscure vegetables of the Orient, the overflow from the produce store on the corner. He felt an irrational
surge of rage, and shoved a box of bok choy violently away with his foot, cursing, drawing frowns

and Cantonese mutters from the produce clerks. Little blue flames of real racism darted momentarily through Karp's consciousness, only to be efficiently snuffed out. Thus has New York survived over the centuries.

Riding up in the elevator, he calmed himself. It was the encroachment on his role at the office that was behind it, he thought, not the damned veggies blocking his door. He was supposed to keep the system honest; that was the core of his job, but in practice it had become "only as honest as was consistent with politics," hence the monstrosity of a trial he'd just witnessed. He breathed deeply, willing the churning in his gut to cease. What was wanted was calm, a happy daddy, home, no tensions dropped on the family, shelter in a heartless world. A pleasant, stress-free evening . . .

The elevator door opened. His son Zak was standing there at the open door to the loft, as he often did when he heard the sound of the elevator. Through an excited grin he crowed, "Dad! Mom's home!"

"She is?" The churning returned, amplified, cubed.

"Uh-huh. She was here when we got home. Some guy got blown up is how come." He ran back into the house.

She was home indeed, sitting in her usual place on the couch in front of the immense, purchased-with-ill-gotten-gains plasma TV set, watching the

news, flanked by her two boys. The mastiff Gog
was at her feet, staring at Blue the guide dog, daring him to start something, Blue meanwhile utter-
ing little growls at intervals, signifying his position
that if Gog wanted to start something involving
Giancarlo, he'd better bring his lunch.

Karp stared at his wife. She was thinner than
she had been and tanned, not a resort tan, but in
the red-leather way of outdoor working stiffs.
The haircut was a mistake, he thought; no more
thick curls artfully sculpted to draw attention
away from the false eye. Maybe she didn't care
anymore. He said, "Well. She's back."

"For the funeral," she said.

"Funeral? Zak said something about a someone being blown up . . ."

"Pete Balducci. You didn't hear?"

"No. Oh, boy, Pete Balducci. That's terrible!
When did it happen?"

"This morning. In Queens. Jim Raney called
me and I came right in. I thought about going
to . . . you know, someplace else, but I came here."
She looked up at him. The familiar illusion that he
could see emotion in both eyes, pain in this case.
"I hope you don't . . . that you're not pissed . . ."

"Marlene, don't be crazy. You live here. It's
your loft."

She turned back to the TV. "I made gazpacho
and a bean salad. And tacos for the boys. It's a
hot day."

"Sounds great," he said. Some more neutral chatter. The twins discussed how to catch the Manbomber. Giancarlo opted for an elaborate sting, Zak for careful forensics. The parents joined in. Karp's voice sounded false to his ears, as if they were all reading a script for a sitcom that would be canceled after three episodes.

Karp was about to ask where Lucy was, when she walked in, carrying two grocery bags. Zak crowed out the big news. Lucy calmly put the groceries away and came into the living room, where she embraced her mother. It was a stiff, almost formal contact, like that between ambassadors from rival nations. Energies Karp could feel but not identify coursed around them as they exchanged pleasantries—love, longing, fear, resentment, all of the above. The boys felt it, too; a gelid silence fell. As usual, it was Giancarlo who forced the play. "I'm hungry," he declared. "Is there anything to eat?"

With which they all trooped into the dining room, where a truly delicious warm-weather meal was served and eaten, and everyone spoke around their real feelings, and pretended to be an intact and happy family. Toward the end of the meal, remarkably, they became through the grace of love and temporary amnesia an actual intact and happy family. Around the table hearts grew light, the old family jokes cracked out, there was laughter.

Then Marlene started to weep, silently, so that it took a while for the others to notice. The boys grew quiet, first Zak and then, after a whisper from his twin, Giancarlo also. Lucy leaped up and announced an expedition to Little Italy for Italian ice cream. In full sergeant-major mode, she overcame their objections (can't Mom come, too?) and drove them from the loft, also dragging along the two dogs.

When they were gone, Marlene released the first of many howls and rushed into the bedroom, where she flung herself down on the bed. Karp followed and sat by her, gently rubbing her back, at a loss. She used to do this, he uncomfortably realized, after she had killed someone, such sessions occurring from time to time during their marriage rather more frequently than Karp had anticipated when he stood with his bride at the altar. Stroking a weeping woman did not take up much of Karp's attention; his mind wandered. He thought about what she had looked like then, the first time he had ever seen her, hurrying down a corridor in the courthouse, a rookie ADA, arms full of legal documents, a pencil stuck rakishly in her thick, dark hair. He never really looked at her then, because she was so beautiful that his glance slid off her face like raindrops glancing from the skin of a simonized Buick. And he was married to someone else at the time, too. But it was also that something in him intuited that she didn't like the gape-mouthed stares that men sprayed her with as she did her work. He didn't truly study her until after they had become lovers, by accident really, and even then he would do this slyly. If she caught him, she would say, "What?" and he would always say, "Nothing." Or invent some triviality, make a little joke. Her beauty was a secret of their marriage.

That perfection was now long gone. A bomb had exploded in her face years ago and taken her eye, and incised tiny scars around her face that plastic surgery could not entirely conceal. She used to hide these with artful makeup, but no longer.

"What?" she said. She had stopped her crying and was looking up at him from the pillow.

"Nothing. Are you okay?"

"No. What an idiot I am! Somehow, I thought I could just waltz in, my little pied-à-terre in the city, stay a couple of days, go to the funeral, flit back to the farm. I didn't think . . . I didn't think about what it would be like, seeing their faces. Or I thought it would be harsh and cold and recriminatory, and I could get to snarl back, a change of clothes and out the door. **I didn't think . . .** the story of my fucking life! I can't bear to look at Giancarlo groping around, and knowing that it's **my** fault, and Zak desperate to protect him and everyone else in the world, doomed little gunman, just like his fucking **Mom**. And Lucy . . .

looking at me like she's **waiting** for something, for me to . . . what? Confess? Repent? Kill myself? I love them, but they're knives in my heart, and every minute I'm with them I'm quaking in terror that some monster I raised when I was being Wonder Woman will crawl through the window and . . . I don't know, hurt them **more.**"

"That's ridiculous, Marlene. What happened to Giancarlo, the whole West Virginia thing, wasn't your fault. You might as well say it was **my** fault. I was the prosecutor on the scene. If I hadn't figured out how to arrest those guys, they wouldn't have been in jail, and if they hadn't been in jail, they wouldn't've broken out, and shot Giancarlo in the middle of their jailbreak . . . I mean, things **happen**. Kids get hurt. There's a whole system we set up to distinguish culpable causes from the other kind, otherwise we couldn't have life. We'd blame Henry Ford every time someone got hurt in a car wreck."

"Maybe we should," she snapped back, refusing comfort. "Maybe the world would be a better place if everyone took ultimate responsibility for every act, down to the seventh generation. Anyway, it's not just Giancarlo. It's not even the family. Even under the strictest definition of culpability, you won't deny that I'm directly responsible for how many homicides? Thirty-four, I believe. Half of an entire family wiped out, because I was enraged that some hillbilly moron shot my kid. So I sent for my Asian gangster pals. Kill them all. I actually said that. And they did."

"That's a different story," said Karp. "Yeah, you're an unindicted conspirator in a mass homicide. That's true."

"And this doesn't bother you?"

"Yeah, it bothers me. It was wrong. Even though you probably saved the lives of an even larger number of other people, cops and women and children. A little Hiroshima morality there. In any case, none of the alleged killings took place in the County of New York, so I personally don't have a moral conflict, and also my sense is that you were operating under extreme emotional trauma, and that would take some of the sting out of it if it ever came to law. Besides which, I'd argue that you can't be held responsible for all the events that occurred in a gang war, with heavy firearms on both sides. Your guys were just a lot better. I mean it's not like Tran lined all the Cade boys up against a wall and mowed them down. So you could go back to West Virginia and confess. And you know what would happen? First they'd cut you a sweetheart deal, because they have no legal case against you at all, and then they'd probably give you a medal for getting rid of the Cades for them. You want to do that? Pay your debt to society?"

"It's a shame you're not Catholic. You would've made a hell of a Jesuit." She sat up in bed, against the headboard, staring fiercely at her husband. "It has nothing to do with a debt to society. That's **your** thing. Fuck society! It's a moral wound. I have no place left to stand."

"You could go see Mike Dugan. Get absolution. Isn't that what you're supposed to do?"

"I don't have the energy for it. More to the point, I don't have good intention. To be forgiven you have to make an act of contrition, you have to promise in your heart that you won't do it anymore. And I can't do that. I'm still moving in a cloud of violence. What do I do all day? Train attack dogs. **Attack** dogs!"

"So quit."

"And do what? Be a lawyer? A housewife? How long before someone shows up and says, 'Hey, Marlene, I got this little problem you could help me with.' And I'd do it, I'd be in the thick of it again, with the bullets flying." She sighed and hung her head. Karp could see strands of silver nestling in the dark pelt. "Sometimes, at night, out at the farm, I take out my pistol and hold it and I stare down the barrel and I think, Oh, why the fuck not?"

Without a thought, Karp found his hands on her shoulders shaking her. "Shut up!" he cried. "Shut up! **Shut up!**"

He jammed his mouth against hers, roughly, and bore her down beneath him. She was stiff for a moment, her jaw clenched. Their teeth clashed painfully. Then she relaxed. Her felt her nails at the back of his neck. They barely undressed. He didn't know any other way to fight the death in her.

Lucy kept the boys out a good long time, ice cream and a visit to the little museum that exhibited common objects blown up to monstrous proportions, and a trip to the music-video emporium on Canal Street, where they rummaged through racks of old CDs, searching for the kind of weird music Giancarlo liked. When they entered the loft, they heard the sound of splashing and soft parental murmurings from the hot tub.

Lucy raised her finger to her lips and walked in a comically exaggerated tiptoe, ushering them in this way to the other end of the loft, where the childrens' rooms were located. Giancarlo paused and took a deep breath, his beautifully fluted nostrils expanding. He smelled the attar of roses his mother used in the bath and on her body. And other scents.

His brother whispered, "Is she going to stay?"

"Maybe," he replied. "Anyway, she's here now."

Felix was mildly pissed that the bitch hadn't wanted to come over and see his new place. He'd helped her clean that shithole soup kitchen up, he'd smiled and charmed the old bags—"yes, sister, no, sister"—and he'd shown her his new photographs, him and his daughter, a little pale girl with an uncertain smile. He'd made up a whole line of bullshit about the girl, so fluent and detailed that he believed it himself. Felix always believed the lies he constructed, which contributed in no small way to his success as a con artist and a seducer.

As yet he hadn't touched her, not really, just a brotherly hug or two, but he could see that she liked it, liked the attention. It wouldn't be hard once he got her in the apartment. But she wouldn't come. She had to go home for dinner and she had stuff to do, she said, after. Which had to be bullshit. Like guys were lining up to date her!

He found a connection on Tenth and Forty-Second Street, and bought some black beauties and Valiums and Tuinals. He popped a couple of the downers immediately to calm himself, take the teeth-grinding edge off the uppers he was on. The tranks were starting to kick in when he opened the door to his apartment and switched on the overhead light. It didn't light. He cursed, slammed the door, and walked farther into the room. He smelled something then, faint and familiar, but before he could figure out what it was, something struck him on the back of the head and he fell into a deeper darkness.

7

FELIX CAME OUT OF THE FOG IN A SPLASH
of cold water, with a crushing pain in the back of
his head and the discovery that he could not
move. He blinked the water from his eyes and
saw Rashid's face, floating there with a peculiar
expression on it, avid and self-satisfied, like a
nasty schoolteacher about to mete out punishment to an errant boy. Felix also observed that
the reason he couldn't move was that he was
secured to an armchair with duct tape. His right
arm was affixed to his side, his torso was tied to
the chair back, his ankles were similarly
restrained, and his left arm was stretched out and
taped to the kitchen table. The hand itself was
heavily wrapped in silvery strips, except for the
little finger, which hung free over the table's
edge. Without seeming to, Felix tested his bonds,
and found no give; he was an expert in this field
and recognized the work of someone who knew

the art. He noticed that the big shaven-headed guy, Carlos, was standing behind Rashid, holding something in his hand. Off to one side, just within Felix's field of view stood the other one, the beard, Felípe.

Felix cleared his throat and said, "What the fuck is this, Rashid?"

"What is this? You want to know? Listen to me. Firstly, we Arabs invented numbers, did you know that?"

"Numbers?" Felix was trying to arrange his thoughts, come up with something, but it was impossible, with the pain in his head and the mounting fear in his belly. His eyes were fixed on his little finger hanging helpless over the table's edge.

"Yes, numbers. One, two, three, four. And also zero. Zero is an Arab invention. Many years ago, of course."

"Yeah, that's great," said Felix. "And look, Rashid, I don't know what this is all about, but you got to admit this is a little extreme, whacking me on the head. I mean there's no reason for . . . I'm doing good for you guys, right? I mean the bombs, and the girl is coming along real good, just the—"

"Shut up! So, since we invented numbers, of course we can count. I have counted my prepared devices and instead of twelve there are ten. That is two missing. Did you think I would not **notice** two missing bombs? Today I hear that this old man has been blown up in Queens, and I think, Can there be a connection? I tell you, Felix, my mind boggles. Is he really so stupid that he believes that **I** am so stupid that I don't **notice** this event? But it is so. You are a stupid man, Felix. I tell you, I warn you in every way, and yet you do this." He made a little clucking sound. "So, you must be trained like a donkey now, with the stick, so you will see we are serious men." He gave a quick command in guttural Arabic. Carlos moved swiftly into position with a pruning shears and snipped off the first two joints of Felix's little finger.

Over Felix's howl, Rashid asked, "Now, where is the other bomb?"

"What happened to your hand?" asked Lucy when Felix showed up at the Holy Redeemer kitchen that evening.

Felix lifted the hand, which was swathed in bandages, and presented a rueful smile. "I caught it in a crusher at the recycle plant up in Morrisania. Took half my pinkie off. My second day. I could get workmen's comp, but meanwhile I'm on the bricks again. Some shit, huh?"

"That's terrible, Larry! What are you going to do?"

"Well, the violin playing is out." He uttered a brave little laugh; she smiled at him.

"You seem to be taking it well," she said.

"Hey, what else can I do? If I didn't have bad luck, I wouldn't have no luck at all. At least, as long as there's people like you in the world, I won't go hungry."

He gave her a glittering smile. She turned away and dumped some carrots she had cut up into a huge pot.

"Thank you. How's your little girl?"

"Oh, Sharon's great. Hey, that's some good news. I got custody of her. You know, I got this job, so my parole officer fixed it for me. She's at my place now."

"By herself?"

"No, no, there's a nice old lady down the hall, glad to watch her." He paused and offered another smile. "So . . . want to meet her? I told her all about you."

"Sure, I'd love to. Bring her around for supper. We have chocolate cake tonight."

"No, what I thought was, she's kind of shy and maybe the first time, you could come by our place. We could get takeout, you know, like a family evening."

His eagerness was palpable. "Well, it'd have to be next week," she said. His face fell, and for an instant she saw something boiling behind his eyes.

"Oh, that's too bad," he said. "Sharon'll be real disappointed."

Lucy said, "I wish I could, but I've got something of a family crisis myself." Someone called to her from the depths of the kitchen, and smiling an excuse, she went off.

Felix had to hand it to himself. Introspection was as foreign to him as Hungarian, but he realized in a vague way that he had a short fuse and that this had meant trouble for him in the past, and so he was proud of not having picked up a knife or something heavy and killing the little bitch right there in the kitchen. Losing a piece of his body had concentrated his mind more than it was used to, besides which he was clean and sober for the first time in a while, the Arabs having found and lifted his pills. But he **had** to get the girl alone, he had to get her to talk about this fucking gook the Arabs were so interested in. They were going to clip another joint off if he didn't tell them about the other bomb, so he did, but it was already planted, they couldn't move it, so it would eventually go off. Rashid had asked a lot of questions about the target and Felix had answered truthfully. In the end, Rashid had shrugged and acquiesced. And why not? What the fuck did they care where the bombs went off. Then Felix had made what seemed now to be an error. He had to disarm them, make them see he was still on the team, so he'd spun a story about the girl, the girl was ready to pop, she loved him, she'd do anything for him, he was that close to getting the story on the gook. It had worked, too. Rashid's eyes lit up.

That was the insurance. They could get another mule maybe to do the bombs, some skinhead, some wacko, but this they couldn't replace, the relationship. So he had to deliver, and soon. That would get him in good again, buy him a little time to figure out how to kill the three of them.

"How did it go?" asked Karp.

From the doorway of Karp's office, Collins said, "About as well as could be expected. Obviously they moved to dismiss after our case in chief, and Higbee blew them off. Then I chewed Burns up pretty good, the lying scumbag."

"Good. Good for you."

"And we started on Selwyn the ballistics fraudster."

"And?"

"Okay, I guess. But you know how it goes with this technical shit. One expert says one thing, the other expert says another. Who knows what a jury will do with it? I didn't stipulate to his expertise and I got the bit about him being fired from Jersey onto the record. Higbee sustained me. That's all we did, cross and redirect. Klopper was rare. I guess he figures if it's confusing once it'll be more confusing six times, and that'll add up to reasonable doubt. Judge let most of the repetition stand. So who knows?" He hesitated, then asked, "Did you come up with that thing?"

"Not yet," Karp admitted. "It's probably an idle fantasy, old neurons firing at random. And it's a little late for it now anyway. I'm sorry."

Collins shrugged, made a what-can-you-do gesture, waved a good-bye, and walked off. As he left the courthouse he loosened his collar and headed toward the subway for the ride uptown. Crossing White Street, he heard his name called. He turned and saw it was Hank Klopper.

Klopper pointed a blunt finger and said, grinning, "You **momser,** you did good in there. I was sweating."

"That's nice of you to say so, Mr. Klopper," said Collins, continuing to walk. Klopper fell into step beside him.

"It's Hank," said Klopper. "Not that it's gonna do you much good, given how things are in the city nowadays. Cop shoots Muslim? Half the people in the city would be lining up to buy the bullets, give 'em the chance."

"And half wouldn't."

Klopper laughed. "Point taken, but that still doesn't help you, because you need a hundred percent to convict. Sad but true. I could walk Jack the fucking Ripper right now if he was sporting a badge."

"We'll see," said Collins, moving away from the corner. "Nice talking to you, Hank."

"Can I give you a lift? West End Avenue, right?"

"How do you know where I live?"

"Hey, if you don't know where **I** live, you didn't do your job. Didn't Karp teach you to do a full bio on the comp?"

Collins stopped walking. He had not done such research, and was a little guilty about it, and was conscious that he was being flattered. He realized that for the first time he had reached the professional level where top-end defense lawyers thought it worth their while to treat him collegially. And avoiding a long subway ride at 110 degrees F. had its attractions. If Klopper wanted an opportunity to feel him out privately, two could play at that. He nodded agreement and they both turned east on White.

"So, you gonna be a lifer with the DA or are you planning to emerge into the broad uplands someday?"

"I like the work I'm doing."

"Sure, what's not to like? Except the salary. You got kids?"

"Clearly you know the answer to that," said Collins.

"Yeah, just making conversation. We're down here."

They entered a subterranean parking garage on White near Franklin. The temperature dropped ten degrees.

"This must cost you," said Collins.

"More than my rent on my first apartment. But leave my car out in the sun and the lunatics

all day? Forget it! Also it's new. My second childhood, my wife says, a Porsche Carrera convert-
ible, yellow. I had it three months."

They descended a flight of dark, gray stairs to
a parking deck.

"Anyway, I understand idealistic," Klopper
went on, "shit, it's hard to believe, but I was idealistic, too, way back when. I worked poverty law
for a couple of years in Nassau County, then did a
hitch with the DA out there. Meanwhile, it's
gonna cost you probably a quarter million to edu-
cate each of your . . . holy fucking shit!"

This last phrase was shouted. Collins saw the
Porsche in its stall, gleaming like a lone lemon at
the bottom of a crate, and he saw bearing down
onto it an immense Ford Expedition that was cutting to back out of the stall opposite, a little faster
than was wise. It was clear even from a distance of
twenty yards that the driver of the SUV was using
only the rearview mirror and couldn't see the low
sports car, and that the huge rear bumper of the
Ford was not going to clear the Porsche's yellow
snout. Klopper shrieked in anguish and ran forward a few steps. Collins hunched his shoulders
and screwed up his face in helpless anticipation.
He heard an expensive crunch, the tinkle of
falling glass. Or perhaps he just imagined it,
because the next thing he remembered was waking up on a bed in St. Vincent's Hospital.

● ● ●

Karp actually heard the explosion as he walked north on Centre Street, but did not register it as anything that should have claimed his attention. A lifetime in New York had inured him to loud noises, and even the current age of terror had not changed that. It was a dull thump, felt more through the feet than heard. He was thinking about his wife, about the passion and terror of the previous night, and about whether she would stay or not. He did not like feeling helpless, but this seemed to be a consequence of marriage to Marlene Ciampi. He was used to it, as he was to loud noises.

Marlene watches Peter Balducci laid to rest in St. John's Cemetery, Queens, less than a mile from where he was killed and where he had lived nearly all his adult life. That was the good thing about getting killed in Queens, she thinks, a short commute. She suppresses the thought, as she does with the other irreverent thoughts she has at funerals. Isn't there a tribe that has clowns at funerals? That would be something she would have liked to do, had she been such a tribeswoman. A Catholic funeral, of course, very old-fashioned like Pete was, no cremation for Pete, but a proper burial next to the wife, and the Knights of Columbus turned out, elderly guys with strong peasant faces, dressed in sable cloaks and white-plumed bicorne hats. A rotten day for a funeral, she thinks, hot, sunny, no shade, everyone in black and sweating bullets, not a breeze moving the yew trees. It should rain on funerals, the black umbrellas out like shiny toadstools.

The daughters are there, crying, supported by their husbands. She didn't know them. Pete was a professional friend, would call for a drink every so often; he took a quasi-paternal interest in her. They would meet in a bar downtown somewhere, Pete, Raney, and Marlene, and catch up. An amusing guy, Pete, a good storyteller, a gambler in retirement, Atlantic City, Foxwoods, the track, also the stock market. He was always pushing penny stocks at her and Raney.

One thing they didn't ever talk about was the connection between them, which was that Raney had saved her life the time that a devil cult had kidnapped her, and she had saved Balducci's by shooting the first man she had ever killed, one shot through the head, from a bad angle in poor light. Only the first of many. No, Marlene, keep away from that line. Let's listen to the words of the priest. Let's think about eternal life, that life has a purpose, that God exists, and loves us. Marlene still believes God exists, although she is no longer sure that the Church as now constituted is His official spokesperson. She acknowledges the flames of hell, and hopes that there is a purgatory. She figures she will spend about 187,000 years there, unless her daughter's prayers get her out. She was not kidding when she told her husband about thinking suicidal thoughts. Now she balances in her mind different degrees of catastrophe. Do they still plant suicides in unhallowed ground? She would like a nice funeral like this one. She imagines Karp and the kids at the graveside, then imagines another graveside, with her standing there in black and Karp or one of the kids, or maybe all three or them, in boxes, and it's her fault. Which picture is your favorite?

Switch that off, we don't need that right now. Standing on one side is Raney, stiff-faced, not a weeper. On his other flank is Nora, Mrs. Raney, a pale Irish beauty, actually from the Republic, an immigrant nurse, and on her other flank in her stroller is plump little Meghan, aged two. Marlene steals a look at Nora. She's the weeper, dabbing at her eyes, her cute little Irish nose getting red at the edges. Marlene has only just met Nora, has never been invited out to the bridal bower in Woodmere. It's still hard for her to think of wild Jim Raney all settled down and domestic. No more flirting with Marlene at any rate, which they'd done a good deal of, and some occasional light necking, back when. Maybe that's why she hasn't been out to Woodmere. Her dirty secret, pathetic nonaffairs with a string of guys, mainly boyish Irishmen, irresponsible, hard drinkers, antithetical to her hubby. Not much energy left for that nowadays, maybe she should do it, that might be a way out, to convince herself she was In Love with an irresponsible lunk who'd beat her as she so richly deserved, unlike Karp, who just took it and took it. Hideous, really to be loved like that when one was such a destructive piece of shit.

The funeral moves into its final act: the family and friends are tossing bits of soil into the grave, crouching on the obscenely green artificial grass rugs that cover the raw earth, wielding a chromed trowel. Marlene doesn't toss. Instead she stands by the baby and watches Jim and Nora do so. The baby is sleeping, a pink doll. Could Raney even imagine placing this one in danger for the sake of some imagined general good? No.

There is a wake at the house in Rego Park afterward, a lot of retired cops getting drunk. Marlene has a glass of wine and makes her excuses. She gets out on Woodhaven Boulevard going north and here comes a life decision, rarely so clear-cut as now, with the freeway ramps and signs looming just ahead. East on the Long Island Expressway, back to the dog farm, or west on the same thoroughfare, taking it to the 278 turnoff and down to the Williamsburg Bridge into Manhattan, and . . . what? A little more torment? A slide back into the life they had before, some time in the city, and then having the boys at the farm for the summer, with Karp coming out for weekends? She rolls under the railway bridge and she's in the wrong lane for the eastbound. She's about to change lanes, when a truck appears on her right, she slows, horns honk, she sighs, and lets the traffic ease her into the ramp that leads back to the city. She wishes all her decisions might be like that, from now on, settled by mere fate, like a scrap of litter driven by the hot breeze of the roadway. She tells herself it's just a day or so, a week. It can't hurt. Besides, she's dying to stroll down Mulberry Street again and shop Italian.

Lucy's appointment was uptown and on the other side of the isle of Manhattan, and it was hot and it was the rush hour and she was oddly exhausted, so she took a cab rather than the subway and a crosstown bus. She glanced at the driver's ID, waited for a stop at a light, and then said, "How are you today, Mr. Saadi?" in perfect Palestinian Arabic. It was one of the small pleasures of taking a cab, but one she did not allow herself too often. The driver's head whipped around. They almost always did this, even when rolling, which was why she had waited for a stop. She had more than once narrowly avoided accidents; New York's cab-drivers are not used to being addressed in their native tongues by American girls. Then the usual: She was not a Palestinian? Surely she was, or could not speak the language so well. Sometimes

Lucy omitted the linguistic-freak explanation and let the cabbies imagine a life for her, a family. She got invitations to dinner this way, in Bengali, Urdu, Arabic, Farsi, Gujarati, and Spanish, and quite often proposals of marriage, on behalf of a son, a cousin, the cabbie himself.

She had to break Mr. Saadi's heart, but tipped him lavishly to make up for it and left the cab. She was at Fifty-Seventh and First Avenue, where the archdiocese of New York has its seat. She was not going to the archdiocese proper, the huge and imposing structure at 1011 First Avenue, but a few buildings north of it, an undistinguished office brick faced with the kind of shiny white material used in tunnels and public lavatories. She ascended to the tenth floor and walked through a glass door that was inscribed in gold lettering. The Lucia Foundation.

Lucy breezed by the receptionist with a smile and a wave. Although officially a limb of the cardinal archbishop's domain, the Lucia was very much a family affair. Her mother had founded it upon ill-gotten stock market gains and named it after her great-grandmother, a woman of strong feelings, courage, and deranged mind. Pazza Lucia, as she was known by Ciampi family historians, was a scion of the di Messina, a noble house of Palermo. She'd run off with a gardener laddie around 1890, the dad had sent men to clip the gardener laddie and bring the daughter home, and Pazza Lucia had, according to the Ciampi family historians, stood in a doorway with her lover's blood all over her nightgown and blown the assassins to hell with a shotgun. Then an exciting escape to New York, with the cops and assorted Sicilian cutthroats at her heels, and a marriage to Paolo Ciampi, also of Palermo, but from a lot lower down in the social order. From this liaison the Ciampi clan, numbering now in the hundreds, had sprung. Here and there in this line—which produced mainly respectable artisans and their wives, and latterly a sprinkling in the more stable professions—appeared a flash of zany fire, when the old ladies in black would mutter **marrone!** and tell the old story again. Thus the ladies in black explained Marlene's exploits.

There was a portrait of Lucia di Messina hanging just outside the director's office. It was not a good portrait, being cooked up from a faded sepia photo, but it looked enough like Lucy's mother, especially around the eyes, to give Lucy a little chill.

She knocked, heard a hail, and walked through the door. The executive director of the Lucia Foundation was Father Michael J. Dugan, a Jesuit in bad odor with the Society of Jesus, which was nearly enough by itself to recommend him to Marlene when she decided to give umpteen millions to the Church. Putting Dugan in charge had been a condition of the gift, and so he was elevated from second seat in a collapsing parish to his current post, where he was tasked with dispensing money at levels sufficient to immensely improve his standing with the hierarchy. He was also the closest thing Lucy Karp had to a spiritual advisor.

Dugan came around from behind his desk—a board on filing cabinets—and embraced her, kissing her loudly on the cheek.

"Are you still allowed to do that?" she asked.

Dugan laughed. He was a stocky man of around sixty, with a thick head of black hair and a knobby, pleasant face. His eyes were blue, intelligent, and marked with pain, although she noticed when she pulled back to look at him that there was less of that than heretofore.

"I don't know," he said, "but why should you be the only Catholic in the country to remain unfondled by a priest?"

She sat in a canvas director's chair. All the furniture in the place was cheap, classic, and functional. He took a couple of canned drinks from a small refrigerator and gave an Orangina to her.

"You're looking sprightlier," she said. "Not so borne down. Surprising, given what's going on. I heard some of you guys are afraid to wear clericals on the streets."

"So I hear. It's funny, I was a flannel shirt guy for years, but since these sex stories started to break, I'm practically always in a collar. A natural contrarian: you say tomato, I say to**mah**to. That or showing the flag as the ship goes down."

"Is it?"

"I wish I knew. It's certainly the biggest thing to hit the Church in my lifetime, maybe not even excepting Vatican Two. It's 1517 again and the same kind of idiots are still in charge, and they may make the same kind of mistake. Their problem is that in this country there's no Church at all without the women, and the women are more steamed about this than they were about the Pill. If they bolt . . ." He waggled a hand. "But you didn't come here to talk about the future of the one, holy, Catholic, and Apostolic."

"No, I came by unannounced to see how you're spending the foundation's money. I am a trustee, you know."

"You want to see the books?"

"No, I trust you. Isn't that why they call them trustees?"

The priest laughed. He had a nice one, and Lucy recalled that when he was working in the hardscrabble parish, he hadn't laughed all that much. He really does like being in charge of something big, she thought. Yet again she wondered what had gotten him into so much trouble. Definitely not diddling altar boys. He said, "I saw a nice white stretch limo in the latest issue of **Corrupt Charities Today**. I might just pick one up."

"As long as you take the poor for a ride, Father."

A somewhat less enthusiastic laugh here. "Merciless! How's your mom. Speaking of contrarians."

Lucy hesitated, sucked it in, and resigned herself. "Speaking of merciless contrarians. She's back home. For a funeral, she says. Strictly temporary. She thinks she's toxic, cursed of God, a danger to her family."

"And what do you think?"

"She's suffering. Which is good, actually. If she was just breezing along with what she's got on her conscience, I could hardly bear to look at her. On the other hand, she won't change. She won't really repent, won't really just accept she's a lawyer of a certain age with two boys to raise, and get a job and act normal, and, I don't know, have a **life**. Everything has to be an opera with her. Guns, knives, danger, corpses strewn around the stage. She'd rather be in dramatic self-exile than say, 'Hey, I had a past like everyone else, and screwed up big time, and I learned my lesson.' I pray for her, but . . ."

"Yes, but," said the priest. "The great 'but' of God." They both thought about this in silence for a moment, making one of the infinity of little surrenders that religious people make in the course of daily life, and then Dugan asked brightly, "And you? How have you been keeping? You're looking pretty good, which suggests you're still in love."

"She blushes to admit it," said Lucy.

"How's the boyfriend?"

"The boyfriend is in Boston, far enough away so that I don't get into trouble. We exchange steamy e-mails. Thus my miserable body remains intact while my heart is all loaded up with foul lusts. I wonder if it's worth it, sometimes. Every time I see him I say to myself, Oh, hell, why not? Let's just dive into bed and cohabit along with the rest of the adult and preadult population of the country."

"Why don't you?"

"Oh, thank you! Is that official advice from the magisterium now? You're supposed to say, 'Sex is a sacrament of marriage, my child.' "

"Sex is a sacrament of marriage, my child." In a pontifical tone.

She laughed. "Yeah, right. The way it's supposed to work is first you get sexually mature, then you fall in love, then you get married and have kids. Sixteen, seventeen, eighteen. Only now it's sixteen, seventeen, and thirty-two, and no one is going to stay chaste that long except saints or the not interested, and I'm neither."

"So you came all the way up here to bitch and moan about your steaming loins? Re-read Augustine." He mimed, shouting out to a crowded shop: "Next!"

"Actually, I consider it an act of charity.

Priests used to spend half their time listening to the sexual agonies of the young, and since the young no longer have sexual agonies to relate, you all must have a big titillation deficit. I think it's an issue for the Curia."

Dugan raised his eyes to heaven. "See! This is what it's come to. Mocked in my own office by a snip of a girl. How long, oh Lord?"

They both chuckled, the chuckles died down, Dugan's face grew sober, and they made eye contact at a deeper level than they had before. A subtle change occurred in the atmosphere of the room, as if the two of them had suddenly entered a sacred space.

"And . . . ?" he said quietly.

"I think I've met a demon," she said.

"Uh-huh. Who's the afflicted?"

"A guy down at Holy Redeemer. He calls himself Larry Larsen, but I doubt that's his real name. He just breathes lies. And he seems to want to get close to me, I mean personally. He's always asking me questions about my life, about my folks, friends . . . the other day he was pumping me about Tran."

"That's interesting."

"Why?"

"Because there are probably people who'd like to know where Tran is, and it's probably common knowledge in some circles that you were as close to him as anyone."

"He's not a cop," she declared. "I guess he could be a bounty hunter, but he doesn't even seem organized enough for that. Asking about Tran is just making conversation. He's curious about the family, too. I figure him for a low-level grifter who got possessed pretty early. There's not much left of him now. The problem is he has a little girl. I'm concerned."

"You could contact the authorities."

"Yeah, and what do I tell them? Beelzebub is squatting in one of their parolees? The guy is perfectly presentable—good looking, sexy, well-spoken. But he has absolutely no idea of how he appears to a person with any spiritual discernment. Of course, that probably hasn't been a problem in his life, given the modern world. The nuns go out of their way to avoid him without being able to come right out and say what it is. They're not supposed to think stuff like that. They've been taught to use psychological language like everyone else."

"How sure are you?"

"Oh, it's the real deal all right. The thing is pretty brazen. It's almost like we're having a conversation while the poor schmuck is running his little scam on me, all oblivious. What do you think I should do?"

The priest sat back in his canvas chair, making it creak. He tented his hands in front of his face and considered his reply. This was not the first time that the fifteenth century had intruded into his life through the medium of the Karp women. The mother definitely belonged in a viperous ducal court in the Italy of that era and the daughter should have been having visions in a convent and making miracles for the peasantry. He knew that Lucy had been having visitations from Saint Teresa of Avila since age seven, so it was only a matter of time before other sorts of spirits came calling. Few men are as inoculated against superstition as old-style Jesuits (more so, oddly enough, than actual materialists), but Dugan did not dare to dismiss Lucy's report.

"I take it your guy would not take kindly to an attempt at exorcism?"

Lucy snorted. "No, he thinks the demon **is** him now. It's way too late for that."

"Is he apt to be violent?"

"Not that I've actually witnessed. But when you cross him, or don't do what he wants, you can practically see the flames shoot from his eyes. I'd say he'd be violent if he thought he could get away with it."

"Then you ought to bail out. Don't mess with him."

She grinned and said, "Oh, you don't think I'm up to handling one little demon?"

The priest didn't smile now. "No. I think you very well might be able to 'handle' him. And how proud you'll be of it."

"Uh-oh."

"Right. You're already so stuffed with pride that you think the rules don't apply to you, and the ones you do keep you keep with such heroic virtue that it's nearly as toxic as sin. Do you honestly think that a self-respecting demon wouldn't prefer you to some loser? Don't you understand that professional exorcists go through elaborate training to prevent just that from happening?"

Lucy dropped her eyes and bobbed her head impatiently. "Okay, right, you made your point. What about the child?" She tried to keep her voice even, but it quivered a little.

He pushed a pad across the desk. "Write her name down and anything you know about her. I'll check her out through my cookie-baker contacts. Meanwhile, keep out of this guy's way."

"He's not going to be like that. I think he's fixated on me. And I'm damned if I'm going to let him chase me away from Holy Redeemer's."

"Yes, you **would** say that," sighed Father Dugan. "I suppose I'll just have to rally whatever pathetic forces God has left and see what can be done."

8

AFTER FELIX'S FINGER HAD HEALED ENOUGH,
Rashid began to send him on errands again. He
drove a pickup truck lettered with the name of a
firm he had never heard of, and his destinations
were scattered throughout the city and the surrounding suburban counties. Once he drove
almost to New Paltz to pick up a load of fertilizer.
Most of the time, he dropped his deliveries off at
Haskell's Plumbing and Heating in Long Island
City. Some of the items, small bottles or cardboard boxes, he took to the house in Queens and
gave directly to Rashid. The Arab now treated
him like a dog, and Felix pretended to be a
changed and more doglike man. No more wise-
ass remarks, no more funny tricks. Felix was a
competent actor and the role seemed to convince. There were no further problems. He
drove, he picked up, he delivered.

He also learned. Rashid gradually slipped back

into the familiar pedantry. The man had hardly a
fact in his head that he did not wish to share, and
not just once, either, because he thought that
Felix was stupid. This was true, in the sense that
Felix had problems acknowledging that any person knew more about anything worth knowing
than Felix himself did. Felix only learned
through personal disaster. But there was nothing
wrong with his intellect, and so he put up with
the Arab's mocking tone and allowed himself to
learn about bombs, explosives, and fuses.

Also, he started to collect. He did not steal.
But instead of the fifty pounds of ammonium
nitrate that Rashid ordered, he would use his
own slim funds to buy seventy-five and keep the
difference. The same with the other chemicals
and the bits of electronics, and the detonators.
He rented a storage locker in Long Island City
near the plumbing place, and kept this stuff
there. It made a convenient lab, as well, nothing
fancy, just the minimum: a table, a chair, some
pans, buckets, plastic containers, an extension
cord and a hot plate, a postal scale, a set of glass
measuring cups, and a thermometer. This equipment allowed him to purify ammonium nitrate
out of commercial fertilizer using chilled
methanol, to mix this with diesel oil and liquid
rubber to make primary charges, to manufacture
acetone peroxide for the initiator charge from
bleach, acetone, and battery acid. He already

knew how to make trembler switches, and the other electronics were easily available. It took him about a month after losing his little finger to assemble the materials, process them, and construct his first bomb.

He was pretty sure that Rashid had no suspicions, but he remained wary. Felix had never been particularly paranoid before: rather the opposite. His base state had been a blithe feeling of invulnerability, which was perhaps the main reason why he had spent most of his adult life in prison. Now, however, he paused before every move, he cast a sharp eye at anyone who looked Middle Eastern, he drove his truck in such a way as to foil anyone tailing him: sudden accelerations and turns, backtracks, roundabout routes down nearly deserted roadways.

It was the finger; they shouldn't have taken a part of him away, that was his thinking, it had turned him into a different kind of person. The old Felix would have struck back instantly with some ill-considered action that might not have worked. He had been way too hotheaded in the past, he saw that now. Funny, because he considered himself to be a fairly well-organized guy. He wrote lists, he kept an appointment book, and always had. But now for the first time, he found himself able to think things through from a number of angles, as if he could see himself on a chessboard, taking various actions, with the other players making their moves, and him making countermoves to theirs.

This business with the girl, for example. He had gone down to the church hall and hung around and watched her. He was a familiar enough character around there by then that several people came up to him and made conversation. Some bums. An old fart, another nut, the guy they called Hey Hey, a pain in the ass. And a new guy, old, with a white beard. Felix didn't like the way this one looked at him, and there was something wrong with his mouth. Felix had left the hall right after that, with no plans to return. Not fear, exactly; he was sure as shit not afraid of a little old guy he could break over his knee. What was it? Maybe the guy knew, maybe he recognized him from before? Anyway, that whole scene was over. It was not going to work the way he had thought it would. The Karp girl was not going to fall for him, was not going to convey the information he wanted via pillow talk. In the old days, this would have made him crazy, maybe provoked him into an assault. No longer. Now whenever he felt that old urge to violent action, he looked at the pink stump, caressed it, felt its absence, calmed himself, and planned anew. He would pull back from the girl for a while. He'd keep in touch, sure, but ease up on the pressure. He'd look for an angle, a chance to either grab her or grab someone she cared about, and then they would see about her snotty attitude. That was another big thing about the new Felix, thought Felix: No more Mr. Nice Guy.

"So are you going to be around tonight?" Karp asked as he tied his tie before the cheval mirror in their bedroom.

"Yes," said his wife from the bed. "I will. I intend to spend a leisurely morning grocery shopping on Grand and Mulberry streets, and then pass the afternoon bent over a hot stove, preparing a terrific meal for my family, which has clearly been eating **rifiuti** since God knows when."

"It's not garbage at all," Karp protested. "We have the four food groups. There's milk. I think Lucy does a good job."

"There are forty-three takeout containers in the refrigerator, and the freezer is full of frozen Milky Ways."

"We like them. They're in a food group."

"It's **chozerai,** in the language of your people."

"In the language of my people, who the fuck asked you to leave?" said Karp, and immediately after, "Sorry. I didn't mean it that way, but really, it's a little much, Marlene."

"I know it is," she said in the dulled voice she often used now. "I'm a bitch on wheels, yes, I know it, and I'm ruining everyone's life."

He sat on the side of the bed and took her

hand, which was damp and warm, like the day.

"I didn't mean it that way. Obviously, we're all glad you're back, but everyone's on eggs wanting to know what's going on—are you here, are you there, in out . . . ?"

She winced and held up her other hand, its palm toward him. "Butch, don't **hover!** Give me a little room—I'm sort of in pieces right now, okay?"

"Okay." Tightly.

"Oh, God, I'm sorry again! And here you are with this horror show at work. Look—could we just take it one day at a time like the drunks do? Let's say I've come back to support the family in a crisis. Our cover story. How's Collins?"

"He seems okay, although they say you can't tell with concussions. I guess it was a lucky break, what happened, with that woman backing up and setting off the bomb. Klopper's in worse shape, but apparently he'll live, too."

"I'm surprised Jack didn't make an objection, you taking the case personally."

"I was surprised, too," said Karp, happy to be easing into a neutral topic. There was no one he'd rather talk to about things than Marlene, always excepting those things he couldn't talk to Marlene about. "I thought he'd go ballistic, because he's always said that trial work is a full-time job and I'm still the chief ADA, and also the racial thing. But he didn't peep. In fact he positively beamed at me. 'Good, great, keep me informed.' The hottest trial on the docket, involving blacks and cops, the two major interest groups he's got to have on his side, and they're on opposite sides in this one, and he's smiling. Why is he smiling?"

"He's smiling because he's not going to run again," said Marlene without apparent thought.

"Not run? But he's the DA."

"Yes, now he is," she said, "but when he was a little Irish boy, he wasn't the DA, and someday he won't be the DA again. Not everyone dies in office, you know. He's not the pope."

Karp checked his watch and threw on a jacket. "I have to go," he said, leaning down to kiss her. "I'm glad you'll be here. Call me old-fashioned, but . . ."

"Old-fashioned!"

"Yeah, and so is Jack Keegan, and even though he's not, as you point out, the pope, it's totally inconceivable that he would not run, and now that I think about it, it strikes me that for the past week or so, the man has been . . . what? Uncharacteristically merry? Maybe he's starting a new medication?"

She pulled the sheet up to her chin. "That sounds right," she said. "Find out what it is and get some for me."

After Karp left, Marlene wrapped herself in her old silk kimono and went into the kitchen. She loaded the big hourglass espresso pot, sliced a bagel into the toaster, and sat hunched in the folds of the kimono while boiling and toasting proceeded. The kimono was the oldest garment she owned, made of heavy silk brocade, printed with plum blossoms against a deep violet ground. It smelled of incense, smoke, perfume, Marlene's body. "Guinea slut" was what her roomie had called her in college when she wore it. She wondered idly where Stupenagel was at this moment, and envied her, familyless, a stranger to guilt.

The espresso pot shook in its usual threatening way, and issued forth its unique scent. The pangs of exile! She had to stop and blink the clouds away as she poured the coffee into her favorite cup, which (of course!) was a hand-painted mother's day gift from the preblind Giancarlo. I am not going to break down weeping in my own kitchen, thought Marlene, and brutally wiped her eyes with the frayed collar of the kimono. She buttered her bagel, sat, chewed, drank.

"Is there any coffee left?"

She jumped, startled. Her daughter had appeared behind her, silently, as was her way. She was neatly dressed in a baggy Filipino silk shirt and khaki Bermuda shorts. Marlene jumped a little.

"Yes, there's plenty," she answered. "I hate it when you sneak up like that. You should carry a bell."

"Good idea, Mom. I'll stop by Leper's World

and pick one up." She poured a cup and sat down at the table.

Marlene said, "I'm sorry, kid, my nerves are no longer the best. As I recall you were a normally boisterous little girl. How did you develop the catlike tread? The Asian influence."

"Yeah, I guess. He always said American women were like water buffaloes. I remember when I was seven or eight we used to sit silently for hours, just watching things in the park. First it was agony and then I got to like it."

"If a parent ever tried that it'd be childrens' court and a foster home. Have you heard from him?"

"Uh-huh. I got a remailed envelope with a post-card inside of the Eiffel Tower, with a circle around the top. On the other side he'd written in French, 'Appolinaire's favorite restaurant: the only place in Paris from which one cannot see the Eiffel Tower.' How about you?"

"Yes. Same thing. Except mine was a postcard of Chartres Cathedral. It said 'wish you were here' in English. I guess he made it to France."

"Or he wants us to believe that's where he is," said Lucy. "I miss him."

An uncomfortable silence here, while they both sipped. It was Marlene's fault that Tran was no longer in the country. She'd **used** him in her lust for revenge, without considering for one second what it would mean for him or for Lucy. She knew it; it filled her with shame; it was something that stood, reeking, between her and her daughter.

Noises from the far end of the loft told them that the twins were up. From Giancarlo's room came the hum of the accordion, from Zak's, synthesized weapon noises from the computer. Marlene said, "Maybe I'll make them French toast. And you?"

"No, I have an early lab and they don't like me to eat a lot before."

"But you'll be home for dinner, yes? I'm going to do a shop, cook up something nice—veal marsala, maybe."

"I'm going to have to miss that, too," said Lucy. "I'm going up to Cambridge tonight for a couple of days."

"Oh, that's too bad," Marlene said, more disappointed than she thought she would be, or revealed. "Seeing Dan?"

"Yes, and Mary. I'm staying over at Mary's."

"How're things going with Daniel?"

"About the same. Friendly." In a flattened tone.

"Just friendly?" Not taking the hint.

"Yes."

"Thanks for sharing."

Lucy put her coffee cup down and looked her mother full in the face. "Uh-huh. Look, Mom? There's not going to be any intimate girl talk going down around here as long as there's this **stuff** between us, as long as I don't know who you are, as long as I don't know what my whole **life** is going to be like. Am I going to have to take care of the twins and Dad, and go to school in the city? Am I going to go back to Boston? I mean, if you have life problems you have to work on, fine, I'm willing to help, but I can't take this void. Hello, Ma? Hello? No answer. Do you realize that we've **never** had a conversation about what happened in West Virginia? What really went down, how Tran got involved, why you split for the farm after Giancarlo got out of the hospital."

"I can't talk about that stuff."

"Why not? You're worried about the legal ramifications? Funny, that never bothered you before."

"Now you're being nasty."

Lucy bobbed her head, bit her lower lip: a gesture of agreement. "Yeah, sorry. Meanwhile, are we going to talk? Am I inside this with you, like family, or am I just one of the other people who clean up the messes you make?"

"You know, Lucy, I've already got a mother to nag me. I don't need another one."

Lucy waited to see if this was going to be the last word. Her mother lit a cigarette and examined the pattern of the tin ceiling. Apparently it was. She stood. Her face became a neutral mask. "Fine," she said. "Then I'll see you when I see you." Lucy kissed Marlene lightly on the cheek and left the kitchen. Marlene heard her saying good-bye to her brothers. Then, she imagined, one of the girl's silent exits. No slammed doors for Lucy; rather the opposite.

Marlene finished her cigarette and her coffee, showered, and dressed in a cotton sun dress. When she came out, her boys were in the kitchen staring into the refrigerator.

"There's nothing to eat," said Zak, meaning "bad mom."

Marlene demonstrated that there was, although it required loving preparation: French toast, Canadian bacon, banana smoothies according to the secret Ciampi recipe. They ate. Giancarlo chattered away, filling the void for all he was worth, for there was a void there, a strain that had never before existed between Marlene and her sons. They'd always been easy together, the three of them, and Marlene had made it clear that even though they were twins, you knew what the differences were and treasured them. For her, this had been a welcome relief from her ever-fraught relationship with The Lucy. Now, however, Giancarlo's manner was almost hectic, too many puns, jokes, merry tales of the life of a street musician; Zak was more than usually taciturn, but his face spoke his need for a signed and notarized lifetime guarantee from his mother that she would stay, and be sane, and allow him to protect her.

Did they want to come grocery shopping with her? They did not. They wanted her desperately, but not enough to take a chance that anyone they knew would actually see them walking on a public thoroughfare with their mommy. She left then, so as to complete the trip before the heat got bad. "If you want faithful," she remarked to Gog the mastiff as they hit the street, "get a dog." The dog indicated his agreement with this proposition by shaking his massive head, spraying drool over the boxes of Chinese vegetables arrayed on the sidewalk. The produce clerk on duty watched her pass without comment and turned on his hose.

Karp said, "Delay almost always favors the defense, but not this time."

"Because . . . ?"

"Because, Murrow, of the events: the terror, the Towers, and the bombs. We're at war and the cops are soldiers. With time, that has to fade. The police will reveal themselves as the same lovable slobs they've always been. So they'll want to keep moving, keep this jury. Why shouldn't they? They're winning."

They were in the tiny library outside the homicide bays on the sixth floor. Karp had commandeered a desk in a cubicle for his work on **People vs. Gerber & Nixon,** the papers for which were stacked in teetering piles on the table and on the floor around Karp's chair.

"But you have a plan," said Murrow, gesturing at the paperwork.

"Of course, but I don't know what it is yet. That's why I'm going to ask for a week's recess. I know there's something here I missed, and I have to find it before the defendants get on the stand."

"What makes you so sure they'll call them?"

"They **won't** want to. Nixon will insist on it. This case is about their word against our witnesses and evidence. He's told the lie so many times he believes it and he wants the jury to believe it, too. You get that a lot with the classic bold-faced perjurer, and sometimes they roll their counsel."

"Do you know who the new guy is yet?"

"No. They're going to have to stretch to get someone to fill Hank Klopper's shoes. But it doesn't matter who takes it. Like I told Collins just before he got blown up, these guys are going for the perfecta. They want to be not merely judged innocent, but totally exonerated, reinstated on the cops, and for that to happen they have to go up on the stand. What they'll be hoping is that I go after Nixon and Gerber tooth and nail so it looks like I'm badgering the simple but honest cops. Which I'm not going to do."

Murrow waited to learn what Karp **was** going to do, but his boss changed the subject. "This is going to be a load on you for the duration. Tony Harris will take over the admin as the acting chief ADA, but he'll need a lot of help with the details. Whisper the right things in his ear. If he has to face down any of the bureau chiefs on anything, let me know and I'll go up there and break some dishes. They may try to end run around Tony to Jack, but I'm not sure that's going to work right now."

"Why not?"

"I don't know why, but Jack has become somewhat disengaged lately. He's been taking Fridays off."

"It's the summer, Butch. People do."

"I don't."

"People. Human beings. I'm not talking Lou Gehrig, Cal Ripken, the Statue of Liberty . . ."

"Fuck you, Morrow. The point is, he never did it during the previous ten summers I worked for him, so why now? Getting old? Why don't you find out?"

"Why he's taking Fridays off?"

"No, why he all of a sudden turned into a human being," said Karp. "Find out why he's smiling."

"I've seen your man," said Father Marcus Skelly.

"And what do you think?" Lucy asked.

"Let's walk down the street here a little ways, if you don't mind. My Lord, it's hot. I don't recall it being this hot in Mexico, but maybe I can't stand it as much as I could when I was a younger man. Although they do say it's the cold that gets you when you make old bones. How about if we stopped in here and I bought us both a Coca-Cola?"

He pushed open the door of a coffee shop. They were on Twenty-Ninth just east of Eighth, a block or so from the soup kitchen run by Holy Redeemer. Lucy went in past the politely held door. The air was chilled and smelled of toast and bacon. He selected a booth in the back.

"You're being mysterious, Father."

"Marcus. I'm retired. And incognito. When Mike called I almost laughed. I told him I was long out of the business. But if you know Mike Dugan, you know he's a convincing son of a gun, so here I am. I haven't been in the city for years."

"Mike said you were at a monastery." A waitress came by and they ordered Cokes.

"Not as such. The Benedictines give me hospitality and I ride a little circuit up there, saying mass for the nuns and other duties. Last rights more than anything else, I'm afraid. The monastery's St. Hilda's. It's up by Lake George. A pretty piece of country."

"So I've heard. And you knew Mike in Latin America?"

"Yes, I worked for the Jesuit Refugee Service in Guat City, and of course you know he was very active up-country there. Quezaltenango."

"I don't know. He never talks about it."

"Well, I can understand that. Parts of it were very bad. He was a diocesan chancellor and his bishop was murdered. And he was jailed there for a time."

"What did he do?"

"Oh, I imagine the usual things a chancellor does." The old priest looked away as he said this and fiddled with the straw in his Coke.

"No, I mean what did he do wrong? He was a bright star, on staff at the Gesú, a chancellor, and then the next thing he's assigned as an assistant in a pokey little parish that hardly needs an assistant."

Skelly looked up. His eyes were gray, red-rimmed, but still alight with intelligence. He had a small, round head with a shock of white hair sticking up above his forehead, Tintin style, and a very short white beard. A deep scar marked his lower lip and made his mouth cock peculiarly when he smiled. "I think you need to ask Mike that. I'm not at liberty to say."

"But you know."

"Yes."

"Was it bad? I mean, dishonorable?"

"You know Michael. What do you think?"

"I think not."

"You'd be right, then. I'll say this: the Society was cross-wise with the Vatican at that time about what was happening in Latin America. Mike was a casualty of the era."

"And what about you?"

He smiled faintly. "Oh, I'm not the man Mike Dugan is. I'm more of a shadowy figure altogether.

In any case, after Guatemala blew up, they pulled me out and let me wander around Rome for a while, a little recuperation, a little research, and then I drifted into an obscure little office that deals with problems like the one you brought to Mike."

"Exorcism."

He laughed. "That word! No one can say it anymore without thinking of that ridiculous movie. The poor old Church wants so much to be modern and hasn't the first idea of how to go about it. Well, they say, we were wrong about Galileo so let's not also be wrong about Freud, or whoever, even though Galileo was right and Freud, as far as we can tell, wasn't any more right than a gypsy fortune-teller. So they're real careful with the E word nowadays. Demons? We don't believe in demons, not really. We believe in pathology and repressed psychosexual la-de-da and temporal lobe tumors, and let's put the man in the MRI machine first, before we call for the bell, book, and candle artist."

"You regret the passing of the Inquisitions?"

He laughed, a short bark. "To a point, miss, to a point. But back to your man. What are we to do about your man? I had a nice conversation with him, about you, as a matter of fact. He feels hurt, feels you don't trust him, the poor fella."

"What did you make of him?"

"An interesting case. Do you know anything about him? His background?"

"Not a thing. He's a con, he admits that, armed robbery. He never talks about his past. He's well-spoken, knows the city pretty well, I get the feeling he was from here, maybe born and raised here before he went upstate. Middle class or above maybe."

Skelly was nodding. "Yes, yes, and you know, he reminds me of a boy I was brought in to help some years ago. This kid, he was around nine, had been taken away from his parents and placed with a foster family, and he'd started to do bad stuff: torturing cats, writing obscenities. He had violent rages, too. The foster family—they were Catholics as it happened—looked into the background and found that the family had been part of a Satanist cult. You read a lot about these cults, but they're actually fairly rare. That's not the devil's style nowadays. Anyhow, the kid had seen a lot of bad stuff, he'd been sexually used, the usual. Apparently the Satanists had told him they had prepared him as a home for a demon, cooked up a fancy name for the thing, as if a real demon would let a human know its name, and the kid came to believe it. That's when they brought me in." He took a long sip of his Coke, and sloshed the ice around with the straw, as if searching for even richer veins of soft drink.

"What happened?" she asked.

"Oh, there was something there, all right. Nothing fancy, like the prince of darkness, although you know, that's what confuses people, it's not dark at all, it's light and glorious, and gorgeous to behold. No, this was just an ordinary one, but it was socked in there in an unusual way. You call on demons and they come. Why should they look a gift horse in the mouth? But the feel of it is different. Most people who pick up an unclean spirit can't wait to get them out, at some level, although it's sometimes hard to tell. That's why you need a cooperating patient if you're running an exorcism team."

"You have a team?"

"Oh, gosh yes! Usually half a dozen people at a minimum. It's an around the clock thing, you know, for days sometimes. I used to be able to count on losing ten, twelve pounds."

"I had no idea."

He smiled at her. "Well, we don't advertise it, do we? In any case, with this kid, there was a funny feel to it. The integration was far along. I mean the thing had humanized itself and the boy had become demonized, if that makes sense. The point is, I had the same feeling talking to your man. I'd say there was ritual satanism in his background, the poor fella."

"What do you recommend, Father? Marcus."

"Well, you know, I don't think there's a thing to be done. I suppose that if we could lay our hands on a wonder-working saint, we could try that, or if Jesus came again, He might look in on the man. I honestly don't know. As you picked up yourself, he hasn't a clue. And of course, he's very dangerous. About as dangerous as a man can be, in fact. Although he may commit no crime at all. He might just quietly spread hell on earth to everyone he meets, perfectly legal, too. Or he might take an ax or a gun and break into a school. I might try to make him go away; sometimes that works."

"He'll just go bother someone else, won't he?"

"Yes, it wouldn't be particularly Christian of us, would it? We'd be almost as bad as the cardinal archbishop there, shuffling his nasty priests. On the other hand, he seems to have an intention toward you, a focus. Blocking that might set him back a little. I mean to say, we can only do what we can do."

"What **will** you do?"

A deprecatory chuckle. "Oh, you know, tricks of the trade, tricks of the trade." He suddenly looked doubtful. "You'll keep this mum, won't you? I don't believe it's exactly canonical anymore."

Lucy made a lip-pinching gesture, then asked, "Will it take long?"

"Oh, consider it already done, my dear," said Father Skelly, and he gave her a sly look.

9

MARLENE HAD BEEN BUYING HER MEAT AT Agnelli's for nearly twenty years, and she superstitiously attributed to her patronage the fact that it was the last Italian butcher surviving in the ruins of Little Italy. When she had first moved to Crosby Street, back in the days when living in lofts had been the illegal dodge of the penurious rather than the privilege of the wealthy, there had been half a dozen Italian butchers. All but Agnelli's had been replaced by Asians. Marlene had nothing against Asians, but she is not going to buy meat from one—fruit, yes, meat, no—racism, maybe, but there it is.

She puts the dog into a stay and walks in to the dingle of the bell. Agnelli's is an old-fashioned place, which Marlene does not mind at all. The floor is hexagons of black-and-white tile, the ceiling is tan stamped tin, supporting lazy ceiling fans, each with a pigtail of flypaper.

The windows are nearly obscured with hand-painted signs announcing specials, but space has been left for a shelf of bright green excelsior, on which rests a tray of pork chops and a tripod of legs of lamb, decorated with lace paper doilies. Within, two sides of the room are fronted by gleaming white porcelain and glass display cases. Salamis and hams hang from chromed racks. The man behind the case looks up when the bell rings and, when he sees who it is, says, "Hey, look who's here! Long time, Marlene!"

Joe Cotta the assistant butcher is dark and squat, with the big-eyed, friendly face of a little boy. He has been the assistant butcher at Agnelli's for nearly as long as Marlene has been a patron, but she does not recall ever seeing him alone in the shop before. Joe is terrific with a crown roast, but he sometimes forgets to collect the money, and it is painful to watch him make change. She says, "How's it going, Joe?" and looks around for the responsible adult, but there does not seem to be anyone out front. Maybe Paul Agnelli is cutting meat in the back.

"Oh, not too bad," says Cotta. "Not too bad. We ain't seen you around much, Marlene. What, you're going to the supermarket?"

"Never, Joe. How's the veal today?"

"Veal what? We gotta roast, we got scallopine . . ."

RESOLVED   205

"I'm making it marsala. So . . . you're all alone here or what?"

Cotta reaches in the case and lifts out a limp white slab of meat. "Look at this here, for marsala? It's like paper."

"Looks terrific . . . give me two pounds." Cotta wraps the meat in white waxed paper. Marlene moves her position to see if there is anyone in the cutting room, but from what she can see of it, it looks empty.

"Mrs. A stepped out?"

"Oh, no, the two of them're down at the court. I'm here all by myself." He hands her a neatly wrapped package with a smile.

"Court? What, a traffic thing?"

"Oh, no, Marlene, it's real serious." He lowers his voice and leans forward confidentially. "They said Paulie did a—what do you call it, the kind where you go with a girl's too young and like that?"

"Statutory rape?"

"Yeah, that. Anyway, Paulie's in big trouble, because she says he did, even though he didn't. A colored girl. Mrs. A? Holy Jeez, I thought she was gonna have a heart attack. They got Biaggi for the lawyer, but Mrs. A says he's not doing much."

"Nick Biaggi? Oh, **marrone!** He must be seventy-five. Why don't they get someone else."

"I don't know. You know Paul. He thought it

was all like a joke, and then it hit him he could go to jail."

The bell dings and an elderly woman in black comes in. Joe Cotta starts to move away toward the new customer, but Marlene waves her package at him, and says, "Joe, that's two pounds at five ninety-five a pound, makes eleven ninety, and I'm giving you a ten and two ones." Cotta takes the bills and rings the sale up and places them in the cash drawer. Marlene hands him a business card. "Joe, listen, tell Paulie to give me a call at home. I'm a little worried about this, and I still know a lot of the players in the sex crimes bureau. Maybe I could help."

"Uh-huh. Okay, I'll tell him, Marlene." He turns away. "Nice seeing you again. Mrs. Alloni, what can I get for you today?"

Marlene forgets about getting her dime, places her veal in her net bag, and walks out into the heat. She snaps her fingers and, like a shadow, the dog falls into step. She makes a few more purchases and walks home. There is a dark blue Ford parked in front of her building. It is not the sort of vehicle one usually finds on Crosby Street in the middle of the day; her pace slows, her pulse rises.

She feels a surge of relief when Jim Raney gets out of it.

They hug, a little stiffly. "To what do I owe?" she asks.

"I need to talk to someone," he says. "I think I'm going crazy."

She steps back and looks him in the face, and sees someone who has not been getting all the sleep he should: pouchy eyes, little lines. No more Peter Pan.

"You better come up, then," she says.

She makes iced tea. The boys come out and say hello, and help unload the groceries, checking them out for anything interesting (yes! tortoni cups). Raney is an old pal, practically an uncle. Zak asks him if he's still hauling that old Browning around and Raney says that he is and they will have to drag it out of his cold dead hands, and Zak explains to him how much better off he would be with the Glock or the Beretta. Giancarlo tells the Irish joke about the old guy who calls the airlines and asks how long the flight was from New York to Dublin and the girl says, "Just a minute, sir," and he hangs up and says, "Jaysus, I'd no idea they'd got so fast." Then Marlene chases them out and sits down across from the detective at the kitchen table.

"So. What's driving you crazy? And may I say that you came to the right place if you're into the blind leading the blind."

"Yeah, well, I thought you'd be sympathetic being as how you got a history with this thing. This is about Felix Tighe."

"The late Felix. What about him?"

"You know his ex-wife was murdered."

"I didn't know. Was it in the papers?"

"Yeah, but she changed her name. Married a guy on the job, as a matter of fact. They had a little girl, nine. The perp got her, too."

"Wait, this was that thing in Forest Hills? That was Mary Tighe?"

"Yeah. And the way they got done, it was a Felix kind of scene. Mean. Sadistic."

"But he's dead."

"Right. So after that a skell named Steve Lutz, who was a chief prosecution witness at Felix's trial, gets killed by a bus bomb. And, of course, there's Pete Balducci, one of the arresting officers, who gets it with another bomb. And now, just the other day, who has a bomb placed in his car?"

"Henry Klopper," says Marlene. "Who happened to be Felix's lawyer."

"Yeah. And as the other arresting officer, I'm starting to get a little nervous."

She stares at him, and then a laugh bursts from her throat. After a second or so, he laughs along with her.

"Yeah, it's really hilarious, Marlene. I knew I could count on you."

She wipes her eyes. "God, I'm sorry. It's just— I don't know—it's so **Friday the Thirteenth**. Hey, evil man comes back from the grave and starts killing the people who put him in jail— happens all the time."

"You can see why I haven't brought it to the attention of the higher authorities: 'Uh, Chief, I cracked the Manbomber case. I know who the guy is, and you won't even have to go for the death penalty, because the fucker's already dead.' "

"Okay, coincidence," says Marlene, "always our first thought, but that's looking a little thin after four incidents. So maybe a surrogate, an agent. Felix met someone skilled with explosives in the joint and they fell in love. With his dying breath, Felix gives him a list of people to clip."

Raney is nodding. "Uh-huh, yeah, that was actually my first thought. But what's wrong with it is Mary and her girl, Sharon. If they got it with a bomb, that story would look a lot better. Them being raped and tortured to death, you'd have to figure a really sick fuck, another Felix, practically, for the job. So that's a hard trifecta—devoted to Felix Tighe, who as I recall wasn't the kind of human being to generate a lot of devotion, plus the sophisticated bomb-making skills, plus the psycho angle. Not many guys around could rape a little girl in front of her mother and then slice the two of them up the way he did."

"He paid to have it done that way."

"Right, I thought of that, too. Except Felix didn't have any money that we know of. His mom had the fortune, but that all got eaten up with civil suits because of that chicken ranch day-care center she was running. He could've had some stashed, but if you were a fucking totally depraved, skilled bomber and a guy who's doing twenty-five to life gave you a shit-load of money for doing a set of crimes that would have every single fucking cop in the universe on your ass forever . . . I mean, why wouldn't you just say, 'Sayonara sucker'? Come to that, Felix was no dummy himself. How could he believe in a deal like that? It's not like he was the Mob. He couldn't really get back at somebody who shafted him."

"He could pay in installments," she says. "The perp sends him clippings and he releases another wad of cash, but that assumes money, and it assumes another agent faithful to Felix on the outside, the guy who's writing the checks, and then you've got the same problem. So, where are we going with this?"

She can see some color coming back into Raney's face now, and his swimming pool eyes are lit with more of the old fire.

"Okay, just let me spin the whole thing out," he says, his hands gesturing in circles. "This's been rolling around in my brain all month. Maybe you'll call the guys with the butterfly net after you hear it, but I got to tell someone."

"Be my guest. You want some more tea?"

"No, I'm good." He takes a couple of deep breaths. "So, now I'm thinking, not friendship, not money—a cult. There **was** a cult, if you recall. Felix's dear old mom ran it."

"Irma Dean, the day-care queen."

"That was her. Worshiping the dark forces and all that shit. The thing was, she thought that Felix was the reincarnation of his late dad, who she thought was the next thing to Satan. And she raised Felix in all of that, just like we got raised in the Church."

"But Felix wasn't into that," Marlene objects. "Or am I not remembering this right? It was the other brother who was the demonic assistant. Felix was in denial because she was bonking him. They had that whole sexual thingy together, Felix and Irma."

"Yes, but what if there was another brother? Or, if not another brother, a—what d'you call it—an initiate. Felix dies in prison, and that unleashes the revenge killings. Now **this** bastard is the spawn of Satan, et cetera."

"Stretching it."

"Yeah? Shit, Marlene, I know I'm stretching it! Stretching is all I got, because what I **really** believe is beyond stretching. It's beyond fucking **sane!**"

She watches him sit back in his chair and rub his face. "And what is that, Jim?"

"I think he's alive," he says. "The minute I walked into that crime scene in Forest Hills and I found out who the vics were, I said to myself, Oh, shit, Tighe's escaped. **He** did this. It was a fucking signature, practically. And then I remembered he was dead. Supposedly. I actually called the fucking prison, Auburn, and confirmed it. The body went out to a cousin here in the city. But what if . . ." he floundered, "I don't know, some strange mix-up?"

"He **is** dead. You think he snuck out of Auburn like Sleeping Beauty? Christ, you **know** they autopsy all prisoners who die inside. What, he's carrying his brains and his guts in a shopping bag while he does these crimes? Also, there's Judge Horowitz."

"How do you mean?"

"I mean Horowitz was the only other person specifically targeted by the Manbomber. The bastard wanted him so bad that he took two cuts at him before he got him, and as far as I know the judge had nothing whatever to do with Felix Tighe. The judge in Felix's case was old Tim Rooney, as I recall, now deceased. So that weakens the link between the Manbomber and Felix. I assume that you all've checked out all the people Horowitz might have pissed off."

Recalling the FBI presentation, Raney says, "Yeah, yeah, a million cross-checks, but there's no clear pattern, and there's no obvious bad guy that all the deaths would benefit. There were people who might have wanted to hurt Horowitz, but nobody recent and the others are still in prison.

That's basically the argument that the bombs are random, and anything that looks like a connection is coincidence—the whole six degrees of separation deal. But in this case I don't buy it."

Without thinking very hard about it, Marlene says, "I agree," and is rewarded with a grateful look. In fact, she doesn't know whether she agrees or not, but only that it is pleasant to be brought out of herself in this way, to be distracted by the needs of someone who is not a family member.

"That's great, Marlene. So, I'm not going nuts?"

"Not any more than you were already. The question is, what do you want to do about it?"

"I don't know, to be honest. I can't talk about this with the cops. They'll put me on the rubber gun squad. I can't assign anyone to investigate and I don't have any real time to investigate it myself."

She waits for him to continue. When he doesn't she says, "Ah, the pregnant pause."

"Just look into it, Marlene. Nothing big-time. I don't know what you charge, but . . ."

"Oh, right, a NYPD lieutenant is going to pay a PI for an investigation. Don't be ridic."

"So . . . what does that mean? You will, you won't . . . ?"

"No, you've got the juices flowing, now. And we owe it to Pete, just to check it out. He would've if it was you or me."

He gives her a searching look. "You're not just, like, humoring me?"

"No, I think it's something that has to be checked out," she says quickly. "And let me start by going over the Tighe file. I can get that from Butch. I want to find out what I can about the devil cult and whether Felix had any likely near and dear. The third brother issue. Then we should investigate the cousin, find out what he did with the body. I'd like to see the grave. Or the ashes."

"He probably flushed them."

"I would have," she says, "but you never can tell about families."

Lucy got to South Station in Boston early in the evening, and took the T to Kendall Square, near the Massachusetts Institute of Technology. Dan Heeney, her so-called boyfriend, had an apartment near there, a three-bedroom in a modern building he shared with a couple of other geeks. She had a key, but she rang the bell instead.

"This is a surprise," said Dan when he opened the door. "Wow. Why didn't you call?"

Lucy eased past the startled young man and into the apartment. The living room was large, light, and filled with more than the usual amount of furniture, electronic equipment, expensive monitors, and fast-food detritus. There were no obvious signs, however, of a female presence.

"I just came by to use the bathroom," she said. "All toilets in New York are closed until further notice to counter the terrorist threat."

Once locked in the bathroom, she made a quick inspection. The room was, naturally, disgusting, which was a good sign. Dan's roomies were Maruf, a Pakistani engineer betrothed since the age of ten, and Wan, a chubby genius to whom sex was a distant rumor. The boyfriend, in contrast, although somewhat softer than was fashionable, had the milky radiance of a quattrocento angel. Girls followed him down the street with jaws agape. Lucy had never been jealous before, nor had she before Dan had anyone to be jealous about, nor had the fellow ever given her any cause for jealousy. Yet she was jealous, and enjoyed being so, and enjoyed watching herself in the throes of jealousy; it appealed to the romantic and literary side of her nature. It made her feel Sicilian, and closer to her mother, although she would have jumped in front of a subway train before admitting this to herself.

A quick check revealed no indication that a female had ever visited the squalid place, or that the sexual act had ever transpired on the premises. No condom wrappers in the wastebasket. No hairpins. She was actually poking through it! Degrading! Marvelous! She popped out, approached the bemused boyfriend, and threw her arms around him.

"Hello, sailor," she said. "Got a kiss?"

He had. It took a while. Kissing was, remarkably, the extent of their intimate relations and they made the most of it, until cyanosis presented a real danger.

"I **really** just came to Cambridge for that," she said through heavy gasps. "I guess I'll go home now."

"Being it's you," he said, "I would almost believe it." He led her over to a love seat, moved some books and a pizza box out of the way, and sat her down. More of the same. She was going to have red marks all over her face from his beard, but she didn't care.

"Okay, let me guess," he said in the first intermission. "You decided that you would finally let me slake my lusts, as you put it."

"Yes, I sensed that you're finally ready to make a lifelong commitment, so that the church can be reserved and lust-slaking can be at least contemplated."

He sighed. "The concept of 'too young' still evades you, I see."

"It does. But that's okay. I don't mind a little heartbreak. I don't mind being spurned now in favor of some future woman who might be better than me. I'm slavishly devoted to you. I admit it."

"So this visit is just to, I don't know, crank up our frustration to an even higher level?"

"Speak for yourself," she said airily. "My mind is set on higher things." She pulled away and looked him in the eye. "Seriously. I needed to get away and I needed to see you. My mom's back."

"Uh-oh."

"Yeah, but the fact is, while she's deigning to grace our happy home and watch the boys, I can get away."

"You could get away anytime. Your dad's an adult."

"Oh, please! Did you ever see him in the kitchen? And if it was you, you'd do the same, wouldn't you?"

A nod, a reluctant grunt. Dan Heeney was from West Virginia, the son of a union official who'd been murdered along with his wife and young daughter, an event that had both precipitated the current crisis of the Karp family and brought Lucy into his life. He often had the odd feeling that suffering on such a scale was part of what made him attractive to her. And her to him. He could not imagine going out on a date with a regular girl, talking exclusively of pop music, movies, classes, gossip.

"Anyway, I don't want to talk about that part," she said. "I just need to be with some dumb-ass materialists for a little while."

"At your service, ma'am," said Heeney.

"Them saints visiting you again?" In the mountain accent he used to lighten things, and when he was nervous.

"Not saints, no. I have a thing going with a guy—don't laugh—I think he's a demon."

"With the head turning around backward and strange powers?"

"Uh-huh. He wants me to have his pagan love child so he can rule the world. I'm thinking it could be, like, you know, cool."

She looked at him sharply, then punched him in the shoulder.

"Ow! What was that for?"

"You were checking me out to see whether I was joking. How **could** you!"

"Well, hell, **I** don't know which of all the stuff you spout is for real. It **all** sounds like Twilight Zone to me."

"Actually, I'm a little scared," she said.

"Really?" He saw that she was not joking, that she was pale and worrying her lower lip between her teeth. He felt a chill himself. He came from a family where courage was the expected thing, but he had never met anyone with the guts that Lucy Karp had shown him last summer in West Virginia. He didn't want to think about what could frighten her.

"Uh-huh. I brought in an expert in the field. He thinks this guy is the real thing."

A laugh popped out of his throat. "Oh, come

on! So you have to find the hidden chest with the secret ring in it? The parchment with the spell written in blood."

She gave him a sad look that was harder to bear than if she had exploded in anger.

"No, those are metaphors. Devils don't have horns and angels don't have wings. The unseen world operates through bodies, but they don't control them like robots. It's not like in the movies. That's why it's scary. It's all spiritual; it's in your head and your heart. The actual violence, it's not from scarlet rays of power, it's just some guy decides that his life will be just great if he chops up a bunch of little girls. I mean, it makes **sense** to him because a **being** has convinced him that his own pleasure and power are more important than the lives of the little girls and their families and all that. And that means . . ."

She stopped abruptly and examined his face, which had upon it an expression both cautiously neutral and doting. She touched his cheek and smiled. "You don't believe any of this, do you? You think I'm a lunatic."

"Yup."

"I know. And it must be so relaxing. Secular humanism, the La-Z-Boy of philosophy. It's all waves and particles, isn't it, operating according to fixed laws, right?"

"You got it."

"And the mind is just chemicals, and the spirit is just a fantasy, right?"

"Right."

She nestled against him and he put a protective arm around her. She felt like a bird, delicate and hot. "Fine, then," she said. "Alleluia, I'm converted. And could we go out tonight? I want to breathe smoke and drink whiskey and listen to loud stupid music and mindless conversation, and dance until my feet hurt and then I want to go to bed with you and torment you with my partial unavailability."

"Sounds like a plan," he said.

Judge Amos Higbee was a cocoa-colored, bulky man with a passing resemblance to the late Justice Thurgood Marshall, a resemblance he did nothing to disguise; he cultivated a brush mustache and a rumbling slow delivery.

"Mr. Karp," he growled, not looking up from his papers, as Karp walked in to his chambers. "Mr. Karp, I'll ask you to wait for your colleague. Have a chair."

Karp sat and thought about Higbee and the triplex chemistry that would develop between them and whomever the detective's union had hired to replace Hank Klopper. Karp ran through the likely members of the defense bar in his mind. Eliminate anyone who hadn't defended a cop. Foolish of them not to pick someone with experience in that particular and peculiar brand of defense. An upside-down trial. He'd explained it all to Murrow, but he doubted that the young man could fully comprehend the true weirdness of such a trial. For every instinct of a defense lawyer, reinforced over hundreds of hours in the courtroom and library, was to attack the police, their methods, their skill, their honesty and integrity. And the prosecutorial bar was conditioned to establish just the opposite, which is why the prosecution of rogue cops was such a kidney stone to a DA's office, and why it was so rarely done, and even more rarely successfully done. A cop had to do some truly lunatic act, impossible to cover up, or do some ordinarily horrendous act in front of a video camera. Neither was present here, which was why it was a bear. He needed a couple more days, a week, which was why he had asked for this meeting. He didn't think whoever picked up the D would object.

＞Object. Keegan hadn't. Why? Karp thought again about Keegan's puzzling good humor. Murrow hadn't come back with anything yet. He'd have to lean on him. Why did Jack seem almost to want him to take the case? Because he wanted it lost? Or won? The case was extremely tough, but Karp was the best litigator on the DA's staff, and thus provided the best chance at a victory. On the other hand the DA had never registered any particular anxiety about winning the case. In fact, he had been conspicuously silent and offhand about it, as if he didn't want either credit or blame to touch him. Or maybe he thought the case impossible and wanted to stick Karp with the loss. Why? Karp losing a case with a black victim and a white defendant would simply confirm the opinion in a large segment of the African-American community that Karp was a bad actor, a racist, but why would that be to Keegan's advantage? He could fire Karp any time he wanted if he wanted to curry favor with that segment, and he hadn't, not even a couple of years ago when he was involved in a serious race with a black candidate. Could Keegan have turned nondevious in his old age?

A knock on the door. Higbee said, "Enter!" in his basso, and Roland Hrcany stepped through the door. The former head of the homicide bureau of the New York DA greeted the judge and took a seat.

Karp became conscious of the amazed expression on his face, and that Roland was aware of it, and was enjoying the effect of his entrance. He'd trimmed his hair, Karp noticed, as Roland shook hands with Higbee and traded pleasantries. During his long career at the DA Roland had worn his blond hair long, brushing his jacket color. Together with his brutal features and his weightlifter's body, it had given him the air of a professional wrestler, but this had not detracted at all from his effectiveness in the courtroom—helped it, probably. He had one of the best records ever for felony convictions, and had been forced out when someone had tape-recorded one of his famous, obscene misogynist-racist tirades.

The business was quickly accomplished. Karp asked for an extension of the recess, Roland objected. Again, topsy-turvy. The defense was always asking for delay, the state for celerity. Higbee commented on this dourly, and made his decision. The trial would resume after the weekend, as originally scheduled, with the same jury.

Hrcany and Karp left the chambers and stood uneasily together in the hallway outside.

"This is a surprise," said Karp. "I was under the impression your practice was restricted to celebrity hit-and-run cases, the dope in the limo, stuff like that."

Hrcany grinned, not pleasantly. "Well, you know, Butch, I've always been tight with the cops. When Hank went down, O'Bannion called from the detectives' endowment and asked me if I'd come in as a closer, and I said I would."

"A closer, huh? He can only throw twenty pitches, but nobody can hit them. Ninth inning, three on, no out, he retires the side."

"Right. A kind of legal Mariano Rivera."

"That what they told you, Roland? The detectives? Just waltz in there, put our boys up on the stand, let them tell their sad story, and boom, acquittal. The seats in the jury box won't even cool off."

"Something like that," said Hrcany. "I was surprised to find you were on the case. I thought that was Jack's big no-no."

"I was confused about that, too," said Karp. "He doesn't seem the same old Jack, playing the political angles and all that. A minor stroke in the paranoia lobe is what I'm thinking. I can't make up my mind whether he's hoping against hope that I'll pull it out of the fire, or that he knows it's lost and I'm his choice for going down with the ship."

"The latter. Definitely."

"We'll see. Now tell me the truth, Roland. Did you know I was up for the People when you took this case? I mean, is this yet **another** chapter in your—what is it now?—your twenty-two-year effort to see which of us has the bigger pecker?"

Hrcany laughed briefly. "Don't flatter yourself. I happen to think that it's a shame when a pair of detectives who don't have a single mark against them as far as bigotry is concerned get second-guessed on a shooting behind an infamous out-door drug market. Second-degree murder, my ass! Fucking immigrants come to this country, first time they ever saw indoor crappers and civil liberties, they think it's a free ride, they can do all the shit they want and they're invulnerable. Then some cop does his duty and if it happens the guy is of a certain race, you PC assholes drop the courthouse on him. I think it sucks. That's why I took the case."

"You were an immigrant, Roland. You told the story a million times, how you and your dad came here after the Hungarian revolution with only a couple of suitcases and—"

"That was completely different."

"Why? Because you were white?"

"Oh, fuck you!"

"You know, Roland, I think that your single flaw as a lawyer is that when you tell a serious fib, your earlobes get a little red. It's more obvious since you cut your hair. You've been dying to grind me to powder on a courtroom floor for years and now's your big chance."

Hrcany glared for a moment and then chuckled. He clapped Karp on the shoulder. What an absolutely peculiar relationship I have with this man, thought Karp.

"Now that you bring it up, I think I **will** enjoy it."

"Unless you lose," said Karp. "See you in court, counsellor."

10

LUCY AWOKE IN DAN HEENEY'S BED WITH A
dense, living headache and the usual dry, crusty
tongue that follows an evening of debauch. She
was an infrequent debaucher, but a somewhat
more frequent one than she might have chosen to
be, for she dreaded more than almost anything
developing a rep as a prig. **More** of a rep, actually.
She was a college student; college students got
plastered; ergo, she got plastered. Unfortunately
for the happy operation of this syllogism, Lucy had
inherited her mother's vast capacity. She could
drink copiously while remaining at least somewhat
functional, and thus absorb enough poison to generate ferocious hangovers, as now.

She slid out of bed, taking care to keep her
head level, found her knapsack, extracted a
toothbrush and two Advils, and clomped
painfully to the bathroom. She observed that
she was dressed in underpants and a T-shirt.

The presence of the panties was a good sign, because she could not remember getting into bed, or what (if anything) had transpired in it. Nothing much, it seemed, as usual. She washed her face, popped in the Advils, and sucked a pint of water from her cupped hands. The water stung the knuckles of her right hand, which she now saw were split and swollen. Uh-oh. She brushed her teeth and stared balefully at her image in the smeared bachelors' mirror. Yet again God had failed to answer her prayer, for she did not look any more like Cameron Diaz than she had yesterday.

She sniffed. Someone was making coffee. She went back to Dan's bedroom and donned shorts and sneakers. The somewhat of a boyfriend was sitting at the kitchen counter reading the **Globe**.

"Hello, slugger," he said.

"Coffee."

"Help yourself. How do you feel?"

She ignored this until she had poured a mug, added enough milk to make it lukewarm, and drank half of it down. Then she said, "I'll survive. I guess I got pretty loaded last night."

"You were fine until you started on the margaritas. How much do you remember?"

"I remember going to Blue City. I remember meeting Mary and a posse of geeks. We listened to music and then we went to Christie's and danced, and then . . . a party?"

"Yeah, we ran into Penny Hogarth and she invited us to her place to drink margaritas. How's your hand?"

"It hurts. Car door?" Hoping against hope.

"Car door not. You coldcocked Paul Maslow."

"I don't know any Paul Maslows."

"You made his acquaintance last night, for sure. You really don't remember?"

"No. I think I remember drinking margos out of a pitcher. Why did I hit him?"

"Oh, he's a famous asshole. Harvard grad student, very postmodern. He thinks it's cool to insult people. It was a pretty interesting party, mostly grad students, people there from every nation, as they say, all of them drunk out of their gourds. Anyway, Maslow got into a rant about the Catholics and what a bunch of morons they were, anyone who believes that malarkey was supporting pedophilia and misogyny, and that the whole thing was a racket so that a bunch of guys could live off the fat of the land and fuck little boys to their hearts' content. As I recall, you got in his face about it, and he said something nasty to you that I didn't catch, and then you started to curse him out in a bunch of languages. It was pretty damn funny, if you want to know: you'd say one thing and all the Chinese guys would crack up, and something else and all the Koreans would go bat shit. The Pakistanis, whatever. And he was getting all redded out because they were laughing at him and he didn't know why and he said, 'Oh, shut the fuck up you stupid cunt,' and sort of pushed you, and that's when you slugged him."

"What did I hit him with?"

"Fists. Darlin', you were a blur is all I can tell you. You must've hit him about six times in two seconds. Where'd you learn to punch like that?"

"It's a family tradition. My grandfather was a pug back in the forties. He taught my mom and she taught me, instead of how to frost a cake."

"Anyhow, one second you were standing there yelling at each other and the next he was on his ass with blood pouring off his face. I think you broke his nose. You never saw so many snotty East Coast intellectuals sober up so fast. The cops got mentioned and I dragged you out of there. You were raving in some language, Latin it sounded like."

Yes, now it was starting to come back. She felt the heat roll up her face. "Oh, God, I'm sorry! Have I ruined you socially?"

"I doubt it. It's probably the first fistfight over religion in Cambridge since ole Willy James was teaching down at the med school. People will be telling stories about it for years. Including Maslow, probably, only he'll make you a six-four abortion clinic bomber he defeated in single combat."

"But you're not mad at me?"

In answer, he rose, knelt by her chair, and

embraced her. She fell against him and groaned. "Jesus! Beating up on people about religion! Good Lord, I should know by now, anti-Catholicism is the anti-Semitism of the smart. In this neighborhood people don't even hesitate before dissing the poor old Church. Okay, the guy was an obnoxious turd, but still . . . resorting to blows? Where did **that** come from?" Knowing full well.

He said, "Oh, hell, darlin', don't fret you none: back home a man who took off like that on someone's religion'd be lucky to get off with a busted nose."

She smiled. "Corn pone."

"Sister, we'ns from **West** Virginia. Corn pone's considerable south of where I hail from."

"It makes me all shivery when you talk like that: **war ah hay-ul fum.**"

"And why would that be?"

"I'm an extreme exogam. Like the mom. I always figured it would be an Asian, but you came along instead, with your sly, cosmological hillbilly ways." She tugged a golden lock; he moved with the pull.

"But," she said, when they were breathing again, "that's it for the booze. I'm on the wagon for a good long while, which means I will be an even less fun piece of dry toast than I was before. I'll understand if you want to kick me the hell out."

"Oh, yeah, with my dad and my brother both drunks. Seriously, though: you think that's a problem for you?"

"Extreme violence under the influence? You saw it. I'd classify that as a problem. Sometimes it even happens when I'm cold sober. It scares the bejezus out of me."

"Because of your mother, right?" He was the only other person in the Greater Boston metro region who knew the full story of what had happened in West Virginia.

"Right," said Lucy, and sighed. "Because of her."

She started with a call that evening, after the delicious veal marsala and the wine, and the rum cake and tortoni, served by candlelight, with poor Karp carefully grateful and the boys on their best behavior, unnaturally so, and the two of them going to bed like the little angels they were not. She was pretending to be the perfect mom and they the perfect mom's family. She found she didn't mind: she'd always thought that honesty and letting it all hang out and confrontation were absurdly overrated. If a little pretense and good manners got you through the day, well then, Marlene Ciampi would not say it nay.

Besides which it gave her a scrap of an excuse for getting into a little something here with Paul Agnelli. He hadn't called by nine, so she called him at his mother's, where he'd been holed up since the collapse of his marriage.

"Hi, this is Marlene Ciampi, calling for Paul Agnelli?"

"Marlene? From the neighborhood?" Mrs. Agnelli's voice was cigarette husky and uncertain.

"Yes, that one. How are you, Mrs. Agnelli?"

"Oh, well, you know, the usual. We haven't seen you in a while. You been out of town?"

"Yes. Look, Mrs. A, did Joe Cotta tell you I was by today?"

"Joe? No, he didn't. You were by? We must've been out."

"Right. Did he give you my card?"

"Card? No, what card?"

"Well, it doesn't matter. Is Paul in, by any chance?"

"Yeah, he's right here." A muffling of the receiver through which Marlene could hear the maternal shout. She waited. Marlene had known Paul Agnelli since early childhood. Her grandmother had lived above the shops on Mulberry a few doors down from the butcher's, and Marlene and her brothers and sisters had been frequent visitors. Paul and she had chased each other with chicken feet in and out of the remains of Little Italy from the age of seven. Somewhat later, there had been a little discreet smooching in the meat cooler, among the hanging joints, nothing serious, and then she had soared into Sacred Heart and

Smith, and he had stayed in the butcher shop and married Karen Boone, a blondie not from the neighborhood, and he and Marlene had smoothly transitioned into a relationship limited to wise-ass remarks across the gleaming counters.

"Hey, Marlene! What's up? Nothing wrong with the meat, I hope."

"No, the meat was great, like always. Look, Paul, I was talking to Joe today and he told me a little about the fix you're in, and I thought I'd call, see if I could help out."

Silence for a moment here. "Well, I'm sorry he bothered you with that, Marlene. I got to talk to the guy about spreading my business around to everyone."

"Oh, for crying out loud, Paulie! I'm not **everyone**. I'm practically your oldest pal, even if I didn't let you squeeze my tits in the cooler. Or only from the outside. In fact, I'm kind of insulted you didn't come to me in the first place. I mean, let's face it, Nick Biaggi is for when you got a problem with your lease, not when you're looking at jail time. So, what's the story?"

Bitter chuckle. "You got a week?" Lowering his voice. "I really can't talk to you on the phone here. Ma's around the corner with her ears, they're like those radio dishes—they probe the galaxies. Can we like, sit down somewheres?"

"How about Russo's? Ten minutes."

"You mean tonight? Right now?"

"Yeah. Unless you got a previous engagement."

"I'm going out," she said to her husband. "A client."

He looked up from the TV. "Doggie business?"

"No, legal. Paul Agnelli the butcher's in a jam. You guys've got him up on a statutory rape charge."

"Paul the butcher, huh? He probably did it, then, or the cops wouldn't have collared him. Come to think of it, I always thought the guy had short eyes. The way he handled those chickens . . ."

"Darling, there is nothing in the least perverse about Paul Agnelli's sexuality, as I know from personal experience. In fact, it's a little **too** normal, if you want to know. This man has broken more hearts south of Houston Street than there are lamp posts. I was actually surprised when he got married."

"Then she said she was eighteen. You'll cop him to abuse two."

"Something like that. I'll see you later." She whistled for the dog.

"Remember, we screw the clients only on the invoice," he said, happy she was going out on legal business rather than the other kind. "If you're not back by three A.M., I'm going to start worrying."

She laughed and left.

Russo's was practically the last working-stiff saloon left below Houston Street, every other joint having being infected with gentry disease. It had a floor made of black-and-white hexagonal tiles, a ceiling made of thickly painted tin, a juke-box with a lot of Perry Como and Connie Francis on it, and a clientele that included a substantial number of elderly men with few teeth and dark clothes. These persons sat at the scarred wooden tables, nursing glasses of inky wine, not talking much, with their hats on and their collars buttoned up to the top collar button. Russo's smelled of cigars and old beer.

Agnelli was waiting for her when she walked in with the dog. Gog whimpered and licked his hand, for he was one of Gog's favorite people. Marlene kissed him on the cheek, smelling a heavy cologne that was not quite up to its fight with the undertone of blood and pork fat. She sat and they looked each other over in the unself-conscious manner of old acquaintances. Paul Agnelli was almost parodically gorgeous, in the classic Italian heartthrob manner. He was dark, thickly haired, sloe-eyed, powerfully built. Tonight he was in cutoff jeans, a red body shirt, and several gold chains. He smiled like a Colgate ad, and told her she was looking good. She returned the compliment, with, she thought, a good deal more truth in it. They ordered a bottle of the house faux Barolo. It came in a labelless green bottle with two squat juice glasses. No stemware at Russo's. Without being asked, the barman brought a bowl of draft for the dog.

"Old friendship," said Marlene, and they clinked glass on it. "Okay, she said she was eighteen, right?"

"No, no, you're off base there. I never touched this girl. I don't know her from fuckin' Adam. Eve. I swear on my mother's head, Marl. The cops came to the shop, asked me did I know Cherry Newcombe, and I'm like, 'Who?' They show me a picture, same deal, I thought it was like some kind of clerical error. They wanted Joe Agnelli, Frank Agnelli, whatever. But no. She says I picked her up at the Red Mill on Barrow. You know it? Right, it's a meat market, excuse the expression. Am I known there? Yeah. Do I pick up chicks there? Yeah again. Did I pick that one up? No, ma'am. They say I got her drunk, and did her in the backseat of my car. She's fourteen."

"Uh-huh. What do they got?"

"Oh, you'll love this. They took my car, right? The Trans Am. And they say they've got fibers, they've got DNA from this girl in my backseat. Secretions. And they said that after it happened, I mean allegedly happened, she provides a semen sample and they want a DNA from me. So I figure, okay, that'll do it, clear everything up like in the papers, you read about some poor **stronzo** in jail for ten years on a rape he didn't do, the DNA test gets him out. But here it works the other way, because they say it's a match. Then they arrest me. I call Nick Biaggi, hell, he's the only lawyer I know. I mean, there's you, yeah, but to tell you the truth, with all this other stuff you been doing these past years, I kind of forgot you were a lawyer."

"Yeah, me, too. So, you got any idea how these samples could've got to where the cops say they ended up?"

Agnellis shook his head and took a swallow of wine. "No, I do not. I mean it's crazy, the girl wasn't in my car and I never fucked her, so how could they have this stuff? It's fucking Twilight Zone, Marlene. It's driving me nuts." He examined her face. "You believe me, right?" She nodded, patted his hand, made comforting noises. "I mean," he went on, "aside from anything, you know me, for cryin' out loud. Did I ever chase young pussy? Even when I was a kid? You remember Mrs. Notale from the dry cleaners?"

"There was a rumor you were porking her in high school. She must have been well past thirty back then."

"Right, see, I mean some guys like young, some don't. It just ain't my thing, little girls. Also, the fact of it is this girl is black and, what can I say, I never been attracted to that flavor. So the whole thing is fucked."

"Yes, except for the forensics. Okay, Paulie, if

you want, I'll contact Biaggi and you give him a buzz, too, tell him I'm on the case. I'll nose around and see if we can figure out who's trying to frame you."

"Frame me?"

"Well, **duh,** Paulie. Those samples did not just walk into your car or that girl's pants. Someone wants you in jail bad enough to commit a serious crime to put you there. Any idea who would want to screw you that bad?"

Agnelli had a stunned look, with his brows twisted into lumps and his mouth half-open. "Jesus Christ! You know, I never thought of that, not for a minute."

"Well, start thinking about it. You need to get me a list of recent sexual partners."

He cocked his head, puzzled. "My sexual . . . ?"

"Yeah, Paulie. Where did they get the semen? Unless off the floor of the dirty magazine section at the newsy on Spring . . ."

"Geez, Marlene, you mean somebody went to a woman I been with and, what? Got a **specimen?** Christ, that's **disgusting!** Who would do a thing like that?"

"You tell me," she replied. "Speaking of which, what kind of numbers are we talking here? Amateurs? Pros? Focus on the time period around when they charged you."

But Agnelli was shaking his head. "No, come

on, Marlene, I'm a guy runs a butcher shop, not some kind of Frank Sinatra."

"But you get your share."

He shrugged. "Tell you the truth, these days I'm not chasing so much as catching. I don't know what's wrong with guys nowadays, maybe they're all faggots or they're working too hard, or it's easier to dial up porn and beat off, but I run into, I don't know, these rafts of women going like **years** between one piece of ass and the next: I'm talking about right in the shop, married ladies, or I go out after work, some saloon, you strike up a conversation in a bar . . . I mean hello, how you doin', buy you a drink, and she's like cut the small talk, let's fuck. It's a fucking drought out there."

"You're a public service, Paulie, God bless you, but I need some names."

"Names," he said, and drew from his back pocket the traditional little black book. It was the size of a pastrami sandwich, stuffed with cards and loose slips of paper, and held together by rubber bands. "Let's see, this is August, and I got picked up April twenty-third . . ." He thumbed through some pages. "It's not like I got a computer system here, but . . . okay, Tina Farnese, there's one about that time, I mean it started then. She's local, a customer, married. Nellie Simms, also local, a painter, I thought she was a lezzie, but no. I mean she paints buildings, not art. Another woman I met at Bocce's, Brenda or

Brandy, a real psycho, I didn't even ask for her number."

"Description? Residence?"

"Nah, it was just that one time and I used a rubber. She supplied it, too, as I recall."

"So, just those two, you think?"

"Three, but yeah. Like I said . . ."

"Right, you're not Frank Sinatra. Tell me a little about Karen."

"Karen?" His large, warm brown eyes clouded. The furrows showed again on the brow. "What about her?"

"Oh, you know. If they found you whacked in an alley, the first person the cops would talk to would be her. So someone gives you the shaft big time, that's who I'd want to look at, too."

He waved his big hand as if to swat the possibility away. "Karen? Oh, shit, Marlene, why would Karen do something like that? Hell, I'm supporting her and the kids: why would she want to put me in jail?"

"Remind me why you broke up? I always thought you were reasonably okay together."

"Yeah, me, too. And, you know, it's amicable, like they say. No horseshit about visiting rights and whatever, support money gets paid right from the bank. But, the short version is Karen didn't want to be married to an Italian butcher anymore. She got involved with this arty group on Broome, and then she's out two, three nights a week, and all of a sudden it's sell the store, sell the building, take the cash. And do what? Open a fucking gallery? Be beautiful people? I mean she went kind of nuts, if you want to know the truth."

"What's this about selling the store?"

"Oh, well, we own the building. My grandfather bought it in twenty-eight for twelve K. Last winter I had a Chinese fella come by and offer two point three mil for it. Incredible, huh?"

"Manhattan real estate," said Marlene. "And Karen thought you should sell?"

"Oh, yeah," he said. "We fought like cats and dogs over it."

"What makes you so sure he's not lying?" said Karp. He was feeling pretty good just then. His wife was snuggled up in bed with him and they were talking about a case about which she was making lawyerlike noises. His dream: Marlene would miraculously outgrow being Marlene; she would have a legal practice; they would go to the movies on the weekends, unarmed, like regular people . . .

"Because he's not stupid and it'd be a particularly stupid lie. The smart lie, as you pointed out earlier, is to say, 'Yeah, I boinked her but she said she was eighteen, she'd been carded in the bar, he had every expectation that she was of age.' This is not the thirteen-year-old baby-sitter situation, which is the usual stat-rape case. Speaking of usual cases, I'm dying to know why you guys are pursuing this one so vigorously."

"I don't like it when you say 'you guys' like that. This is a Laura Rachman deal."

"What, she doesn't work for you?"

"We both work for Keegan is how she would put it."

"But I wish I knew what the real deal was," she said. "Nudge, nudge."

"You may nudge all you want, but you're not going to get pillow talk from me about active cases. Why don't you go talk to Rachman? She'll talk to you. You hired her, as I recall."

"Yes and I also recall her qualifications were not quite up to snuff, but I admired her guts and aggressiveness."

"No good deed goes unpunished," said Karp. "This could be a reprise of the Hirsch travesty. Laura likes to try middle-class white guys, whether they did it or not."

"You're loving this, aren't you?" She propped herself up on an elbow and regarded him closely and not with approval. "Miraculously I'm in both domestic habitation and nonviolent employment and I'm going to go up against your least favorite bureau chief, and maybe even make a monkey out of her. What a nauseatingly self-satisfied grin that is!"

With which she rolled on top of him and drove

her hard little knuckles between his ribs. "Take that, Mr. Patriarchy! And that! And that!"

Karp was writhing and laughing. "Stop it, Marlene," he hooted.

"Stop it? Stop it?" she said. She moved her point of attack. "How about this? Should I stop this, too?"

"No, not that," he said. "Don't stop that."

Felix sat in the shade smoking a cigarette and watched the two fake-Spanish Arabs unload the sacks of fertilizer from his truck. It was hot and miserably humid, and the Arabs worked stripped to the waist, carrying the eighty-pound burdens on one shoulder, the other hand perched grace-fully on the opposite hip. Felix did not do physical labor himself, but he did not mind watching it take place, rather enjoyed it in the present circumstances, watching the sand niggers do nigger work in the blazing sun.

Rashid had said this was the last shipment for the time being. Other things would be found for him to do. Felix had said that there seemed like a lot to do, with all that ammonium nitrate to use up, and Rashid had given him one of his cold glares. Felix had acted suitably frightened off; he was getting good at playing the rabbit, actually enjoying it in a way. Rashid had no sense of humor and even the most parodic cringing, Igor in a bad Frankenstein movie, was accepted at face value. It would add to the fun, thought Felix, when he finally made his move and had Rashid all naked and hogtied on a plastic sheet in his secret storage locker. Still, he would like to know what the little fuck wanted with all that stuff. Felix had been keeping track of the buys over this last month and a half, and it came to nearly seventeen thousand pounds of ammonium nitrate. Add six percent fuel oil and shredded rubber (which he had also purchased), and you had just about nine tons of ammonium nitrate-fuel oil high explosive. Felix had been studying on the Internet and understood what that much high explosive could do. It was absurd to think that they were accumulating a tonnage like that to make pissy little pipe bombs. The pipe bombs had to be a distraction of some kind, besides a means of knocking off a number of individuals the Arab didn't like.

The Arab. Felix wished that he could rat out the Arab, get him kicked out of his cushy job in the infirmary, return him to the general population maybe, maybe arrange to have him shanked. But obviously he couldn't do that without the Arab ratting **him** out in return. So that was another blocked revenge, a frustration. The Arab, Rashid, and the girl, a trifecta from hell. Which he was not going to go crazy about.

Think. Plan. With that much ANFO you could take down a street of buildings, knock out a bridge or a bunch of major tunnels. Felix thought that he'd like to see a blast like that. On the other hand, maybe . . . if he just knew what their plans were, he could go to the cops, tip them off in return for a free ride—new ID, money, a fresh start somewhere else, the Islands, South America. Possibilities were opening up here; it could really work out for him if he played it right. The details were going to be the problem, though. How to feed the cops just enough to hook them, and stay out of their hands, and move into position for the big score. It would probably mean giving up the session with Rashid, but okay, he might be able to pay to have that done. That was the mature response, and he could not help feeling some pride about it. Hooking the cops was not a problem. He could get on it right away. The Karp business, he would have to figure out a way to integrate that into the master plan. And the girl. That was different. His mind bounced against the idea of her. He had to stay away from her, he'd already decided that, but for how long? And why had he decided? He couldn't quite recall. Part of the strategy.

He needed a new strategy, that was clear. He took out his little book and one of the fine-point Pentel markers he liked and began to write down the things he had to do to get it rolling. Yeah, the girl had to be central here, was his thought, although he could not have told you why. He might have to give up Rashid, but not her.

11

KARP READ ONE LAST TIME THROUGH THE
background material describing each member of
the jury in **People v. Gerber & Nixon**. He was
not a great proponent of the theory that the case
is either won or lost when the jury is impaneled,
because he still believed in juries and believed
that a perfectly designed prosecution case would
compel any jury to convict. The defense bar did
not believe this for a second, which was why in
expensive cases like this one they spent small for-
tunes on jury consultants. Of course, Karp understood that he was not getting, nor had he ever gotten in his long career, a jury composed of a random selection of New York voters. As the courthouse saying had it, juries were actually selected
from the pool of people too stupid to avoid jury
duty. Although there were a huge number of

college-educated professionals in New York County, world center of finance, publishing, the media, the arts, an island city studded with medical and educational institutions, none of these were on his jury. Instead he had a plumber, a house painter, a retired naval petty officer, a retired electrician, a carpet installer, and a clerk in a tire store. Those were the men, average age forty-seven, one black, one Hispanic, the rest white. The women were a waitress, a postal clerk, a home health aide, two homemakers, and a retired bookkeeper, average age forty-four, two black, three Hispanic, two Asians, the rest white.

Collins had used his peremptory challenges to seat as many minorities as possible, and Klopper had used his to do the opposite: the state wanted the bleeding hearts, the defense wanted the Fascisti. They'd collected the inoffensively ordinary. Collins had at least kept the panel free of singletons, which was the one place Karp thought that jury selection counted a little. If you needed a unanimous verdict, you didn't want one jury member feeling isolated, rushed, pressured.

Yet the character of the jury was not foremost in Karp's mind as he packed his files into cardboard folders in preparation for the walk to Part 34 and the trial. What held that place, and itched like an unhealed wound, was his failure to find what he had been looking for since he took the case, since, in fact, his last conversation with

Terrell Collins. The key, the lever, the angle, the fatal discrepancy that would torpedo the testimony of the two lying cops. And he had looked until his eyes filled with grit and tears: all the transcripts of the trial and the grand jury, the medical examiner's report, the Q&A done immediately after the crime, the ballistics reports that explored in boggling detail the fate of each of the seven bullets that had passed through the body of the victim, where they were probably fired from in relation to the victim and where they had finished their flights.

He had pored over the report by Hugo Selwyn, the defense's ballistic man. Selwyn told a story that explained the bullets' fates in a way favorable to the defense. This story, naturally, required an implausible number of bullet miracles to have happened, implausible to Karp, who'd seen zillions of such reports, but perhaps not to a jury of high school grads and dropouts. Bullets did occasionally do weird things; even Karp, even the state's own ballistic guy would have to admit that. But not seven little miracles, that was pushing it, and Karp would have to convince the jury of that. Not easy; millions of people still believed the Warren Report and its own miraculous bullet.

A quick stop in the men's room to check appearances: no lettuce on the teeth, no egg on the tie. He practiced an honest look, adjusted the knot and the collar. A little butterfly here, as just before a game. Nothing else gave that feeling. His sole addiction.

He was thinking about the bullet, as he walked into the courtroom and took his seat at the prosecution's table, and suddenly he stopped, right at the edge of the table. It was almost there, on the edge of his mind: it was the bullet, one of the seven . . . no, not the bullet per se, something to do with how it got shot, something wrong with the defense's story, not a ballistics thing, something clear, an impeaching fact, undeniable . . . and damn it! It had skittered out of reach. Being Karp, he found it easy to blame himself: getting old, stupid to take this case, a loser, twenty years ago he would have had it on the first try, the brain cells not what they once were, too many other worries crowding the case out, the kids, Marlene . . .

He realized he had frozen behind the table, and that people were starting to stare. He sat down and arranged his materials. He nodded to Roland Hrcany, who was seated at the defense table, looking relaxed and confident, along with the two defendants and another lawyer, Barnett, from the detectives' endowment. Karp wondered whether Roland ever had butterflies. In their long relationship it had never come up. Karp supposed he himself looked relaxed and confident to all the many defense lawyers he had faced. Over at the Legal Aid Society he was genially known as the Prince of Darkness.

Nothing was as it seemed in the institution whose whole ostensible purpose was divulging the truth. The judge entered and they all rose.

A male voice says, "Auburn Correctional Facility," and Marlene says, "Yes, this is Marlene Ciampi and I'm at the district attorney's office, New York County. I'd like some information about the disposition of the body of a prisoner who died in custody."

She looks around the office she's poaching. Yes, that wasn't a lie—she really is at the district attorney's office. The man says, "Just a minute, ma'am," and puts her on hold. While there, she hears a recorded ad encouraging her to apply to become a correctional officer. The cheerful voice mentions pay, pension, and benefits, and omits the regular inundations with urine and feces, but Marlene thinks it sounds pretty good—steady work, not all that demanding, she doesn't really mind being besmirched with human wastes . . . and then a man comes on the line wanting to know who she is and what she wants, a deputy warden, no less. Marlene tells him; he says he can't release that information over the phone, and Marlene says it's vital to an ongoing investigation and speed is essential and she would be glad to have a subpoena drawn up but hopes that isn't necessary because she would also have to have the DA send a note to the head of the department of corrections, cc to the governor, wondering about were we all playing on the same criminal justice team or what. The man asks for her number and she gives him the number of the DA and the extension at the desk she has appropriated. He calls back in five minutes, with the name and address of the cousin to whom the late Felix has been delivered, and the funeral home that has actually received the body. Marlene thanks the deputy warden, hangs up, and dials information. Number of Evan Murphy and Sons Morticians, in New York? Sorry, no listing. Again, number of a Bruce Newton, address in Queens? The mechanical voice gives her a number. Interesting, a phony funeral home and a real cousin.

She checks her watch. Time for her appointment. If you had an appointment with the DA you were supposed to wait down in the tiny lobby at the DA wing entrance on a little side street off Foley Square, but Marlene just flashes a ten-year-old ID card and slips past the guard station into the waiting elevator. Dumb trick, but it gives her a little lift. A dumb Marlene trick, Karp would have said.

"Can I help you?"

A woman stands in the doorway of the tiny office, dark, petite, wearing her hair short and her tan linen suit crisp. Marlene slides off the edge of the desk and holds out her hand. "I'm Marlene

Ciampi. You must be Ms. Palmisano." The woman shakes hands with her, but the uncertain expression stays on her face. She stows her briefcase, which Marlene notes is highly polished leather on a shoulder strap, equipped with brass fittings that look as if they'd come off a Clydesdale.

"Did they call up?"

"No, I was in the office for something else and I just came over to sex crimes. I used to work here."

Marlene can see the wheels spinning. A smile appears on the little pixie face. "Oh, of course. I should have recognized the name. You're a famous figure."

"Infamous maybe." A shared chuckle, a little social small talk. They sit. What can she do for Marlene? Marlene says, "I didn't mention it to the secretary . . . I've just been retained by Paul Agnelli."

A puzzled look, the social smile fades. "You mean retained to represent him?"

"Yes, I thought we could talk informally, see where we stand."

Palmisano nods. She sits stiffly behind her desk, like an old-fashioned schoolteacher facing an errant pupil. "I don't see where we have much to discuss, Ms. Ciampi. Unless you were thinking about pleading guilty."

"What, you mean to the one thirty-point-twenty-five?"

"Right, the rape in the third. Cherry Newcombe was fourteen years of age when your client had sex with her in the back of his car. And she looks fourteen. Have you ever seen her?"

"No. But it doesn't matter what she—"

"Here's a picture," Palmisano said, opening a folder on her desk and pulling out an eight-by-ten glossy print. Marlene looked at it. It showed a pretty light-skinned African-American child, her hair in the traditional bunches and a sad expression in her huge liquid eyes. The photo showed her from the waist up, wearing what looked like a fancy little-girl's party dress, with ruching down the front and puffs at the shoulders. She had no breasts to speak of and looked about twelve.

"When was this taken?" Marlene asked.

"At about the time of the crime in question."

"The **alleged** crime. I understand you have good forensics."

"We have terrific forensics. Everything we need to convict."

"Uh-huh. The problem is my guy says he didn't do it."

Roll of eye. "Well, **duh!**"

"Yeah, but as you know, the usual defense in a case like this is to say I thought she was eighteen. My guy's story is he never heard of this girl."

Palmisano tapped the photo. "Look at this face. No jury would ever believe that anyone would believe this girl was legal, or that any **normal** man would regard her as a sex object."

"Yes, but on the other hand, she got into a club where you have to be not just eighteen but twenty-one. Your case is based on her being in the club and the defendant encountering her there and seducing her out into his car. And I guarantee you that if she was in the Red Mill on the night in question, she did **not** look like she does in that picture. I notice that you don't present any testimony from anyone at the Red Mill regarding the alleged victim's presence in the place on the night of, or that she was seen in the company with the defendant, or what she looked like on the night."

"Why should we? We know she was in his car and we know he had sex with her."

"Yes, I know you think that, but the problem with it is, I know my client. My client is a sexually active man, even something of a lothario, but what he definitely does not have is short eyes. He's also something of a mild bigot. Therefore, a little black girl would be his absolutely last choice for a sexual target."

With a shrug Palmisano replies, "Tastes change."

"Not that much, they don't. In fact, as I'm sure you know, the constancy of sexual tastes is the basis of almost all rape investigations. Look, imagine that the basis of a case was that a lifelong committed lesbian had seduced and had passionate sex with a man. And say you had gallons of semen, all the forensics in the world. Wouldn't you at least wonder if someone was fooling around with the evidence?"

That one hit home, thinks Marlene. The other woman goes white around the mouth, narrow around the eyes. "What are you implying, Ms. Ciampi?"

"I'm not implying anything. I'm wondering why you don't think this feels all wrong."

"Maybe because I haven't sold out," Palmisano snaps. "I can't believe you coming up here, trading on your reputation, trying to catch a break for some scuzzball kiddie rapist." A little shrill here, the last few words.

"Calm down, counsellor," says Marlene in a quiet voice. "Let's keep this civilized."

"Fine! You came, you made your pitch, and now I don't think there's anything useful we can say to each other at this point. Have a nice day, Ms. Ciampi." The woman turns slightly away from Marlene, pulls a fat file from an in-box, arranges a yellow pad and some pencils, and begins ostentatiously to pretend to work.

Marlene doesn't move. Instead she stares fixedly, silently, at the side of Terry Palmisano's head. A minute passes. Two. Palmisano whips around, her chair squealing.

"What? Why are you still in my office?"

"Gosh, you know, I really think you're under

the impression I came up here to make an argument for my client."

"Didn't you?"

"No, I came up here because you're making a major error. You're participating in a frame-up based on rigged evidence. I don't want to have to demonstrate that in court. I want you to look into it yourself. Is the victim kosher? Did anyone get to her? Is there anyone benefiting from Agnelli taking the fall? And so on. I'm doing you a **favor.**"

Palmisano rises out of her chair. A bit of dark hair falls out of the mousse's grip and dangles fetchingly on her forehead. There are blotches of dark red on her cheeks. "Oh, give me a break!" she cries. "What I really want to know is how someone like you sinks into becoming a slimeball shyster. What's the secret, Marlene? You figure we'll all roll over and play dead because of hubby up on the eighth floor? 'Doing me a favor?' What kind of moron do you think I am?"

"I don't know what kind of moron you are," says Marlene, fixing Palmisano with her eye. Palmisano suddenly realizes that Marlene has only one eye, and recalls vague stories of how she lost it. She also recalls other stories about this woman. She wonders if she has gone too far. Marlene continues, "But you need to remember, before you impugn my character, that I was killing sexual predators with my own hands— these hands—while you were still in high school.

I invented this office; I hired your boss. The idea that I would for some putative career advantage take on the case of someone I knew to be a child rapist is absurd, and would be seen as absurd by anyone who knows me."

"Please leave my office!"

Marlene gets to her feet.

"You need to ask around, Terry. There are still plenty of people in the system who'll tell you you're way out of line. Meanwhile, take another look at that evidence."

"Out!" Pointing to the door.

"As for me," Marlene says, pausing in the doorway, "my only curiosity is whether you are a witting or unwitting abettor of this conspiracy. And I intend to find out which."

Good exit line, she thinks, and then feels the lash of shame. She hates bullying like that, and descending to the level of made-for-TV movie tough-girl dialogue. She wishes that just once her life would shift of itself from the groove of grand opera to something closer to normality: Gee, thanks for pointing that out, Marlene, you saved us from a massive error. Briefly she considers going to Laura Rachman and putting the squeeze in there, but decides she doesn't have the heart for another confrontation. And it **would** be one, if she recalled Laura rightly. She pauses in a lobby cul-de-sac, takes a seat on a pile of cardboard case file crates, unlimbers the cell phone.

• • •

Daniel insisted on putting Lucy on the train at South Station, over her objections. Secretly, though, she was glad of it, since it showed he was, beneath the chromium surface of his intellect, a soppy romantic just like her. He helped her up the stairs as if she were wearing a brocade hobble skirt and not a pair of baggy shorts.

"If you dare to run along the platform crying my name and waving a handkerchief like you did last time, I'll never speak to you again."

He ignored this. "That's strange," he said, gawking, "it's all in Technicolor. I was expecting black and white. And there should be big whooshes of steam."

"You're such a dodo," she said, leaning into him, putting her face into the hollow of his neck. "If we were married, we would never have to do this. I'm feeling such a pang, now. This is really painful, you know?"

"Okay, let's do it."

"Seriously."

"Yeah, I'll ride into Manhattan with you and the conductor can marry us, like the captain of a ship. We can have our honeymoon in Providence."

"That's right, mock my little-girl dreams, grind them under your booted heel. Someday, when you're married to the phony blonde goddess of your perfervid imaginings and I'm buried in an obscure convent grave, you'll think back on this moment, and I hope you feel really, really bad."

The conductor made the usual announcement.

After they stopped kissing, she said, "Oh, this is awful. You're awful."

He stepped down to the platform. "Sell the emeralds in Mombasa," he called out. "Trust no one! I love you!"

The train pulled out. He ran down the platform after it waving a red bandanna, shouting, "Lucy, Lucy, don't leave me!"

She got some looks in the car, indulgent ones from an old lady, interested ones from a couple of teenage boys. That was something she'd noticed, when you didn't have someone interested in you, no one was interested in you, but when someone was, a lot of guys were. Maybe it was pheromones. She rummaged in her bag and brought out a falling-apart Everyman Catullus, and read dirty poetry in Latin all the way into the city.

"Ah, Jimmy, let it ring," said Nora Raney. "Let the bloody machine pick it up."

It was Raney's Regular Day Off, the baby was asleep for once, and Raney was in bed with his lovely wife. He was not quite **in media res,** but there was heavy breathing and athletic writhing going on. A few years ago, Raney had done an uncharacteristic good Irish son act and taken his mother back to County Clare, the family home place. There was a tedious little Great Famine museum there in Crusheen, which the old lady had dragged Raney off to one fine morning, and there she was, in a green museum guide uniform, Nora Muldoon. And wasn't it love at first sight? Yes, it was. Although the book on Irish redheads was unfortunately true, and there were blazing fights enough, Raney was happy as a king. Especially in the rack; Raney had been around the block a time or two, but he had not been prepared for the passion that a twenty-six-year-old convent-bred Irish country maiden could generate when at last she got her hands on a lawfully wedded husband.

So he cursed the interruption, but lieutenants of police do not let the phone ring, and policemen's wives must live with that. He reached across his wife's marvelous cream-and-pink breasts to the bedside instrument and read the caller ID numbers in the tiny window. Cursing again, he placed the receiver next to his ear. He thought he might caress one of the breasts while he talked but she batted him off with a flurry of blows, and moved as far away from him on the bed as she could.

"This better be good, Ciampi," he growled.

"Why, did I interrupt something? Is that strenuous breathing I detect? What, Raney, a **nooner?** You dirty dog!"

"I was mowing the lawn. What d'you have?"

"Well, the funeral home they gave was a

fugazy. The next of kin is real on paper, although whether he's really a cousin or just someone screwing around with us remains to be seen. Anyway, the idea that it was a scam of some kind remains in play. How do you want to handle it?"

"Could you check out the cousin? I want it nailed that it's a scam before I go in to the bosses, because if he really did go out of a maximum house live in a coffin—holy shit, heads are gonna roll right up to Albany. But I'll look like a horse's ass if it turns out it's a clerical error or some garbage like that."

"No problem, Raney. I'll get right on it. Now could you do me one?"

"Anything you want, babe."

"Owen McKenzie, a third grade at the Five— you know him?"

"To look at. He came on the squad in my last year there. Why?"

"He's the arresting on a case I'm interested in. What's he like?"

"Middle of the pack. Not bad, not a superstar, either."

"Not a Jim Raney."

"Not. Why're you interested in his case."

"It's a statutory rape case. I'm defending the guy."

"Oh, fuck, Marlene! You know I can't screw around with a made case."

"Hello? What happened to 'anything, babe'?

Besides, I'm not asking you to screw with it. Just call McKenzie and tell him there's a possibility that it's a frame, that the evidence is planted, and that he should talk to me. The story is we're interested in stopping what could be a major embarrassment for the department and to him personally. Plus the possibility of a collar on a corruption case that'd be a lot more juicy than one more pissy little statutory rape clearance."

A pause. "This is legit, Marlene? I mean, I'm a family man now, it's not like the wild west old days. I got to worry pension, health insurance . . . I mean, you're not presuming on our old friend-ship to, you know, win a case?"

"Jesus fucking Christ! You, too? What hap-pened, it was on the TV I suddenly became a scumbag ambulance chaser? Look, you want the whole story? I ran into an old pal from the neigh-borhood, he definitely did **not** do the crime, he's totally wrong for it, the forensics are a little **too** good to be true, and the victim is a choir girl who just happens to hang out in a major meat market for the over-thirty set. The whole thing is yelling 'frame, frame.' And, in the extremely improbable event that I'm wrong, I will plead my client to the top count, and no harm done, plus I will kiss your ass in Macy's window."

Raney had to laugh. He agreed to call the detective and hung up. His wife was not laugh-ing. She had the sheet pulled up to her neck, her arms akimbo and a blue glare in her eye.

"Sorry, that was business," he said, and reached, but she slapped his hand away.

"Business, was it? The famous Marlene, was it?"

Raney fell back on his pillow and laced his hands behind his head, gritting his teeth at the ceiling. "Yes, it was. She's helping me out."

"Helping you out. It sounds like you're helping **her** out. And putting your career at risk in the bargain. **Anything, babe?**"

"Nora, there is nothing going on between Marlene Ciampi and me."

"But there used to be."

"There **never** was."

"But you wished it, didn't you?"

"Yes. I had a lustful attraction for her, okay? That never went anywhere. I've told you this a million times."

"Have her over, then."

"What?"

"I want to set eyes on the woman across me own table, with you sitting right there. And God help you, James Raney, if you're not telling the truth, because I'll know. And here's Meghan wailing now, and so you've missed your chance at me milk white body, and serves you right!"

Felix was attending a council of war. The little shithead actually called it that, a council of war, when he told Felix he had to be there. It was held in the dining room of the Queens house. Rashid sat at the head of the dining room table, with an easel and a chalkboard behind him, flanked by Carlos and Felípe (or whatever their real names were), and the other seats at the table and some folding chairs arranged in a couple of rows were all filled with young men that Felix didn't know. There were fourteen people including him, and none of them was speaking English. They were drinking mint tea, which Felix thought was wacked on a scorching August day; he wanted a beer himself, but Rashid had said no beer, so he had got himself a liter bottle of Mountain Dew. Felix had no idea that Rashid was running so extensive an operation.

After about twenty minutes of this yakking, Rashid rapped sharply on the table with his tea-spoon. Somewhat to Felix's surprise, he spoke in English. He explained that since they all spoke different dialects of Arabic, and some did not speak Arabic at all—here a number of men glanced at Felix—he would speak in English, their one common tongue.

In English he spoke and it went on for some time. Rashid hit all the points in the fanatics' hand-book: oppressed peoples, revolutionary vanguard, imperialistic lackeys, Zionist murderers, world Jewish conspiracy, lie of the Holocaust, bourgeois materialism, spiritual growth through violence, striking a blow in the Zionist-imperialist center, history is with us, my brothers. At the end there was applause, rather more polite than fervent. Felix wondered why there wasn't more God talk. The Muslims in jail were always on you about Allah this and Allah that and the Koran, but not these guys, or anyway, not Rashid. Maybe a different kind of Arab, not that he gave a shit himself.

Rashid was now at the chalkboard talking about the great blow, and here Felix's interest perked up. He had been wanting to know what all that high explosive was for and here it was: a plan to simultaneously truck bomb the four tunnels leading into Manhattan. Rashid assigned the various terrorists to different teams. One man in each team would drive the truck, another would drive a motorcycle, on which the driver and he could make their escape. Felix noted with interest that these were not the suicide type of Arab. Another team member would be responsible for driving the car to which the bombers would transfer after ditching the motorcycle. The two fake-Spanish guys, Carlos and Felípe, would be responsible for assembling the bombs, which would be packed into septic tank pumper trucks. Two young men, one thin and one fat, Omar and Fuad, were introduced as technical support for the two fake Spaniards, although to Felix they looked more like a pair of goofy high school kids than hardened terrorists. Rashid explained that a small septic tank service firm had been acquired for that purpose. There was laughter at this, the stupid Americans.

Rashid sketched maps and indicated the location of safe houses, provided timetables, delineated phases one, two, and three, and provided all the minutiae of a carefully designed plan. Felix was impressed in spite of himself, and felt the first inkling of what it would be like to be part of something larger than Felix. To be the master of an organization was something he had never considered, but now as he saw Rashid swell like a frog or a strutting pigeon, he could imagine himself in the role. As master, of course, and not as the flunky he was just now. As Rashid droned on, Felix entertained himself with fantasies of taking over Rashid's organization, or better yet, starting his own terrorist band. It could work. Explosives were easy to get, he knew how to make bombs now, and getting a couple or three guys together wouldn't be a problem, for drivers and bomb planters and gofers. None of this political shit, except maybe as a cover. Blame it on the Muslims or the niggers, that would work, but basically you'd go into a city, make a couple of spectacular demolitions, and then do extortion.

That was another thing that interested him. The scale of Rashid's operation meant he had to have a ton of money from somewhere. He was keeping all these guys in couscous or whatever, he seemed to have bought a whole business to use as a base, and another one as a source of septic tanker trucks. He bought houses and cars and fake IDs without strain. Obviously money was the key, because without it, you'd have to steal vehicles and rent, and that was what would get you caught. It could not be in cash, as he had previously thought. There had to be accounts, wire transfers in and out. He would have to find a way of getting his hands on some of that money.

Rashid was asking for questions; there were surprisingly few, considering the complexity of the plan. Felix wondered whether all these guys had worked together before. He raised his hand. Rashid acknowledged him with an imperious gesture.

"Yeah, Rashid, I noticed you didn't give me an assignment. I'm not on this thing?"

"No, Felix, I want you to continue what you have been doing," said Rashid, "also, if you would stay after the others have left, I have some special instructions."

It took an hour or so for the place to empty, the men departing alone or in twos at intervals, so as not to draw attention. They spoke to one another in Arabic as they awaited their turns to leave, and ignored Felix. Finally, when only Rashid and the two fake Spaniards remained, Rashid turned to Felix and said, "The chief wants this Karp business taken care of, and also the information from the girl. I was under the impression that this was nearly in your hands."

Again Felix felt that odd repugnance associated with the thought of approaching Lucy Karp. "Hey, she clams up. She doesn't want to talk about your guy. I misjudged the situation. I don't think the soft shit is going to work with her. Sorry. I think we need to pick her up and work her over." His words hardly sounded convincing to his own ears, and it was all he could do to keep the humble, remorseful expression on his face.

What the terrorist said next was therefore something of a relief. "It does not matter. There is no need to deal with the girl directly. She has a brother, two brothers, and one of them is blind. They are often out of their house. The blind one plays music on the street." Then something in Arabic to the other two, who responded with laughter. "It should not be hard to pick one or both of them up. Then the sister will of course provide us with any information we want."

"You want me to pick up the kid?"

"No, someone else will take care of that. I want you to deliver another device. The wife must be eliminated first. She has a truck."

Felix smiled and thought about the bomb he had already made for Marlene Ciampi, killer of his brother. Oh, good, that saves me a bomb. He began to consider who would get it.

"What about Karp?" he asked.

"He'll be taken care of in due time. We have a plan for everything, as you saw just now. First you will make this one delivery and then we will see."

"Yeah, but it'd be good if I was a little more into the planning end, so I could get an idea of how everything fits together. I mean, why are we still planting these little bombs when you've got this big blast coming?"

Rashid responded with an icy glare, and, "You know, Felix, you are still on what we can call probation because of your recent betrayal. You will therefore be told only what you need to know. Don't get above yourself is my advice."

Felix made himself grin engagingly and nod. "Sure, whatever you say, Rashid."

"Excellent. I will give you the device shortly. And now, if you will excuse us . . ."

It was a dismissal. Felix left the room and as he did so, a notional lightbulb lit above his head as he realized how he was going to get the money out of Rashid. A smile bloomed on his face.

And on Rashid's. He turned to his two companions. "Well? What do you think. Is he hooked?"

They nodded and smiled and agreed that he truly was.

12

THERE WAS SOMETHING WRONG WITH THE air conditioning in Part 34. The temperature outside the grimy windows was moving toward eighty, and inside the packed courtroom the ambiance was approaching that of the midsummer subway at rush hour. They brought in two large fans at Judge Higbee's order, so that it was like standing in front of the kitchen exhaust of a deli, without the greasy smell.

Karp didn't mind the heat particularly, although he noticed that Roland Hrcany was a little more red-faced than usual. He actually felt sorriest for the jury, who were fanning themselves with their instructional pamphlets: "Your Jury Duty, An American Privilege." The defendants didn't seem to be sweating at all. Perhaps they had rolled in Arrid.

But on the stand, Hugo Selwyn also seemed to be feeling the heat. He had a big bandanna out and often mopped his face with it, establishing a certain **Inherit the Wind** tone. The ballistics expert was a big man, in his mid-sixties, with a thick mop of silvery curls, like a cartoon senator, a bolo tie, and a powder blue three-piece suit. With his solid jaw and canny blue gaze, he looked like central casting had sent him over to play an expert witness. Karp imagined he garnered a good deal of his custom off his looks, that and his willingness to provide an expert opinion favorable to the defense, whatever the ascertainable facts might be. Selwyn had been on the stand once already, before the bomb had knocked both Collins and Klopper out, during which time the defense had been at pains to establish the man as a legitimate ballistics expert, and, according to the transcript Karp had carefully read, Collins had done a good job painting him in whore's colors.

Roland had a big easel set up next to the witness stand, upon which a gigantic color diagram of the crime scene, generated by a computer, Karp imagined, with the positions of Gerber, Nixon, and the victim, Onabajo, marked out according to the defense's theory of the case. The trajectory and final fate of the seven bullets also appeared, each bullet's path marked with a different color. Karp thought it was an effective chart, if largely fictional, and thought it was clever to use a computer diagram instead of a photograph, which was what Collins had used when he presented the state's version. There was a lot of blood in the photograph, a lot more than you saw even in slasher movies. That was one of the big shocks of real-life crime, just how much blood got spilled in a fatal shooting. The defense did not wish to draw attention to the blood.

Roland was taking the old fraudster through the expert testimony with his usual skill. Seven bullets, and they each had names by now. On a smaller easel off to one side, but well within the jury's view, was a photographic blowup of all seven, lined up like little soldiers, and exhibiting various states of deformation. They were all Federal 115-grain jacketed hollow-point nine-millimeter bullets, two fired from Nixon's Smith & Wesson Model 915 and five from Gerber's Ruger P89, and those that had hit something solid had turned into little mushrooms. Roland asked his expert to explain how each bullet had ended up where the cops had found it. Bullet one (B-1), the jury learned, had exploded from Detective Nixon's pistol while it was pointed seventeen degrees below the horizontal, entering the body of the assailant . . .

"Objection," said Karp. "Mr. Onabajo is not the assailant in this case. He is the victim. Mr. Gerber, the defendant, may be called the assailant if counsel so wishes."

"Sustained," said the judge. "Modify your question, counsel."

The body of Mr. Onabajo, then; it had glanced

off Mr. Onabajo's hip bone, exited Mr. Onabajo's body, ricocheted off a fire hydrant, and buried itself in the tire of a parked vehicle. Was the position of the muzzle of the pistol consistent with struggling over the weapon? Could Mr. Onabajo's hand have been on the weapon when it was fired?

Objection from Karp. Calls for conclusion outside the alleged expertise of the witness. Sustained. Roland objected to the use of the word "alleged." Judge told Karp to watch it.

Karp sat down feeling fairly good about this first tapping of the foils. It was going to be an interesting trial, an enjoyable trial actually, if that wasn't the wrong word to use about any participation in this hideous disaster. Roland and he had been trained in the same school, were about equal in skill and knowledge, and were meeting as adversaries for the first time, the difference being that Roland really wanted to crush Karp, and Karp did not particularly care about Roland. He wanted to get Gerber and Nixon, though.

The rest of Selwyn's testimony went off without objection. Roland knew how to phrase questions well enough, and Karp was never a lawyer to load on purely tactical objections designed to break the flow of the witnesses' narratives. He'd take care of Mr. Selwyn on cross. The only thing preventing Karp from being as happy as he ever got in a professional setting was that nagging thought—he had missed something, and it had to do with the bullets in some way, and unless he thought of it pretty soon, it would be too late to insert into the trial.

At three that afternoon, Marlene prepares to leave her loft for the purposes of placing under surveillance the residence of Bruce Newton, the cousin—according to the New York State Department of Corrections—of the late Felix Tighe. Her boys, with whom she had been spending a rare maternal day, are not pleased.

"Can we come?" asks Zak.

"No, it's work. I'll be back in two hours. And Lucy will be home soon."

"It's okay, Zak," says the brother, "we need to see Bogart and get some more skag. We're almost out and I don't want to have to kick cold turkey again."

"Yeah, right," Zak agrees, "But we have to knock over a convenience store first to get paid. Or we could sell your body in the West Village."

"Whatever," says Giancarlo, smiling angelically at his mother.

"I hate both of you," says Marlene. "It was a mistake to have you, and you're both going to foster care the minute I get back." She marches toward the door and trips over her dog, who rises in her path for just that purpose. The boys laugh cruelly.

"Oh, all right!" she snarls. **"You** can come."

Giancarlo says, "See, I told you, she loves the dog more than us."

"You're darn tooting, I do," says Marlene, "he's more useful and he's a lot cheaper to feed." She strikes like a snake, grabs both of them and kisses them both wetly on the cheeks, as they squirm and howl their disgust.

"Honestly," says Marlene in the descending elevator. "Did you ever hear such mouthing off? I was like the perfect mother all day. Jelly omelets and Canadian bacon for brekkie. A special trip to the video store for kung-fu movies. I mean, really! What would **you** do?"

Their flesh would feel the grip of my mighty fangs, snarls the dog.

"Oh, shut up!" says his mistress. "You only say that because you're not a mother."

Marlene keeps her Ford 150 pickup in a lot on Grand. She has her key ring out and is just about to push the little button that switches off the alarm, when Gog the mastiff barks twice. She freezes and looks at the dog. Gog practically never barks, and when he does, it is only in particular situations, as when warning someone off an area he has been instructed to guard, but that bark is a different bark from the one he now utters. This one is higher-pitched, with a little whine at the end. Chill flashes over Marlene's body. She stares at her truck, then at her dog, then spins on her heel and dashes out of the parking lot, fumbling for her cell phone as she runs.

Lucy saw the flashing lights as she crossed Grand at Broadway, and without thinking, began trotting toward the scene, with the pounding starting in her chest. It never occurred to her that a police emergency might be happening on her corner without her family being in some serious way involved. The cordon had been thrown quite wide around the parking lot at Grand and Crosby, the reason for that explained by the characteristic shape of the bomb squad containment vessel truck. She shouldered through the dense crowd—all the neighboring buildings had been evacuated, obviously—and then worked around the police lines until she spotted her brothers and her mother. Her mother was talking to a man in a NYPD hardhat and a white Tyvek suit.

"Mom! What's going on?" Lucy asked.

Giancarlo answered. "The Manbomber tried to bomb Mom's truck."

"You have to be kidding!"

"No lie," said Zak. "Gog sniffed it before Mom got into the truck."

"Mah-um!" cried Lucy.

Marlene broke away from her conversation with the detective and approached her daughter, who embraced her enthusiastically.

"We don't know it's the Manbomber yet, and what's with the hugs?" said Marlene. "Are you getting married?"

"No, Mom, it's my natural reaction when you're nearly blown to bits. It's allowed. Check out the Good Daughter's Handbook, page twenty-four."

"Please, I've already been blown up once. It can't happen again. Ask Lieutenant Tancredi here."

The cop, a heavyset man with a fat brush moustache, rolled an eye. "She's right. There's practically no one gets blown up by a bomb more than once."

"I bet it was the Manbomber," said Zak. "We're going to be famous."

"Not if I can help it," said Marlene, and to the cop, "Lieutenant, when can I have my truck back?"

"Couple of hours, maybe. CSU has to dust, and then they got to stand around hoping that a clue will turn up, the bastard dropped a match-book with the name of a nightclub on it, and a phone number on the inside."

"It was definitely the guy, though?"

A raised eyebrow. "You didn't hear it from me, but yeah. Hell, even your little kid knows it's him." He grinned at Zak, then said to Marlene, ungrinning. "We're going to have to talk."

"Well, you know where to find me. Let's go, kids, show's over."

It was. The bomb truck rolled away, the blue-and-whites cranked up and moved out of barricade position, the technicians and detectives departed, as did the throng. Soon the only police presence that remained was clustered around Marlene's pickup truck, which was still marked off from the rest of the lot by yellow crime-scene tape.

The Karp family went back to their loft. Lucy had to spend a good deal of time being loved by her dog, Magog, who had been sleeping under her bed while she was gone. Marlene observed them rolling around on the floor with a professional eye. "They're not supposed to be one-man dogs like that, but Maggie sure is. How did you manage it?"

"She's a freak of nature like me," said Lucy, kissing the huge black muzzle. "Aren't you? **Aren't you?** Yes, you are."

Marlene did not call Lucy on the freak business, as she had reflexively in the past. They were past that, it seemed, and Lucy had, after the spontaneous embrace down on the street, slipped into the correct formality she had used with her mother since the grim events of the previous summer. Marlene studied the girl. She looked good; there was a glow coming off her as she laughed and played with the dog. She wondered if she had at long last become Dan Heeney's lover, and had opened her mouth to say something that would move them back into the intimacy they had once shared, but the words stuck in her throat. She went into the kitchen and poured out a glass of Barolo. She could have a glass of wine, she thought; she had almost been killed.

A buzz from the intercom: it was Lieutenant Tancredi from the Manbomber task force, and could he come up. The detective had shed his helmet and white suit, and was now in a short-sleeved blue shirt and tie and a wilted cotton jacket. He was accompanied by a younger cop named Fox. She installed them on stools in her kitchen, poured them iced tea, and another glass of wine for herself.

They did an interview. The central questions involved the other victims. Tancredi showed her a short stack of sheets they had made up, a little picture of a dead person, a name, a description. Marlene pointed to Pete Balducci's image. "I knew him. We were friends."

"Pete Balducci," said Tancredi. "Yeah, I knew him, too. A shame. No one else?"

"Some of the other people were involved in the criminal justice business and I knew them by rep or we had some casual contact. Klopper, Horowitz, this Daoud guy was the father of a girl I knew once." This was not the time to bring up Felix Tighe and Raney's odd obsession. See the cousin first.

"Uh-huh, well, that's not unusual, then.

Everyone seems to know a victim or someone who knew a victim. It hasn't added up to anything yet. So—anything at all, anyone you know who'd want to put a bomb in your car? Assuming it wasn't, that all of these aren't, totally random?"

"To kill me? Are you serious?"

The cop put on a mollifying smile. "Well, we have to ask."

"Dozens. Scores."

A frown. "No, I meant I **am** serious."

"So am I. You don't know who I am?"

"No, who are you, ma'am?"

"I used to be a PI. I shot a few people, and messed up a larger number, mostly guys who wanted to beat up their women friends. I discouraged stalkers as a profession. On the other hand, I can't really think that any of them blew up half the city in order to disguise a hit on me. It's a little overelaborate, even for a stalker."

"Why don't you let us be the judge of that. I'd like to have a list of names and addresses."

"Sure. Just a second."

She rose from her stool and disappeared into the loft, returning a minute later with a set of laser-printed sheets. Tancredi looked at them, his forehead knotting.

"What is this?"

"Like it says up there, a list of people who would not be unhappy if I died violently, and might be inclined to do the job themselves. Oh, you thought I'd have to scratch my head over a yellow pad? No, I've been adding to it over the years and I kept it where it'd be found if I got killed." She watched as he glanced through the names.

"Any of these you like especially for this?" he asked, passing the list to his partner. Fox looked through it and stared at her, with either horror or wonder.

"Not really." She realized she had never crossed Felix Tighe's name off. Again, it was on the tip of her tongue to lay out the theory, but the flaws in it dissuaded her. Ridiculous when you thought about it. Tighe wasn't a bomber. He was a knife artist. He liked to get close. She added, "Some of them might be dead or out of town, though. You'll find out. And, look, if there's nothing else, I got an appointment in Queens. Can I get to my truck now?"

When the policemen left, Marlene had a minor nervous breakdown. It came upon her unexpectedly as she poured another glass of wine. Her hand started to shake. It shook the glass right out of it, to shatter in the sink, and she could hardly put the bottle down without knocking it over. Then she started shaking all over, like a malaria victim. She tried to sit on a chair and knocked it over instead, and finally collapsed against the stove, with strange, honking hoots coming out of her mouth and tears gushing from her eyes.

Her daughter found her like this. Without wasting any time on hysterics of her own—for the more extreme mental states were no strangers **chez** Karp—she got the mom seated in a chair and a roll of paper towels handy for sopping up the leakage, and sat next to her with her arm across Marlene's shoulders. When she was sufficiently recovered to make words again, she said, "I wasn't going to take the dog. I could've taken the kids. You know how they run ahead and jump into the truck when I pop the locks. They would have both . . . both of them . . ." More weeping. Then, "I have to go. I have to go out."

"Mom, sit down. You're not fit to go any-where."

"No, this was the capper. It wasn't a random bomb. It's Felix Tighe."

"Who?"

"A case. Before you were born. He was a kind of violent con man, a psychopath. He used to get next to women, move in on them. Strip their assets, dominate them. He liked to torture them, too. One of the girlfriends complained and he beat her up, and the woman in the next apartment called the cops. He came back later and slashed her to pieces along with her little boy."

"She was one of your clients? The victim?"

"No, not at all. I never met her. It was one of

your dad's big cases. He convicted Felix and sent him away, twenty-five to life."

"So this is because Dad convicted him? And how did he get to be the bomber? Or escape from jail?"

Marlene looked at her daughter, who had an expression on her face that no parent likes to see, the one that comes before "Gee, Mom, maybe you ought to see somebody."

"I'm not crazy, Lucy," she said and proceeded to relate Jim Raney's theory of the Manbomber case, adding the information about the way Mary Chalfonte and her little girl had died. "And this just now, like I said, is the capper. Only he's dead, which is why I have to go see the cousin."

Unlike most children, Lucy didn't ask for an explanation of this seeming paradox. Instead, she said, "You're not going out of this house by yourself."

"What!"

"What I said. Look at you, you're still shaking."

"I am not!" Marlene protested, holding out her hand, which fluttered like a pennant in a stiff breeze.

At that moment, they heard the elevator door thump open, and a moment later the sound of the loft door opening.

"Good! Dad can watch the boys," said Lucy, as she snatched the truck keys up from where the cop had laid them.

• • •

The drive to Hampton Street in Elmhurst, Queens, took a good long time, as it was nearly the height of rush hour. Lucy drove: the Midtown Tunnel, Roosevelt Avenue, Elmhurst Avenue, and the street itself, a row of asphalt-shingled or aluminum-sided two-story semi-detached houses with tiny front yards, under maples and sycamores in dense leaf. The streets were spotted with men and women coming home from work, and others going to work, and children playing noisily. The people here were Asians of various flavors, and Latin Americans.

The yard on the one they wanted was unkempt: weeds shot up among the deep mulch of last year's leaf fall. The blinds were closed on the front windows.

"Wait here," said Marlene.

"You're sure you're all right?"

"Yeah, I'm fine. I just want to talk to this guy."

"Okay, but if you're not out of there in twelve hours, I'm calling nine-one-one."

Marlene forced a chuckle and went through the chain-link gate and up the cracked walk.

Ding dong.

The door was hauled open and the guy who opened it did the sort of double take you get when someone expects a caller and gets someone else. He was wearing greasy gray canvas work pants, a sleeveless undershirt (with gold chain and shiny crucifix), and a black ball cap with a Rangers logo on it, bill cocked to the side. He had a broad, high-cheeked tan face, coarse black hair spattered with little white grains, and a drooping Fu Manchu moustache and short beard.

Marlene said, "Hi, I was wondering if Bruce Newton was home?"

The man started to close the door. "No hable inglés."

"But we speak Spanish," said Marlene in that tongue, making beckoning motions. Lucy got out of the truck. "My daughter speaks it very well," she promised. This statement virtually exhausted her colloquial Spanish, although she could follow simple conversation fairly well.

Marlene explained to Lucy what was required. Lucy asked the man if Bruce Newton were available.

"Who're you?" the man asked.

"We're working with the corrections department, checking up on some things. Don't worry, he's not in any trouble." She tried a smile, which was not returned. "Is Mr. Newton at home?"

"No, he's away. On a trip. Business."

"But this is his residence, yes?"

"Yes. But he's not here now."

"When will he be back, do you know?"

"No. Month, two months. I don't know."

Marlene said, "Ask him about the funeral."

Lucy said, "Yes, excuse me, Mr. . . . ."

A pause. "Gonzales."

"Mr. Gonzales. Did Mr. Newton attend a funeral recently? His cousin Felix?"

"Yes. They sent the body to the funeral home and he went there. They cremated him."

"Ask him what funeral home," hissed Marlene, but when Lucy did so, the man professed ignorance. "In the neighborhood, I don't know. He wasn't my cousin, you know?"

Marlene thanked the man, who went back behind his door. The two women returned to the Ford. Lucy drove away. After half a block, Marlene said, "Pull over here."

Lucy did so. "What now?"

"What did you think?"

"Of Mr. Maybe Gonzales? Not forthcoming. Why? Maybe he's got fifteen Salvadorans back there with one green card between them. He's a working stiff, though. He had pipe grease and plumber's dope on his pants, and concrete dust in his hair, too. Construction plumbing, I'd say. Also, he's not a Latino himself."

"No? What is he?"

"I don't know. His Spanish is fluent enough, but still a second language. And it's not a Latin American accent. He's a Spaniard, or someone who was raised in Spain but was originally from somewhere else."

"That's very impressive, Lucy."

Lucy polished her knuckles on her breastbone

and blew across them. "Language is ma game."

"Yes, but you got he was bent and that he was a plumber. And if you go into detective work, I'll break your knees for you."

"It's too late, Ma." Laughing.

"We'll see about that. So, you can't tell where he comes from? From the accent?"

"Not offhand. If I had a tape, maybe I could."

"Let's get one, then," said Marlene, pulling a microrecorder from her bag. "Come on!"

With that, she was out of the truck and heading down to the Newton-Mr. Maybe Gonzales residence, with Lucy following. They slipped down the side alley between that house and its neighbor, crouching low so as not to be spotted from any of the windows. These were all wide open because of the heat, and they could hear sounds coming from the houses on either side— an argument in Spanish, a pop song in the same language playing on a radio, and from the kitchen window of the Gonzales house the dull roar of a fan. And talking. Marlene lifted an eye to the corner where sill met window frame. Gonzales was on the kitchen phone, his back to the window. She held up the microrecorder and pushed the button. The conversation went on for some time, the man speaking nervously in a language Marlene had never heard, which was not going to be a problem because here was Lucy with all the answers in that department.

But when they were back at the truck and Marlene asked, Lucy said, "I have no idea."

"What? Why not?"

"Because there are around sixty-five hundred languages spoken on this planet, and I can speak fifty or so with some fluency and can identify maybe fifty more, and those are only the really common ones. There are hundreds of languages that I've never even heard, each one of them spoken by millions of people. On the other hand I can probably make some guesses."

"Like . . . ?"

"Well, clearly not in the top forty, because I know all those. Not an Indo-European, not Asian. Could be an Amerindian tongue or something out of Africa—I would guess Africa, because, like I said, his Spanish isn't really American, plus I have a gut feeling it's in the Afro-Asiatic family. The gutturals, the dentalized t's, the glottal stops, the voiced implosives . . ."

"I thought you just said it wasn't Asian."

"No, Afro-Asiatic takes in north Africa and the Middle East—Arabic, Hebrew, Amharic, like that."

"That guy could have been an Arab, huh?"

"I don't know about that, but he probably wasn't Gonzales from San Salvador. I'd figure a guy from the Middle East who grew up in Spain."

"I'd like it if he was an Arab. Bombs and Arabs go together in my mind, I'm afraid."

"Yes, racism is alive and well in New York," said Lucy. "Give me the tape. I'll play it for some people and we'll find out."

They drove back to the city. Marlene smoked one Marlboro after another, which was something she did not often do, and never did out at the dog farm. It's working at this again, she thought, it's not good for me. I should be happy, getting somewhere with this case, getting along with my daughter, but all I can think of is I'm back in the salty soup and something awful is going to happen to the kids because of it.

"What's wrong, Mom," Lucy asked, after they had driven almost to the tunnel in virtual silence.

"Nothing," Marlene said. "I'm just a little tired. You can slip in there behind that bus."

Felix was in the crowd that watched the removal of the bomb from Marlene's truck. He wore a Caterpillar cap pulled down low on his forehead and wrap-around sunglasses, and blue mechanic's overalls with the sleeves hacked off and **Larry** embroidered in red on the breast. He watched the bomb squad work with interest as they x-rayed the bomb and then did some things he couldn't see, because they set up screens for the guy in the Kevlar suit to work behind. In any case, the thing didn't go off and they placed it successfully into the bomb vessel and drove it away. It was a shame there wasn't a dual circuit on the thing, Felix thought, radio and trembler, because then he could've set it off and watched the bomb guy fly through the air.

The bitch had escaped, however, and he had to call Rashid and tell him about it, which he didn't really feel like doing, because the little fuck would carry on like it was the end of the world and Felix's fault. Seeking to delay the confrontation a little, he walked up Broadway to West Houston, found a coffee shop, slipped into the john, swallowed a handful of pills, drank a cup of coffee, and then went to the pay phone he'd spotted in the narrow alley near the restrooms.

To Felix's surprise, however, Rashid listened calmly to the story. He asked about the dog and then said, "A bomb dog, interesting. Who could have imagined she would own a bomb dog. In any case, it is no big thing. We will succeed another time. But it is important that you come here right away."

"What, your place?"

"Yes, immediately."

"What's up?"

"Immediately," said Rashid in a harsher voice and then hung up.

Felix slammed the phone down and karate-kicked it a couple of times, leaving it askew on the wall. He went out into the street and walked aimlessly north, keeping up a rapid pace, pounding the anger out of his system. It was really important to remain perfectly calm just now, plan it out. Being a nigger's nigger was something Felix simply could not bear for another minute. He thought he could, but no; it made him too crazy, and he could not afford to be crazy anymore, not hanging out like this, with no resources, carrying explosives around. All it would take was one cop . . . no, it had to stop.

He got to Sixth and walked uptown. Before long, he passed the window of a kitchenware shop, stopped short, examined the display, and went in. There he purchased an eight-inch carving knife, which fit neatly into the long, narrow tool pocket that ran along the leg of his overalls. If he saw an opportunity, if only one of the fake Spaniards was around, he could take him out silently and get the drop on Rashid. Once he had him tied up there shouldn't be any trouble about the money, or anything else. A good plan, and simple. If he could keep calm.

He turned east on Eighth Street, feeling a lot better as the pills kicked in, more confident that the plan would work. This was a lot better than what he had thought back after the council of war, blackmailing Rashid by threatening to go to the police with the plan to blow the tunnels. And also no fun involved. And supposing there was an organization behind Rashid, he could maybe get to them and still pull some money out of them for not telling. And then, of course, rat the fuckers out.

From Eighth Street and Broadway he took the R train to Steinway Street in Astoria. He played a little eye game with a cute Latina woman on the subway, and thought briefly of pursuing it, but no, this was more important, and he didn't want to lose the peak of the high, the uppers making him confident, giving energy, the downers making it mellow and suppressing the jaw-grinding twitches. He nearly floated down the few streets to the house and was almost to the door when he stopped. Something was wrong. The windows were closed, for one thing, and the blinds were drawn. It was a broiling day, they should have been open. Another thing: Rashid's green car wasn't parked where it usually was, and neither was the truck that Carlos and Felípe drove. He climbed the stoop and pressed his cheek against the little window at the side of the door. No sound, no movement.

If there was no one home, why had Rashid told him to come, why had he been so insistent that he come? He put his hand on the doorknob and turned it. Unlocked? He pushed a little and then froze as the explanation hit him. He spun on his heel and took the four steps of the stoop in a single leap. He was running full tilt down the walk when the house exploded behind him.

13

"HOW DID IT GO?" MARLENE ASKS AVIDLY
when they reach their seats. Raney has met her
in a Bayard Street luncheonette not too far from
police headquarters. He carries his suit jacket;
his shirt collar gapes open, unusual for Raney,
who had a rep in the department as a snappy
dresser. "Gentleman Jim" was one of his nick-
names. It's the heat, she thinks. It's over ninety,
and his face is flushed and beaded with sweat.
She, on the other hand, loves the heat, and is
lettuce crisp in a white linen pants suit.

"Okay, I guess," he answers, dabbing at his
brow, grateful for the way the air conditioning
is drying his face and back. He would like a
beer, but he's on duty, and he's strict with himself about that: the good lieutenant. "At least
they didn't kick my butt out and bust me down
to patrol. But, obviously, the situation has
changed."

"Changed? Oh, right, you mean the explosion in Astoria. They think that's it?"

"They sure as hell want it to be. The evil Manbomber gets his just deserts and they avoid the expense of a trial. Of course, it'd also show how incredibly dumb-ass these guys were and make the department and the bureau look even stupider than they do now for not nailing them months ago, but they're not thinking that way yet. So, we got a couple of dead guys in the ruins, and there's your culprits. It's neat enough, at any rate. The explosives check out, exactly the same as the ones used in the Manbomber bombs, plus you got bits and pieces of a bomb lab, they all check out, too—the same technology. There's no question in their minds that this is where those bombs got built." He looks around and signals a waitress. After she's taken their order and hustles away, Marlene says, "But you're not convinced."

"Hey, Marlene, I mean what the fuck—who am I to be convinced or not? I buy that it's the right place—the forensics are rock solid. But there's a couple of things. One is that at least half a dozen witnesses described a guy with a ball cap and dark shades around the blast sites, the parking lots, the buses, the theater that got bombed, and we even got a useless sketch out of it. They disagreed on the details, but two things they all agreed on: the guy was a moose—not that big but strong, a bull neck, shoulders—and that he was white. Now the guys in Astoria: okay, they had to put together the pieces a little, but neither of them added up to that guy. Not built-up, not Caucasian. These were average-sized, light-brown types of people. So what happened to that guy, Ball Cap, and who the fuck is he?"

"But you like him for Felix?"

"Oh, shit, I don't know! What we do know was Felix was a bull and that he was white. We know that and so there's **another** coincidence we got to explain away. The second thing is we canvass the neighborhood, talk to people about that house. They all agree, it's a bunch of Latinos there, working stiffs, they figured maybe illegal immigrants, three regulars, and from time to time a bigger group of them. One of the neighbors is an elderly PR lady, she says one of the boys came over and brought her little doggie back when it ran away. Said he wasn't a PR but he spoke good Spanish, guy told her he was a Bolivian. Nice guy, she said. She said there was another guy, a fourth guy, living there, too, not a Hispanic, a white guy, always wore a ball cap pulled low. She says he was a hunk. A guy who works out. Okay, the time of the blast, she sees this guy staggering around just outside the house. So he was there, he survived the blast. Was that Ball Cap? If not, there's coincidence three hundred and fourteen."

"On the testimony of one old lady?"

"Yeah, I know, and it's not my case, so I can't

poke around in it. She could have been wrong. The guy could've just been a bystander. But doesn't it nag the shit out of you? Anyway, we didn't get into that at all. I had my captain there, Stacy, and Deputy Chief Inspector Moellen, from the Manbomber task force, and a couple of his clones and drones. Lechman, the bureau liaison guy. I led off with my double murder, the pattern of the relationship, Felix, and then the bomber so-called coincidences—the targets connected to Felix: Lutz, the witness against him, Balducci, the cop who collared him, the lawyer, Klopper, plus you. Then I added the Latino guy in Elmhurst who speaks Arabic on the phone . . ."

"It's not Arabic. We don't know what it is."

"It's close enough for these guys," says Raney. Their order comes and they are silent for a few minutes, chomping. A little badinage with the waitress here, about the heat, the only subject just now in the city. Worse than the bombs, she jokes, and leaves them and Raney takes up his thread: "Anyway, the problem is there's nothing solid, no linkages. Over and beyond the fact that Felix is officially dead, we got no connection between Felix and any terror group, and he's got no background in bomb construction. Also, from day one we've been more or less denying the idea that Manbomber is an Arab thing, out of al Qaeda or what have you, because the fingerprints are all wrong. There aren't the expected

targets—prestige structures, government buildings, Israeli interests, synagogues. Plus, according to Lechman, there isn't a peep on the intelligence network about any operation like this. So
they're playing it like a psycho, a Unibomber on
steroids, maybe multiple guys with a grudge. So
they don't want to hear about your Arab, especially when it looks like it's closing time for the
Manbomber."

"And the Felix angle? If they wanted a psycho,
you couldn't ask for a better. What about that?"

A rueful smile, eyes rolling upward. "Oh, that.
Well, when they heard I was Peter's partner on
the Tighe arrest, it was clear as daylight.
Detectives get obsessional about suspects, and
here's a clear-cut case. It's unusual that the suspect's dead, but . . ."

"They shined you on?"

"More or less. The fact that the funeral home
seems to be fake was the only thing that saved me
from being asked to take a leave of absence and
see the department headshrinker. They want me
to check out the prison, see if there was maybe an
inside guy or a clerical mistake. They'll think about
the double murder as maybe being connected to
Felix, but they don't buy the connect between
Felix and the Manbomber, or that he's alive. Uh-
uh, that's a bridge too far."

"So, we have to go up to Auburn?"

"There's no 'we' about it, Marlene. I'm taking

a puddle jumper up there tomorrow morning. It's all arranged."

"I can't come? I'll buy my own ticket, if that's the problem?"

"No, that's not the problem." She notices that Raney looks uncomfortable. Is that a faint blush? He clears his throat, takes a swallow of his club soda. "I thought it was better to leave you out of it, I mean when I presented the thing. Also . . ."

"Yes?" Dryly.

"Okay, you want the embarrassing truth? Girl, if I went off for an out-of-town overnight trip with you along, Nora would go ballistic. She already thinks I'm halfway up your pants."

Marlene guffaws in an unladylike fashion.

"It's not funny, Marlene. You don't know her."

"It's hilarious. You want me to call her? Tell her I wouldn't have you on a plate, even though I did chew illicitly on your face a time or two?"

"Oh, please, that's all I need. But you can tell her whatever when you come over. You're all invited this Saturday."

Roland Hrcany was taking his sweet time with the fatal bullets and his expert witness. It was now the morning of the second full day of this testimony and they had just started on bullet four of the seven that had helped kill Moussa Onabajo. Karp could understand why he was going so slowly. The roaring of the fans placed strategically around the baking courtroom made it difficult for the jury to hear the testimony or the questions. He could see several of the jurors leaning forward, cocking their heads, cupping ears. Those were the ones still interested in the case. Others, stunned by the heat or by the usual boredom, had given up entirely and were frankly dozing. And Roland was going slowly because lies, which were what he was selling now, were always more complex to convey than the truth. This last was one of Karp's deepest beliefs, that the truth was always clear and simple, and one he clung to despite almost daily demonstrations to the contrary.

Bullet number four was the first really magical bullet, and Karp was, unlike the majority of the jurors, truly interested in how the defense intended to play it. The first two had come from Nixon's gun, shot during the struggle, causing only flesh wounds. The third had been Gerber shooting the struggling Nigerian through the chest to save his partner. Police ballistics and the People's case maintained that bullets number four, five, six, and seven had been fired at the victim after he had fallen to the ground, helpless, hence evidence of intentional homicide. But no: it turned out, according to Hugo Selwyn, that number four had been fired while the victim was still hanging on to Detective Nixon, still allegedly scrabbling for the detective's pistol, still a danger to the officers. That the bullet itself, squashed flat against the asphalt of the parking lot, had been found under Mr. Onabajo's body, was explained by a marvelous set of rebounds within the corpus of Onabajo, enabling the projectile to end up looking "as if" it had been fired into a recumbent man.

Bullet five had done a little dance around Onabajo's pelvis before winding up in the soft asphalt right next to its predecessor slug, in remarkable coincidence. Bullet six had bounced off a spinal process of the Nigerian desperado and was directed in a downward direction, ending up within six inches of numbers four and five. And now for bullet number seven. Karp let a smile slide onto his face, and he made sure that Roland and the jury saw it. He leaned forward in his chair and clasped his hands, as if riveted by a performance.

For bullet number seven was the worst bullet from the point of view of the defense. It had not participated in any of the merry bone dances of its earlier associates. It had been a simple gut shot, entering three inches to the left of the midline, blasting through the soft liver and exiting through muscle, fat, and skin tissue into the pavement, penetrating deeper than the others, and carrying with it (which the police department forensic experts had already established) bits of liver tissue, undershirt, shirt, skin, and beer, this last from a spill on the surface of the parking lot. It was like a scientific core from an ancient glacier or a redwood, recounting history in neat layers.

As Karp had expected, Roland admitted all this, as it gave him a chance to reiterate the position that the other three shots **had** glanced off bones. He asked Selwyn whether the trajectory and rest position of the fourth bullet could be explained in any other way than the way the state had explained it, and Selwyn, naturally, answered in the affirmative. Easel charts were brought out and set up, and, guided by Hrcany, Selwyn began to describe how hydrostatic forces generated by the hollow-point bullet entering soft tissues could have deflected the projectile so as to make it turn nearly ninety degrees and plough into the pavement, as it would have had to do if Gerber had shot Onabajo while Onabajo was on his feet and struggling. There was even a chart of partial differential equations to support the trickology. Karp rose to his feet.

"Objection, Your Honor. No foundation."

A stunned silence for a beat or so, and then mutters among the courthouse cognoscenti. "No foundation" is an objection associated with exhibits. You object in that way if, for example, the photograph of a crime scene is not a photograph of how the crime scene looked at the time of the crime. Judge Higbee said, "Explain yourself, Mr. Karp."

"These equations violate the Law of the Conservation of Energy, which law, Your Honor, with all due respect, lies outside the purview of this court. It's like supposing perpetual motion or antigravity—"

Roland raised his voice. "Your Honor, I must protest! Counsel will have plenty of time to cross-examine our expert."

Oh, don't stop there, Roland, Karp hoped to himself. And Roland did not, adding, "In any case, it's outrageous for counsel to advance himself as an expert in ballistics."

"It's outrageous for your witness to do so," said Karp in a stentorian voice.

Bang of the gavel, amid titters. "Sit down, Mr. Karp," Judge Higbee snapped, "Objection overruled. Jury will disregard Mr. Karp's remarks. Proceed, Mr. Hrcany."

Roland did so and Karp sat back, ostentatiously reading through his notes, seeming to ignore the remainder of Selwyn's testimony. He was well satisfied with his move. Whichever members of the jury had been dozing had been awakened by the gavel and by the dueling lawyers, which was what all juries yearned for, having been trained for it by television. He had also recalled for the jury the state's original trashing of Selwyn's reputation, which would make it easier for Karp to impeach him during cross-examination. A neat little tactic. Roland could never resist putting in an extra twist of the knife, and thus the perfect straight line had been set up. And Karp had almost nailed it, the key to impeaching the cops, something about the position of Nixon and Onabajo, that had to do not with Gerber's five bullets, but with Nixon's two. So close, but not quite in hand.

Lucy was walking up Crosby Street from Howard, on the shady side, for it was a blazing day, and her mind was full of deep thoughts. She had come from doing a number of necessary errands and was looking forward to shedding her sticky clothes, taking a cool shower, and lying nearly naked on her bed and having a conversation with her boyfriend. It was not exactly phone sex.

Among the places she had visited was the language collection at Columbia, the office of a professor of Semitic languages, and the offices of the Lucia Foundation. At the first she had learned the identity of the language on the tape her mother had made of the man who called himself Gonzales. At the last, she had experienced a somewhat spiky interview with Father Dugan. Giving away millions of dollars had eroded his pastoral chops, or maybe he was less interested in her problems than he had once been, since his daily work now consisted of sticking Band-Aids of various sizes on the world's festering, incurable wounds. She had brought up the demon and been told to stop being silly; she'd had her exorcism, the man wasn't hanging around anymore, a little less mysticism, please, just now. And there was no such person as Sharon Larsen in child protective services, so she could forget about the swine in good conscience. The romance issue, her sacred virginity? Gosh, here was a project to get Thai preteens out of the sex trade, made it kind of hard to focus on Lucy Karp. Maybe it was time she stepped up to the plate—drop the guy as an occasion of sin, or do the sin and take the consequences, but for the love of Pete, stop this endless shilly-shally. She had not exactly walked out in a huff, but he'd received a call and taken it, and she'd slid away while he was on the phone with someone who had two hundred and fifty thousand starving children on hand.

So she was in the process of kicking herself for being a spoiled brat, but dragged up a smile nonetheless for the whores hanging around outside the brothel just south of her front door. The girls were cheerful Fujianese for the most part, their clients, men of the same nation, sweated labor shipped across the oceans to the Gold Mountain in containers, like spare parts. Lucy, while officially disapproving both as a Catholic and a feminist, thought it rather distinguished to have a whorehouse on her street; and since she was the only local available who spoke their language, she had become a great favorite among the soiled doves. She explained a littering ticket, described the procedures at a free clinic, warned against a Ponzi scheme. Amid giggles, then, the girls informed her that she had a boyfriend, a man asking them about Lucy, where she was, when she would return. They knew enough American to understand what he wanted, although of course they had said nothing. They pointed, laughing. **That** man.

He was lurking in a deep entryway across the street. Even in the shadows she could tell it was the guy from the soup kitchen, Larry or whatever his name was, the demon. She left the group of women, moving toward Grand Street and her door. He spotted her and accosted her just as she was getting her keys out. She saw at once that he had been sleeping rough, for he was unshaven, dirty, and there was a peculiar scorched smell about him, as if he had rolled into a trash fire.

"Lucy, could I talk to you a second?" She looked him in the face and what she saw there prompted a faint nausea: violence and terror roiling behind a scrim of pathetic sincerity. She swallowed heavily and said in what she meant as a cheerful tone, "Sure, Larry, what's up?" Going to the prom, Larry? Want to split a milkshake? He must see it in my face, she thought, the horror—but no, clearly empathy was not Larry's strong suit.

"Look, I'm in trouble," he continued. "I really need some help."

"Why? What's wrong?"

"Oh, man, I got myself into a jam. I been out on the street for two days."

"What did you do?"

"I didn't do anything!" he said indignantly. "Why do you think I did something? Jesus!"

That's incredible, she thought, he's working on my liberal Catholic guilt and sure enough, I feel guilty. She said, "So what happened?"

"I was just looking for work, you know? So a guy I knew told me to hang out on Eleventh and Fortieth with all the illegals, I figure I could get some day work. So a guy shows up, says his name's Carney, he's got a job unloading trucks. I go with a couple of other guys, Spanish, Latinos, you know? In his pickup truck. We go down to a warehouse in Chelsea and we unload semis all day, appliances, stereos. Then Carney pays the other guys off and the split. And he says to me, 'You want to make some extra?' And I say yes. What else, right. So he says, 'Settle down, it's not for a couple of hours.' I get something to eat and go back. Now it's like ten at night. A semi pulls up and I start unloading. It's all cigarettes, and I figure, Uh-oh, this can't be legal. I'm about to go to the guy and tell him I can't afford to get mixed up, because of my parole thing, when all of a sudden, this big black SUV screams up and four guys get out. I'm in the truck, and the driver says, 'Wait a second,' and he goes out and I hear yelling, so I like, peek around the side, and I see these guys have got Carney and the driver up against the wall, and they're hitting them with pistols. Then I hear shots, and man, I just took off. They saw me and they shot at me, but I got away. I went right up a razor-wire fence, tore the shit out of my clothes and my back. I've been staying in a burnt-out building, scared out of my mind. They were yelling in Spanish. I figure Dominicans, they're into cigarette smuggling."

"You have to go to the cops, Larry," she said. Her voice sounded strange in her ears, strangled.

He shook his head violently. "Nah, I can't do that. I can't get busted. I mean, I was working an illegal scam. They'd put me back in jail."

"But you'd be safe."

He laughed bitterly. "What, are you kidding? You think these guys don't have people in the jail? I'd get shanked the first day." He snapped a look over his shoulder, the universal gesture of a confidence to be offered. "Lucy, I don't know, I'm really in trouble now. I got a sister in Plattsburgh I could stay with, me and the girl, I could get away from this fucking city . . . but I got zilch, man. I got no cash at all. They killed him before I got paid."

"How can you do that?" The words blurted out without thought, almost without volition. She meant the lies, but he didn't understand. He said, "What? Do what?"

"Nothing," she mumbled. She felt the violence

cruising beneath his skin, like a shark under tur-
bid waters. Lucy was already reaching into her
bag. She knew the man was lying, but his terror
was genuine. He had the true look of someone on
the run, but she suspected he was closer to the
source of the evil than he had let on. It didn't
matter. She was seized by a visceral passion to be
free of him, to not occupy the same air. She
plunged her hand into her bag, brought out her
wallet, and snatched all the currency out of it.
She thrust the sheaf of bills at him. As he took it
from her, there appeared on his face a mask of
sincere gratitude. Little tears glistened in his
handsome eyes. "Gee, Lucy, thanks! God, I'll
never forget you for this, I mean it, and I'll pay
you back, I swear it, every penny . . ."

She felt the pressure of a fixed smile on her
cheeks. She couldn't wait for the elevator car.
Instead, she inserted her key, murmured a quick
good-bye, slipped inside, and slammed the door
on his professions of eternal gratitude. Then she
ran up four flights of stairs, faster than she had
ever run them before, as if the devil were on her
tail, until, at the last landing she had to sit, panting and nauseated, with her head down between
her knees.

"What's wrong?" her mother said instantly upon
seeing her. Lucy would have tried to sneak by her

room, but the dogs caught her, which was one of the problems with having dogs. Besides, she desperately needed a cold drink.

"Nothing," she said as she got a bottle of mineral water out of the refrigerator, with the dog Maggie whining hello and nudging at her thigh.

"Not nothing. What happened?"

"I said nothing, Ma." She poured water into a large glass full of ice, and added a chunk of lime. She drank and wiped the dribbles from her chin with the back of her hand. The dog rested its hot head on her knee, and got the desired scratch between the eyes. "I gave all my cash to a street person with a sob story, is all. And then I ran up the stairs to punish myself for being such a sap. Still. It's hot. I almost got heatstroke."

The mother inspected her, using a surface-penetrating sonar more accurate than anything the Pentagon had. "You weren't mugged, were you?"

"No, Mom, just conned." To change the subject she pointed to the kitchen table. This item, its surface mottled with a century of immigrant life, had belonged to Marlene's grandmother and was the largest horizontal surface in the house, far larger than the table in the dining room. It was covered with legal folders and papers. "What's all this?"

"Paul Agnelli's case. I told you about this?"

"The butcher, uh-huh, the statutory rape. Are you going to get him off?"

"It's looking a little better. This is the material I got from the DA, and from Paulie's old fart attorney. I can't believe he didn't see this right off."

"See what right off."

"There's no rape kit. The alleged vic didn't go to the hospital. In the Q and A she says she was so upset she went home and showered off. She didn't report it until the Wednesday after the Friday it allegedly happened."

"I love the way you always say 'alledgedly' even when you're talking to me."

Marlene cast a sharp eye on her daughter to see if she was being needled, but Lucy had nothing on her face but frank interest, and could that be a hint of admiration?

"Yes, well, it's a good habit to get into in this business. Anyway, aside from the girl's testimony, their whole case is forensic—his car showed hair, fibers, and fluids from the girl on the backseat, plus matching semen on the girl's underwear and skirt. Paul says he can't imagine that any woman he slept with during the right span of time would have participated in a scam against him. Which is a problem for us, because we know there had to be a scam, and the girl had to be in on it. Do you know a real estate guy named Fong?"

"Hiram Fong?"

"Is he in local real estate?"

"I guess. He has an office on Mott with a big-character sign out front. A tong guy."

"You know this?"

"Everybody knows this, Mom," said Lucy, meaning everybody who spoke the half-dozen most popular dialects of Chinese and had lived in Chinatown her entire life, and knew the sociology thereof. "Why do you ask?"

"Oh, just a notion. This Fong made an offer on the building Paulie owns and Paulie turned him down. I'm trying to think of an angle here. Why would anyone go through all that trouble to frame a Mulberry Street butcher? A rival Italian butcher? A grudge from way back? A spurned lover? All possible, but not likely. Somebody had to get to Cherry Newcombe and get her to make the complaint in a fairly elaborate and risky way, and somebody had to get to a source of Paulie's semen, and absent any evidence that Paul Agnelli is such a monumental son of a bitch that two women would go out of their way to shaft him for free, it means that someone put up a nontrivial amount of cash, or put the scare in, to make them do it. Fong sort of fits the picture as the kind of fellow who could do either or both."

"So, you're saying what—he sends his yellow minions secretly after Agnelli, finds out who he's been balling, gets a fresh sample from her by threat or payoff, and frames the guy so that he'll sell the butcher shop? It doesn't sing to me."

"Me, either. There's a missing piece, but I don't know what it is. I should go see McKenzie, the arresting officer, see what he has to say for himself." She regarded her daughter with a considering eye. "Would you like to be momma's little helper on this one, too?"

"I'd be glad to help in any legal endeavor."

"Is that **legal** as in pertaining to the law, or **legal** an in noncrimonous?"

"What do you need, Mom?" asked Lucy, ducking this jab.

"Fine out what Fong is up to, his rep, and would he pull something like this? Just pick up on the street stuff. Nothing involving break-ins, torture, or bribery."

"Like you usually do, you mean? Okay, Mom, not a problem."

"There'll be per diem expense money."

"Fine. Oh, and that guy the other day, not really Gonzales? He was speaking Tamazight."

"Tama-what?"

"Tamazight. It's spoken by about three million people in the Atlas Mountains of Morocco and Algeria."

"Arabs."

"Berbers. These guys were raised in Tamazight, and then went to Spain at a fairly early age, or else they were raised in Spain with Tamazight as a cradle tongue."

"Guys? We only saw one guy."

"Well, him plus whoever he was talking to on the phone," said Lucy.

"Thank you, and **duh!**" said Marlene. "The old lady's brain has half-rotted away, but she passes the falling torch to the next generation. Which God forbid."

Felix went into a restaurant on Lafayette and counted his money under the table. It came to sixty-seven dollars. He had been so astounded when the little bitch yanked the cash out that he hadn't done what he should have done, which was getting her to go to the bank and cleaning out her account, and then going with him to pick up his supposed daughter. He'd had her eating out of his hand for a while there, he could see it in her eyes. The plan had been, once he had some serious money and her credit card, to rent a car with her, drive to some alley, tonk her on the head, into the trunk, and over to his storage locker. Then after he'd had his fun, and she'd told him what he wanted to know about this slope Rashid was so interested in, he'd see what the information was worth. A bonus in more ways than one.

He took the last of his pills with the ice water the surly waitress had placed on the table, along with the teapot. Jesus, these fucking people, drinking tea in weather like this! They were giving him the eye from the kitchen, because of the way he looked. That was one thing he would have to take care of. First get more pills. He took out his little notebook and made a list. Pills. Clean up. Clothes. No, clothes first, then clean up. He changed the list. Bag. Call Rashid. That was going to be fun. The waitress came over and stood stolidly over him with her pad ready. He ordered a beer and pointed to a picture of something that looked like spaghetti. He figured how bad could they fuck up spaghetti, even if they were chinks.

Three hours later, Felix was feeling a lot better than he had in a couple of days. The blast at the Astoria place had shaken him up more than he had admitted to himself, mainly because of how dumb he'd been. When the bomb hadn't killed Karp's wife, they'd decided to write him off, and he hadn't seen it coming, had walked up to the front door like a moron. Of course, they figured he couldn't be trusted anymore, and since they knew he knew their big plans, they'd decided to take him out, along with the evidence at the Astoria place. He had stayed in the locker the night before, which was like being a fucking pizza in an oven, worse than the joint, and had come out in the morning completely wiped, with hardly carfare in his pocket, hungry, raggedy-assed, and burned in several places. It had been inspired to go after the girl, and even though he hadn't made the big score, he'd scored enough. One advantage of hanging out with all those losers at the soup kitchen is that he'd learned a

lot about how to survive in the city's underground—where to get a shower, a meal, cheap
clothes, unofficial medical attention. The city was
apparently loaded with people with nothing better to do but to give stuff to piss bums.

So the late afternoon found him in Midtown
on the west side, fresh from a shelter shower and
shave, dressed in plaid Bermudas, an I Love NY
T-shirt, a Mets cap, plastic sandals, cheap sunglasses, and carrying a plastic fabric sports bag
from St. Ignatius High School in Weehawken, all
from the Goodwill on Twelfth Avenue. He was
clean and indistinguishable from the other million or so tourists wandering the city. A tourist
was nearly as good as a workman for invisibility.
Now he entered Penn Station and found a phone
booth on the Amtrak level. He dialed Rashid's
cell number. After a few rings, the Arab's voice
came on the line. "Hello, you little piece of shit,"
said Felix cheerfully, "remember me?"

There was a long pause on the other end, and
Felix realized with delight that the Arabs had
thought he'd been killed in the explosion.

He heard Rashid say, "Felix?" and heard the
fear in the voice. Felix had to laugh, it was going
to be so good. It was going to work out for him
now for sure.

14

RASHID REPLACED THE TELEPHONE AND with a broad smile mimed firing a rifle into the air, with appropriate sound effects. His two companions smiled as well, a little hesitantly, as they had never seen their dour commander in such a mood. One of them, Felípe Gonzales, born Habib Bouazizi, said, "So what did he say?"

"What we expected," said Rashid. "He threatens, he wants money. He knows our plans and he will tell the authorities. I was very frightened." He giggled.

The other man, Mamoud Yahia, called Carlos Perez in the land of the enemy, said, "I don't understand this. If he goes to the police, won't they find out who he is? And then what will happen to the chief?"

"Naturally he won't go to the police himself," said Rashid dismissively. "He does not want to risk being identified. He will call, or write a letter. Even if they happen to arrest him, they will have no idea who he is, and he has no interest in telling them the truth. It will never occur to them that he is a man convicted of a crime nearly twenty years ago, and who is officially dead."

"So, maybe he will not go to them at all," suggested Carlos.

"Of course, he will go. He is a stupid vengeful man, and he was chosen for that reason. We cut off his finger, we blew the house up in his face, of course he will want revenge, and he will think that revealing the tunnel plot will hurt us the most of anything he can do. He has attempted to blackmail us just now, and we will indeed give him something to show that we are frightened of him. He will take the money and go straight to the police, and think he is being oh so clever. Believe me, the chief has thought this through very carefully. You see, in an operation like this, in enemy territory, you must have a number of independent layers of deception . . ."

Both Moroccans sighed inwardly and settled back for yet another lecture. They were patient men, cousins, born in the mountains south of Fez, moved as infants with the family to Ceuta along with thousands of others, with money pooled from the whole clan to pay the smugglers for the short but perilous trip across the straits. They had been intermittently schooled until age ten or so and then dropped out to help sell ices and snacks on the streets of Seville, the family business. Later, as young men, they had drifted into the vast African lumpenproletariat scratching a living doing what the Europeans no longer wished to do themselves.

Their parents died, family ties became tenuous; God faded, they drank whiskey and went with women, they wore the cheap, flashy clothes of young Euro proles, and spoke Spanish. To each other, though, they continued to converse in the language of the middle Atlas, their cradle tongue. Habib was a little quicker, Mamoud handled the more physical aspects of their hardscrabble life. Through a connection, Habib found them a job in a gravel quarry. Someone approached them in a café, he had money, he bought drinks. Could they get their hands on any explosives? They could, and for some months they flourished. Then the special police broke down the door of their little room, and in short order they were in prison, where they spent ten months, after which they were deported back to Morocco.

Rashid had found them living in a packing crate in the shantytown that surrounds Ceuta. He was looking for a couple of boys who knew their way around explosives and wanted out of the packing crate life. At first they thought he was a gangster, because he never talked about Allah or the Koran or jihad, and their experience taught them that people who wanted to blow things up very often wanted to do it in the name of God. But no, Rashid was political in a different way. He told them he was an Egyptian, and that he worked for a great man, greater than Nasser, another Saladin. This man was at war with the United States, not like the stupid and backward Islamists, but like a modern person, an educated person, with modern beliefs. The United States was objectively evil, the greatest barrier to the aspirations of all oppressed peoples, the sponsor of racism and Israeli genocide. All the peoples of the world who were not the lackeys of the United States were kept poor, and let this monster once be destroyed and then a new and glorious world of prosperity and peace would miraculously dawn.

Habib and Mamoud did not necessarily believe what Rashid had to say, but it was clear to them that Rashid believed it, and believed in his mysterious leader. More to the point, he had money, and a magical way with official papers. And they were tired of the packing crate and one meal of couscous a day. Within a week of meeting Rashid they had new clothes, and a nice room in a newish apartment block with a TV set, and they had Dominican passports with the right visa stamps and a couple of airplane tickets to New York. Rashid told them about Latinos, how if they wore gold chains with elaborate crucifixes, and a certain kind of clothing, and spoke only Spanish, they would be invisible in New York City. And it was true. For two years, they lived the Latino life in New York. They learned ductwork and danced to salsa, and slept deeply. Then, some months ago, Rashid had appeared and called them into wakefulness.

". . . so you see that in order to conclude phase two, we have to do the following things: one, destroy or evacuate all organization sites that the criminal knows about; two, place the criminal in danger from us—he must know we want him dead—so he will wish for revenge; three, insure he has no money, so he will want to blackmail us; and, of course, four, provide him with a detailed plan, so that he will have something substantial to betray. Now, phase three begins with—"

Habib interrupted, "Rashid, we know all of this, you have explained it to us many times. What you have not explained is what we are going to do about the woman and the girl. They saw me at the house in Elmhurst. They are asking questions about Bruce Newton. Soon they will know about Felix and the chief. And then what?"

"Let them ask questions!" said Rashid in an irritated tone. Under the drone of his own voice he often fell into a pleasant enchantment, from which it was disturbing to be yanked by impertinent ignoramuses like Habib. "Let them—what can they learn? The Newton identity is a real one and will last until the operation is complete. He really is traveling abroad. As for you, what did they see except a Latino workman who knows nothing."

"I do not know," said Habib. "They seemed dangerous to me. That girl spoke better Spanish than I do. And why would the wife of Karp and his daughter be interested in Felix at all? It does not make sense."

Rashid put on one of his annoying superior looks. "Not to you, perhaps, but there are elements you do not know. Anyway, you are out of that house. We are out of the Haskell premises to which Felix made his deliveries, leaving evidence that it was a storage place for large quantities of explosives. Our two volunteers for martyrdom have achieved martyrdom in the house in Astoria. So the police think that the Manbomber is over, and the Manbomber **is** over. Now Felix comes and tells them about another plot, against the tunnels. Can they afford to ignore it? No, but now they strike at shadows—**two** organizations, or one very large organization, Islamic or not? They do not know, and so they run around like headless chickens. This is the highest art in this kind of business, to create phantoms, and while they chase these phantoms, you strike deeply in the most unexpected place."

Habib shrugged and said no more. The whole thing seemed unnecessarily complex to him. The two Muslim kids from Brooklyn, Omar and Fuad—they thought they were working for Hamas right up until the time he and Mamoud had rapped them on their heads and left them in the basement of the Astoria house. He was uneasy about that, too. It seemed unnecessary. And blowing up the house. He'd done it himself from a truck parked down the street, pushing the button when he saw Felix approach the door. More waste, a perfectly good house, incredibly luxurious to someone like Habib, and for what? You want to blow something, he figured, you blow it and get out, if you can. All this fancy figuring—Rashid said it had come direct from the chief, which did nothing to allay Habib's concerns. If the man was so damned smart, why was he in prison?

There is a technique to demolishing an expert witness on cross. Karp knew it as well as any other good lawyer, although he had not had much occasion to use it in his career. The typical defendant in a New York criminal trial does not have the money to pay experts, so most of the forensic and ballistic experts in those trials are state witnesses, and wrecking them is therefore a defense skill. Nevertheless, Karp was pretty sure he could do the job on Dr. Hugo Selwyn.

First, establish the anticredentials. Terrell Collins had begun this process before he'd been bombed, and now Karp was finishing it. He made sure the jury understood that Selwyn was a hired gun, without credibility among serious ballistics experts. As he did this, Roland Hrcany hung about his heels with objections. We've had all this, Your Honor, we brought this out already, there's no need to go over this, expertise is a matter of opinion, witness has ten years' experience, counsel is harassing my witness, and so on. Not too many of these, not enough to piss off the judge or irritate the jury, but enough to give Selwyn some respite from the hammer blows, and break Karp's concentration and tempo.

Karp finished this line and turned to the evidence itself. As the defense had done, he addressed each of the seven bullets in turn, tracing their paths, not just on the chart but in real space, pacing out the distance and indicating on his own body the unlikely rebounds and gyrations that the bullets would have had to go through to fit Selwyn's theoretical trajectories. The jury was not dozing anymore. Juries liked physical action; they liked seeing a gigantic but graceful man acting out a little drama right there in front of them, despite the heat. It was like being in the Garden, a little, watching the Knicks.

Karp pressed at the witness: "So you really, truly believe, that bullet number five did not leave Detective Gerber's gun and shoot directly through the prone victim and into the asphalt, but instead ricocheted off the victim's shoulder blade and hip bone while he was standing up, yet leaving no evidence that the medical examiner was able to find that such a richochet ever occurred?"

"Objection. He's answered that already. This is more harassment, Your Honor."

"Sustained. Move on, Mr. Karp."

"Yes, Your Honor. Mr. Selwyn, turning now to bullet number six . . ."

As he said this, Karp faced the jury and rolled his eyes to the ceiling, making a "what can you do?" gesture with his hands. It only took an instant. A ripple of titters ran through the jury box. Roland looked back, flushing, the judge frowned, Karp carried on with bullet number six, smiling, thinking that there was nothing quite so delectable as a stolen moment with the jury. Walking back to his table, he cast his eye over the packed courtroom and was surprised to see his daughter standing behind the back row of the spectator seats. He shot her a look—anything wrong? She flashed a thumbs-up. Karp turned to face the witness.

Now he cranked up the volume a little, his gestures a little broader, his movements a little more dramatic, his expression of wonder at the whoppers of the witness a little more insolent. Occasionally Roland made Judge Higbee slap him down, but with no great enthusiasm. Judges retaining any level of self-respect—and Higbee was one—do not like naked and preposterous lies told in their courtrooms.

And now the last bullet, the one that had hit nothing but meat. The jury perked up; they recalled this one from the direct testimony.

"You took high school physics, Dr. Selwyn, did you not? Yes? Now during that course, did you happen to come across the Law of the Conservation of Energy?"

"I must have." Cautiously.

"I should certainly hope so. Could you explain to the jury what that law says."

"Objection. Relevance. The expert is not obliged to prove his expertise, Your Honor."

The judge said, "You're going somewhere interesting with this, Mr. Karp?"

"I believe so, Judge."

"Then I'll allow it. Proceed."

"Doctor?" said Karp.

Selwyn rambled through an explanation about how energy is conserved, plus a little high school physics on vectors and how a moving object could be made to change direction. Karp said, "I see. So that means that if I took this ball . . ."—here Karp reached into his pocket and pulled out a pink rubber ball of the type known to generations of New Yorkers as a Spaldeen—". . . and—with the court's permission—put energy into it like so . . ." —bouncing it hard on the floor—". . . on each bounce, it will lose energy, correct? There's no possible way for the ball to get more energy while it's bouncing, right? Unless I add it by some outside force. A stickball bat, say?"

Selwyn agreed that it was so. Karp snatched the ball out of the air. "And the same would apply to a bullet, correct?" Having obtained agreement, Karp switched to a discussion of Selwyn's theory of hydrostatic rebound, that the seventh bullet, striking the soft tissue of the victim's still upright and dangerous body, had set up a shock wave that, rebounding against the bony structures, had been able to deflect old number seven so that it happened to land right where the final four bullets had landed, embedded in the parking lot, within an area the size of a dinner plate.

Karp said, "Sir, now I show you People's exhibit number thirty-two, which has been identified as taken from the parking lot at the crime scene." This was a huge photo of the small blood-soaked area of the parking lot, with the victim's outline drawn in chalk and the four bullet holes in the asphalt clearly numbered. "Is it true that you claim that despite all these gyrations you say that the bullets have been through, reversing directions, bouncing off things, they all ended up in this small blood-soaked area under where Mr. Onabajo fell that night? Just through chance alone?"

"Well . . . as I said, bullets can do some pretty remarkable things."

"Remarkable, yes. Now I show you People's exhibit thirty-three. These are cross-sections of the paths the four bullets made into the asphalt of the parking lot. Will you tell the jury, after examining this display, which of the four bullets penetrated most deeply into the asphalt?"

Selwyn leaned forward and examined the exhibit on its easel. "Number seven."

"Very good, number seven. And that's a function of its energy, correct? The more energy, the deeper the penetration, right?"

"Well, yes, if the density of the receiving material is the same."

"True enough, and we had a city engineer do tests to establish just that, to show the jury that within the area in question the asphalt was essentially homogeneous, so that therefore you, as a ballistics expert, would have to attribute the difference in depth entirely to differences in projectile energy at impact, correct?"

"Yes."

"Now, Dr. Selwyn, a bullet must lose energy when it strikes an object, correct? Like my Spaldeen a moment ago, bouncing lower with each bounce?"

"Yes. But varying materials will—"

"Thank you. My next question is: Where did the energy come from that drove bullet number seven deeper into the ground than the others, which according to your testimony bounced off any number of solid objects?"

Selwyn licked his lips. "I'm not sure I understand."

"No? You just testified under oath that bullet seven struck the victim while he was standing. According to you it then set up a bouncing shock wave, that forced the bullet in an entirely different direction, out the victim's back, and into the asphalt, yes?"

"Yes, but—"

"So where did the necessary energy come from, the energy that is demanded by the immutable laws of physics?" Here Roland made a gallant effort to give his guy another second or two to think his way out of this, but the judge instantly overruled his objection as to relevance, and told the witness to answer.

"Bullet seven didn't hit any hard structures and therefore lost less energy."

Snap goes the trap. "Didn't hit any hard structures, thank you. Then where did the energy come from that changed the course of the projectile, hm?"

"The bullet's own kinetic energy."

"But, sir, you yourself just taught us that an object in motion tends to remain in motion unless acted upon by an outside force, is that true?"

"Yes."

"And according to you, this bullet was absolutely shot from Mr. Onabajo's body, having changed its path by one hundred or so degrees. Your hydrostatic rebound would have had to have added energy to the bullet for that to have happened, yet the only source of hydrostatic pressure came from the bullet itself, correct?"

"Yes, but it's more complicated—"

"Your theory of bullet seven violates one of the central theories of physics, does it not?"

"No, it—"

"The ball somehow has bounced higher rather than lower on the second bounce!"

"No, I—"

"You're a scientist, doctor. Isn't it true that it's a scientific precept always to go with the simpler of two explanations? Occam's razor I believe it's called."

Selwyn mumbled in the affirmative.

"And isn't the simplest explanation for the condition and penetration of bullet number seven the fact that Mr. Onabajo was lying on his back helpless when Detective Gerber shot it through his gut?"

"No."

"And confronted with this straightforward situation, you concocted a ballistic solution out of whole cloth to earn your pay from the defense?"

"No."

"And one last thing, Dr. Selwyn—" here Karp swung around so he could eye the jury, "when you were studying physics in high school . . . did the dog ever eat your homework?"

Objection, roars of laughter, bang of gavel, remonstration from the bench, to which Karp replied, "My apologies, Your Honor, withdrawn. And nothing further."

There was a silent pause after that when

everyone looked at Roland, to see if he would attempt to repair his sweating and hapless witness on redirect, but Roland wisely declined, and the court recessed for lunch.

"You were terrific," said Lucy as they walked away from the courtroom, ignoring the massed cameras and microphones lurking in the hallway, and the cries of the reporters. "I didn't think they allowed one-liners like that."

"Technically, they don't. It just came to me and I let it out. Selwyn looked exactly like a kid I knew in junior high, not his face, but the expression on it, someone caught in a hopeless pathetic lie."

"Will you get in trouble?"

"Not really. Higbee is pretty straitlaced and he'll probably call me into chambers and give me a mild spanking. On the other hand, he wasn't averse to seeing a lying witness embarrassed."

"Why did Roland do it? I thought he was pretty good."

"Roland is very good, but he's playing the hand another lawyer left him, which is always sticky. Klopper likes to use a lot of expert trickology, figuring the jury will lean toward the defense if there's enough confusion thrown up. Dueling experts? Hey, there's your reasonable doubt. Roland has a different style. He's going to want to put the jury in the shoes of the two cops. Dark night, fearsome criminal struggling for the officer's pistol, do you really want to second-guess two sworn officers? Would **you** have acted any differently?"

"But Onabajo wasn't a fearsome criminal. He sold fake Rolexes in Herald Square."

Karp laughed. "Some people would consider that a death-qualified crime. But in Roland's summation he'll argue that they had the victim confused with a very bad guy, and when the man went for the cop's gun, their instinct took over. Of course, they regret it, he'll say, and also there's some doubt about the position of the victim in relation to the two guns, reasonable people can disagree, blah blah blah, let's call it a tragic confrontation and move on, which is why he decided to keep Selwyn's testimony. The subtext is, do you people really want some cop to get killed in a dark hallway because he's afraid of using his gun?"

"It won't work, though, right?"

"It might. Unless I can show that these are not the hero type of cops from Nine Eleven, but the cowardly, murdering-type cops from before. That means I have to impeach one of the cops, show they're telling a bold-faced lie up there on the stand. I have to show guilty knowledge and prevarication, which always trumps the tragic circumstances defense. To tell you the truth, it's driving me crazy, there's this gigantic hole in their story but I can't put my hand on it. It's like it's too obvious to be seen. Where are you taking me, by the way?"

"We're having a picnic in the park."

"No kidding? To what do I owe? It's not my birthday, is it?"

"No, it's just that it occurred to me that it's summer and everyone is sort of lazing around except you, and also that when I was going to school in the city we used to spend a lot of time together, playing b-ball, and hanging out, and we hadn't done hardly anything together, so I thought, I'll just run down to the courthouse and get my father to eat a healthy and delicious lunch instead of a lump of grease **chozerai . . .**"

"Oh, no, not **healthy . . . ?**"

"Yes, and it's all bought. All you have to do is enjoy."

They walked a block or so to Columbus Park, behind the courthouse, and sat in a sycamore's shade, where Lucy had laid out a blanket and a Styrofoam box, and set her mastiff to insure nobody else ate it while she was gone. There was a salad with lumps of some sweet flesh in it, cold soba noodles with a spiced peanut sauce, a kind of iced tea in large, gaudily printed bottles, and a bloody sheep's thighbone, which was flung at the dog.

"Gosh, Luce, this is a meal fit for a king," said Karp, "supposing the king was training for the triathlon. What is this?"

"It's abalone salad."

"Is that like a bologna sandwich?"

"Almost," she said, laughing, and they ate their lunch companionably, not talking much, while Karp tried to think of what good deeds he had done in order to deserve such a daughter, and as always came up blank. Lucy in the meantime was exercising her primary religious talent, which was not, as some might have thought, her ability to see apparitions of the saints, but rather simply keeping still and reflecting in peace and gratitude. This had a radiating effect on the other lunchers. The dog fell into a dream of chasing men, and Karp lapsed into a semitrance, during which he forgot for a few moments the details of **People v. Gerber & Nixon.**

"There's that guy again," she said.

Karp snapped into full awareness. "What guy?"

"No, you can't see him anymore, he went behind a truck. But I'm sure it was him. I saw him on Spring Street watching G.C. play music. Then I saw him again when I went into the DA entrance. A big brown guy with a fringe beard, wearing workclothes. I'm sure he was watching me just now."

Karp suppressed a tremor of fear. "Any idea who he is?"

"No, but I think I saw him going toward that work site at the back of the courthouse, on Baxter."

"That would explain what he's doing around

here. They're replacing all the ductwork and pulling in a new climate control, which is why you can smell lead in the courtrooms. How worried are you about this?"

"Not very. Actually, I was more worried about this other guy who was hanging around the kitchen. I told you about him already. I ran into him outside our place the other day. Apparently he knew where to find me and was looking for me. I gave him a wad of cash and took off."

"Was that wise?"

She smiled at him. "Oh, you know me, the softest touch in the city. I give the most to the ones I can't stand."

"Hello?"

"It's sort of a Catholic thing, Dad. Weird."

"Indeed. You'll let me know if either of these guys bothers you again, okay?"

"Okay."

"No, **really.**"

"Really," she said, almost meaning it.

When Paul Agnelli walks into Russo's, Marlene is finishing her second glass of wine. She looks meaningfully at her watch.

"I know I'm late, Mar, I got into a thing with a son of a bitch purveyor, Frascato Brothers, all of a sudden he wants cash on delivery, like we haven't been buying fucking lamb from them for thirty years." She can smell the meat on his clothes. He still wears the greasy boots he wore at his shop.

Marlene tosses back the remains of her wine and signals for another round. They move to the dimness of a booth. "They're worried about you because of this thing?"

"Yeah, and fuck them all! All of a sudden I'm cancer in the business."

"How's the trade been?"

A hand-waggling gesture. "A little off. People know me, they know it's horseshit; also, where they gonna go for my veal? But I need to get clear of this, you know? Soon."

"Yeah, I know. Look, the reason I wanted to meet with you—were you aware that there's no rape kit on Cherry Newcombe?"

"There's not? They told me they had it."

"Yeah, well, you know, the cops are not obligated to tell the whole truth to a suspect."

"Well, fuck, that means she never got raped, the lying little cunt."

"No, it doesn't mean that at all. The cops still have a semen match with you, like you told me, but it's not from a rape kit. I checked. It's from her clothes. Underpants, to be exact."

"Like Clinton and what's-her-name."

"Just like. So the question is the big one I asked you when I first took this on. Sexual partners. I have in fact spoken to Tina Farnese and Nellie Simms. They're both fairly active sexually, they recall you fondly, but I didn't get any inkling that they wanted to do you a bad, or would help someone who wanted to do you one. On the other one you told me about, Brandy or whoever . . . ?"

"No way. I got out of bed right after and flushed the condom."

"Then think harder, pal, because for some reason Terry Palmisano is after your Italian ass."

Agnelli drinks wine, wipes his mouth with the back of his hand, and in a wounded tone says, "I thought as much as I can think about it, Marlene. I mean, give me a break! Besides the occasional old times' sake fuck with Karen, there was only those three, I swear on my mother's head."

"The occasional **what?**"

"You know, weekends, the kids? I go over the house, pick up Patsy and Jerry, I bring them back, and usually Karen cooks up something. I bring over a little meat, veal, sweetbreads, shanks, what's good that day. You remember Karen with the food, she's Martha fucking Stewart, Betty Crocker, whatever. So we sit around the table, eat, do a bottle of wine, get a little lit up, to tell the truth. It's civilized, you know? I figured it was good for the kids. Anyway, so we tuck them in, and then, what the fuck, you know, in the eyes of the Church we're still man and wife, so . . ."

"So you had sex with your wife."

"Yeah, what is that, a federal crime?"

"No, but I guarantee you that's the source of the semen sample. Jesus, Paulie, talk about dumb!"

But his head is shaking, lock to lock. "Uh-huh, no, no way, uh-uh . . ."

"Face it, Paulie—"

"No, and here's why: Even if she wanted to shaft me, how the fuck is she gonna support herself, dress, feed the kids, unless I'm there cutting and selling meat six days a week? She makes shit at that little gallery job she got. It's just not in her interest to see me making license plates upstate."

"Unless Hiram Fong pays her two point two million for your building."

"Where the fuck did you get that?"

"From my own little girl, who got it from the lips of a Cantonese person who shall remain nameless, but who works for one of Fong's business rivals. Everyone seems to know that Fong is assembling a big block of property around your street. The smart money says it's new housing for the huddled masses of Asia. He's been making out like a bandit since downtown business collapsed after Nine Eleven. Anyway, you don't want to sell, but if you're in the slams and you can't pay child support and she goes to court on it, you won't have a choice. Unless you think that Slow Joe and your mom can run the place without you."

"Nah, no way." He dismisses the notion with a wave of his hand, takes a deeper drink of wine. "I can't fucking believe this. So what's the story with this girl? She's got to be in it, too. Somebody got to her?"

"For sure. It turns out that Hiram is mobbed up in his own Chinese way, so it was either money or muscle, maybe both. Okay," here she claps her hands once, sharply. "Now that we know where to look, I've got a better chance of unraveling this. Paulie, don't look so glum, this is good for us."

"Yeah, right. Christ, the mother of my children! And for what? So she can stand around in black clothes and drink shitty wine with a lot of phony baloneys? I ought to break her neck."

"I don't want to hear talk like that, Paulie. We're going to put her in jail, you'll have to be satisfied with that."

"Jail? She could go to jail? Jeez, that'd be awful! What'll I tell the kids?"

She rolls her eyes to the tin ceiling, pats his hand, slips from the booth, thinks, Husbands!

She says, "Paulie, I'll be in touch. And keep your mouth shut about any of this. We don't want to tip off the bad guys."

Dully: "Yeah, uh-huh."

"I mean it, man! Especially Karen."

15

THAT FRIDAY, RANEY TOOK THE 9:00 A.M.
U.S. Air flight from La Guardia to Syracuse and by
11:00 he was in a rented Taurus with the AC on
high, driving through the seared fields of central
New York State toward Auburn Prison. In his
eighteen years on the job, Raney had been to several state prisons, and when he arrived he found
this one a typical maximum-security joint, ugly,
noisy, stinking of that characteristically nasty male
primate-and-disinfectant smell you got only in
monkey houses and men's prisons. As always,
Raney wondered how, having once been in a place
like this, any sane human being could ever con-
template doing anything that would have even the
tiniest chance of bringing him back to one. Yet he
knew that something like two thirds of the people
here had been in the slams before, and often many
times before. The criminal mind: a deep mystery.

They took his gun and sent him to the admin

block, where he sat in the cheaply paneled but heavily air-conditioned office of Ewell V. Molson, the deputy warden for administration. Molson struck Raney as the sort of geek who might conceivably have written on an application once that he wanted to go into corrections because he was good with people. He regarded Raney and the world through small black eyes, like coffee beans, and wanted more small talk than Raney did. After this was clearly exhausted, he tapped a thick file on his desk. "This Felix Tighe. Not one of our big successes. Didn't adjust, a bunch of disciplinaries. Poor impulse control—hell, not unusual here—resistance to authority, a fighter . . ."

"I'm not thinking about hiring him," Raney could not resist saying.

Molson decided that this was a joke and curved his thin mouth up at the corners for a half second. "No. Anyway, he got shanked in a fight, a little race riot in the yard. He was an Aryan Nation kind of guy. Killed a guard in that fight, too."

"Really? I didn't know that."

"Well, we didn't exactly call the networks, and since he died right after, we kind of let it slide. According to our medical records, the stab wound became infected, he went into septic shock, and passed away." He paused. "I shouldn't say this, but small loss to the world. Anyway, to get back to the reason for your visit, there's no doubt that he's dead. He was autopsied and cre-mated right here in Auburn."

"Cremated? I thought his body was shipped to his cousin in New York."

"Nope. According to these records, a con-tainer of ashes was shipped."

"Can I have a copy of that file?"

Warden Molson was accommodating as to copies. He was similarly accommodating in set-ting up interviews with the staff of the infirmary. Shortly, therefore, Raney found himself in a cramped office that stank of rubbing alcohol and iodine, talking to a cadaverous man who was apparently the medical director of the institution. This interview took a while, because Dr. McMartin spoke very slowly, and sometimes lost the drift of what he was saying. Raney believed the man was a stone junkie, like ten percent of American physicians, but blowing the whistle on the creep was not any part of his business. McMartin confirmed the official version—stab-bing, infection, failure to respond to the antibi-otics, septicemia, death. He had signed off on the autopsy.

"You didn't do it yourself, Doctor?"

"No, I meant I supervised, ah, supervised the autopsy as per . . . protocol, of course. But, ah, I was assisted by . . . my assistant there."

"Named?"

"Outside, down the hall." A languid wave of

the hand. "I'm afraid I have a lot to do, seeing patients, so if that's all . . ."

Raney thanked the man and went down the hall from the medical director's office. There, in a wide space in the corridor he found a tiny cubbyhole with a young man in it. This person, lard-colored, crop-headed, pimply and tattooed, had a short-sleeved set of green scrubs on, with a nametag that read T. AMES, and a frightened look in his wet blue eyes.

Ames was obviously expecting him. He also confirmed the official report. The information that Felix's body had been shipped to New York was clearly wrong. Where did the detective hear that? Someone called the prison on the phone? That explained it. The copies of the records sent to the front office often had mistakes. The filing was done by prisoners, and they didn't really much care where they stuck the forms. Nope, Felix had died, Ames had watched him die, had arranged for the cremation, and sent the ashes parcel post to, let's see here, a Mr. Bruce Newton, in New York City . . .

Raney knew the man was lying but had no way to nail him with it just then. He wasn't even a cop up here. His eyes had wandered while Ames went through his routine and had been seized by the contents of a bookshelf raised above Ames's tiny desk. There were some medical and first-aid books, a **Physician's Desk Reference,** some thick manuals for medical equipment, a prison regulation handbook, and some other volumes.

"You a reader, Ames?" Raney asked, standing to peer at the titles of these.

Ames followed his eyes to the shelf. "Sure. I got a lot of time on my hands." A false, scared smile.

"That's pretty high-toned stuff you got here. Fanon, Lenin, looks like some French guys— hey, there's even one in Arabic script. You read Arabic, too?"

"No, that's something . . . ah, we had a Arab guy here a while ago, he must have left that."

"Yeah? He still in the joint?"

"No, he paroled out."

"And he left his book. Well, well." Raney jotted down all the titles and laboriously copied the intricate calligraphy on the spine of the Arabic volume. He left the prison feeling both frustrated and excited.

Lucy was a block and a half away when she saw the man try to kidnap her brother Giancarlo, at the junction of Crosby and Howard streets. It was a pretty good place for a daylight snatch. The area is almost entirely industrial, with scant street-level foot traffic, and what traffic there is consists largely of Asian people who would rather not get involved with the authorities, as their immigration papers are not what they should be. A Ford van, dirt-colored and battered, had been drawn up to the curb, with its side door slung open, and a large man was trying to haul the boy into it. Giancarlo had dropped his accordion case and it had popped open, spilling the instrument on the pavement like a dead snail. Both brothers were howling, this noise accompanied by barks from Blue, the guide dog.

Then it was all over. Lucy was just starting to run, a shout was just forming in her own throat, when she saw the kidnapper's white T-shirt turn scarlet around the big knife that Zak plunged into the small of the man's back. The man dropped his grip on Giancarlo and did a hideous little pirouette with his hand behind his back, reaching in vain for the black grip of the knife. In the next second, Giancarlo kicked the man in the groin and Blue clamped excited jaws around the back of the man's right knee. He fell like a tree onto the bed of his van, screaming something. The driver gunned the engine with a roar and a cloud of exhaust, and the van took off north on Crosby, with the man's legs dangling from the open door and, for a few yards at least, the dog hanging from a leg. The van passed Lucy too quickly for her to get the plates.

She ran up to her brother and clamped on the hug of steel, then held him at arm's length for inspection. His shirt was torn, but he seemed all right. "My box!" he said, and she had to let him inspect the button accordion with his hands. While he was so engaged, she grabbed the other brother's arm. "Did you recognize that guy?"

"I don't know. I recognized the driver, though. He's a Latino guy I've seen around listening to G.C. play."

"I've spotted a guy like that, too. Big, shaved head, little beard, gold chains, Latino-looking. I thought he was following me," she said.

"I saw that one too, I think." He looked away nervously, then at his sneakers. "Luce, you're gonna tell the 'rents about this, right?"

"Well, **duh,** yeah I am. Aren't you?"

"Hell, no! We'll be grounded for life. They'll never let us play on the street anymore. And if Dad finds out I was carrying a knife, he'll go ballistic."

"When did you start carrying?"

"After . . ." Zak gestured to his brother, lowered his voice, "you know, when he got hurt. It's a good thing I had it, right? And it's gone, too. It was a Bucklite Goliath, sixty-three bucks."

Giancarlo was packing away his accordion, and added, "He's right, Luce. Our lives will be totally over if you tell. Also, what'll they do if they know? Call the cops, the cops'll do zero. They're not going to put a twenty-four seven on us, so what's the point? Mom'll grab us up and take us out to the island, where we'll waste away in boredom. And my career is just getting hot. A guy the other day invited me to an open mike in the East Village, and an Irish guy was here the other day and he said I was gonna be as good as Johnny Connolly. You should find out who these guys are. I mean, why did they pick me?"

"**I** should find out? What am I, Wonder Woman?"

"Yes," said the twins. "Puh-leeeeze, Lucy?"

"Oh, shut up and don't be ridiculous!" she snapped. "Of course we have to tell them."

"You asked me to find out why the boss was so happy," said Murrow.

"Yes," said Karp distractedly. That had been a while ago, he recalled, before this trial had eaten up his working life. Why was it important to know that? He couldn't quite think of it. He was running through autopsy reports for perhaps the twelfth time, trying to find the one thing he really wanted to recall, the thing that would impeach Frank Nixon and Eric Gerber on the witness stand. First bullet, entry right flank, exit right back, damage done: superficial, not mortal; second bullet, upper left arm, damage done: not mortal . . . he looked up. "And did you?"

"Possibly. Judge Patrick F. Toomey has retired from the federal bench."

"Uh-huh. Well, so long, Pat. This is what's got

Jack Keegan singing bird songs? Why, did he think Toomey was a bad judge?"

"I have no idea, but it does create a vacancy in the Southern District of New York."

"And . . . what? You think Jack thinks he's got a chance?"

"An excellent chance, I'd say. A practically preemptive chance."

"I don't see why. It's a presidential appointment, and the president, the last I heard, unless they had another coup d'état, is a Republican."

Murrow gave him a peculiar look. "You really don't understand how this works, do you?"

Karp said, a little sharply, "Don't patronize me, Murrow—you got something to fucking say, just spit it out."

Murrow took a deep breath. "Yes, the president is a Republican, but both U.S. senators from the state are not Republicans. In fact, they are both famously liberal Democrats. Which means, the president is not going to get what he really wants, an anti-abortion, pro-gun, pro-death penalty fascist Republican. There's no way in hell those two senators are going to pass on that kind of candidate, and as I'm sure you know, regardless of party, U.S. senators have essentially veto power over judicial nominees from their states. So the administration is thinking, Why not go with a Democrat? But it would have to be a very special kind of Democrat. It would have to be an Irishman first of all, because it's an Irish seat on the court that's going to be vacant. Obviously, you'd also want unimpeachable legal credentials, tough on crime, and if not pro-death, then at least neutral on it, and most of all, anti-abortion. Big time. Can you think of anyone we know with all that going for him?"

Karp could. "This is actually going to happen?"

"I hear it's practically a done deal. The beauty part for the White House is that it manages to shove a bamboo splinter under one of Hillary's red nails. She has to explain to her liberal witch constituency why she's backing a man with that kind of record, whose wife, by the way, is cochair of New York Right to Life."

"And if she doesn't go for it?"

"Then she can run for re-election next time without even the small part of the Irish vote that she had last time, and without the help of the regular party. Jack's paid his party dues, he deserves it, and the old bulls'll never forgive her if she fucks him on this one. Oh, it's rare. It's nearly as good as Clarence Thomas as a fuck-you message."

"Holy shit," said Karp.

"Yeah." He studied his boss briefly, a bemused smile on his lips, as if standing before a museum exhibit about a lost civilization. "Tell me, no offense, but you really don't get all of this, do you?"

"It's not that I don't **get** it, Murrow. It's not like it's particle physics. I don't spend any time thinking about it, is all."

"No, I guess not. But assuming what I just said is true, you do realize that it means the DA is up for grabs. Have you given **that** any thought?"

"What do you mean?"

"I mean that Keegan will have the gift of it. Within limits, he can pick someone to fill out the last year of his term."

"No, it's a gubernatorial appointment and the gov is a Republican."

"True, but Keegan could preempt that by appointing a profoundly nonpolitical acting DA during the time of his confirmation hearings, at which point the gov would not like to look like he was politicizing the office by trying to push some Republican back in there for the final year of the term. The **Times** wouldn't like that. And that leaves . . ." He paused and looked meaningfully at Karp.

Karp pointed a finger at his own chest. "What? Me? You have to be joking."

"It's you, boss."

"What about 'Ku Klux Karp'?"

Murrow waved a dismissive hand. "Yes, but that's going to disappear when you win this trial, and put those two white cops away for killing a black man. You see all those pickets out in front of the courthouse? They're going to be your best friends if this goes down right. That's why Keegan hasn't said anything, and why he wanted you to take this trial. He's waiting to see how it goes."

Karp suddenly realized why Keegan had made no objection to his taking on **Gerber & Nixon**. "And if I lose?"

"Then the governor will be able to present you to the great and the good as Jack's first choice, an excellent lawyer, blah blah, but he has this unfortunate reputation, doesn't really seem to understand black lives are just as valuable, blah blah. The great and the good will know that he tried to be nonpolitical, and then he can go ahead and appoint someone his party owes a favor to."

"You have this all figured out, huh?"

"It's not particle physics," said Murrow, "and I happen to be interested. Are you?"

"Am I what?"

"Going to win?"

"I might. But I'd have more of a chance if you left me alone so I could find out how I know these fuckers are lying."

Lucy parked the boys in the loft and made them swear that they would not budge from the place until an adult returned.

"Are you gonna tell?" asked G.C.

"I will definitely tell if you're not here when I get back."

"Where are you going?" he asked.

"Out," she said, and left. As she headed uptown on the baking train, she writhed in a moral quandary more uncomfortable than the damp heat. Clearly the thing to do was tell the parents, call the cops, kidnapping was serious, not something to fool around with. On the other hand, G.C. was right. Confronted by an actual threat rather than her own guilt-driven paranoia, Marlene would instantly snatch both of them back to the far reaches of Long Island, would register them in school out there, and keep them in paranoid security behind razor wire, protected by a herd of mastiffs, and that would be the effective end of the Karp family. Better to identify and neutralize the threat first. It did not occur to her that she was doing here what her mother had taught her, nor did she doubt for a moment that she was equal to a gang of kidnapping thugs of whatever size and resources. She had resources of her own; another thing learned at her mother's knee.

An hour later, Lucy was giving out candy bars and cigarettes in a dim underground vault lit by candles stuck in bottles and jars. It was a disused railway tunnel, bored into the rock of the Hudson shore to service a Lackawanna Railroad pier that was never built. It was difficult to access, dry, cool, and extensive, and had both official and unofficial connections to the remainder of New York's many-thousand miles of tunnels. For these reasons, it was popular with that segment of the homeless who wanted even less to do with the authorities than the more sociably inclined destitute. New York City has a substantial population living almost entirely underground—no one knows how many, but estimates run to several thousands. The "regular" homeless called them the mole people.

Lucy was now walking through their largest settlement. As in the city's sunnier precincts, a certain proportion of the population was evil, and several of these regarded Lucy with bad intent as she moved past, but they knew that if they tried anything with her they would immediately be torn into tiny little pieces, in as painful a manner as possible. Lucy had been coming here since age fourteen dispensing small gifts and her particular brand of hard-headed goodness. For her the place was as safe as church.

Deeper into the tunnel, the railway engineers had carved bays out of the living rock and lined them with brickwork, intending them to hold the sidings of the notional railway. These were now the sites of separate communities, and the most populous of them, which Lucy now entered, was known as Spare Parts. The ruler of this troll kingdom was also called Spare Parts for the place was named for him. She found him on his throne, a sprung couch set up on railway ties, lit from below by a Coleman lantern's hard glare. The effect was stunning, like a pagan idol on an altar, although this god could and did come down from on high to reward and punish. Spare Parts the

man had a cleft palate and a harelip, one brown
eye and one pale silver eye, and only one ear (the
other being a scrap of greasy cartilage), all stuck
on a head the size and approximate shape of a
half-deflated basketball. Other than that, Spare
Parts was only slightly smaller than Shaq O'Neill.
Lucy climbed up and sat beside him, an unusual
privilege.

"Hello, Jacob," she said. "I brought you a
Dove Bar. I hope it's not too melted." She
removed it from its insulated bag and handed it
over. The big man took it in his filthy paw and,
raising it high, let the whole thing slide into his
maw. Lucy politely looked away and tried not to
pay attention to the wet noises. Spare Parts did
not like people watching him eat.

"Ank 'ou, 'ucy," said Spare Parts, when the
sounds had ceased. "I 'ove 'ove 'ars."

"You're very welcome, Jacob," she replied.
They conversed briefly about the underground
world, mainly about deaths and sicknesses and
recoveries, together with tips and hints, about
who could use what kind of help, and how to
manage things so that the needy would accept
what they needed. It was strangely restful, like
something from a fairy story. As usual, Lucy
found that she could understand him fairly well,
her skillful brain supplying the dentals and
palatals that the man could not pronounce. She
imagined that he didn't speak to anyone as much

as he spoke to her. After an interval of silence, she said, "Have you seen Grale?"

"'E's a'oun'."

"Is he still, you know, down with the rats?"

"Not nany 'ats 'eft now."

Not many rats left. David Grale was a religious maniac and a serial killer. The people he killed were feral humans who lived in an ancient and unrecorded tunnel. It was rumored in the upper tunnels that they lived on human flesh. For sure they lived on rats. Grale considered it his ministry to cut their throats.

"If you see him, tell him I'd like to talk with him again, okay?"

"Ih I shee 'im I'll 'ell 'im," said Spare Parts, after a pause. Spare Parts didn't care for David Grale. Compared to David Grale, Spare Parts was the borough president of Manhattan.

"What's wrong with the boys?" Karp asked. Marlene was driving the truck east on the Belt Parkway, heading for Raney's house in Woodmere. The radio was tuned to an oldies station, the Isley Brothers telling the listener to keep holding on, keep holding on . . .

"I don't know," she answered. "They do seem a little subdued."

"Subdued? The pair of them look like the after picture in a Prozac ad. Usually they're up to meet new people they can embarrass us in front of. Whatever it is, Lucy's in on it. She barely met my eye when I came in," said Karp.

"What can I say, our children are master criminals. I belief in Old Vienna, ve haf called zis **eine** ab-reaktion. In order to define zemselfs ze **kinder** must go srough a period in vich zey reject zhe parental walues."

"Thank you, Doctor. Although, given the differences between your **walues** and mine, it's surprising that they knew what to react against. Or that they didn't become saints."

"Actually, if you noticed, they did become saints, at least Lucy and G.C. did," said Marlene.

"Yes," said Karp. "Are you going to claim credit for the assist on that one?"

"No comment. And how was your day, dearest?"

"Not bad. Murrow thinks I'm going to be the next DA." he explained the theory about Keegan, the federal judgeship, politics, and the trial. Marlene nodded, as if he were telling her something she already knew.

"Yeah, that makes sense," she said. "It was just a matter of time before Jack got his slot. He's been wangling for it for years; it's practically a courthouse joke. And who else are they going to get besides you? Congratulations, sweetie."

"Not so fast. There are a lot of qualified people," said Karp, to which she snorted, "Oh, please!" and then, musingly, "I wonder if it'll change you. Nothing else has."

"Well, I haven't got it yet," he said, choosing to ignore the last remark. "According to Murrow, I have to win this trial to be eligible."

"I guess," said Marlene, as if this was obvious to small children. "How did it go today?"

He shrugged and rubbed his face. The feeling of being on the edge of some trial-winning revelation had not dissipated after leaving the courtroom. It still tugged at his mind, making him uneasy with domestic relations. Even the song on the radio seemed to be a part of the puzzle— keep holding on, **to what?** Soon it would be the birds in the trees and the drops of water on the windows that held high significance, and the slope down to madness.

"Hello? Ground control to Major Tom . . ."

Karp shook his head, as if to dislodge an insect. "What? Sorry, I was thinking." The radio turned to a discussion of California dreaming.

"About what?"

"I don't know. The trial. Anyway, Roland had Gerber up there all day. I could see that it was killing him to do it, but they must have insisted."

"How was he?"

"He looked pretty good. Roland spent most of his time getting out their story about the victim trying to sell them heroin, but. . . ." He pointed.

"You need to get off on Twenty-seven east, on your right here."

"I see it," she said. "Well, they can't be too morose. Giancarlo is playing his accordion back there."

Karp twisted around and peered through the rear window of the pickup, but the matching window of the camper back was dirty and he could only make out shadows. He could hear the tweedle of the accordion, though. It sounded fairly morose to him, but he didn't know anything about music.

The Raney home in Woodmere was a postwar brick bungalow, immaculately kept, on a pleasant street of similar ones. Marlene pulled the truck into the driveway, and they all got out, trooped around to the front, and Zak pushed the bell. The door flung open.

"Now here you are and very welcome all of yez, but Raney's not home and there's no dinner at all."

"You're Irish!" said Giancarlo.

This was even more obvious to those of the Karps with intact vision. Nora Raney had bright red hair done up in a once neat but now dissolving bun, pale freckled skin, grape green eyes, a snub nose, and not much in the lip department. She stood in the doorway, dressed in pale blue surgical scrubs, with a whining red-haired toddler, a miniature of the mom, on her hip.

"That I am," she said with a laugh, "and don't I rue the day I came to America and married a policeman. Well, don't stand there like statues, come in!"

They entered the house. The living room, Marlene saw, was furnished with a combination of Mom and Dada stuff, the kind of solid dark pieces that Irish immigrants bought in the 1920s when the man of the house got on the civil service, and lighter, brighter young-marrieds gear from Ikea and the Door Store. It was the same sort of furniture (substituting Italian for Irish) that Marlene had supplied her own home with twenty years ago, and she felt a pang of . . . something. Regret? Sorrow? Fear? Yeah, fear was a lot of it, always bubbling up, tainting all the homely sessions of her life. Smile, Marlene, she told herself, this is supposed to be fun. She caught Nora looking at her. Could she smell it, too? No, that was just the young bride checking out the old flame, who wasn't even really an old flame anyway. Good for Raney, though, and the kid was gorgeous.

They were in the kitchen, where a pot was steaming on the stove and piles of potatoes sat in a plastic basket on the table.

"There's not a bite in the house except those spuds . . ."

"Gosh, you really **are** Irish," said Giancarlo, and got the back of his mother's hand lightly across the top of his head. But Nora laughed, and said,

"Yes, and isn't it a bloody parody. And I was going to make a potato salad to go with the barbecue that Raney's supposedly bringing home, but he's not home. He came down from that prison he was visiting and checked in at headquarters, and there he's sat with no word since he called at half three this afternoon. And I would have been here to go to the shops, y'see, but Moira Flannery asked me to take a shift for her, and I couldn't say no, could I, because hasn't she covered for me a thousand times when Meghan was a babe? Well, and so here we are, I swear it's just like the Great Famine, but at least there's beer."

Bottles of cold Harp lager were distributed to the adults. Zak grabbed one, was yelled at, allowed a swallow, and then set to peeling potatoes with his brother. The others went out the back door and lounged in the somewhat scruffy yard, and got acquainted. Nora was a surgical nurse by profession, and seemed to know a lot about the Karps. She exchanged some phrases in Gaelic with Lucy ("And that exhausts me knowledge of the dear old tongue, I'm afraid"), listened to Marlene's version of the adventures she'd been through with Jim Raney (in which Raney came out a deal more heroic than he apparently had when he'd recounted them to the bride), and then the women got into child-rearing practices. Karp was content to listen to their talk as he might have the sound of the surf. Lucy drifted inside to supervise the boys, who, from the sounds they made, were spending more time flicking bits of spud at each other than actually peeling.

They were all well into their second beers when Raney arrived, laden with meats and looking wilted and whipped. Beers were provided him, he showered and changed into cutoffs and T-shirt, the fire was started, sweet smoke rose to heaven, the party ate the burgers and hot dogs, plus a French potato salad that Lucy had pulled together while Nora, the slut, had taken her ease like a duchess. Who piled compliments on Marlene, for her talented daughter.

"Oh, the Karp show has only started," said Marlene, who had by then lost track of the beers. "G.C.!" she called, "give us a tune!" One never had to ask him twice. Zak trotted out to the car and returned with the box. Giancarlo played "The Night We Had the Goat."

Nora said, "Ah, that's grand, but say, can you play a slip jig at all?"

Giancarlo launched into "The Windy Stairs," and then "Up in the Garret," with Nora doing a credible dance with the baby jouncing and giggling in her arms.

Meanwhile, Marlene had sidled up to Raney.

"Tell me," she said.

"The short version is there's something bent going on. We don't know who's in on it yet, but I think I got them interested enough to get an investigation going. The doc up there is a junkie, and they showed me a kid supposedly in charge of the ward where Felix supposedly died, who was lying through his teeth. The orderly station had a bunch of books there that belonged to someone who was not the hick pretending to be in charge, two in French, one in Arabic."

"Oh, hot damn!"

"Yeah. In French we got **Reflections on the French Algerian War** by Mouloud Faroun and **The Black Book of Jihad** by Gilles Kepel. In Arabic there's an admiring biography of Sabri al-Banna, a.k.a. Abu Nidal. Close associate in the old days of . . . ?"

"Not what's-his-name: the B'nai Brith bomber?"

"Him. Feisal ibn-Salemeh. Resident at Auburn. It was a pretty slick setup. Salemeh was in total charge of the infirmary for years, and it'd be nothing for him to slip Felix out. They even had this ringer all ready to pretend to be in charge of the prison clinic if anyone came by."

"I can't believe that no one connected him with the bombings."

"Hey, he was in jail, under an assumed name. The guys who knew about his background weren't talking to the people trying to find the Manbomber. We'll be having a conversation with ibn-Salemeh's lawyer, I'm pretty sure. He was the conduit, apparently. And it would've been cool if Feisal had remembered to take his library when he ducked out. Auburn will be crawling with feds and state cops by tomorrow. Of course, the feebs immediately cut us out of it, but who gives a shit about that. I just want Felix."

"And the cops are happy with this?"

"More or less. At least One PP isn't looking at me like I'm a nut anymore. The main thing the Felix connection does for them is to explain the bombing pattern. Yeah, it looked random, because Felix was settling scores and there was no connection between him and anyone with bomb skills. Now there is."

"But besides Judge Horowitz there's no one who's died in the bombings that has a connection to Salemeh. Or is there?"

Raney's face had grown grim. He stared at his dancing wife and then back to Marlene. "Well, there's you. The Karp family is on both bad guys' lists."

"Oh, right. Shit!"

"And there's Daoud got killed, the baker. Also the theory is the bombing so far's been a sideshow, and that they're saving it all up for some big bang. Or were until their base blew up on them. I'm not supposed to tell anyone this . . . but, we got a tip. They're planning to attack the tunnels: Lincoln, Holland, Queens, and Battery. According to the rat, they have fucking tons of high explosive manufactured and ready to go. They were planning on using septic tanker trucks to carry the bombs in."

"Oh, great! This is going to do wonders for traffic."

"Tell me about it. Anyway, the interesting thing is, they played us the tape of the guy who called it in. He had his voice disguised, but it was obvious that it was a regular American voice, no accent."

"Oh-ho."

"I'd bet on it. Once you have the general out-lines, the plot is pretty clear. Salemeh gets Felix out of Auburn and ships him to his pals in the city. Why? Easy. The whole world is searching for skulking Arabs and Felix is an all-American-looking guy. By the way, there's our fella in the ball hat for sure now. So he plants the bombs, buys explosives, whatever. But since Felix is Felix, he's not a happy camper at all. Did you know he was a big racist? Oh, yeah, he doesn't miss a trick, Felix. So he probably wasn't happy taking orders from a bunch of Ay-rabs. So he does a few operations on his own, bombs or peo-ple he had a grudge against, that double murder right here in Queens. Which couldn't have made Salemeh's people too happy. So they break up."

"Wait a minute, what makes you think that there are any Salemeh people left? Who died in the Queens house?"

"Two brothers named Alfiyah, Omar and Fuad, from Brooklyn. Palestinians, born here but very hot Islamists. Dying to be martyrs, according to the neighbors and police intelligence. So to speak. I guess they got their wish."

"But they were recruited by someone."

"Oh, yeah, they were just the kind of assholes Salemeh liked to recruit—disposables, okay to put together bombs and then get rid of them. It might have worked, too, except for Felix. I'm guessing that Felix might have helped that house explode. It's a Felix kind of thing. But they're still in business, so since Felix doesn't ever let go of a grudge, as his good-bye present he lets us know what he learned about their plans."

"I like it. Did the bosses?"

"Not all of it. Now, needless to say, they love that Arabs are in the picture now. Arabs they can handle. They're a little spooked about putting a dead guy out on a wanted bulletin, they want to wait for—"

Raney was snatched away with a jerk on his wrist by his wife, who pulled him into a reel. Marlene had no idea that Raney could do Irish dancing. Maybe Nora had taught him. Before Pete Balducci's funeral it had been several years since she'd seen Raney, and she probably would have let him drop out of her life completely had they not met there. Why? They'd always liked each other. Sexual guilt on Raney's part, her own withdrawal from the world after going crazy, and more so after what had happened in West Virginia.

No, let's not think about this shit, Marlene, let's just have a normal evening with friends, and my, didn't they make a handsome couple, dancing to the wild music. Zak was banging out the tempo on a beer tray with a piece of wood from some toy. Lucy was bouncing the baby on her lap in time. Marlene went over and sat on a wide chaise next to her husband.

"Happy times," he said. She didn't answer, but laid her head against his shoulder. He put an arm around her. He was still nursing his first beer.

Karp watched the dancers turn. He was listening to the music, but through his head still traveled the lyrics of that song, about keep holding, keep holding on. It was almost there. The weight of Marlene's head on his arm was pressing it against the pipe frame of the chair, making it tingle unpleasantly. The ulnar nerve, the median nerve, the axillary nerve were tingling. He knew that because . . .

He knew that because . . .

A drop of water fell on his hand. He looked up at the sky, darkening to deep blue with approaching evening, but clear of clouds. Not rain, but a tear. His wife was crying; her cheeks were wet with it.

"What's wrong?"

"Nothing. Life. I'm in terror."

"What? What is it?"

"I can't have this. Peace. Felicity. Friends and

music and the kids happy and us together. I feel like the skeleton at the feast."

"That's . . . not true, Marlene." He had almost said, "That's crazy."

"It's okay. I'm being an idiot. Jim thinks Felix Tighe is still alive, and on the loose."

"What? I thought . . ."

"That he died in prison, like everyone else thought. Well, he didn't, and he's b-a-a-a-a-ck! Apparently, he's also the Manbomber. At least he distributed the bombs. There's probably a cell connected with our old pal ibn-Salemeh. It looks like he masterminded the whole thing from prison."

"Are you serious?"

"Deadly. I'm sure the details will emerge, but just now they're keeping it all real dark." A howl sounded over the music. "Shit, what does that dog want?"

"Hamburgers?"

"No, it's something . . . I better go check." She heaved herself up and went through the chain-link gate to the driveway. Gog was whining and fretting and when she opened the camper back door, he stuck his face in hers, drooling buckets.

"What is it, pal? What's up? Calm down! Be quiet, everything's okay." She walked around the truck, looked beneath it, walked down the drive-way past Raney's sedan, and out into the street. There were some kids on a bike riding around in the twilight. They zoomed past, shrieking, and the mastiff growled. That was it.

"It's just kids, you big silly. Calm down. It's all right. Look, Magog is fine. Settle down!"

She poured the rest of her beer into the dog's dish and walked back to the party.

Which went on. They finished the beer and started on the Jameson. Nora was imposed upon to sing "West Coast of Clare" and "Four Green Fields," which she did in a pleasant contralto. A Pogues poster had been discovered in the bathroom, and Zak announced that his brother could play nearly everything on "Rum, Sodomy and the Lash," so they had to hear some of that, too. Then Marlene tickled her son until he consented to play "Lady of Spain," which he did off-key, while she sang the lyrics with drunken vigor. Karp watched this resignedly. He didn't much care to drive and he would be driving tonight, but it was worth it to see her having fun. So she drank a little too much, so what? He was feeling better than he had felt in a long while because solution to **Nixon & Gerber** had just that minute popped into his head.

The shot through the arm, not mentioned in the original testimony from the medical examiner because not contributory to cause of death, but noted in the autopsy report. Everyone focused on the fatal bullets from Gerber, ignoring Nixon's non-fatal ones. Keep holding on, keep holding on, like in the song, like they both said the victim had.

But he hadn't. He **couldn't**. Karp knew he would have to check when he got back to the office, but he was as sure about it as he was about anything.

Now it was full night. Little Meghan had been put to bed. Raney was on the couch nodding. Karp was making eye signals to his wife.

"We should go," he announced. He looked out the narrow window that gave a view of the driveway. "You need to move your car, Jim."

"Oh, hell, I'm sorry. I wasn't thinking." Raney rubbed his face and started to look for his keys.

"Ah, would you look at the man, too plastered to back a car down a drive!" said Nora cheerfully. "And the old lady's got to do it for him." She snatched a set of keys from a china bowl on a side table and went out.

Karp supervised the boys' retreat, gathering up shoes and socks and various bits of boyish equipage. Lucy supervised her mother. Raney walked them out to the front walk and they were all standing there in front of the house watching as Nora Raney backed her husband's Pontiac out of the driveway. There was a small drop where the lip of the driveway met the road, ordinarily a hardly noticeable little bump. But it was quite enough to trip the trembler switch in Felix Tighe's last bomb, which was fixed by its magnet to the chassis right under the seat she sat on. No one else was even scratched by the blast, although Raney burned all the skin off his hands trying to reach his wife.

16

"WE MUST EXPECT SOME REVERSES," SAID Rashid with a confidence he did not really feel. "We are in combat with a superpower, just we few, but the central plan is still intact."

"How? How is it intact?" demanded Habib, the false Felípe. "Felix blows up the wife of a policeman with one of our bombs, after the bombings were supposed to be over because the bombers blew themselves up in Queens. Now they know that all that was a fraud, and the search for us is still on. We should have killed that piece of shit when we had our hands on him, and then this would not have happened. But, no, we had to have your circles within circles of deception. I think we should leave the city and regroup somewhere else."

They were sitting in the dingy office of Scarpese General Contractors, the last of the businesses Rashid had purchased over the years.

This was their final redoubt, the storehouse of the explosives that they had garnered and made with such care. It was located on St. Nicholas Avenue in Inwood, a neighborhood of upper Manhattan occupied almost entirely by Caribbean and Central American Latinos. The premises consisted of a three-story red-brick workshop/office and a large yard guarded by a high chain-link and razor-wire fence. In the yard were several large flatbed trucks and big black industrial boilers on pallets.

Rashid walked over to the grimy window of the office and looked out on the yard, as if to assure himself that the physical assets of his operation were still there. He had not really recovered from the news that ibn-Salemeh was under investigation by the FBI, that the whole business about Felix Tighe had been discovered. Admit your mistakes, then move on: that was one of ibn-Salemeh's precepts. Rashid had to admit that he had been mistaken about Tighe. He thought the man was just interested in money. He also had no idea that Tighe had the brains to build a bomb himself, with stolen materials, but there it was, and now the television was saying he had been running his own vendetta with what were supposed to be random attacks. That's how they had known that his death was fraud. He had put his signature on everything.

"Leave? No, that is out of the question," said

Rashid. "The plan will go through. But staying very quiet is a good idea. Staying quiet in place. Our papers are good, we have green cards, we pay our bills, we live quietly, we work, day by day we advance the plan. There is no reason for anyone to bother us. However, we cannot allow Felix to be taken by the police. They will sit him down with an artist, or perhaps even have him go through visa photos, and then our faces will become known, mine and yours, Mamoud and yours, Habib. So he must be eliminated."

"What are we going to do about Rifaat?" asked Mamoud, called Carlos.

All three of them glanced toward the door, where in the next office, a man lay on a cot, scarcely breathing. The child's knife had nicked an artery and the man was slowly bleeding to death. There was no possibility of getting him any medical attention. Rashid lifted two hands palms facing, the classic gesture invoking fate. "He will live or he will die, as God wills. Is the target still staying in that storage place?"

"That is what Saad tells me," said Carlos-Mamoud.

"Let him do it, then. Tonight. See he has the necessary equipment and drive him away afterward."

"Saad? Are you sure? I could do it."

"No, you are critical to the plan. You can not be risked at this stage. And why not Saad? He will be happy to get revenge for his brothers. He already thinks Felix caused the explosion. Make sure there is no body found. Use the casting furnace here. Oh, and be sure to collect the ashes. Perhaps we can still convince them that Felix has always been dead."

Lucy convinced Karp with some difficulty that he was **not** needed at home in the aftermath of the Raney bombing, and that the best thing he could do on the Monday was to go to court and resume trying the **Gerber & Nixon** case. So he had, leaving his stricken family: the boys silent and prone to fits of weeping; Marlene red-eyed, smoking continuously, and sitting in her rocker, creaking gothically back and forth by the hour, and dry as a stone, with an expression on her face that he did not remember ever seeing there before, a look of ashes. And Lucy, girl of steel, even Lucy looking a little rusty under the eyes as she made sure the family ran along, that there was food on the table, and clean clothes and the floor mopped and the dishes done.

So here he was, having, to his shame, put absolutely everything out of his mind except the business at hand. The first thing he'd done, even before leaving for work, was to get in touch with Dr. M. K. Shah, the assistant medical examiner who had done the autopsy on the victim and testified about it during the prosecution's case in chief. Dr. Shah was a little surprised to have the chief assistant district attorney call him at his home at eight on a Monday morning, to ask him about an incidental wound in an autopsy he'd done months ago. He assured the gentleman from the DA that the wound to that particular victim's left arm was of no importance in the demise of the victim, having severed no major blood vessels. Yes, he recalled it well, because it was the first bullet he had recovered—it had smashed the humerus and lodged under the collar bone, painful, yes, damaging, yes, but not contributing to the death . . .

That was not, however, what Karp wanted to know. When Dr. Shah finally understood what the question was, and that the DA was making no criticism at all of the way he had handled the autopsy or testified at the grand jury and at the trial, he genially confirmed Karp's surmise and announced himself ready to take the stand again at a moment's notice to establish the fact in open court.

In that court, the first business was Karp's cross-examination of Detective Eric Gerber. It was brief.

"Detective Gerber, you've just testified that you shot the victim, Mr. Onabajo, because you thought he was about to overpower your partner, Detective Nixon, and take his weapon, and what I'd like to hear from you is how you knew that."

"He was shouting at me: 'Eric, he's got my gun!' "

" 'Eric he's got my gun,' a cry for aid, yes, but from where you were standing, you couldn't actually see that struggle, could you?"

"No, the suspect was in the way. He had Detective Nixon locked up."

"Locked up? Locked up, how?"

Gerber's right hand went to the collar of his jacket and gripped it. "He had him by the collar. Detective Nixon was wearing a leather jacket, and the guy had a bunch of it in his fist. He couldn't pull away."

"I see. Now in demonstrating that, we see you're using your right hand. But Mr. Onabajo was using his left hand, of course. Is that correct? He was holding your partner's jacket with his left hand?"

"Right, his left."

There was a humorous murmur at this. The judge scowled it down.

Karp smiled, too. "So, you are absolutely positive that while he contested for Detective Nixon's weapon with his right hand, he was holding tight to that officer's leather jacket with his left hand, locking him in, as you say."

"Yes."

"From where you stood, did it appear to be a powerful grip?"

"Well, yes, the jacket, the leather, was all bunched up."

"Detective Nixon was not pushing him away, was he, or using his hands to pry loose that powerful grip, was he?"

"No, he wasn't."

"Why was that?"

"Because he was using both hands to try to keep his weapon away from the suspect."

"Away from the victim, yes. But he was able to fire, was he not? Two shots?"

"Yes."

"But these shots did not make the victim release his powerful grip, did they?"

"No. Not that I could determine at that time."

"And that's why you fired five shots from your pistol, to get him off your partner?"

"Yes."

"Thank you, Detective. Nothing further, Your Honor."

Karp caught the surprised look that passed across Hrcany's face. Karp knew he hadn't expected this. He had expected a lot of questions about the five fatal shots from Gerber's gun, which Hrcany, in his direct questioning, had been at great pains to demonstrate were all necessary to subdue a desperate criminal clawing at an officer's weapon.

Marlene stirs. The dog is hungry. Lucy has taken care of everything else, but Gog will accept food only from her own hand, as he has been trained to do. So she leaves the rocker and pours kibble and two cans of beef liver dog food into his trough. She eats a banana and pours out some of the coffee Lucy made that morning. The daughter is out with the boys. Marlene doesn't know where, except that they are away from her and therefore safer than they would be if she had them all on her knee. She sips the stale coffee, not tasting it, and watches the dog eat. The dog tried to tell her about the bomb, and she hadn't listened to him. Gog was bomb trained, Magog was not. Marlene should have known why Gog was upset, but she was too drunk. She checked her own truck but not Raney's sedan. So that was her fault, too.

She finds herself in the room she used to use as an office, a bright room that occupies the end of the loft that looks out on Crosby Street. In former days it had been a jungle of house plants, but now only one brave philodendron survives. She believes that Giancarlo still waters it. It would be the sort of thing he does. She had given all the other plants away, or allowed them to wither.

This is automatic pilot, she thinks, the simulacrum of an active life. She is aware that if she stays in her rocker and never speaks to anyone and never acknowledges anyone speaking to her, her family will call in medical help, and she will find herself in a looney bin, with kindly people trying to help her out of her depression. In fact, she is not depressed. She is in a state perfectly suitable for a woman who has lived a life of willful violence and is now suffering the moral consequences thereof. How else should she be feeling but bereft, miserable, guilty? She knows that mental health professionals do not think in such terms, which is one reason she wants to stay out of their hands. Lucy understands this, but Karp does not, and Karp will be in charge if she has what they will call a breakdown. So she is careful not to have one. If the authorities still existed that once dealt with people like her, the kind that used to burn at stakes, or immur in towers, then she might seek that sort of professional help, but no kindly people, please. Therefore she goes to work.

On the agenda today is Cherry Newcombe. Marlene has put some of Paul Agnelli's money on the street. She has a wide acquaintanceship among the demimonde of lower Manhattan. She knows people who will watch other people for a fee, and ask questions in ways that practically insure that they will be answered truthfully. So she has learned that fifteen-year-old Cherry has recently come into some money, serious money, and that she has clothed herself in splendor, having bought a number of tiny, shiny garments suitable for evening wear, plus a remarkable number of expensive shoes, some gold jewelry, and the hire of a car to take her around to the clubs. Other moneys have been spent on her boyfriend, Gambrell, twenty-two, who is apparently multiply guilty of the crime for which Paul Agnelli has been brought before the bar of justice, to wit, porking Ms. Newcombe, an underage female, but no one seems to be after Gambrell. Even more of this new cash has gone, as far as Marlene's people can determine, to a man called Carter "Smoke" Belknap, a dealer in cocaine. Belknap's usual place of business is a parking lot on Essex at Delancey, next to a club called Boot Kamp, which is, not incidentally, a favorite of Cherry Newcombe's.

Marlene now packs a nylon bag with the implements she will need for the evening's work: a black cotton jumpsuit, black Converse high-tops, a silk balaclava, nylon rope, plastic cable ties, duct tape, and a nine-millimeter Beretta 92FS semiautomatic pistol, fitted with a Jarvis threaded barrel. Marlene had sworn never to use a gun again, but she now construed that oath to mean never use one as an adjunct to some legal, professional activity. What she was about to do was a crime. And a crime in itself was the last item she tossed into the bag, a SRT Matrix sound suppressor, also called a can silencer, the ownership of which in the state of New York is a felony.

She takes this bag, the dog lead, and Gog the dog and leaves her home. It is a long time until dark, but she wants to visit Raney and tell him what happened. She announces this mission to the dog and adds, "Maybe he'll shoot me. Save everyone a lot of trouble." Her voice sounds strange to her ear, hoarse, as if still suffering from the effects of the last significant noise she can recall making, the scream that shot from her throat when the bomb went off. The dog says nothing, as he has learned not to indulge her in these moods. Besides, he knows she is immortal, as the gods must be if the world is to make sense.

Lucy took the twins to Washington Square. This time they did not complain that they were not babies and could wander the city streets at will. Lucy foiled Zak's attempt to slip out with a six-inch chef knife stuck in his waistband under his shirt, and was deaf to his arguments that they required weaponry of some kind, preferably a gun. At the park, Giancarlo unlimbered his accordion and began to play "Brokenhearted I'll Wander," a tune suitable for their collective mood. Lucy sat on the bench next to Giancarlo; Zak took up a position at some distance, where he could scan the crowd for danger and call in air strikes. She pulled a **Post** from a wastebasket. The Raney murder was still front page, fed by the anastomosing story about the fantastic escape of the killer Felix Tighe from Auburn Prison, his association with the terrorist chieftain ibn-Salemeh, the possibility that Felix was the Manbomber, that he had murdered his ex-wife and her child and now the wife of the man who had arrested him fifteen years ago. There was a big picture of Felix, as he had looked at the time of his arrest, and a more recent one from the prison.

"What's wrong?" said Giancarlo, after his song was done.

"Nothing."

"Yes, there is. You said, 'Oh, good Christ! Oh, Jesus!' under your breath when I was playing."

"It's fine, Giancarlo, I just thought of something I had to do. Play on!"

He shrugged and did. People paused in their walking by, and a number stayed to listen, so sweet and sad was the music. Soon afterward, a weedy teenager with a tin whistle arrived, and a bearded man in his mid-twenties came and opened his violin case and began to play, and then a pretty young woman with a Gaelic drum, a **bohdran,** and the four of them started in on "The Heather Breeze," as if they had been playing together forever. It was music squeezed from the rock of misery, designed over the centuries to make you forget the cruelties of life for the space of a song.

Hours passed in this way. They ate lunch from the cancer wagons. Lucy checked in with her father, and with her mother, getting neither, but leaving messages. When work let out, more musi-

cians came by and they played the sun down.
Someone mentioned an open mike night at a cof-
feehouse on Christopher and so they all trooped
over there, Lucy being happy enough to stay in
the safety of the crowd. Giancarlo formed a band,
with four people who were all twice as old as he
was, to be called Blind Boy Please Help. They
made forty-eight dollars. The thought passed
through Lucy's mind that it would be very pleasant to wander the world in this way, with her two
brothers, playing innocent music and letting
events drift by. She looked at Zak while she was
thinking this, and got a bright smile, an unusual
sight on that face, and she knew that he had been
thinking just that, too. Her cell phone buzzed;
she spoke briefly into it and switched off.

"Who was that?" Zak asked.

"I have to meet a guy in about an hour."

"A boyfriend?"

"Uh-huh. Leo DiCaprio. He saw me in the
street and fell in love. He wants to marry me, but
I don't know . . . I don't want to be, like, spoiled."

"He's a jerk, and he's probably about five-
three. No, really, who?"

"A guy I want watching our backs," she said
and would say no more.

Karp could see that Roland was as rattled as he
ever got, which was not much. He seemed a little

hesitant with his next and final witness, the powerfully gripped other detective, Frank Nixon. Nixon was wearing glasses today, rimless ones, instead of his usual contact lenses. His dark blond hair was swept back, combed close against his skull with water like an altar boy's, and he had a shirt on that was a size too big around the collar, making him look like the guy on the beach who got sand kicked in his face. The signal here: a mild and unthreatening fellow. He had a sharp high-cheeked face built around a ski nose and a set of pale, smart blue eyes.

Roland spent a good deal of time on the first moments of the altercation, when the victim allegedly went for the detective's weapon. Karp understood that he was doing this because Karp had focused his questioning of Gerber on those moments, and that meant that Karp thought they were vulnerable, that Karp would concentrate on those moments during his summation. He would ask the jury if it were reasonable that a man shot several times could hang on with a powerful grip. Roland meant to fix in the jury's collective mind that it **was** reasonable, that it **did** happen, and that two cops were swearing that it happened in just that way.

It was a simple trap and Roland was walking, nay running, into it, singing tra-la-la. When the direct questioning of Detective Nixon was completed, therefore, all Karp's work had been done

for him by the opposition, which is every litigator's highest hope. Karp now rose and paused.
He looked at the witness; he looked at the judge
and the jury. From the beginning of this trial,
from the moment it had become known that the
defense was going to place the defendants on the
stand, and expose them to cross-examination, all
the speculation in the press had been that this
examination would make or break the trial. And
when the word got out that Karp was taking the
case, they went into a frenzy of anticipation, for
Karp was the best cross-examiner in the recent
history of the DA. He had just demonstrated this
by his demolition of Hugo Selwyn, the ballistics
expert, and everyone was looking forward to dramatic fireworks. It was going to be like on TV.

"I have no questions for this witness, Your
Honor," Karp said, and the courtroom gasped
and burbled with noise, requiring the judge to
wield his gavel and threaten to clear. When order
had been restored, Roland announced that the
defense's case was concluded. Higbee's eyes
flicked to Karp's, who said, "Your Honor, may we
approach the bench?"

The judge dismissed the jury for five minutes. When the two counsels stood beneath the
presidium, Karp said, "We have a rebuttal case,
Your Honor, and since it's closing on three
thirty, I would suggest carrying it over until
tomorrow."

Roland said, "Your Honor, we'd like an offer of proof here. It's inconceivable to me that the state could rebut the defense case except by a repetition of previous material."

"Your Honor, I believe I know my responsibilities under the rules," Karp replied. "Our rebuttal case will include new material impeaching the defendants' testimony, as required."

It was an easy call. The judge brought the jury back in, told them what was going on, and what a rebuttal was, and dismissed them for the day. Reporters mobbed both attorneys outside the courtroom. They asked Karp why he hadn't cross-examined. They asked if he was throwing the case. If he was throwing the case because the cops were white and victim was black. Or Muslim. Karp brushed by them silently, as he always did. The more perspicacious among them noted that he was smiling happily, and wondered why. The reporters had Roland Hrcany, however, who loved to talk with the press, and he supplied enough information for two. He was glad to explain that the reason that Karp had not cross-examined was that the direct had been done with such skill, and the story was so obviously true, that any cross would have been otiose and harassing, and that's why Karp, for whom he had the greatest respect, had wisely declined to pursue it.

• • •

The street outside of Raney's house is full of parked cars when Marlene pulls up, both private and police vehicles. She must park a block away and walk back. As she does, she passes men she recognizes from the cops. They recognize her, too, and many give her hard looks, for most of them think that she should be wearing an orange jumpsuit up at Bedford instead of walking free on the streets.

Inside the house it is crowded, hot, and noisy with voices and music and the clink of glass against glass, for they are waking Nora Raney in the grand old style. Jim Raney is a famous and popular cop and his wife was a charmer. There is an open bar, much patronized. The place smells of many colognes, whiskey, smoke, and beer. Marlene steers her way through beefy men and hard-faced women with short hair (none of whom resemble the lovely policewomen of televisionland), all with drinks in their hands. Raney is on the couch in just the place he was sitting when his wife grabbed up the keys and went out to move his car. A woman who shares his bright Irish good looks sits next to him on the couch and an older woman sits on the other side, dabbing her eyes: the sister and the mother. In an armchair nearby, a red-eyed, red-haired woman dandles little Meghan. Nora's sister over from Ireland, Marlene guesses.

She meets Raney's eyes, which are red-

rimmed, too, as if he had been swimming in chlo-
rinated water. He is very pale, the freckles stand
out on his forehead. His hands are wrapped in
bandages. He sees her and makes a motion of his
head, of his eyes. She understands and leaves.
The backyard is empty, the Weber grill sits where
it sat on the night of the explosion, a burger lies
mummified on the grate. Marlene lights a cigarette and wonders again why she has stopped
drinking.

After a few minutes, Raney comes out. "Give
me one of those," he says.

She pulls out a Marlboro, lights it, and raises it
to his mouth. It is intimate without being sexy.
They are comrades of a special type.

"It's a good wake," she observes when half the
cigarette has vanished.

"Yeah, pity Nora couldn't come. She always
said that. 'Pity old O'Hara couldn't come.' At the
guy's wake. Are you going to ask me how I feel?"

"No. I believe I can guess. I wanted to tell
you . . ." No, when it came down to saying the
words she couldn't, not about the dog and it
being all her fault. There was no point to it. It was
self-immolating self-indulgence. ". . . how sorry I
am. I liked her."

He just looked at her, waiting. She said, "What
will you do, Raney?"

"I don't know." He lifts his hands. "There's
some deep damage, they tell me. The bosses are

going to consider this a duty injury, trying to rescue a victim, so if I throw in my tin, I'll get a three-quarter pension. I might do it. I could've lost my enthusiasm for police work, all things . . ."

"They'll get him."

"Yeah, and there's been a hundred forty-eight cops through here in the last couple of days and every single one of them looked me in the eye and said, 'Don't worry, we'll get him.' I said the same thing myself to families. Like it matters."

She helps him to a final drag and then crushes out the butt under her shoe. He says, looking up at the milky hot sky, "I mean, it **does** matter. If he came in here right now, I'd shoot him like a dog, and I wouldn't feel a thing. 'Don't worry, we'll get him.' **Of course** they'll get him. He's fucking doomed, now that they know it's him. There's no place he can go. But I got no feeling about it, you know? It's like a fucking meteor came through the roof and killed my life. My wife. So, I might not feel anything for a while. But definitely not wanting revenge. I'm not like you, Marlene."

"I know."

"I thought I was, but I'm not. I just want to take Meghan and go hide now. Get out of the city. Her folks want us to come stay with them in Clare. The west coast of Clare, like in the song. You want to hear something funny? If we hadn't had you over, I'd be dead and you'd be here talking to her. And she wanted you over to get a look at you because she was worried we used to get it on, and she wanted to check you out. I got to get back in there or they're going to send a search party. They all want to help, but I'll be glad when it's just me and the girl again."

Marlene has nothing to say to that. He looks around the yard, as if he's seeing it new. He adds, "I still see her, you know. And hear her. Opening cabinets. Walking, her step when it's quiet. My ma says it's the communion of the saints, the dead are all around us. I don't know. I can't believe all that about playing harps in the white robes, either. You ever think about that?"

"Death? A good deal. Although even if harps and white robes exist, they're probably not in store for me. Lucy's the expert on faith, though. You could talk to her."

"I don't know. I wish I had it. I swear to Christ I do. I wish I had it like my old lady and my gran did. Or Nora. The fucking Irish! Aside from the music it was the only decent thing we ever had and we get over here and get a little money to jingle together and a warm place to shit, and we let it go like a used Kleenex."

With that he walks back into the house. She leaves the yard and goes down the driveway, past the scorched place, her feet crunching on broken auto glass, and down the street to her car. The drive takes unusually long, for they are checking the tunnels, as they have at unsched-

uled intervals since it was revealed that the Manbomber's plan was to blow them up. The
expressway is backed up for miles. She takes out
her cell phone and has a long, interesting conversation with Detective McKenzie, the arresting
officer in the Agnelli case. Then Marlene plays a
CD of the Pavarotti **Rigoletto** on her stereo, and
smokes in the chill of her air conditioner. She
doesn't care if it takes four hours to get back to
the city. She has to wait until dark before she can
go to work.

Lucy and the boys walked down Crosby south of
Broome. It is a narrow dark street, almost devoid
of traffic in the night. Someone has painted the
streetlight shadows of the hydrants and parking
signs with black paint on the pavement, produc-
ing the ambiance of a stage set.

"Give me your knife, Zak," Lucy said.

"You took it, remember?" he answered
grumpily.

"She means the one in your sneaker," said
Giancarlo.

"Yeah, that one," said Lucy, who had only suspected. "But I'll give it right back."

He handed over a big Case jackknife. She
knelt next to a manhole cover and tapped a syn-
copation on it. Again.

A minute later there was a heavy rattle and

scrape and the manhole cover was raised from below, and slid to one side, and a tall, thin man jumped out, so quickly that it might have been a piece of stage magic. He was wearing a dark sweatsuit with the hood up and had a rucksack on his back and a heavy belt such as utility workers wear, from which dangled a number of tools and pouches. The sweatpants were tucked into rubber knee boots. His face was mushroom pale and he had a long pale beard. A dank smell rose from him, alien but not unpleasant.

"Hello, David," said Lucy. The man smiled and the smile illuminated his face in a way that was not entirely pleasing. Both Zak and Lucy, who saw it, felt a chill, and Giancarlo, who did not, sensed that chill and drew closer to his twin. There was something inhuman in the look, not cruel or uncaring, but rather beyond humanity entirely, the look Lucy imagined must have appeared on the faces of one of the tormented torturers with whom God has so generously supplied the Catholic Church.

"I'm glad to see you, Lucy," said David Grale. "You know, besides Father Dugan, you're the only person I miss up here in the world. And look at you! You've turned into a lovely young woman!"

Lucy felt herself blush and was glad of the night. At one time she had maintained a crush of gargantuan proportions on this man, when he was a Catholic Worker and a fellow servant of the poor. And she was not called lovely very often.

He turned to examine the twins. "And these are your brothers. All grown up, too, I see, and I see God has sent an affliction to . . . which one are you?"

"Giancarlo."

"Great things often arise from the afflictions God sends. You're a believer, I think . . . yes?"

"Yes."

"Yes. And your brother is not. Isn't that mysterious?"

Grale walked across the pavement and sat on the deep windowsill of an art gallery, right on the little sawteeth set there to prevent such sitting. They stood in a group in front of him, like tourists gawking at an exhibit.

"Dear, would you possibly have a cigarette on you?" he asked.

She did and he lit one up, inhaling luxuriously and blowing a column of smoke.

"I love these," he said, "and, you know, I don't think I have to worry about lung cancer." He grinned. "They said you were having some trouble," he said.

"A little. You know about the Manbomber, right?"

He'd heard nothing but rumors. Grale did not do current events. She quickly filled him in, especially about the more recent revelations:

that Felix Tighe was alive (and she had to explain who he was) and had set off a bomb that had killed a cop's wife in the presence of all the Karps; that a man of Latino or Middle Eastern appearance had tried to kidnap Giancarlo, and one other thing.

"I know Tighe. He called himself Larry Larsen and said he was a homeless ex-con, you know, down at Holy Redeemer. He was pretty curious about my connection with Tran. You remember who Tran is?"

"The Viet bodyguard, yeah. Why did he want to know about Tran?"

"I thought he was just making conversation. I mean it's pretty unusual to know someone like that and Tighe is a con artist. You know, they want to find out all about you so they have some kind of angle . . . that's all I thought it was. But now, that there's this connection with ibn-Salemeh, that explains it. They wanted to find out where he was, and they figured I'd know."

"Do you?"

"Of course. And that was the reason for the snatch on G.C. They figured if they had him, I'd tell."

"Would you?" asked Giancarlo.

"No, silly. I wouldn't care if they gave you a million nuggies," she said, giving him one. "But there's another thing. You remember when we used to talk about spiritual stuff and about how dumb people were if they believed that 'spiritual' meant 'good'?"

He nodded. "Yes. I miss those discussions. As I recalled we talked about saints and demons . . ."

"Yes. Anyway, I think Felix is one. I mean he's inhabited. I told Father Dugan about it and he sent a guy around, a priest, and the guy agreed. He put a kind of zinger on Felix and Felix stayed away from the soup kitchen after that. I saw him in front of our place a little while later. I gave him some cash and he booked. But now, with all this, with the Arabs coming after us and him, too . . . and my parents can't know this is going on, they have enough to deal with right now, and . . . you were the only one I could think of."

He finished his cigarette, stubbed it out carefully, and placed it in a tin box he took from his pocket, nodding all the while. "I see. So you want me to marshal the armies of the night to look after you and your brothers." He grinned again, more wolfishly this time.

"Yeah, just until they catch them. Can you do that?"

"I'll need a little while to set it up. I'm sure Spare Parts will help out once he knows the story. Actually, I'd very much like to meet this Felix. I must say, I'm a little surprised at you calling on me. I thought you had scruples about . . ." He gestured vaguely, taking in all of society's norms and the corpus of Christian morality.

"I guess you were wrong," she said. "About Felix, you'll be careful, right? I mean—"

"Oh, you think if I confront him and he happens to not survive, I'll be infected?"

"Yes."

"Darling, who do you think lives down there where I live? What do you think I'm doing down in the deep tunnels?"

Actually, she hadn't thought about that at all. "So how do you keep from, you know . . ."

"Being infected? I don't. I trust to the Holy Spirit to keep them all under control." He laughed and, lowering his voice an octave, said, "My name is Legion."

"That's not funny."

"No. It's a shame. It's hard to be in polite company anymore." He rose and hoisted his pack onto his shoulders. "It was nice seeing you, Lucy. Boys. Don't worry, we'll keep an eye on you all." His mad eyes met hers. "God be with you," he said.

"And also with you," she replied.

He walked over to the manhole and lifted it with a tool he took from his jangling belt. In a moment he was gone. The lid clanged dully into place.

"Boy, that was great!" exclaimed Zak. "God, Luce, you know all the cool people. How come I don't get to meet cool people like that?"

"He's an insane serial killer, Zak," she said.

"Yeah, wow!" Zak exclaimed, his face shining. "Neat!"

It is dark by the time Marlene enters Manhattan. Policemen and camo-clad Guardsmen populate the entranceway to the Battery Tunnel, and trucks of various types are pulled out of line for inspection, including Marlene's. There is an altercation between Gog and the NYPD's bomb dog, which Marlene has to sort out, with much exhibition of identity papers. **Vere are your paperz?** No longer an ironic line, it seems, in New York. They clear her without a thorough search of her truck—silly them—and she creeps through, her many felonies unrevealed.

As she turns east on Houston her cell phone buzzes. One of her street informants: Cherry Newcombe is on the move. Marlene drives into the Lower East Side on Essex, parks in a certain lot near Delancey. It's still a little early, so she goes into the camper and lies down on a foam pad with her dog, who is transported by this act to paradise. She allows him to nuzzle her face and then wipes herself off with a towel kept for that purpose. She stares into his brown eyes and hopes that she may come back as a dog: a short intense life where morals and ethics are reduced to mere loyalty seems good to her just now. "Why was I not made a dog, like thee?" she purrs. Oh, shut up and rub my belly, the dog replies.

She dozes and wakes with a start. Voices and the occasional sound of thumping music. She strips her clothes off and gets into the jumpsuit, sneakers, and balaclava. She loads her pistol and screws in the suppressor. Peering out the camper's side window, she sees that a black Lincoln Towncar with custom gold trim is sitting in a dark corner of the lot. A white guy is leaning in the passenger window. He walks away and she slips out.

There is a black man sitting in the driver's seat listening to Usher sing "U Remind Me." Marlene looks in the passenger window and taps on the frame with the butt of her weapon. "Get out of the car," she says politely.

Smoke Belknap looks at her without expression. "It's in the glove. You want the money, too?"

"I don't want either. I'm not after dope or money. I want you out of the car."

"Well, then fuck you, bitch! You want to cap me, go the fuck ahead. You not getting my ride."

Marlene shoots Belknap twice in the car stereo to make her point. The pistol makes a thirty-decibel sound, about the same as clearing your throat in church.

"I don't want your car, either. Get out now. Take your keys."

Belknap gets out, slamming the door. "Then what the fuck **do** you want?"

"I want you to make a call to one of your customers."

After some protest, Belkap places the call, and after a good deal more protest, he himself is placed in his car trunk. When Cherry Newcombe comes out of the nearby nightclub on the promise of a sachet of particularly pure and cheap cocaine, Marlene kidnaps her and forces her into the back of the camper. There she is introduced to Gog, who does his insane carnivore act, which is not entirely an act, while Marlene explains what she will let the dog do if Cherry does not tell her right now the truth about Paul Agnelli, Mr. Fong, the ex-wife, the phony rape charge, how Agnelli's DNA had arrived on Cherry's underpants, and how Cherry's fibers and other traces had arrived in the back of Paul's car.

After urinating in terror on Marlene's foam pad, and after she stops crying, the girl is forthcoming into a tape recorder for some time. It is a complex plot, and Cherry does not know all the higher details, but enough. She's been paid three thousand dollars for her participation, which amounted to her testimony, a used pair of panties, and a selection of hair and secretions. A Chinese man had paid the fee and taken the stuff; that is all she knows.

Afterward, she starts crying again and asks Marlene what will happen to her, what the cops would do, what Fong will do when he finds out.

She starts to cry again. Marlene looks at the girl, the absurd sex-ruined child in her expensive tiny dress, and finds that she feels nothing at all.

"I don't care," she says honestly. "There's a trunk-latch button inside the car. Go let your dope dealer out and maybe he'll give you a freebie."

Marlene climbs into her truck and drives away. As she drives she feels that something is amiss, that she has forgotten to do something. When she has parked and is walking toward her door, she realizes what it is. In the past, when Marlene participated in acts of violence, she always became nauseated, and threw up. But she's not nauseous now. She feels fine. She feels nothing at all.

17

DR. SHAH WAS A GOOD WITNESS. WHEN asked a question he would cock his head slightly to one side and knot his brow, demonstrating that he was making an effort to utter the whole truth, and in his answers he was precise, answering just what was asked. His diction was precise, too, featuring the clipped accent of the vanished empire. His mien was distinguished without being threatening: a pale brown man of about sixty, slightly overweight, with graying sides to his full head of dark hair. He was heavily diploma-ed as a forensic pathologist, and had worked as an assistant medical examiner for fourteen years. Karp watched the courtroom as he took his seat. He felt a tension that had not been there yesterday. All the jurors were alert and staring.

"Dr. Shah," said Karp, "when you first appeared here as a witness some weeks ago, what was your goal, in your testimony?"

"Why, my goal, as required by the law, was to attest to the cause and manner of death."

"And so you discussed those wounds of the victim that taken together produced the shock and exsanguination that were the immediate cause of death, and only those, correct?"

"That is correct."

"But there were other wounds, were there not?"

"Yes, there were."

"Doctor, I would like you to tell the jury about one of those wounds, the wound from the bullet that we have been calling during this trial 'bullet number two,' which was the second bullet shot from Detective Nixon's weapon. What was the path of that bullet and what damage did it do?"

Dr. Shah said, "Yes, well, based on the transcript of my notes, that bullet entered the anterior deltoid muscle at an oblique angle and struck the anatomical neck of the humerus, shattering it, and then rebounded back into the axillary region of the torso, striking against the posterior surface of the clavicle. It caused a greenstick fracture of that bone, and came to rest two centimeters from the medial end of the clavicle, where it was retrieved by me during autopsy."

"Thank you. Now, in plain language, Doctor, what were the physiological results of this damage?"

"The damage was localized, of course, and not

life-threatening, but neurologically quite severe. No major blood vessels were damaged—the brachial and subclavian arteries and veins were intact. But the bullet shattered a large bone mass, sending a hail of bone splinters down and medially—that is, toward the body. The ulnar nerve, the median nerve, and the radial nerve of the left arm were all completely severed proximal to the insertion of the deltoid."

"And what would have been the medical results of such damage?"

"The voluntary muscles of that arm would have been paralyzed."

"I see. And after such damage, would the victim have been capable of exerting a powerful grip on something with his left hand?"

"Oh, there is no question of powerful. He would not have been able to grip at all. He would have had no control of that arm whatsoever. It would have been hanging like a dead fish."

"Thank you, Doctor." Karp nodded to Hrcany. "Your witness."

Karp had to give Roland game. When confronted by a hostile expert who is not bullshitting at all, the only strategy is to get him to tell a slightly different story than the one he provided for the opposition, and hope that the jury will take this as reasonable doubt. So Roland had the doc go through the list of nerves in the arm and to say yes or no as to whether those nerves were cut. He was able to prevent Shah from expanding on his answers, to point out, for example, that these other nerves didn't matter, that the major motor nerves were the only ones that counted. Unfortunately, Dr. Shah bridled under this treatment, and became more and more impatient, so that when Roland finally said, "So, Doctor, it's not correct to say that Mr. Onabajo's arm was entirely deprived of neurological impulse, is it?" the medical examiner did not give a simple "no," but burst forth with, "Not relevant, sir, not at all. The left arm was completely paralyzed." After which Roland had to ask the judge to direct the witness to answer the question asked, and to tell the jury to disregard the doctor's answer.

The jury did not like this at all. Karp could see it on their faces. They had heard a solid impeachment and they were shocked. A pair of cops had lied under oath and had been caught in a lie by the testimony of a patently decent man who clearly had no interest in anything but the truth. You need to sit down now, Roland, Karp thought, take the hit and move on and try to fix it in summation, but even as he thought it, he knew Roland would not: it was his one failing as a lawyer. Karp had spoken to him about it any number of times when Roland worked for him in the homicide bureau.

"Dr. Shah," said Roland, "you're a Muslim, are you not?"

"Yes," said the doctor, puzzled, "but what does—"

"Objection, Your Honor, relevance," said Karp instantly.

"Withdrawn; nothing further," said Roland and sat down, with the courtroom burbling around him.

The judge called a recess after that, and Karp went back to his office. In a normal case, this would be the time when a defense attorney who had just seen his case go up in smoke would call and propose a deal, because juries did weird things. For an ADA a bird in the hand was often better than taking even a small chance that it would fly away, and also, with a plea, you got to see the defendant stand up there in court and unravel all the lies. But he knew Roland would not call. The clients would not press him, because they had slipped into hallucination— they believed the story they were telling. It was truth for them, and they had a whole culture backing them up, rather like the Southerners who maintained in the face of all evidence that the Civil War was not about slavery. But the real reason was that Roland Hrcany could not ever admit that Karp had beaten him in a direct head to head. You wanted courtroom lawyers to be scrappy, but Roland carried it to extremes, and his rivalry with Karp, twenty years in the festering, had become toxic.

So there was no call, and the court assembled again. There was no chance of a surrebuttal, because the medical facts could not be disputed. Roland needed to make the jury forget Dr. Shah and his clarity, and concentrate instead on the confusion in the nightclub parking lot. And he did. And he was good, too. He did the little speech about how much we owe to the people who protect us, **especially in these trying times,** and went on to compare Nixon and Gerber struggling with the gun to the desperate struggles that went on all over the city all the time, **especially now that we've been attacked by people who don't share our values**. Maybe people like Dr. Shah, hm? Which was not said, but left lying there like a wrapped gift of garbage for anyone to pick up.

And then the usual about the state's obligation to prove guilt beyond a reasonable doubt, and then a list of all the reasonable doubts—the conflicting on-scene witnesses, the disagreement about the ballistics, and who knew what a desparate individual might be capable of, doctors didn't know everything, look at what they told you was healthy, and then unhealthy, and then healthy again! Against that you have testimony from two experienced, brave, decorated officers. They didn't have to come up on the stand; the law cannot compel any defendants to appear as witnesses. They came voluntarily because they wanted you to hear the truth from their own lips. Their testimony agrees in every detail. The man was hanging on, he was grabbing the gun, he didn't let go even though shot twice.

It was rare, and when Karp rose to begin his own summation, he could see concern on the faces of some of the jurors. It was time for a Mark Antony opening. Karp utterly abjured any hostility in his mind or heart regarding New York's Finest. Cops were great and glorious and everyone knew that, and everyone wanted to support the police. Unfortunately, however, cops were human, and humans make mistakes, like the two defendants did on the night they killed Moussa Onabajo. What they should have done then was to say, Oh my God, we made a mistake, no, a whole series of mistakes. Karp counted these off on his long fingers. One: we accosted an inebriated man in the dark because we thought he was somebody else and we tried to get him to sell us narcotics. Two: because he wasn't a dope dealer he felt insulted and he abused us, but we persisted until he struck at Detective Nixon with his fists. Three: we did not identify ourselves as police officers. Four: in our anger we violated the police department's own rules of engagement— we drew our guns. Five: we panicked and shot a defenseless, harmless man seven times and killed him. **That** would have been telling the truth, but these men did not want to tell the truth. They feared the sanctions that the law provides for mistakes of this magnitude. So they made their final mistake: they lied. You did not hear the truth from their lips, but only self-serving lies.

Karp then went on to enumerate the lies and the testimony that established that they were lies beyond a reasonable doubt, focusing on the ballistic and medical evidence. He explained that Nixon was just as guilty as Gerber, even though he did not fire any fatal shots: they were acting in concert, and Nixon had started the assassination. He just wasn't as good a shot as his partner.

After that he said, "These facts are incontrovertible. For whatever reason, in whatever nighttime confusion, these two defendants at some point decided to kill Moussa Onabajo, and they did kill him, in violation of the law, for no reason except that he had made them angry by insisting that he was not a dope pusher and thereafter assaulting one of the officers, who never identified himself as a policeman, with his fists."

Karp moved to one side of the jury box, so that the jurors had a clear view of both him and the defendants at their table. "Now, let me confess something, ladies and gentlemen: if these policemen had come forward in the trial with the truth, if they had come forth crying, "God forgive us! It was dark, we were frightened, we made a terrible mistake, we violated our oath and our department's rules and gunned down an innocent, harmless man,' then I believe that the state would have had an almost insurmountable task in bringing in a conviction for second-degree murder. Not in this season, and not in this wounded city. But they did not do that, they did not do the decent and honorable thing, they did not emulate the brave men who died wearing the shield of New York's Finest. Instead, they came before you arrogant in their lies. They sought not expiation or healing, but impunity. **Impunity!** Look at them! They don't think they did anything wrong."

Karp spun and pointed his long arm at the defendants. Gerber had the look of a stunned ox. Nixon, bless him, had an actual half smile on his face, the gelid expression of a schoolboy caught in a fib. Karp gave it a couple of beats—not a sound but the whirring of fans—and went on.

"Ironically, Mr. Onabajo came from a nation where policemen and soldiers assault citizens, and kill citizens with impunity all the time. And it is likely that if Mr. Onabajo had been on the streets of Lagos and not New York he might not have defended his reputation with such vehemence. He might have run away. He might have confessed to a crime he didn't commit in order to avoid a worse fate. But he thought he was in a different kind of country, a country where even a struggling street merchant like Mr. Onabajo had dignity, and the protection of the law, where he could practice his religion, and earn an honest living, and care for his family, a country where despite his race and religion he was safe from being murdered by police officers just because they didn't like the way he behaved. Was he wrong about our country? I don't think so. I think we still have that kind of country, despite the terrible pressures of recent events. I hope you think so, too. If you do, if you think we still live in a nation where the police cannot shoot down a man with impunity, then on the basis of the evidence you must find, beyond a reasonable doubt, to a moral certainty, that Eric Gerber and Frank Nixon are guilty of murder in the second degree."

Judge Higbee's charge to the jury took another two hours, a fair and unobjectionable charge, right out of the book. Prosecutors usually take pains to define reasonable doubt and moral certainty, but Karp thought that the facts were so heavily on his side that he felt free to omit this part, confident that the judge would cover the points sufficiently, as he indeed did. Higbee was taking no chances of being reversed on that score. The jury trooped out at 4:10, looking serious, even grim, as homicide juries mostly did. Karp hoped the jury room was cooler than the courtroom. He figured on a fairly long deliberation, because he sensed that it would be difficult for them to reach consensus in a case this troubled and controversial. Therefore, he left the office at about 6:30 and walked slowly home. For once, he had not needed a reminder to take his cell phone with him.

To his surprise, that instrument sang out just as he was about to enter the elevator that went up to his loft. It was a court officer. They were back. Karp trotted over to Lafayette and grabbed a cab in front of the Holiday Inn, taking it the six blocks back to the courthouse. The pack of placard-carrying protesters in Foley Square had grown larger—hundreds and hundreds of people—and there were cops in helmets setting up gray crowd-control sawhorses in the streets. The press had been alerted and was lying in wait at the DA's entrance. Policemen had to help him through that mob. Cameras, reporters, and technicians packed the hallways outside the courtroom. They shouted for his attention like feeding gulls.

The usual butterflies as he took his seat. The little rituals of assembling the court. Time stretched. Then the court clerk took the sheet of paper from the jury to the judge, the clerk asked his dreadful question, the foreman rose, answered, and it was over: startled wails from the police families, applause from some others, gaveled into silence by Higbee.

Then the short formalities of thanking the jury, disposing of the convicts, the exit of the judge, and then chaos, a blur. People slapping his back, pumping his hand, the pressing crowds, the cameras and microphones. He gave a brief press statement, answered a few questions, ignored the personal ones, and broke away into the DA's wing. From his office he could hear cheering from the square.

The phone buzzed and, as he had expected, the DA wanted to see him.

When Karp walked into the DA's office, Keegan got up from his desk and gave Karp the full politician's handshake, with forearm grip and shoulder slap.

"Congratulations, kid!" said the DA. "Would it be insulting to say I always knew you could pull this one off?"

"Only mildly. I didn't realize I could win it until a little while ago."

Keegan laughed and gestured Karp into a chair. Sitting down behind his desk, he lifted his feet up and waggled his prop cigar. They discussed the details of the case for a while and then, in a convenient silence, the DA said, "Butch, we need to talk about something else. I guess you've heard the rumors?"

"About you and the federal bench? Yeah. Any truth to them?"

"The president will put my name in day after tomorrow."

"Congratulations to you, then."

Keegan nodded his thanks. "It just goes to show you: naked and shameless ambition pays off. What about you? Have you thought about what you want to be doing?"

"What I'm doing now, I guess. Maybe take a few cases to keep the juices flowing, if it works out."

Keegan looked at him steadily, as if waiting for something else. He shifted his gaze to the tip of his Bering. "The governor will be asking me for names to replace me, a courtesy. I understand from his people he'd like nonpartisan types. Good government, above the fray; I mean until the next election. It'd be a year and change. I'm intending to put your name in."

Karp felt his face flush. Even with Murrow's warning it was still a shock. He managed to say, "Thank you. I'm flattered," with the aid of some heavy throat clearing.

Keegan said, "I heard them cheering the verdict. We don't hear that very often."

"No. And that should tell us something about the system. When do you think we'll know? I mean, about the governor."

"Oh, a matter of days. But don't worry. I think it's all wired." A political smile here, and a cool assessing look. What's he looking for, Karp wondered. Probably for the first tender blossoms of corrosive ambition. Again, he found himself wishing that he trusted Jack Keegan a little more.

"Good thing we won the case, then."

Keegan burst out in startled laughter.

• • •

When he got back to the office, he saw that Murrow had arranged a celebration. Terry Collins was there, in a wheelchair, together with a large number of the more senior ADAs. Karp was surprised to see that they had waited so long after work to wish him well. He was one of those men who, without being popular, inspires great devotion in his subordinates, a fact that had entirely escaped his notice. He was prevailed upon to make a speech, and did, thanking all the little people who made it possible and saying he wanted to devote his career to advancing world peace. He was just starting to relax when his secretary tapped him on the shoulder and said that his wife was on the line.

"You're on the news," she said. "You won your case."

"I did. Let's hope we don't need any favors from the police anytime soon."

"Yes, always looking on the bright side. Well, good for you!"

"Thank you."

"I expected you home by now."

"They threw a little party, but I was just about to leave. Anything wrong?"

"I don't know. I just found out one of your ADAs is concocting evidence. Does that still qualify as wrong?"

"I'll be right home." said Karp.

● ● ●

"This is bad," said Karp, after Marlene had told him her story. "How sure are you that Palmisano knew about all this?"

"I'm **not** sure," said Marlene. "But it's hard to figure it otherwise. Look, Cherry Newcombe was paid off to lie and to supply underwear and physical samples to an agent of Fong. We know Fong wanted Paul's building and Karen wanted Paul to sell it to him, which he wouldn't. So they concoct this rape charge. There's no rape kit. The only evidence is the traces of Cherry in Paul's car and Paul's semen on the undies. The cop, Detective McKenzie, says he never handled the underwear, that Palmisano just announced that she had obtained it from Cherry, and that Palmisano ordered all the forensic work on it, the DNA matching and all. But Cherry says she gave all the stuff to Fong's guy. By the way, McKenzie said Palmisano seemed to take an unusual interest in the case, which he thought was more or less a piece of shit until the DNA undies turned up. He definitely did not believe Cherry's story, but, as he put it, quote, the woman was on my ass like Agnelli had whacked the president. She wanted him nailed, unquote. Paul swears there is only one likely source of such semen at the necessary time—Karen Agnelli and the fuck he gave her for old time's sake. That means that Fong must've slipped the mystery panties to Karen, Karen must've added the stain, and then taken it directly to Palmisano. Palmisano therefore lied to McKenzie about where she got them. Why would she if she wasn't bent? Q.E.D."

"It's not Q.E.D., Marlene. You have no direct evidence that Karen gave Terry Palmisano anything."

"True. Why don't you ask her?"

"Who, Palmisano?"

"No, Karen Agnelli. She's down at the Human Bean, waiting for you to show up. I called her a couple of minutes before you walked in."

"I'm being manipulated," said Karp.

"Yes. Relax and enjoy it. She's a small, cute blonde; she'll be dressed all in black, by Prada."

"And you arranged this by . . . ?"

"Telling her I knew all and that it was her only chance to stay out of jail." She checked her watch. "Go. You know where it is, right?"

He stood and looked at her with a grumpy expression. "Yeah, corner of Broome and Crosby. You know, Marlene, there are other ways of doing all this shit, ways that many smart people have worked out over the years, ways we call—what's the word?—legal procedure. How come you never use any of them?"

"I do, unless they become inconvenient."

"Speaking of which, how come little Cherry was so forthcoming with her story? Or do I want to know this?"

"You don't."

"And I guess you realize that whatever else happens in this abortion, she can't be called as a witness because you fucked it up with strong-arm stuff."

"I do. But all you need is Karen, and she's ready to fold."

"You're sure of that."

"Yes, I have utter faith in your interrogatory abilities."

"Present company excepted."

"Oh, just go, Butch!" she said sharply. "I can't be cute just now. I want this to be over."

Rashid had promised Felix twenty grand for not telling, and had delivered five of it, and Felix had gotten himself cleaned up and into a decent Midtown hotel and bought himself a bunch of clothes and a couple of nights with an expensive whore. Five grand did not, however, go as far in the city as it had when he went into the joint, so he called Rashid and asked for the rest. Rashid yelled at him and accused him of revealing the plans about the tunnels. Felix denied doing this. He said it must have been one of Rashid's people. He added that if Rashid did not come through with the rest of the cash, not only would he confirm the cop's suspicions, but also give them detailed descriptions of Rashid and his two pals and the names and descriptions of the guys at the famous council of war. Rashid had sighed, a defeated man, and asked Felix where he wanted to pick it up. Felix then named a place on the corner of Tenth Avenue and Thirty-Ninth where they had just demolished a building, a lot filled with rubble surrounded by an easily penetrated chain-link fence. Eleven at night. This night.

Felix was early, to check out the scene, make sure it wasn't a set-up, not that they would ever try anything. One guy, he'd said, and sure enough, here was the one guy with the shopping bag he'd specified. The only light came from the street lamp and the neon on the avenue; Felix stood in the shadow of the adjoining building and watched the man pick his way across the rubble field. The man was twenty feet away when Felix stepped out into the light. The man stopped short when he saw Felix; no, it was a kid, a teenager, dark skinned, in jeans and a T-shirt, an Arab. Felix motioned him to come closer, but the kid didn't move. Instead he reached into the shopping bag.

That was wrong. Felix saw the gun in his hand and the flash and the crack of the bullet over his shoulder. The kid kept the gun pointed at Felix, but nothing happened. The kid looked at the gun, puzzled. A jam. He yanked at the slide. Felix started to move.

In the prison yard there had been any number

of debates about what to do if someone was trying to kill you. Jimmy Hoffa was often quoted—
charge a gun, flee a knife—after which someone
would always say, "Yeah, and look where he is
now." But Felix had always thought that was good
advice, if you couldn't instantly duck behind
cover and get to a car. The thing was, you
couldn't outrun a bullet, and you had to figure
that a target closing on the shooter would do a lot
more to mess up his aim than one running away,
where the guy could get into position and
squeeze off shot after shot. And if you did have to
take a bullet, it was better to be on top of the guy,
rather than ten feet away, where he could fill you
with holes at his leisure and you couldn't do shit
back to him. If the guy was a pro, you were probably dead anyway, but you had to figure a small
chance was better than no chance at all. This kid
was definitely not a pro.

The Arab kid cleared his jam and brought his
pistol up, just a little too late. Felix was on him,
knocking his gun arm aside with his left and
going in low with the knife. The kid screamed
and fell off the blade onto his knees, trying to
hold his belly closed and mumbling something in
Arabic. Felix stepped behind him quickly and
slashed his throat.

Lights flicked on in the windows of the apartment across the street. A car stopped on the
avenue and a man stepped onto the curb. Felix

heard a woman scream and he saw the man on the curb take a cell phone out of his pocket. Felix knew what number he was dialing. There was, naturally, nothing but newspapers in the shopping bag. He ran for the shadows, toward the river.

At Eleventh, he passed a storefront belonging to a glass company and examined himself in a mirror hanging there. He had been wearing black clothes, so that was all right if he got rid of them soon, but there was blood on his hands and face. He cleaned the knife handle and dropped the knife into a sewer, went into a dark saloon on Twelfth and washed his hands and face, then headed back to his hotel.

There were two police cars parked in front of the hotel, and several uniformed officers on the pavement at the main entrance. Felix was stunned. How did they know? Or maybe it had nothing to do with him, maybe he could just breeze by. No, too dangerous. No one looked at your face in a big commercial hotel, but if for some reason they had already associated him with that dead Arab, like maybe he had a note— "Meet Felix Tighe"—in his pocket, **that** could trigger this. No, that was crazy, the Arabs didn't know he was there. Or maybe they did. Maybe Rashid had dropped a dime on him, when the kid hadn't shot him. But no, that would mean the Arab in Auburn would be screwed . . .

No, fuck the Arabs, the Arabs couldn't

have . . . but maybe some clerk had recognized him from the pictures they had in all the papers, on the TV, that **Most Wanted** program, he'd just made that this week. In any case, he knew he was sweating bullets, and he knew that cops could smell it on you, the fear, and he couldn't do it, he couldn't stand to bluff his way past. He couldn't think anymore, and he was getting close, he couldn't just spin around and run, that would have them on him in a second.

So he ducked into a steak house, and asked the cashier where Radio City was and then stepped out in the opposite direction from the hotel entrance. He walked over to Times Square, bought a nylon duffel, an eight-inch hunting knife, and a change of clothing: jeans, T-shirt, cheap sneakers, work gloves, a raincoat, and a wide-brimmed bush hat. He changed into these in the men's room of the clothing store, tossed the bloody clothes into a trash can, and headed west again. He couldn't take the chance of staying in a fleabag; that would be just where the cops were likely to look. He would have to drop out altogether, to go underground.

Fortunately, from his chasing after the Karp girl, he now knew something about the underground, about places cops hardly ever went. As he walked again toward the Hudson, he was conscious of a feeling he had not had in a while, the feeling of eyes upon him, rational paranoia. He found he didn't like it. He had loved being dead, and now his face was all over town. He was probably the most wanted man in New York at the moment. How to render himself invisible again? As long as his face was unknown, he'd been invisible as a uniformed workingman, and invisible in tourist gear. That wouldn't work anymore. He had to disappear, he had to become someone else, someone everyone saw but didn't look at. His memory threw up a few candidates, and one in particular, who had the added advantage of having some kind of screwy relationship with Lucy Karp.

Felix dry-swallowed another Dexedrine capsule to keep his brain working in the necessary high gear. The new plan gelled in his mind, giving him a little jolt of satisfaction. He was starting to feel on top of things once more. This was his natural state of mind, one entirely unaffected by his recent history, which was that aside from the few murders he had been able to accomplish, every plan he had hatched since leaving prison had ended in failure. The constant inner voice was crooning to him now, telling him he was the king of the world, untouchable, a little god. He turned south on Ninth, and headed toward the Penn Station area and Holy Redeemer.

"How did it go?" Marlene asked. It was after midnight, Marlene was watching celebrities make chitchat on the TV, and Karp had just walked in, looking worn and disgusted.

"That is a piece of work, little Karen," he said, sitting down on the couch. "You were right, though. She doesn't want to go to jail. In fact, that was actually the first thing she said to me when I sat down. No 'hello, how are you, glad to meet you,' just 'I am **not** going to jail.' "

"It's true, no one has manners these days," she said, as he kicked off his shoes and plopped down with a sigh on the couch next to her. She muted the chatter on the set. "So, is she?"

"Probably not, since she's the only conspirator who knows the whole story. Fong's guy, whoever he is, acted as a cutout between Cherry and Karen. You know what the chances of us finding an anonymous Chinese gentleman who does not want to be found are. Fong we have nothing on without Karen, and nothing on Karen without either Fong or Palmisano. Conceivably we could have assembled a circumstantial case against the bunch of them using Cherry's testimony, but you messed up the possibility of using the girl as a witness."

"And if I hadn't muscled her, we wouldn't know any of this."

"Wrong, Marlene. You could've told me your suspicions, we could've brought the girl in, had a talk with her, with her parent along, as required by law. We could have read her the perjury statute, and the penalties therein, and she would've cracked."

"You're sure of that."

"Dear, the day I can't break a lying fifteen-year-old girl is the day I hang it up. And with that, we could've raided Fong, and audited him, and traced the payoff to Cherry, and maybe even found the guy who picked up the material from her. And then we would've had Karen Agnelli in a bind. As it is, we have to give a walk to the chief conspirator to nail the peripheral ones, which is not how it's supposed to work. Why the hell did you do it?"

She stared at the pretty people on the screen. They seemed to be having a good time, even without sound. What was the answer to her husband's perfectly legitimate question? She didn't know. It had something to do with velocity. She'd taken on Paul Agnelli's problem and she didn't want it anymore. She wanted to go away again.

"The bomb," she said. "Raney. Nora. The kids."

"I don't understand: what has all that to do with Agnelli?"

"Ah, don't **grill** me, okay? I know it doesn't make sense. I've stopped making sense, okay?" She picked up the remote and made laughter fill the room.

Karp snatched the remote from her and clicked the set off. "This is important," he said. "What's going on? Talk to me, Marlene!"

She turned to face him, so that her remaining eye could fix his. "You want to know what's going on? It's just blood lust, darling. I want to get the people who killed Nora Raney, just like I wanted to get the people who shot Giancarlo. And I couldn't so I took it out on a dumb-ass dope dealer and a silly teenage girl. I know it's crazy and irrational, I know that it's the law's business to find those people and put them away. And, lest you get all bent out of shape, I have no project under way to find them. Or Felix. But the feeling is in me. I want to see their blood. Should I go see someone about this? Yes. Will I? Probably not. I don't believe in psychotherapy. It's a faith, like Catholicism. You have to believe, on the basis of exactly zero evidence, that your malad-justments are due to the fact that Dad diddled you at age ten or Mom didn't love you. Or that your brain soup has the wrong kinds of molecules in it. And I don't."

"So, what **do** you believe?"

"I don't know. In fate. In doom. That I can't be with the people I love because my presence puts them in danger. That I'm an instrument of justice manipulated by powers outside this plane of exis-tence, divine or demonic, I can't really tell. I need to get back to the island."

"Do you understand how crazy what you just said is?"

"Yes, I do, actually. Which means I'm probably

still technically sane, at least in the eyes of the law. Speaking of which, now that you're going to be DA, my exploits are going to come under a good deal more scrutiny. I've just more or less admitted to you that I've committed serious felonies. Let me enumerate: possession of a silencing device, one count; criminal possession of a weapon, two counts; prohibited use of weapon, two counts; menacing, two counts; unlawful imprisonment, second, two counts. I think that's it. It's enough."

"What're you doing, Marlene?"

"I'm confessing to an officer of the law. Maybe jail is the best place for me."

Karp stood up. "No, you're just messing with my head," he said coldly. He felt cold, in fact, the cold of outer space. His wife was receding from him at speed, like an astronaut cut from her tether. "You can't confess to your spouse, as you very well know, but feel free to contact the police. I'm going to bed. You'll let me know your plans."

In the morning she was gone, with her dog and many of her cold weather garments. On the kitchen table was a workmanlike note describing in sufficient detail all the hoops that had to be gone through to get the boys registered in school, and a list of household reminders and contacts—doctors, plumbers, repairpersons, and all the various entities necessary to support a middle-class family in Manhattan. Marlene was severing.

His daughter asked him what was wrong when she came into the kitchen, so he supposed it showed on his face. "Your mom's off again. She left a note."

Lucy read it. "This is not good. It reads like she's not coming back."

"My thought, too."

"Well, don't worry, I can handle this stuff. Do you want me to make coffee?"

"No, sit down."

He sat, too, at the kitchen table, with Marlene's note fuming between them like a contract with the devil. "Listen, you are not, repeat not, going to leap into your mother's role around this house. You're still a kid, you're in college, you need to have a college kid's life. In fact, I think it would be a good idea if you finished up at Boston."

"I can't do that," she said instantly. "How will you manage? What about the boys?"

"I'll manage fine. If I need help, I'll hire it. In fact, I might even rent this place out and get an apartment in a doorman building. With a full-time housekeeper. I'm going to be a big shot with a car and driver and a bodyguard. And the boys are almost twelve. They can mostly look after themselves."

Lucy was about to object that the boys could not look after themselves, and would get into any number of scrapes if they were once outside the eagle eye of their sister, but then thought better of it. Being the district attorney was a completely different thing from being a mere minion thereof, even the chief minion. Her father would have police at his beck in any reasonable numbers. The Karp family had outgrown amateur security. Something in her sighed relief, and also whispered more enticingly of escape from the swamp her family had become and into if not precisely the arms of her boyfriend, at least into his daily presence.

"Okay," she said. "I guess you're right."

"You're sure? You're not going to go up there writhing in Catholic guilt?"

"No, I'm fine," she said, and gave him one of those illuminating smiles. "Sad but happy."

After the public announcement of John Keegan's nomination to the federal bench and the somewhat later and lower-key announcement that Karp had been nominated to fill his term, the usual King Lear power magic occurred on the eighth floor of the courthouse. Keegan immediately became a nullity as far as the DA's office was concerned, and all his power and influence flowed to Karp, even though Keegan was still formally the district attorney. Because Keegan was not actually retiring from public life (indeed, might even be said to be rising in it), there was no dimunition of phone calls or visits to his office. But as far as the DA's operations were concerned, Karp was in practical terms the DA. Those satraps—bureau chiefs and others—who had crony or political associations with Keegan, or who had rivalrous relations with Butch Karp, now either had to start looking for other work or, if they wanted to stay, had to come and render obeisance to the new magnifico.

To Karp's wonder, this latter group seemed perfectly natural in their expressions of congratulations and support, even though several of them, to his certain knowledge, hated his guts and had badmouthed him and worked to undermine him for years. During these sessions he experienced feelings he could not recall having previously, swollen bullfrog feelings, satisfaction of boot-on-neck feelings.

"What's the matter, boss? You look queasy," Murrow observed after one of these sessions.

"I **am** queasy. I can't get used to being brown-nosed shamelessly. I want to say, 'Oh, fuck you, you slob, kissing my ass will not preserve your miserable job for a single day,' but I don't. Somehow it's not allowed. Strange."

"Yes. And we recall Lord Acton's famous apothegm, don't we?"

"Yeah. Are we corrupt yet?"

"I certainly am, since I'm browned by a lot

more people than you are, being more accessible. I kind of like it, because I know that the hatred focused on the guy who guards the access to the great man and speaks with his voice is a thousand times greater than the hatred focused on the great man himself. And I'm really such a nice guy. So let them writhe in the dust."

"I'll pretend you didn't say that, Murrow," replied Karp, thinking now about power and how very much of it he had: that there are few public officials in American life whose power is more absolute within a defined sphere than that of a district attorney.

"Speaking of writhing," said Murrow, "Ms. Rachman is out there. You want her to come in, or should we make her sweat some of her make-up off."

"No cruelty, Murrow," said Karp. "Send her in. And stay yourself."

Laura Rachman came in in a suit so bright blue that it looked like it had been snipped from a French flag. She was wearing a white blouse and a red, white, and blue scarf, giving her the look of a Fourth of July float. She sat and they made pleasantries for a few minutes, during which it was perfectly apparent that Ms. Rachman was just as prepared to kiss ass as any other subordinate manager in the office. Karp, however, stifled a particularly fulsome trope by saying, "We need to talk about what we're going to do about Terry Palmisano."

"I've suspended her and she's going to resign."

"You read the investigative report I had the DA squad prepare?"

"Yes. It's incredibly shocking. I had no idea she was involved with a witness."

"Uh-huh, well, the problem is that it was a lot more than being involved with a witness."

"Honestly, I didn't even know Terry was gay," said Rachman, and added, with a rueful laugh, "not that there's anything wrong with that." Karp had observed that there was a class of people who did not register negative information and instead filled the air with non sequitur comments, as here. He said, "I assume you read the Q and A we did on Karen Agnelli."

"Yes, and obviously we've dropped the case. I personally called the husband to apologize. He doesn't sound like he's going to sue, thank God."

"Now, **focus** on this, Laura," said Karp in a more demanding tone. "It has nothing to do with lesbian passion and nothing to do with the husband or lawsuits. It has to do with only one thing: an attorney in this office has knowingly submitted false evidence in a criminal case and wittingly accepted perjured testimony. It's not a question of her resigning; I want her disbarred and I want her in prison. And I want you personally to prepare the case against her."

"Me? Wouldn't that be a felony bureau case?"

"I don't care about the bureaucratic partitions.

It's your mess and you have to clean it up. Next, I've scheduled a press conference for seven-thirty tomorrow morning. In it I will break the story of how an innocent man was framed with the connivance of the district attorney's office. I will introduce you and you will stand up there and endure public humiliation as you explain every detail of this miserable farce. I expect the headlines will read 'Gay Love Nest Corrupts Rape Bureau at DA.'"

Rachman opened her mouth to say something, but Karp shook his head and drove on.

"Next, you will dismiss the case against Dr. Kevin Hirsch, which I'm sure you realize is a pile of horseshit, even without the now suspect involvement of Terry Palmisano."

"Oh, I see we're letting off all the white boys today."

"Only those who haven't done anything. You know, one of the things that breaks the liberal heart is that people who've been oppressed for however many centuries, when they escape from oppression it never occurs to them to say, 'Hey, being oppressed is **bad,** so let's not do any oppression.' No, they pile on to whoever's available with both boots. Isn't that sad and wonderful? But we're not going to do oppression around here. No one's going to use this office to get even. Now, you have patently wasted prosecutorial time on two cases that I know about, in a city that is crawling with bona fide male sexual predators. That's a crime, Laura, a **shandah**. I expct you to come down on those genuine bad guys like a ton of bricks, regardless of race or social status. I want them put in jail forever, if possible. But we are not going to give a free pass to every black female that accuses a white man. We are going to—for crying out loud—**look** at the fucking evidence! Do you understand the distinction I just made?"

But Rachman didn't answer this question. Instead, with a half smile on her face, she asked, "When you say every detail, would that include the involvement of your wife? Including your wife's, ah, interaction with Cherry Newcombe?"

So Laura had done her homework. Karp answered, "Of course. I expect you to be as forth-coming as possible. Also, should you come across any material that would prompt a criminal com-plaint against Marlene Ciampi, I would expect you to pursue it. You would inform me in such a case so that I could recuse myself from any super-visory responsibility. Finally, I want your resigna-tion on my desk by close of business today."

"You're **firing** me?" Rachman's face blanched, making her face paint look more than it usually did like an amateur spray finish on an old car.

"Not at this time. I've asked all the bureau chiefs for their resignations. When I take over officially in a couple of months I'll decide which of them to accept."

"You're sure you'll be allowed to take over officially if that business with your wife comes out?"

"That's up to the governor, Laura. What's up to
me is telling you to do the three things I just told
you to do, failing any of which I **will** fire you. Are
we perfectly clear about all this?"

Apparently so. Rachman left. Murrow said,
"Whew! **That** was certainly a high colonic. Do
you think she's going to go after your wife?"

"She might. She's vindictive enough. But
Marlene's a big girl, with a lot of money and a brilliant legal mind. In any case, it's not a suitable subject for speculation in this office, is it, Murrow."

"No, sir. But **are** you going to can her?"

"I might. But maybe she'll come around.
Maybe no one ever kicked her in the butt
before. I certainly needed kicks in the butt at her
age, and of course you do, too. In any case,
everybody gets a second chance in Karp's All-
Star Technicolor Flying Circus and Peep Show."

Lucy Karp had inherited from her father the
peculiar notion that the cure for emotional
exhaustion was hard work. She put in a morning
serving free breakfasts to kids in a church basement at Third and Avenue B, and then did a food
distribution—dented cans and past–sell date
items at a grocery warehouse on Hudson Street,
and then traveled uptown with a group of

Catholic Workers to hand out a pallet-load of surplus blankets and ponchos at a refugee center in Inwood. In each of these places her language skills were invaluable. New York was full of people who had dropped into the twenty-first century from the far elsewhere and were hurting in various ways. She forgot about her own troubles, which was part of the deal, too, as it seemed that a crazy mother, a broken family, and a case of sexual frustration did not make the top ten among the afflictions of mankind.

She finished at the refugee center at about seven, had soup and bread with the Catholic Workers in a nearby church hall, and walked out onto Dyckman Street to find it had started to rain. An actual cool breeze was coming from the nearby Hudson. She reached into the big military sack she habitually lugged through her life and drew out a Gore-Tex anorak. There was a bodega nearby and she went in and got a coffee and hung out under the red-and-yellow plastic awning, watching the rain increase in volume, and watching all the people who couldn't afford Gore-Tex anoraks trying to cover themselves with newspapers or plastic trashbags.

Then she saw, across the wide street, dimly through the sheets of rain, a familiar figure, the red doorman's coat, baggy cutoffs, the floppy hat with the skeins of fishing line wrapped around it: Hey Hey Elman doing his little dance. He seemed to have seen her and was gesturing and calling her name. She waved him over, but he shook his head violently and beckoned to her. He seemed more agitated than usual, and this might mean that he was having one of his spells. Hey Hey was normally as harmless as a bunny, but sometimes he decided that some passerby had stolen his thoughts and sought to have them returned, starting a conversation with that person from which it was nearly impossible to withdraw. Which meant the cops, and rough handling, and tears, and having to go down to some precinct to get him released to New York Psychiatric. Lucy had done this herself several times and did not look forward to doing it again. Hey Hey was turning in little circles now, flapping his arms—something she had not seen him do before. She tossed her container in the trash, pulled up her hood, and dashed into the traffic.

When she reached the other side of Dyckman, Hey Hey was half a block away, still beckoning. She shouted for him to wait up, but he just beckoned more urgently and skipped away around the corner. They headed west toward Broadway and the park. Just past Sherman Avenue there was a fire site, a five-story building gutted black and gaping with boarded window holes above a heavily gangster-decorated plywood fence. The fence had long since been penetrated by people seeking salvage or a place to shoot up. Lucy saw Hey

Hey duck behind a plywood flap dedicated to the work of RAMON 178. After a moment's hesitation she followed.

Inside, the usual rubble lot, decorated with broken plumbing fixtures, rotting furniture, rusting appliances, and scorched rubble. She saw a flash of red ahead that quickly disappeared into an irregularly shaped blackness, the entrance to the former basement. She stumbled forward through the junk. The rain was coming down harder than before, the breeze had turned into an actual wind, lightning flashed and thunder echoed like cannonades through the Manhattan canyonlands. She laughed to herself and thought, Yes, the pathetic fallacy, the image of my life, chasing a lunatic through a hurricane into a ruin.

She stood for a moment blinking in the dark. Hey Hey was nowhere in sight. She shouted, but nothing came back but dull echoes and the sound of innumerable freshets burbling through the roofless building. When her eyes adjusted she found she was on a brick ledge a few feet above a rubbled slope that led, she guessed, down to the original basement floor. Then there was a sound, a groan, and a sharp, high shout. She scrambled down the rubble and onto concrete.

The air was damp and the damp brought out the smells—burnt things, mold, broken sewage pipes, rats both live and dead. From her bag she took the little Maglite she kept on her keychain.

Its narrow beam shone on standing water; the basement was flooded and she had to walk carefully, feeling beneath the black water with her sneakered foot. Another cry just ahead, and there was a glow. Lucy thought it must be another sick one sheltering in the ruins, like the one Hey Hey had led her to before. She reached into her bag to make sure she had her cell phone.

Candlelight was shining from what must have once been the building's boiler room. The boilers were gone, carted off for scrap, but the walls still held twisted stumps of pipes and the floor was a tangle of rusty plumbing. She saw the candle, stuck in a beer bottle, and saw its light reflecting from Hey Hey's red coat. She moved toward him, saying, "Oh, there you are. Why didn't you wait up, man?" She saw him hang his hat on a pipe. That was wrong. Hey Hey never took off his hat. The man turned. Lucy said, "Oh, shit!" and spun and leaped for the door, but she stumbled on a pipe and he had her. He was incredibly strong. His forearm around her neck felt like a tree limb. It only took a few seconds for Felix to choke her into unconsciousness.

Felix Tighe looked on his work and found it good. The bitch was naked and spread-eagled on a frame of one-inch piping, her legs stretched as far as they would stretch, her arms in a crucifixion position. The wacko had been carrying half a dozen rolls of tape in his belong-ings, which had come in handy; a good omen, Felix thought. He had neglected to buy tape, and he thought it amusing that the victim had supplied tape not only sufficient to immobilize himself but enough to take care of Lucy Karp, as well. The guy's clothes stank, however, and Felix was anxious to get this over with and get back into his own clean ones. Not so anxious that he would leave anything interesting out of his forthcoming session with the cunt.

A clank and a scraping sound told him she had revived. He had three candles arranged to cast light on her face and body and he watched avidly. He loved to see them when they woke up and realized where they were and started to understand what was going to happen to them. The best part of the present setup was that he didn't need a gag. With the thunderstorm and the isolated venue, no one was going to hear her yell. Another really terrific omen.

But the expression on her face was not what he was expecting. She wasn't looking at him in horror at all, but staring at something in the corner of the room, behind him. He snapped a look around; nothing. Then she began to speak, as if to someone standing right there, pausing as if to listen to a reply, and then speaking again. She was speaking in Spanish, not the jailhouse Caribbean Spanish he was familiar with, but a pure, lisping Castilian.

Lucy awoke to pain and a dark, nauseous

headache. Hard things were pressing into her back and her thighs ached. She knew exactly where she was and what had happened to her, but no terror stabbed her belly or made her tremble. Instead, all her attention was focused on a dim figure standing in the corner of the room, a middle-aged somewhat plump woman dressed in the black-and-white habit of the Carmelites. The woman had three small moles on her face, which was otherwise distinguished by a long nose, huge round eyes, bushy eyebrows, and a perfect rosebud mouth.

"Is this one of His jokes?" Lucy asked the figure in her native tongue. "I went through agonies to preserve my precious virginity and now I'm going to be raped and murdered in a cellar?"

"It is somewhat amusing, I suppose," said Saint Teresa. "No more amusing, perhaps, than that a woman such as I, who lived only for delight, and fine clothes, and witty companions should have founded a strict order of cloistered contemplative nuns. You can have no idea of the dullness of the conversation of young, ignorant Castilian girls. If it happens as you imagine, I hope you commend your soul to Him and give thanks that you have had the great good fortune to be tortured to death as He was. What an honor! I knew many who would envy you your situation."

"That's a point of view, Reverend Mother," said Lucy, at which the apparition gave her the kind of God-haunted grin one only ever sees on the faces of people far advanced in holiness, and Lucy burst out laughing.

"Who the fuck . . . what the fuck are you laughing about!" Felix screamed. "You think this is funny? How about this, you think **this** is funny?"

With which he began to torture Lucy with his knife, and was happy to see that she howled appropriately.

"You're not laughing now, are you, bitch?" he said. It was not as good as he thought it would be, and he was starting to get pissed. He asked her where the Vietnamese was, and she told him he was in Paris, but she didn't know any more. Felix didn't think that was worth too much, but maybe something. Maybe she knew more and wasn't telling yet. But she would.

The problem was that he was causing her pain, but not fear, and so it was about as much fun as torturing an animal: okay, but nothing special, not like doing Mary and the brat or the others, before prison. She was not begging for mercy. On the contrary, she seemed to be praying for Felix's soul and forgiving him for what he was doing to her. She also wanted to know about the goddamn looney he got the clothes off of, and he took pleasure in telling her that her looney was resting quietly and would be released unharmed in time to put on his bloody clothes and take the rap for what Felix was going to do to Lucy. To which she had replied only, "Thank God he's all right."

The worst of it was that he needed the fear to get sexy and so far his attempts at raping her had been unavailing. He used the handle of the knife instead, but it wasn't the same. No, he was going to actually have to cut parts off her to get her off this God shit and make her understand that **he** was what she needed to worship, the center of everything, the only thing worthy of any attention at all. The problem with that, unfortunately, is that once you started to cut pieces off they went into shock real fast and checked out, and then it was just meat, and not as much fun, although fooling with the body and thinking about the people who would find it gave him a giggle or two. But he was still a little annoyed that she had turned out to be some no-fun religious maniac. He voiced this thought to his victim as he idly twirled the point of his knife under her small breast.

"I'm not a maniac," she said and cried out as he increased the pressure. She felt no need at all to be stoic.

"I bet you think **I'm** a maniac, though, don't you?" This was a fun game. You asked them a question and however they answered, you zapped them and when they finally agreed with you, you zapped them to say the opposite.

"No, you're not a maniac, either," she said. "You're a demon. **He's** the maniac."

At which she looked over his shoulder at something, like she had before. Felix paid no attention. He grabbed the substance of her breast in his left fist and set his blade for the stroke that would slice it off. He was kneeling awkwardly upon the pipe arrangement, the backs of his knees exposed by Hey Hey's baggy cutoffs, so that it was really no problem for David Grale to roll in, and in one smooth, and, Lucy thought, obviously well-practiced motion, slice through both of Felix's hamstring tendons.

Felix screamed shrilly and flopped around among the pipes like a landed tuna. His knife clattered away. David Grale searched out a short length of pipe and whacked him a few times on the head.

"Don't kill him!" Lucy cried.

"Good Christ, Lucy, look at what he did to you! Isn't that an excess of forgiveness?"

"Shame on you, David," she said, "and thank you. Could you unwrap me, please?"

The fileting knife that Grale used went to work and, in half a minute, Lucy was free. She tried to stand up, but found she could not. He lifted her and carried her a few yards to where some junkie had once made a bed out of cardboard and pink insulation.

"You need to get to a hospital. You still have your cell phone?"

"My bag, if it's still around." As he went to

search for it, Lucy thought, This is odd: I'm naked and bleeding, but I'm perfectly comfortable with him. Maybe I'm going into shock.

There were sounds now, and voices. Into the boiler room came several people Lucy recognized from Spare Parts, and with them Spare Parts himself. The giant came to her side and spread an army blanket over her. "Oh, 'ucy, you 'oor sing! Oh!" cried Spare Parts. On his face was an expression of almost childlike grief. Grale came near, too, and handed Lucy her cell phone. "They're on their way. You may want to call home."

"Thank you," said Lucy, and broke down in hysterical sobs. This lasted for some time. The wounds she had endured were really starting to hurt now, and around the corners of her mind slunk fears that she had been permanently maimed. When she had somewhat recovered herself she asked, "How did you know where I was?"

"People have been following you, dear. The invisible people had you in view. I'm just sorry we didn't get here any sooner."

"Soon enough. Did you call the cops, too? I mean, for him."

"'e'll 'ake 'are ah 'im," said Spare Parts.

"You mustn't hurt him," she said sternly.

"We won't touch him," said Grale, with his most saintly smile.

• • •

Felix awoke and realized immediately that he was being carried on foot by several men. The pain in his legs and the back of his head was enormous, but even worse was his fear. He was a cripple now, and would be for some time. He had to get to a doc, even if it meant turning himself in. He escaped once, he could escape again, but he had to get fixed up. He was being transported in some kind of tarpaulin; there was rough canvas against his face. They were probably taking him to a police station, he thought, because if they were going to kill him he'd be dead by now. Bunch of piss bums. Who could figure?

He had tape against his mouth and around his hands. He tested the bonds and felt a little satisfaction. An amateur job: he could get out of this with a little work, maybe an hour or two—tape stretched and his wrists were mighty. The canvas was damp and he heard the patter of drops against it. They were traveling through the streets. He could smell the rain.

Then the rain stopped and there was another smell, smoke and cooking food, and he was put down for a while. He kept working on his wrists and controlling his breathing. He felt himself being picked up again. They were taking him head first and the general direction was downward, because his head felt lower than his feet. That was good because his legs didn't ache so much when they were a little elevated. This went on for some time. He had about a quarter of an inch of play now between his crossed wrists.

Then he felt his head go much lower and he was sliding. He felt the canvas rush past his face and then smooth damp soil and small pebbles against the back of his head, and then sheer dread as he flew through space. It was only for a moment, however, for he landed heavily on his back and felt the horrible stroke of agony as his useless legs followed and hit the ground. The darkness was absolute. He heard the drip of water and a rustling sound, and smelled a dank stench. He was in a sewer.

He heard something—not so much rustling as a light clicking. He wondered what it was. Then he felt something heavy moving on his leg and something else climb up on his chest. Now he knew what that sound was. There were a lot of them; he could smell their stink, sharper than the sewer gas. Warm weight pressed on his face. He twisted and humped and made noises behind his gag. The rats did him the favor of chewing this away in order to get to his delicious soft mouth parts, and so he could scream and scream as they ate the face off his skull.

—— Now Again

18

"NO, STUPENAGEL, THEY DIDN'T HAVE A point," Karp snapped. "It happens to be the case, one, that the vast majority of black and Hispanic defendants are ill-defended easy outs; and two, that the insanity defense is what it is largely so that people with expensive lawyers, most of whom happen to be white, can avoid prison. It's part of the system, like the kid who sells an ounce of smack gets ten in Attica and the guy who loots a hundred million from the pension fund and wrecks the lives of ten thousand people gets, maybe, six months in a country club jail. I never said it was fair. It's just what we got."

"You seem to have made your peace with it, regardless."

"That shows how much **you** know," said Karp. Her eyes widened with interest. I'm making a serious mistake here, thought Karp. I'm a public official getting drunk with a reporter, and if I'm not careful, I'm going to spill my guts and get into trouble. He then considered that, although he had been in trouble many times before, he had not ever got into this particular kind of trouble. It was not great virtue; he just didn't drink and never had. Then he thought, and here the unbidden idea surprised him, that maybe it was time he did. Was that the booze talking? Was this how it happened, the descent into disgrace? He found he didn't much care and took another sip of the cognac. It seemed to grow smoother the more you drank. Stupenagel was looking at him with a peculiar smile, and her face seemed to glow.

"You never make peace with it," he said. "It just grinds you down, like a pencil in a pencil sharpener. Dickens said something about it, the inevitable hardening of the soul that results from a life in the courts. You just live with it. You have technical pride—is the case as perfect as you can make it? Even though, **even though,** we can put guys in jail behind shitty half-baked cases, because the defense is overworked and second rate a lot of the time and lame, and also, do you have the stones to drop a case when it's not perfect, even though the guy's probably guilty and it pisses off the victims and the cops, and the media make a big thing of it? Thin soup, but that's all we have."

"What happens when the pencil is ground down to the eraser?"

"Oh, well, that hasn't happened yet," said Karp. "I have a very long pencil."

A long honking laugh from the reporter. "So anyhow, you let the big one get away. How did you feel?"

"How do you feel always asking people how they feel? Why does the media do that?"

"It sells. People are voyeurs. They're dead inside most of the time, so when someone's kid gets burned up they like to see the mike shoved in the mom's face. The amazing thing is that the mom usually loves the attention. Was Rohbling the bottom of the barrel, do you think? The most evil?"

"Oh, no way," said Karp instantly. "Rohbling was, in fact, a nut. I argued that he wasn't, but he was. We had an eleven-year-old a couple of years ago who killed both his parents, same thing. Also with a screw missing. But there **is** evil."

"You think so?" she said. "It depends on how you define evil. I had an interview once with a man who ordered the massacre of an entire village in Guatemala. He was right there watching his men murder old women and little kids. He had no regrets. He thought it was necessary to suppress the Communists. Slept like a baby. Wanted to sleep with me, too, although probably not like a baby."

"Did you let him?" asked Murrow.

Karp and Stupenagel both stared at him. The

reporter laughed, that astounding bellow. "Why, Murrow, I thought you'd drifted off to bye-byes. What flattering curiosity, too! As a matter of fact, I didn't, but not because he was a brutal mass-murdering scumbag piece of shit. The problem was he had the most appalling bad breath; it was as if his conscience had crawled into his glottis and died. I have, however, shared my silky body with men who could have eaten that fellow for breakfast. I have unusual tastes . . ."—here she batted her thickly mascaraed eyelashes at Murrow and licked her lips in a parody of lasciviousness—". . . which is probably why I'm not married and driving my little girls to soccer practice. My point, however, was that doing things that most of us would consider grossly evil seems to have no effect on the personality, precisely because no one really believes that anything they do is really evil. There's always a justifying excuse. Eichmann famously went to the gallows with the perfectly clear conscience of a man who just did his duty. Milosevic is outraged that the Hague tribunal thinks he did anything wrong. So evil is something we call other people, people we don't agree with, or else a word we use for a particularly gross violation of the law. Shooting a liquor store clerk is bad. Raping and murdering lots of little girls is evil. The first represents nothing but a difference in power: the winners get to say what's evil. The second is an essentially mean-

ingless verbal enhancer, like 'heinous' or 'inhuman.' Or don't you agree?"

"I don't. Everyone knows right and wrong, no
matter how much they rationalize it or deny it.
Even the Nazis knew they were doing wrong, and
they had a whole elaborate system for making
thousands of murderers think they were doing the
world a favor. But they kept it real dark, even to
the end, and they denied that any of it took place."
He paused. The word "evil" was not one he used
in the courtroom; he didn't think it added anything
to an argument, and it rarely crossed his lips in
everyday speech. He had been surprised, just now,
to hear the word slip out of his mouth. He continued, "Well, it's a religious rather than a legal term,
isn't it? My daughter's take on it is that it's real and
palpable, but then she believes in God and the
devil. She thinks that what makes evil evil is the
lie. Your guy really didn't massacre helpless people, he was fighting communism. The pedophile
isn't really raping children because the children
really like it. Every crook I ever met had an
excuse. In fact, that's how we nail most of them.
They're actually anxious to tell their sad story.
How I didn't mean any harm. How she made me
do it. Lucy thinks that demonic forces actually get
into people and whisper this kind of shit into their
heads, and that's why they do stuff that doesn't
make any rational sense. Man kills wife, kids, self."

"It's a theory," said Stupenagel. "How is little

Lucy, by the way? Not so little anymore. God, how the years fly! I don't know how I'd feel having a little time clock staring me in the face every day. My child is an adult? My child is fucking guys, having babies? Tick tock." She shuddered. "Or maybe not. Has she recovered?"

Karp didn't like to talk about what had happened to his daughter. "I guess. She seems all right. She goes to school in Boston. She just came back for the Christmas break."

"He tortured her, I heard. You must have used mucho chips to keep it out of the press."

"I did and I will continue to do so," he said coldly, and with his sternest look.

"Sor-ry. And you never actually found the scumbag?"

"The case was closed by forensic evidence."

"I heard someone left a cleaned skull in a plastic bag in a church."

"No comment."

"Oh, please! We're just talking. I heard there were little gnaw marks all over it."

"What part of 'no comment' didn't you understand, Stupenagel?"

"Okay, okay. So she's fine. Well, good. Any dish in her life, or is she still on that virginity kick?"

"You'd have to ask her," said Karp, with an increased chill in his tone, and gave her another and more intense blast of the Karp Stare. The reporter let her eyes slide away from his and chuckled. "Maybe I will. I assume she's still with the languages? How many does she know, now?"

"I don't know, fifty or sixty."

"Christ! Yet another thing to be envious about. Here I am traveling in obscure corners of the world and aside from French and Spanish I can barely order a drink or ask where's the bathroom. Speaking of which, where is it? I have to take a slash."

Karp told her. She unfolded herself from her chair like a complex doll. Karp was not surprised to see that, although she had drunk more than the two men put together, she did not weave or stagger.

"Don't go anywhere, boys," she called out. "This is starting to be fun." She slammed the door closed with a twitch of her hip.

"You're rolling your eyes, Murrow," said Karp. "Does that mean you're falling in love?"

"Oh, yeah, I'm totally smitten. Christ, what a monster! But I'll admit to a certain morbid fascination, like watching a crocodile eat a deer. Is she always like that?"

"As far as I know. According to my wife, she's utterly unreliable as a friend and entirely lacking in moral values, aside from bravery and fanatical devotion to journalism. She's very good, too. She gets the story. Marlene says she likes to be around Stupe because she's the only person she knows who makes her feel like a good person in comparison."

"Is she serious? About lusting after you?"

"I think so. We've had some odd moments over the years. The occasional grope. I always say, 'no, thanks,' and she takes it with a laugh, like now."

"What if you said 'yes, please'?"

"Oh, she'd be in the rack in a heartbeat. She has a kind of competititive thing with Marlene, from years back. Marlene apparently didn't put out much in college and Stupe was always stalking her boyfriends with sex."

"And they're still friends?"

"Yes. The human heart is mysterious. The heart has its reasons."

"You're waxing philosophical, boss."

"I'm waxing drunk. I may throw up on the governor. I believe that's what Brenda Starr in the girls' can is kind of hoping for."

"Is that a real danger?"

"I don't know. I doubt it. I'll probably nod off in a while, get up choking on vomit, stagger into the toilet and puke, and then emerge as a steely-eyed and sober public servant with a massive headache. It's my bon vivant mode. Is that a pitying look, Murrow?"

"No. But if you don't mind my saying so, you've had a rough time recently. Maybe you should take a break."

"I do mind your saying so," snapped Karp. "I'm fine. I can do my job fine."

Murrow got up. "Maybe I should take off."

"Sit down!" Karp ordered. "If you think I'm going to let you leave me alone, drunk, with the dragon lady of American journalism, you're nuts."

Murrow sat down. He poured himself another little drink.

A long silence ensued. In the distance telephones rang and there was an occasional metallic clang from the barely functioning heating system.

Marlene had not intended to attend Karp's coronation. She had avoided the city since Lucy's release from New York Hospital in September and thought she would be wrongfooted to appear as the Wife in her husband's moment of triumph. Also, she thought her wide reputation as an unindicted violent felon would not add luster to the occasion. But when she expressed these thoughts during a phone conversation with her daughter, she got an earful, including an accusation that her hesitance had nothing whatever to do with diffidence or finer feelings, but stemmed entirely from her monstrous narcissistic ego and her superstitious, moronic paranoia, the diatribe ending with the threat that if Marlene did not attend this party she would not be invited to Lucy's wedding. Marlene meekly acquiesced; she found she was willing to avoid present pain in the form of her daughter yelling at her even if it promised greater pain in the future: returning to the city, seeing her husband and children. So she'd become a moral coward, too. It didn't matter much. It was just days. When she thought about it, she realized she had gotten her wish. She was more and more like the dogs. She thought she might as well let Billy Ireland fuck her. Why not? She didn't care for the flirty tension anymore, it was too much like having a real personality. But she would only let him do her dog style. That would be most suitable. First, though, this trip to town.

She had, of course, no suitable clothes at the farm. Buy a new outfit? No, she had a closet full of costly garments from her brief stint as an IPO millionaire. But they were all at the loft, which meant she would have to go back there. Could she sneak in and out? No, the boys and Lucy were on winter break from school. Was she so low that she would buy an outfit she didn't need and would never wear again just because she didn't have the courage to face her children? No, that was lower than letting her dog boy fuck her from behind. She was mildly surprised to see that there were still some things beyond her.

So on the Friday morning she left before dawn, having slept hardly at all, and drove west in her truck. The weather reports the night before had been full of the massive storm that had socked Buffalo and smothered Albany and was now whistling down the Hudson Valley like the

Twentieth Century Limited. There were only two inches on the ground when she got out of the tunnel, but traffic was already incurably snarled, even without the tunnel security delays. It was just past 8:30 in the morning when she came up into the gray daylight of Manhattan. The hundred-mile trip had taken her four and a half hours.

"She's been gone a long time," said Murrow. He was starting to feel the liquor, just a trace of blurriness, of fuzzy face, but he was far from drunk. Murrow was of the class, nearly extinct in the city, where children were taught to drink at their parents' table. He had been taking sherry or a light cocktail with his mother from the age of fourteen, and at Brown he had been famous for drinking men twice his size under the table. Karp was over twice his size, but not any kind of a drinker. He looked at his boss and regretted having brought the cognac, for he had not expected the arrival of the reporter, or that the afternoon would have, under her influence, degenerated into a debauch. Karp, he knew, had a tendency to be a little morose, even when cold sober. Murrow did not want to think about how he was going to get Karp into shape to meet the governor in the time remaining. He checked the bottle and glanced at his watch. He prayed for more snow, for blizzards, lightnings, earthquakes.

Karp observed Murrow glancing at his wrist. "Maybe she fell in. Maybe her bladder is the size of the Chrysler Building. Would you like to go to the ladies' and check?"

He spoke with unnatural slowness and deliberation. Murrow thought that Karp had no real idea how drunk he was. That could be a problem. He poured more cognac into his own glass, filling it over the halfway mark. It was one way to keep Karp from drinking much more. If that goddamned woman would just get back and absorb the rest, things might still be rescued.

"No, I think I won't," said Murrow. "She's a big girl."

Two minutes later she reappeared, brandishing a magnum bottle of Veuve Cliquot. Murrow's heart sank; the city was practically shut down by the blizzard and he couldn't imagine where she had found a liquor store open. He expressed this thought, somewhat sourly. "My child," said Stupenagel, "only four things are required of an international correspondent: accuracy, speed, courage, and the ability to find alcoholic beverages any place in the world at any hour." She yanked out the cork with a bang and a flourish.

"Some people think it's vulgar to make a loud pop when you open wine," said Murrow, but held out his glass.

"Well, they're not invited to our party, are they?" she said, pouring. "I was in the can, and I thought, Hey, it's a celebration, we require champagne. And also to wash the cognac out of the system, to clear our heads, polish our wits, so we don't disgrace ourselves when the governor arrives. Is he sleeping?"

"Stunned, I think," said Murrow. "You know, you really are a wicked person."

"Wicked?" she exclaimed. "Wicked. That's a word you don't hear much anymore, except as an intensifier in New England. Wicked good maple syrup. What else is wicked besides witches? I can't think of anything. You wouldn't say 'wicked empire,' or 'wicked dictator,' would you? Evil is the classier term, because it's about power, and whatever we say, we can't help loving power. But I like wicked, the implied cleverness in there, the delight in turning things to one's own advantage, outsmarting the goody-goodies, generating a healthy and renewing chaos. As here. Wake up, Karp, it's time for your champagne. Jesus, it's cold in this office. We won't need an ice bucket for the bottle. Is something wrong with the radiators?"

"They've been fixing the system for months," said Murrow. "That, or it's an experiment to see if criminal justice can be improved by rapidly changing the temperature of the courthouse. They've tried everything else. Last summer they actually had the heat on, or so it seemed. At least this building is old enough so that the windows still open. Why are you so intent on getting him drunk?"

"I'm not **getting** him drunk, Murrow. You can't **get** someone drunk nowadays like you could in Victorian novels." She added in an oily voice: " 'Have some Madeira, m'dear.' " Champagne splashed into the glass that Karp held out. He drank some, finding it cooling after the brandy and quite pleasant.

"See?" said Stupenagel. "He wants to get drunk. Why? Perhaps his life has gotten away from him. Perhaps things haven't worked out the way he planned, and he wishes a few blessed moments of oblivion?"

"Perhaps you're a pathetic, lonely alcoholic who wants company," said Karp.

"Oooh!" crowed Stupenagel. "A new side of Karp emerges. See, Murrow, I may be wicked, but that was **cruel.**"

Karp was starting to feel queasy. He couldn't recall what he had eaten for lunch, but if the past was any guide, he would shortly learn what it had been in full Ektachrome. It was twenty years since he had been this drunk at an office event— that horrible, magical night when Marlene had helped him stagger back to his lonely apartment and his life with her had started. They had all been drinking Olde Medical Examiner then, a punch concocted by some wiseasses from the morgue out of fruit juice and absolute alcohol. The present drunk was rather more elegant. He wondered if he would be quite as sick. But other than the messages from his belly, he felt fine. He hadn't thought about Marlene, or what she was doing, or whether she was really going to show up here with his family or not, and he hadn't thought obsessively about his own future, either, for the better part of two hours. He felt enclosed in a comfortable blanket, the fuzz of it against his face, its warmth relaxing his limbs. Everything was going to be just fine. This was why people became drunks, he thought. If you could feel like this all the time, it might make more sense than he had previously imagined to live in a cardboard box and never bathe. He felt a sudden burst of affection for his fellow drunks.

"I'm sorry, Stupenagel," he said. "It was the liquor talking, not me."

"Oh, no offense, Karp," she said. "If I took umbrage at everything said to me during drunken bouts, I wouldn't have any friends left."

"Assuming you had any at the onset of the bout," observed Murrow in a not quite inaudible voice.

"Murrow, what is it with these little digs?" she said, fixing him with her eye. "Would you like a blow job? Would that calm you down? Excuse me, Karp, this will just take a **second.**" She slid off her chair and stumped across the office on her knees for a few feet, with her mouth open, making vacuumlike sounds, and saying, "You know, some of these little skinny guys have the most enormous schlongs. I hope I don't crack my jaw. I hate when that happens."

"I'm sorry," said Murrow, "I have to have my special rubber underwear or it doesn't work."

When they had stopped giggling and Stupenagel was back in her chair, she said, "What were we talking about before Murrow got carried away by his disgusting lusts? Something important . . ."

"Whither modern jurisprudence?" suggested Karp. "Very important."

"Indeed it is. Well, whither? The age of Keegan is about to end. Now begins the age of . . ."

"Please! I don't want to hear it. It's funny, I've just been thinking about the last time I got drunk in this office. Not this office, one of the big bays down on six. We were having a party, and everyone was pretty well oiled, and some of the guys got weapons out of the evidence lockers and they were playing grab-ass cops and robbers, like a bunch of kids. They had some porno films, too. This was when porn was illegal, Murrow, way before your time."

"What, no tits and ass on demand, twenty-four seven?"

"No, Murrow, back then, in order to see it legal you had to go on a date. You had to wear a jacket and tie and buy flowers and beg and tell lies. Anyway, we watched porn films, and got even more fucked up, bras hanging from the light fixtures. . . . And Garrahy found out about it, and hauled all of us up to his office, standing in rows like prisoners in a roll call, and he just reamed us all new assholes. I never heard anything like it, before or since. Because he thought that the DA was like a church and what we did was sacred, and screwing around with it like we did was like blasphemy. He always said, whatever you do on the job, imagine how you'd feel if it got printed on the front page of the **Times**. He believed that and he lived it. And the people like me who came up under that regime never forgot it. We didn't always live up to it, but when we did something slimy we had the grace to feel bad about it. The sad thing was that when he was reaming us out, we could see how old and weak he'd become: he had to stop and catch his breath between excoriations. Ray Guma said it was the last scoop of ice cream in the carton, that speech. It was close to the end of his term, and everyone figured he was going to hang it up, hoist the jersey up to the rafters, and go out with the cheering. Keegan was head of homicide then, and all ready to step into the shoes."

"But he didn't, as I recall," said the reporter. "Garrahy ran again."

"Yeah, he did. I went up to see him one afternoon. I'd done something that deserved a compliment, I forget what it was. And he started talking about leaving, about how it was time for him to go. What do you think, Karp? He asked **me,** a pissant kid. So I said, 'Oh, **no,** Mr. Garrahy, no, everyone wants you to stay. Everyone will come out and work on your campaign, all the staff.' So, instead of retiring he ran again. I managed the campaign, as a matter of fact. Not that the issue was in any doubt. He got another term, and a couple of months later he was dead. The governor appointed a piece of shit to replace him. Sanford Bloom, an actual felon. I don't think Jack Keegan has ever really forgiven me for that."

The radiator now let out a groan that stopped conversation. It sounded as if something heavy and metallic were being dragged over a number of hogs.

"They must still be working down in the basement," said Karp, reaching over to touch the radiator. "Stone cold. Cold as a well digger's ass. Cold as a bail bondsman's heart."

"That's good, Karp," said the reporter. "Have you ever thought about a career in journalism?"

"Briefly, but I failed the aptitude test. You know, where they make you eat raw zebra that's been dead for a week?"

"Mm-mm!" Smacking those large lips. "Love it! So, are we going to freeze now? We could take off all our clothes and crawl under my space blanket. That always works."

"Do you actually have a space blanket?" asked Murrow.

"I do." She groped in her bag and showed a corner of the thing, red and silver. "Prepared for everything, my motto. Alternatively, Murrow, we could kill Karp and crawl inside him for the warmth, like arctic peoples do with dogs."

"Do they really do that? I thought that was just a story."

She shuddered delicately. "They really do, my boy, and I've done it. Why do you think I drag a space blanket around with me?"

Murrow stood up. "Luckily, I know where there's an electric heater. We may not have to eviscerate the chief assistant district attorney. I believe that's a misdemeanor offense."

"Oh, go ahead!" cried Karp. "I don't mind."

"Be right back," said Murrow, and left.

"Leave the door open," said Karp, too late. "What are you doing, Stupenagel?"

She had crossed the intervening space in an instant, and was settling herself on his lap. "Just getting warm. You don't want me to freeze, do you? Would you like to see a special heat-producing trick I learned in Siberia?"

"No."

"How about a plain vanilla, repressed Jewish lawyer little kissee, then?" She grabbed his head and suited the action to the offer. Her mouth tasted faintly of lemons under the various alcohols, quite pleasant, Karp thought, and also thought that if you were a man, and a woman sat on your lap and ran her unusually long and muscular tongue down your throat you could not, no matter how uxorious you felt, scream like a Victorian virgin and slap her face.

She came up for air at last. "There! Wasn't that nice?"

"Yes. Now could you get off me?"

"What is your problem, Karp? We're a couple of grown-ups having grown-up fun, a few scant moments of delight snatched from the general shit pie of life. Don't you think Marlene does it as much as she can?"

"Does she?"

"Of course. With that hunk out there that trains her dogs. You think they play hearts all evening?"

"She's not out there. She's in town, and I expect her at any moment. With the kiddies."

"Then they can all watch." The mouth descended on him again. I must really be drunk, he thought. This must be another reason people drink, besides forgetting their problems. People drink to remove inhibitions, so they can have pleasures they ordinarily forbid themselves. Was he having pleasures? To an extent. This was pleasurable but also slightly sickening, like eating a quart of rocky road ice cream at one sitting.

They heard footfalls and a clanking scrape, as

if someone was maneuvering a large appliance through the narrow dogleg corridor outside Karp's office. Stupenagel immediately began to bounce up and down on Karp's lap, making the chair's springs squeal, and at the same time crying in falsetto, "Oh, God, oh, God, oh, do it, give it to me, oh, that's so good. Ooooh!"

Karp shot to his feet, dumping the reporter onto the floor and knocking the judge's chair over backward. He staggered, became entangled in the legs of the chair, and went down, too. The reporter was hooting laughter as Murrow peeked in, clutching to his bosom a large electric baseboard heater.

"Did I interrupt something?"

"No," said Karp, struggling to stand. There was something wrong with the message center that normally controlled his legs.

"No, we were just finishing up," said Stupenagel. "It was one of the greatest experiences of my life. I feel like a real woman now."

"Oh, shut the fuck up, Stupe!" said Karp, finally upright.

"I could leave," said Murrow. "Just let me find an outlet for this and I'll be gone."

"Take her with you," said Karp as he picked up his chair.

"No, I want more, more, more," said Stupenagel. "You promised!"

"Gosh, boss, this is just like those lawyer TV

shows, where they're always grabbing each other after court. I'll just plug this in—here—and you can have your privacy back."

"Oh, for crying out loud, Murrow, we're not doing anything. This woman is a maniac."

"You have the right to remain silent," Murrow intoned, as Stupenagel laughed like a maniac.

"Turn it on high," said Stupenagel to Murrow as he plugged the thing in. "I want to be covered with greasy sweat. I want my blood to boil."

The two men looked at her, then exchanged a look. "Perhaps a moderate setting," said Murrow, "just to chase the chill. And now that I've done that, why don't I go check with the state people on when this show is going to get going."

He made to leave, but Karp was up so fast that his chair vibrated on its central springs.

"I'll go," he said, almost bodychecking the smaller man on his way out. "I have to go to the . . ."

He was out the door. Murrow shut it and addressed the reporter. "Well, if you don't mind, I think I'll go back to my desk. I have a few things I need to catch up with and—"

"Oh, fuck that, Murrow! Sit your tiny little ass down and have some more wine. It's Friday, for Christ's sake. You have nothing that won't wait." She poured two glasses full of champagne. He was interested to see that, drunk as she was, she did not spill a drop. He took a glass and sat on the couch. She perched on the edge of Karp's desk. She raised her glass. "Dead friends."

They drank. "Have you even got any dead friends, Murrow?"

"A kid from my soccer team in middle school drowned in a boating accident."

Her snorting laugh. "Oh, perfect! That's so American, which is why I spend as little time as I can in my homeland. Let me show you something." She rummaged in her big sack of a purse, removing files, notebooks, a large jar of French Imodium tablets, an Urdu-English Dictionary with no cover, a ball of soiled tissue, a cell phone, and a thick greasy nylon passport wallet. She opened the wallet and plucked out a creased photograph.

"This was taken in the bar of the Summerland Hotel in Beirut in 1982," she said. "That gorgeous creature in the middle is me, if you can believe it. The other five people in it were all killed on the job." She pointed a finger at one grinning face after another. "Beirut, a bomb, about a week after the picture. This one, a sniper in Sarajevo, this one disappeared in Chechnya. Peru, kidnapped. Guatemala, shot at a roadblock. What do you think of that, Murrow?"

"I think it's sad. I think you need some new friends."

"Nobody wants to be my friend anymore. No, that's not true. I don't want to be their friend anymore. Do you know why? Because they all get killed."

"You need friends in safer professions."

"That's a good idea, Murrow. You could be my friend. We could get married. I could get a job on the style section. Or I could marry Karp. Tell me the truth, do you think there's any possibility that he'd dump Ciampi and go for it?"

"He seemed pretty devoted."

"Devoted. That's a great word you don't hear much anymore, except in obits. 'Devoted wife of Abraham Schnitski.' I could write obits, that might be a good way to conclude my career in journalism. Does he ever talk about her?"

"Marlene? No, he tends to keep the private life separate."

"But come on . . . they've been married years. I can't believe he doesn't play around a little. All these cute little lawyerettes tripping around the office, a good-looking alpha-male man, the aphrodisiac of power. Off the record, Murrow."

"Honestly, I really couldn't say."

"Oh, please, Murrow. I'll let you feel me up."

"Really, I don't know anything that would be worth **that**."

"Oh, fuck you. But seriously . . . never? No chewing face in the supply closet with what's-her-name, the little Irish?"

"No. Strange as it seems, he takes his marriage vows seriously. Many people do, you know. It's a point of honor."

"Good Christ! Honor? I've slipped into a time

warp. As long as it's not just **me** that turns him off. I mean, you don't think it's me, do you? I'm losing it, maybe? Oh, God, my entire life ethos has been based on the idea that men are dogs: show them a damp pussy and they have all the discrimination of a cheap windup toy. Honor is not a concept I have seen much associated with the sex act. What is this, a trend? I hope not. The New Victorians. I could do a feature, if I wrote that kind of shit. How about you, Murrow? Do you keep your honor bright?"

"My honor is my loyalty," said Murrow.

She laughed. "Just as the Nazi SS used to say. And you knew that, didn't you? A man with an historical imagination; it makes me all shivery. If only you weren't such a little Murrow. Have some more champagne." She poured, her hand steady as a cliff. "Murrow, could I ask you something?"

"That's all you've been doing."

"No, really. I have to whisper it."

"Oh, go ahead." He felt her hot breath on his ear.

"Do you see that sprinkler head sticking out of the ceiling?"

Murrow looked up. The ceiling was very high, a characteristic feature of office buildings erected before the age of air-conditioning. The brass sprinkler nozzle stuck up from a dropped pipe that ran the length of the room. "What about it?"

She whispered.

"You might," he said, "but wouldn't you regret it later?"

"I never have before," she said. "It's sort of my trademark." She reached both hands up under her skirt.

During her long drive in, Marlene had rehearsed her speech. She thought that if they could just keep quiet and let her say it, and played along, they could all get through this pretty well. In addition to the crazy stuff, there was a lot of what Marlene still thought of as divine-intervention love in the Karp family. And it was also helpful that all its members were essentially decent people. Except for her. And she wasn't quite sure about Zak, although he was still young.

In the event the thing went off well enough. She sat stiffly in a chair in her kitchen (her former kitchen?) and spoke to the three children, who stood before her in a group. A speech from the throne. She said, "Babies, I'm barely hanging on here, and if you ask me any questions about what I'm doing, or why I'm not here, or when I'm coming back I will die. I'm not going to make up happy stories about it. It's bad and I can't disguise it. I've been a terrible liar, I thought I was being smart, that I was trying for . . . oh, forget that, I don't want to justify what I did. But now all we have is the truth."

She paused, forcing herself to look at their faces, Lucy's patient, Zak's closed and hurt, Giancarlo intently listening, his eyes invisible behind his dark glasses, leaning slightly against his brother. She wished for a cigarette, a prop.

"The truth is that this is a big day for the man I love most in the world and if I have anything to do about it, it's going to be a good day. We are, I am, going to pack all the family garbage into plastic bags for one day and just concentrate on making it right for your father. Can we just do that?"

Giancarlo said, "But if we do that and we're all happy and like that, like we used to be, you'll start crying and you'll have to think about why you're not here with us."

"Yes, but you know, sweetheart, I think I can just suck it in enough so that won't happen. I think for once I can just be here now. It's supposed to be the route to true happiness anyway."

A brief silence and then Lucy said, "That's good, Mom. Did I tell you Dan's here?"

"No. That's great. He's lurking while we have our family conference."

"Yes, and I'm going to go back there and ease him into the flow." She kissed Marlene on the cheek and walked off.

"They're kissing all the time," said Zak. "They never stop."

• • •

Karp reeled into the eighth floor men's room and leaned on a sink. His face felt as though someone was holding a velvet throw cushion gently but firmly down on it. His lips and tongue seemed the size of hamburger rolls. The floor rolled slowly under his feet, which seemed farther away than they ordinarily were.

I'm drunk, he thought. Drunk as a skunk. Or a lord. He sort of enjoyed the rolling-floor feeling, but not the velvet-cushion one. Despite knowing he was drunk, he felt fine, not in the least impaired, or rather not so impaired that a little extra care would not put him right. The Inner Karp, however, informed the drunk that this feeling was exactly what led people to climb into motor vehicles and drive them at full speed down the wrong side of the freeway, under the impression that they were fully in control of the situation.

The Inner Karp also took this opportunity to inquire why Karp was doing this, getting drunk just before such an important and prestigious occasion. Karp strove for an answer; he was interested, too. A phrase floated up from memory: You're wound up so tight that one day you're going to crack and when that happens, look out! His wife's voice. First or second wife? Hard to tell; they had both expatiated on the theme. Can't believe I married a man who doesn't drink. That was definitely Marlene. Days of wine and roses? The drunk drawing the partner down the drain of self-destruction. Not really. Marlene was what she called a maintenance drunk. Come to that, Jack Keegan was pretty nearly in the same class, along with half the cops and judges in New York. And a binge every twenty years was not exactly a ticket to Betty Ford. But why now?

You couldn't discount Stupenagel's presence, the woman did drive him crazy, her challenging routine, daring him to match her drinking, as if that were some kind of achievement. And also not wanting to look like a wuss in front of Murrow. And why had Murrow brought that cognac? To celebrate, obviously, and it had gotten out of hand.

Or had it? Karp splashed some water on his face and dried it on a rough paper towel. Karp did not let things get out of hand, not consciously anyway, and only where his wife was concerned. Marlene was perpetually out of hand. So . . . he **wanted** to get drunk? The room swam, the white walls wavered like the reflection in a swimming pool. Karp fought off a wave of nausea. No, there was a purpose here, the need for some greater access to the reptilian brain. Down there must lie the answer to . . . what? What was the question? Why he felt this way. He had won, triumphed over everything, it had been a great year and the next would be even better. Why then did he feel like everyone knew a secret that he didn't know? He gets to be prom queen but it's all a big practical joke, a pig date on a metropolitan scale.

A toilet flushed, a stall door swung open, and out walked a man named Kevin Battle. Chief Inspector Battle was the chief of staff of the police commissioner's office and one of the major foundation stones of the Blue Wall. He had survived half a dozen PCs and confidently expected to be PC himself someday soon. He startled a little when he saw Karp. Karp was not his favorite person this year, so his smile was even more full and false than it usually was.

"Butch Karp! Man of the hour!" Solid slap on shoulder. "How're you doin' fella?"

"Fine, Chief. You're with the DA and his . . . ?" Karp couldn't actually say "cronies" so he hung the end of the sentence on silence. Battle did not seem to notice.

"Oh, yeah, just sitting around telling lies. You ought to come by and tell some yourself. We were wondering where you'd got to?"

"I'm talking to a reporter. Telling lies myself."

Hearty laugh. The guy was good, Karp thought. He hates my guts and if I didn't actually know that, I would think he was being genuinely friendly. Karp had the same sort of feeling he had when he heard a great musician play or saw a great athlete perform: I will never be able to do that no matter how hard I try. That effortless phoniness. He wondered, not for the first time, whether this defect was a deadly disadvantage in his chosen walk of life.

Battle said, "You want to be careful around the jackals, fella. They'll eat you alive." He washed his hands, dried them, inspected his heavily decorated uniform in the mirror, brushed off a bit of lint. He paused at the door, his sharp blue eyes narrowing slightly as he gave Karp an appraising look.

"You all right? You look a little pale."

"I'm fine, Chief." Forming the words with extra care.

"Yeah? You don't look fine. A little early celebrating, huh?"

"A friendly drink with well-wishers." Change the subject. "So, do you have anything new on the governor?"

"Yeah, we just got the word he's on the Deegan, behind a snow plow. They said figure forty-five minutes. By the way, you know anything at all about this heating plant? Jack couldn't get through to anyone. If they don't turn it on there's gonna be ice on the walls by the time the big fella gets here."

"I know nothing," said Karp easily. "It's a shame, we wanted to give him a warm welcome."

Another hearty laugh, and Battle slipped away.

But before he did, he gave Karp a look. It was a half-humorous, half . . . something else. Pitying? Contemptuous? Karp didn't know, but he had seen it far too often on the faces of Keegan and the various political hierarchs he hung with. Karp had met them all—party bosses, borough presidents, big contributors, judges—in various meetings the DA had arranged in the past months. Karp always got the big hello, the two-handed political handshake, the shoulder grip, but always there was that peculiar look. It was, of course, impossible to confront any of them on it. They'd think him crazy, or crazier than they probably thought him already.

Now it was less than an hour to the event and he still didn't know the punch line of the joke everyone else seemed to know. Maybe the governor would know what it was. Karp thought that if he got a little drunker, he might just ask him.

"Did you hear any of that?" Lucy asked as she entered the guest room and closed and locked the door. Dan Heeney, on the bed, looked up from the Powerbook on his lap and slipped down his headphones. "Say what?"

"Oh, nothing," she said, and lay down next to him. "What're you doing?"

"Well, since Zak told me you have a superwireless node in this building, I've been downloading some stuff from NASA, the new MAP data."

"Map of what?"

"No, it stands for Microwave Anisotropic Probe. It's a deep-space research satellite. It measures the background radiation of the big bang. Are you bored yet?"

"Almost. You're sure you don't want to come to this thing? You could see me in a little black dress."

"I'll see you before you leave. I'll pick lint off of you."

"But we'll go to a fancy restaurant after. We could sit together and play footsie."

"Gee, tempting, but I already agreed to do a conference with a couple of guys at Cal Tech and a guy at Case. Some fairly heavy hitters are supposed to join in. Besides, it should just be family going. How's your mom, by the way?"

"Ruined. Crazy, but holding it all together with masking tape and rusty wires. It's like the House of Atreus when she shows up."

"The who?"

"A Greek myth about getting paid back for your bad deeds unto the fourth generation. The Greeks were an ancient people who lived far across the sea. . ."

"Yeah, ha ha. We'uns din need no furriners up t' th' homeplace. Nossiree bob! We'uns spoke English jes like the Lord Jesus done."

"Barbarian hick. Anyway, it just kills me to see her like that. It hurts worse than torture in a way, you know? Because I don't have any memory of the pain. We don't, really, it doesn't get stored that way. We have empathy, yeah; my dad's got an awful knee injury and when he sees a guy get hurt on TV, it drives him nuts. He says he feels it all over again. That's not the same thing as recall. But spiritual pain goes on and on, because we **can** remember it. What we did to someone else, our sins against them, what we failed to do, how we let down the people who loved us, how we were violated and humiliated in the spirit."

"That's hard to believe," he said. "If I was mooning about, I don't know, the problem of evil or whatever, and I got a tooth abscess, I'd dump that high-tone speculation pretty fast."

"Not the same thing at all," said Lucy. "Yeah, you'd stop those thoughts and go to the dentist and get it fixed and then you'd have the problem of evil all over again, and the memory of the abscess wouldn't interfere with that spiritual pain. It might make it worse."

"Yeah, but it's her problem, not yours."

"Well, see? Physical pain can block it for a while, as can pleasure, which is why they sell so much heroin. And that's all I want to say about it."

She wormed closer and slid the laptop to the

floor. "So, could you render me unconscious right now?"

"We're fresh out of heroin."

"Use your mouth, then," she said.

Why don't they cancel this goddamn thing, Murrow thought again, looking out the window into what seemed a wall of grits, so thick was the fall of snow. He also thought, This is what hell is going to be like, trapped in a room, waiting for an event indefinitely postponed, with someone very much like Ariadne Stupenagel. He wished fervently that he had been a better man heretofore, and instantly resolved upon the reform of his character. He glanced upward past the window to the ceiling, its pipe, its sprinkler head, and the sprinkler head's new decoration, a pair of lacy lavender silk panties. It had only taken her two tries. Murrow wondered whether Karp would hold him responsible for this. Probably. He tried to estimate whether, if they moved the desk and Karp stood upon it, and upon, say, three volumes of the Criminal Code, he could reach it and pull it down. Drunk. Falling, breaking his neck. The scandal . . .

The demon reporter was slouched in Karp's big chair. She was facing the window, muttering and swinging her big bottle like a metronome, clunking it dully at the end of each stroke against Karp's desk. A maddening sound. Every dozen or so beats the bottle would rise into sight and then vanish again as she drank a slug, and then **clunk, clunk.**

Impelled to speak by the Sartrean horror of the moment, Murrow said, "They're going to have to cancel this."

The chair spun around. She pointed the champagne's snout at him like a shotgun. "That's where you're wrong, my son. They'll never cancel this, not if a fucking glacier came down from the Catskills and buried the Bronx. The gov can't be seen to be stopped by a little snow. It would make his little willy seem smaller than the willy of the mayor, and that would never do. Ninety percent of American politics is about who has the biggest willy. And there's another reason." She looked stupidly at the mouth of the bottle for a moment as if the other reason dwelt there, and then stuck it into her own mouth.

"What reason?"

"Ah," she said, "that would be telling. See the way it works is I ask **you** and you tell **me** and then you read all about it. But here's a hint: how could they possibly have picked a situation that would get this event less publicity than holding it on a Friday afternoon the week before Christmas. Okay, they didn't order the storm, but since they have it, they for sure ain't going to waste it. This party is destined for page eleven below the fold, and not even local TV coverage."

"They didn't want to publicize it."

"No, and that's why I'm here. You would be surprised at how many good stories start at events no one is supposed to go to. Embassy cocktail parties thrown by second-rate countries. Unveilings of statues of national poets no one's ever heard of. Friday afternoon coronations of obscure legal bureaucrats."

"But why?"

The answer to this was a snicker. The chair swiveled back until the reporter faced the window. The champagne bottle swung and clunked against the desk. A shadow appeared in the glass of the door. Murrow felt a pulse of relief at Karp's return, until he noted that the shadow wasn't nearly tall enough. The door opened and in walked a small elderly man swathed in a fur-collared overcoat and a fur hat, both thickly encrusted with snow. The man brushed this off and looked around Karp's office owlishly. He did not fail to notice the panties on the sprinkler or that the long, booted legs reflected in the window pane did not belong to Butch Karp.

"You look like you been having a party," he said. "Where is everybody?"

The chair swiveled. "Oh, Guma," said the reporter. "Did you bring anything to drink?"

"What a question!" said Ray Guma, drawing from the deep pockets of his overcoat two unopened fifths of Teacher's scotch.

"What've you been up to, Guma?" asked Stupenagel. Her glass, which had held cognac and champagne, now was half full of scotch. She held it up to the cold light of the ceiling fixture to check for insects and other floaters, a habit born in the third world, where the scotch is often not what it should be.

"Dying," said Guma. "They tell me it's in remission now, but meanwhile I got about twelve inches of gut left and I'm missing half the accessories."

"Oh, spare us the details! To tell you the absolute truth, I thought you were dead already."

"To tell you the absolute truth, I am," said Guma. Murrow could believe it. He had heard stories of Guma's exploits in the old days, and it was hard to credit them to the withered man hunched in his coat on the couch, who had once been infamous as the Mad Dog of Centre Street. He looked like the mummy of a monkey, although his eyes still glowed with a calculating intelligence.

"I'm like in that Christmas carol movie, the ghost of Christmas past," Guma continued. "I hope you've been good, Stupenagel."

"Very, but not through any fault of my own. Being bad has fallen out of fashion, I think."

After a moment's reflection, Guma said, "You know, Stupenagel, you really broke my heart back there when I was jumping your bones. I really thought we had something."

"We did have something, Goom. You had information I wanted, and I had a warm body and we exchanged, quid pro fucking quo."

"No, just come out and say it," said Guma. "You don't have to let me down easy."

Another snorting laugh from Stupenagel. Murrow looked at the two of them and tried to keep the horror off his face, as he envisioned this pair going at it. Where was Karp? Murrow discovered that he had a glass of whiskey in his hand. He definitely did not want to drink anymore. Guma and Stupenagel seemed to have forgotten him. They were talking companionably about events of some years back, when they had apparently had their inconceivable fling. Stupenagel was saying, "Yeah, I spent time in Guatemala, in India, in Mexico, in Argentina, in fucking Sudan, all places where beating up the press is practically like a requirement for promotion in the police, and I didn't get a scratch. I come home to the land of the free and what happens? I get pounded to shit by a corrupt cop. No wonder I drink."

Murrow slipped out like a ferret and went straight to the men's room. He dumped the scotch down the sink and used the glass to drink tap water, as much as he could hold, a trick his mother had recommended as a way to flush the toxins from the system and avoid a hangover. As he did so, he could not help noticing an almost operatic performance from the last toilet stall. Someone was, as they used to say in his prep school, blowing lunch, although it sounded like breakfast, too, and the dinner from the night before. He waited, and was not entirely surprised when Karp emerged.

"Well, that was fun," said Karp when he saw his underling. "Care to join me in a puke?"

"No, I'm a diluter, not an expeller," Murrow said, holding up a glass of New York's purest. "How do you feel?"

"Like a street person has been living in my oral cavity. Can I borrow your glass? Dilution sounds good."

Murrow looked on in wonder as Karp drank. After a long while he said, "Croton Reservoir's on the phone, boss. They're hearing sucking noises and they'd like you to cut back a little."

Karp laughed briefly, put down the glass, and washed his face. "Tell me, Murrow, do you do this often?"

"Not that much anymore. But I did, nearly every weekend, from about age seventeen to a couple of years ago."

"May I ask why?"

"Oh, I guess sex was a lot of it, it helps in going to bed with people you shouldn't really go to bed with. And blessed amnesia, relaxation of every moral code, tolerating boring, stupid people—the usual. And habit. I grew up with parents who drank martinis at five-thirty, every single day."

"Amazing," said Karp, shaking his head. "And you're still alive and halfway competent. I salute you. Is that woman still in my office?"

"Yes, she is," Murrow admitted.

"Still drinking?"

"Steadily. Your pal Guma showed up and brought more jet fuel."

Karp brightened. "Oh, yeah? Good old Guma! Are they playing nice?"

"Sort of. I gather they have a history."

"Yeah, years ago. Being the two most promiscuous heterosexual people in New York with college educations, it was probably a mathematical certainty that they would sooner or later end up in the rack together. It didn't last, though."

"A real shame," said Murrow. "They seem to deserve each other."

Karp gave him a stern look. "Why don't you let **me** be the disapproving puritan, Murrow. It suits my age and status better. Guma happens to be one of my best friends, and Stupenagel is one of my wife's best friends. I realize that neither of them is completely housebroken, and they leave hair on the couch, but they're both the kind of person that they don't make many of anymore, sort of throwbacks to a more dramatic and less politically correct age, and I prize them for it when they're not pissing the hell out of me.

Everything is better nowadays, of course—we don't smoke, we don't drink, we're strictly monogamous, or else if we're not we have to be investigated by the whole fucking legislature and go on **Oprah** to confess, and that's fine and dandy, and it also happens that I was all goody-goody like that, way, **way** before it became fashionable, or required, if you can believe it, but still . . . I detect a certain shrinking of the great human canvas, especially around the neighborhood of the courthouse. Not only do we not have smoke-filled rooms, we barely have mafioso anymore, or political bosses. Instead we have pissant little white-collar criminals on the one hand and brainless thugs on the other. It makes for a lot less interesting life if you're in the business of putting asses in jail. Are we done here, by the way? We hang out together in the men's any longer, people'll start to talk."

"Not that there's anything wrong with that," said Murrow, pushing open the door.

Karp laughed. "Yeah, right. Another cosmic change. In any case, Guma and Stupenagel: both extinct—no, endangered—species. The hard-drinking, I-don't-give-a-shit reporter, and the quasi-legal DA. They're like grizzly bears. Horrible and terrific at the same time. I mean, everyone says, 'Boo-hoo, save the bears,' but would you want one in your backyard, eating the poodle, the cat, little Susie?"

"Why is he quasi-legal?"

"Because Guma is, or was, the reigning expert on La Cosa Nostra in this office, encyclo-fucking-pedic on the subject. He knew them all, the whole Brooklyn Mob, including Murder Incorporated. He was on a first-name basis with every capo regime in the city over the last thirty-five, forty years. He saw them rise and he saw them fall, and helped out in both directions."

"You mean he was corrupt?"

"Not as such. But his relation with the Mob was extremely Sicilian. Guma probably put more Mafiosi in prison than any other living New York prosecutor, but he also let a lot of them go, if he thought it was better for the long-term health of the criminal ecology. Not a strictly legal position, maybe, but one that suited him and the times. It was a risk, too. Swimming with the sharks. The Mob doesn't shoot people like us as a rule, but they'll make an exception for guys who pull shit like Ray pulled from time to time. Giving a break to a slightly dumber and/or less vicious guy so as to grab up a slightly more dangerous gangster—like that. And, of course, that's another thing he's got in common with Stupenagel. College-educated middle-class people usually don't put their bodies on the line in their daily work. That's the way of civilization, of course, which as reasonable men we have to approve, but it's also a little dull. Like you and me, Murrow."

As he said this, Karp experienced a minor epiphany, in that he finally understood why being married to Marlene was necessary to his life. Yes, she drove him crazy, but she also prevented his life from going gray. He thought of the few peers who had been at it as long as he had. Keegan, his caution, his perpetually unsmoked cigar. Others, graying men who wore ratty cardigans in their offices. Some of them had Dickensian eccentricities that everyone excused, but joked about all the same. He shuddered.

"What?" said Murrow.

Karp gave him an inquiring look. "What what?"

"All of a sudden a strange expression appeared on your face, like you discovered the secret of life, or were having a stroke."

Karp let out a short hard laugh and threw a big arm over Murrow's shoulders. "It **was** the secret of life, my son."

"May one know it?"

"When you're older, Murrow. It wouldn't make any sense to you now. Let's go back and join the party and see what excesses our friends have perpetrated in our absence."

"Oh, good," said Guma when Karp and Murrow entered, "you didn't fall in. What the hell is wrong with the heating? My nuts are freezing off."

"No loss to the world, if you ask me," said Stupenagel.

"I didn't ask you," said Guma. "What I asked you was if you could breathe on them to take the chill off, but oh, no . . ."

Karp sat on his couch, a little grumpily, because he could not figure out a polite way of kicking Stupenagel out of his chair. Instead, he said to Guma, "You can't smoke in here, Goom. In fact, you're not supposed to be smoking at all."

Guma admired his big Macanudo and took another puff. "Excuse me, are you speaking as the deputy fire marshal or as my personal fucking physician? Every time I smoke one of these things it takes fifteen minutes off my life, and considering what my life is like nowadays, it's worth it. That's yet another thing that was better in the old days—right, Stupenagel?"

Stupenagel said, "Yes, Karp, we've been sharing some old-fart moments, even though he's, of course, vastly older than I am. Decades. Guma longs for the days when the criminal justice system was even more arbitrary and vicious than it is now, and when, in his phrase, 'you fucking jackals' knew your place, which was to take our split of the graft and stick to the sordid affairs of the lowlifes."

"An exaggeration," said Guma.

"You think the system is arbitrary and vicious?" asked Karp.

"Yes, of course," she said, "don't you?"

"No, not really," said Karp.

Stupenagel swiveled Karp's chair around and stared at him as if he had just wondered why, if the Earth was a ball, the people on the bottom half didn't fall off. Karp noticed this, and also that she had somehow partially undrunked herself. Her jaw had stiffened up and her eyes were no longer floating in a boozy sea. He recalled that this was one of Stupenagel's more valuable journalistic talents, but whether it was a result of ruse or immense natural capacity, he had never been able to tell.

"I mean, it's not what it should be," he continued, "it's a human institution, like the church and the press. Humans are fallible beings."

"There's no comparison at all," she replied. "The press, my sweet fanny! What if every time I wanted to run a story I had to convince twelve high school graduates selected at random that it was true, while some other guy tried to convince them it was false."

"You'd be wrong less often?" suggested Karp.

"Excuse me, but if we had to print retraction notices as often as DNA evidence freed people you guys convicted, we wouldn't have any room for the bra ads, and Guma would stop reading the paper. Can you really sit there and tell me that the American justice system has **any** other purpose than the aggrandizement of fucking lawyers? Oh, and to make sure that rich people don't have to pay for their crimes any more than once or twice a decade. Do you realize that over ninety percent of the people in this country believe that some innocent people are convicted of murder? A hundred and fucking ten murder and rape convictions at last count thrown out because of genetic testing."

"What's the alternative? The Star Chamber?"

"Yes, that's what you guys always say, although we have no evidence at all that the Star Chamber was any less unjust than trial by jury. The reason they invented juries in the first place was so that the English barons could do what they damn well pleased and be tried by their pals instead of having to face the king's justice. It's **designed** to give the rich a better break than the poor—that's what it's fucking **for.**"

"Commie pinko atheist slut," said Guma. "I guess the way they do it in Red China is better."

"No, but the Euros get by without juries very well, thank you, and their crime rates are a tenth what ours are."

"That's a non sequitur," said Karp. "The crime rate has nothing to do with juries."

"No, but it's got to have something to do with your fucked-up system. Hey, you want to warehouse a third of the black male population? Go right ahead! But don't dress it up like it's justice."

"Oh," said Guma, "now she's gonna go with

the oppressed minorities. Wait a second, let me get out my towel."

"Asshole! Tell him he's an asshole, Karp."

Karp, who had occasionally entertained private flashes of the type the reporter was expressing, said nothing, but took refuge in aphorism: "The law is born from despair about human nature: Ortega y Gasset," he intoned, which put a temporary stopper on the conversation. After a moment, Karp said to Murrow, "Listen, go find that woman from the governor's office and get a straight answer out of her about if and when this thing is going to start."

Marlene spent a reasonably pleasant hour watching Zak conquer Asia on the computer, and listening to Giancarlo play some new songs and watching him demonstrate a device that read pages in a book and spoke the text in a creaky mechanical voice. As she had promised, she did not break down. Around noon, Lucy and Dan emerged from the guest room, hand in hand. Marlene observed that her daughter's mouth, already generous, seemed puffed across half her face and that her normally dull skin shone with a milky light, except for the numerous red marks. Lucy engineered a lunch: cold shrimp quiche, salad, and white wine for the big people, zapped frozen tacos and lemonade for the boys. Giancarlo

valiantly charmed and, Marlene noted with pleasure, Dan Heeney stepped up to the plate and
batted a few long balls in that department, too. An
excellent addition to the Karp family, she thought,
and would get along fine with whichever respectable woman Karp would next take up with.

After that it was time to get ready. Marlene
bathed in the big tub she had made long ago out
of a black rubber electroplating bath she had
found onsite when she'd first taken this loft. What
a long time ago it seemed, before SoHo, before
Karp and the children, before the first killing. She
stayed in the bath for a long time, not long
enough to wash her sins away, but long enough to
have a good silent weep, and to prompt her
daughter to tap discreetly on the door.

She dressed in baggy slacks of heavy, braided
black silk, tucked into knee boots and a long wool
tunic that buttoned down the front. By the time
she emerged from the bedroom, the family was
dressed and ready, the boys looking strangely
unformed in jacket and tie, Lucy surprisingly elegant in the little black number.

"Don't rush," said Lucy. "I called. Flynn said
the whole thing's been delayed for a couple of
hours."

Murrow returned five minutes later. "They're
setting up the cameras again," said Murrow. "The

man is entering the building as we speak. They're saying half an hour."

Stupenagel slid out of Karp's chair and turned toward the window. "And the snow seems to be letting up. I can see across the square now." She stepped back and checked her reflection in the glass. She hiked her skirt up and around and tucked in her shirt, then reached into her bag and brought out a compact, which she flipped open.

Guma said. "If you're gonna shave your legs, Stupenagel, I believe I'll ask to be excused."

"I never shave my legs," she replied, examining herself critically in the mirror. She wielded a hairbrush. "I have a Moldavian who likes to yank the hairs out with his teeth, one by one."

The three men watched as she whipped through a quick and efficient toilette, finishing with a blast of breath spray. She looked as though she had been supping tea and ladyfingers for the past three hours, rather than guzzling large quantities of assorted alcohols.

"Well, boys, I think I'll circulate and collect lies. Thanks for the drinks and the philosophy." She hoisted her bag onto her shoulder.

"Aren't you going to take your underpants?" Murrow asked grumpily.

She fixed him with a look down her long nose, one that made Murrow acutely aware of how much taller she was than he. "And what underpants would those be, sir?"

"The ones on the sprinkler head."

She made a show of peering at them. "Lovely. What makes you think I tossed them up there?"

"What makes me think . . . ? Jesus, Stupenagel, I saw you yank them off and throw them."

"Yet another demonstration of the unreliability of the eyewitness. In an alcohol-driven sex fantasy, you imagined me removing my underwear and tossing it up there, but in fact I am wearing the pair I set out with this morning. Would you like to check?"

"Yes!"

"Care to put some money on it, sonny? Say a hundred bucks my loins are enclosed in a pair of chaste and hygienic Hanes cottons, in black?"

Murrow looked desperately at Guma and Karp; the former was intently examining the damp tip of his cigar, the latter made an almost imperceptible negative motion of his head.

"I've been set up," said Murrow.

"I don't know **what** you're talking about, dear boy," she said, "but clearly you're not about to put your money where your mouth is, so I will bid you all a temporary adieu. Butch, if your lovely bride shows up, tell her I said hi, and to give me a call sometime. Guma, let me know when you die, okay? I'll send a wreath."

She left. Both Guma and Murrow blew kisses at the door. Karp sat down behind his desk and said, "Listen, both of you: speaking of being set up, why am I getting these weird looks whenever any of the big boys mentions me being the DA?"

"Weird looks?" asked Murrow.

"Yeah. Like they all know something I don't know. What is it, I'm going to be standing up there being sworn in and a big bucket of blood is going to come down on my head like in **Carrie?** What?"

"That must be about the pool," said Murrow after a nervous silence.

"What pool?"

"The one about how long you'll last before fucking up so bad politically that the governor can ask you to resign with no shit sticking to him."

"Oh," said Karp. "Why didn't you tell me about this before?"

"I thought you'd disapprove. I mean, of my involvement."

"In the pool? You're betting I'm going to get canned?"

"No, I'm running the pool. I'm taking the bets. The line is fifteen to one you won't last the year, and forty to one you won't win election if you run."

"I'll take some of that action," said Guma and laughed, and then Murrow joined him and finally Karp, who said, "Tell me, does Jack Keegan have any money in the pool?"

"Yeah, but he's picking up some of my risk. Like me, he thinks you'll hang in there."

"That's a surprise."

"No it ain't," said Guma confidently. "Keegan knows he's a twisty, ambitious prick, but he also knows that you're the closest thing to a reincarnation of Francis Phillip Garrahy that he's likely to see in this life. And he loved Phil. As long as it doesn't hurt his ambitions he'd like to see one like him in the DA. Which is why he's kept you around all these years, and protected you, when it would've been a lot better for him to have given you the boot. And why he used a bunch of chips with the party of evil to get you the appointment. You didn't realize this?"

"It's particle physics to him," said Murrow and Karp was about to come back with a rejoinder when the phone rang. He listened for a moment or two, and Murrow, observing his face, asked, "Bad news?" Karp held up a shushing hand and continued to listen. He said, "I understand" several times and hung up.

"What?" asked Murrow.

"Bomb threat," said Karp.

"Here?"

"Yeah, it sounded like the real thing, too. They said they're going to take down this building unless we release Feisal ibn-Salemeh."

Rashid clicked off his cell phone, put his car in gear, and drove carefully away. It was his supreme moment, giving orders to Karp in that way. He felt for the first time in his life entirely in control. Except for the car.

He had never driven in this kind of snow before, and the tension of driving racked his nerves. But besides that, he felt everything had worked out remarkably well, a tribute to his organizing genius: the gigantic coup was now fact, all the layers of deception jerked away to reveal the perfection of their plan, nearly six years in the making: assembling the papers and the money, infiltrating the sleepers, buying the necessary firms, gaining the skills. Then those morons had blown up the World Trade Center and suddenly no Arab could move freely around the country and they had had to recruit Felix. A mistake as it turned out, but he had brilliantly compensated for it, and no real harm done, because of the depth, the intricacy of the plan. The bidding for the contract to supply two boilers for the building, which, of course, they won. Everyone knew that Americans thought only of money, so in order to gain access to any place all you had to do is become the low-bid contractor. He had seen that the boilers were put in place, he had led the quick violent action that neutralized the few outside workmen. His troops were completely in charge of the courthouse basement. Rashid had wired the blasting cap to a cell phone ring circuit, and left the construction site and driven a few streets away and made his call. All that was needed now was for Carlos and Felípe to arrive from the Inwood site with a plastic pipe full of acetone peroxide crystals. They would insert the pipe into a hollow drilled into the seventeen thousand pounds of ammonium nitrate that filled one of the boilers. Placing the initiator charge was the trickiest part of the operation, but ibn-Salemeh had been adamant about doing it that way. You had to have a good burn to bring down a prewar building of solid masonry and steel, and the initiator was essential to a good burn. But the peroxide was sensitive stuff and it had to be made fresh before use.

Rashid checked his watch. At this moment Carlos would be installing the initiator into the heart of the great bomb.

He drew the car to the curb, or at any rate out of the middle of the street. He had not counted on the snow, but it seemed to be letting up and would make no difference to the success of the plan. He had to keep moving because they would be trying to pinpoint the location of the cell phone from which the calls originated. He sat for a moment with the heater running full blast, enjoying the quiet of the blanketed city. Then his cell phone warbled. That would be Carlos giving the coded message that the bomb was ready for detonation, that the booby traps guarding it were in place, and that the whole crew was out of the building. He answered the phone and waited. But it wasn't the coded message.

"They're not answering at the courthouse," said Lucy, hanging up the phone.

"It's probably crazy there, with the snow and the governor and the ceremony," said Marlene. "Let's just go."

"Can't we finish this game?" asked Zak.

"No," answered his mother, tossing in her cards, "you'll have your whole life to play hearts. Get your coats!"

So they bid Dan good-bye and bundled up in their warmest and hit the frozen streets. It was the kind of day when not people who love people, but people who own four-by-four high-bed pickup trucks with knobby tires, feel like the luckiest people in the world.

"It seems to be letting up," observed Marlene as she steered east on a nearly empty Grand Street.

"Yeah, from a total white-out blizzard," said Lucy, sitting next to her. "I'm glad it's you driving." In the family, Marlene was famous for her winter driving skills. As she passed Baxter, Marlene found that the sole lane down the center of the snowy road was blocked by a plumbing company van. The driver had skidded sideways and was now doing the worst possible thing, gun-ning his engine, spinning his wheels, and digging himself in even deeper.

"That moron!" said Marlene and rolled down her window. "Don't do that!" she yelled, "Rock it!" The engine up ahead continued to roar, however, and sent up blue clouds of stinking smoke.

"Can you back up?" asked Lucy.

"No, there's a big tow truck behind me," said Marlene, after checking her side mirrors. "Crap!" The tow truck honked its air horn helpfully.

Then the passenger-side door of the van opened and a man jumped out. He walked back to the rear of his truck and examined the situation, which was that the rear wheels were sunk to the hubs and spinning on solid ice. He yelled to the driver, who stuck his head out of the window and yelled back. The wheels stopped spinning. The man opened the double rear doors of the van and yelled something else. The driver stepped down from the van.

"That's Tamazight," said Lucy.

"What?"

"Those guys are speaking Tamazight, like the guy we saw . . ." She rolled her window down and looked out at the man behind the plumber's van, who was now talking into a cell phone.

"That's him," said Lucy. "That's Maybe Gonzales. What're they doing out here? Should we call the cops? Mom?"

• • •

Marlene doesn't answer. She is staring at the man, who has put his cell phone away and is now removing a short length of three-inch plastic pipe from the rear of the van. The tow truck honks again. Marlene understands what she's seeing, and understands what she has to do. She hands Lucy her cell phone.

"Yeah, call the cops. Tell them we've spotted people who are probably members of the Manbomber gang, right next to the courthouse. They've got what looks like big pipe bombs. Give them the details on the guys, and remind them that the governor is in the courthouse right now. Then call Dad and tell him the same thing."

"What are you going to do?" Lucy asks. She doesn't like the look on her mother's face.

"Call," says Marlene and slips from the cab of the truck. She goes to the rear and pops the camper door.

Zak asks, "What's going on, Mom? Why did we stop?"

"A little problem. Look, both of you, it's real important that you stay here with Lucy. I have to go and check on something."

She takes a key ring out of her bag and uses a cylinder key to open a steel lock box bolted to the bed of the truck. The can suppressor is still screwed to the barrel of the Beretta nine-millimeter from the night she used it on Cherry and her dealer.

"What's going on, Mom?" asks Giancarlo. The guide dog whimpers.

She has not cleaned the pistol, has not wanted to think about the pistol at all. Now here it is in her hand again, with her nonblind son staring at it and her with a mix of horror and fascination she cannot bear seeing. She slams the camper door on his protesting cry.

She runs forward. The two men are trudging through the drifts, two men in black coveralls, each one carrying a short length of gray, three-inch pipe capped on each end. She shouts to them to stop. They turn and see her and her gun. They start to run, slipping and sliding in the snow.

Karp is closeted in the DA's office with the DA and the governor of New York and all the senior NYPD people on the premises, and the governor's security chief.

"He was real clear," said Karp, and not for the first time. "There's a bomb in the basement big enough to destroy the entire building and he'll set it off unless he hears from ibn-Salemeh that his release is under way. He said we're not to bring in the feds, not to inform the press, and not to bring any additional police onto the scene. He said they're observing the building and if any move is made to evacuate it, or to move cops in, they'll blow it up. He gave us two hours."

Everyone looked at the governor. The governor looked at Karp. "Are we sure this isn't a bluff?"

"Well, I can't say from the conversation I had with him, Governor, but the connect between ibn-Salemeh and the Manbomber is fairly explicit by now. We shouldn't be in any doubt that these people can build, deliver, and explode bombs. And they don't care about killing people one bit."

The state police security man, a fellow named Lambert, said, "Governor, the limo is waiting right outside the DA entrance on Leonard Street. I can't see how they could learn you're moving, give the order, and explode the bomb before we had you safe and away."

The governor ignored this. "What about the other people in the building? How many are there, Jack?"

Keegan said, "Usually about fifteen hundred, and we have more than the usual number of kids in the day-care center. It's the big day for judicial staff Christmas parties and people like to bring family. There's usually well over a hundred. Do you want an exact count?"

"No, it's more than enough. We're staying." He turned to an aide. "Get Auburn on the phone. I want to talk to the warden."

While this was being done, they heard the

sounds of a scuffle outside, a loud male voice and a higher female one, indignant. Karp stood up and walked to the door. Outside in the narrow corridor, his secretary was facing off with a state trooper twice her size.

Flynn met Karp's eye. "It's your daughter. She says it's an emergency and this lummox wouldn't let me by to tell you."

There is an excavation on the Baxter Street side of the courthouse. Half the street and all of the sidewalk have been taken up and replaced by a pit shored up on three sides by raw two-by-eights. On the fourth side is a ramp faced with perforated steel plates and large enough for a five-ton truck. This is how they moved material for the cooling and heating renovations down into the basement. Marlene sees the two men disappear down the ramp and she follows. A hole has been cut in the side of the building and shored with steel girders. Past that is the basement proper. Marlene sees them enter a hallway. Crouching slightly, she pursues them. She is thinking, These are the people who killed Pete, and Nora and those others, and all the self-pitying feelings of the day and the previous days are gone, and she is focused on the passing instant only, in full predator mode.

She is in a hallway, painted pale green. There

are black bloodstains on the floor and two bodies, both of men in construction worker clothing. A man steps from a doorway holding a Skorpion submachine gun. He fires a burst at Marlene but he doesn't aim low enough and she hears the rounds snapping over her head and whining down the hall. She raises her pistol and without breaking her stride shoots him in the chest and face. He falls in the doorway and she trots forward and steps over him.

Marlene is on a small landing. Steel steps lead down to the floor of the main boiler room. Six men are on the floor of the room. Two of them are the men in coveralls she has chased here and the other four are wearing construction gear. Of these, three are armed with pistols or submachine guns. The scene is very clear and sharp to her, almost unnaturally so, like a museum diorama showing how the Indians made pemmican. There is a rough table in the center of the group, on which lie the two plastic tubes. One of them has been opened and wires emerge from it. These wires are wrapped around others coming from a cellular phone with its case removed. The man wrapping the wires looks up like a high school teacher interrupted at a demonstration of some elementary physics fact. It is Maybe Gonzales, the Berber. Because Marlene has a silenced weapon, they don't realize that she is killing them for a few seconds and so she takes out Gonzales and two of

the armed ones and then there is a return fusil-
lade from the floor and she has to retreat.

Lucy's 911 call got a lot of attention. The 911 system has been trained to take bomb threats very
seriously, and after the operator had determined
that Lucy Karp was a real person, and responsible, and the daughter of the soon-to-be DA, and
that the threat was lodged in the courthouse, the
governor also being onsite, things moved with
dispatch. The recent events in New York had
caused to be created several specialized
Emergency Service Units to deal with terrorists.
One of these teams was lodged in police headquarters, a few hundred yards from the courthouse. Three minutes after being scrambled, two
extremely costly specialized black, four wheel-
drive vehicles were racing up Baxter Street,
loaded with enthusiastic, heavily armed men.

"Where are you now?" Karp asked.

"On Baxter, about a hundred feet from the
north end of the courthouse," said Lucy. "I can
see the construction hole Mom went down. Here
come the cops."

"Cops? Christ, Lucy, we're not supposed to
bring any cops in. He said they'd blow the building if we did."

"Who said?"

"Never mind that! I want you to go away from the building. Take the boys and leave."

"But what about Mom?"

"Lucy, take the boys and go! Run!"

Rashid tried again to raise Felípe on his cell phone, to no avail. There had been no message from Carlos giving the ready signal, but there had been one from the boy he had watching the courthouse, telling of lights and sirens and the arrival of the police in strength. It was the snow, he thought. The initiator had been delayed by the snow and their timetable had been thrown off. No one could have counted on the snow. So he could not really be blamed. But the men were armed, they should have no trouble fending off the police for the few moments it would take to rig the bomb. The chief would, of course, be angry, but on the other hand, as Rashid would explain to him, the success of such an operation would make it possible, perhaps, to win his release with a mere threat. That was definitely the line to take. Against that, there was the loss of Carlos and Felípe, or Mamoud and Habib, valuable men, but not irreplaceable, and a few others. He picked up his cell phone again and dialed a long-memorized number.

His heart missed a beat. He should have heard the explosion from here, the entire city should have heard it. He dialed again and again. Nothing. He does not know what to do now. He sits paralyzed.

A garbage truck-mounted snow plow, its yellow light flashing, is moving down the street. His car is blocking it. The plow driver honks. Rashid backs up too quickly, fishtails, smashes his rear lights against another car. There is a police car behind the snow plow. Its occupant gets out and walks around the garbage truck to see what the problem is. He walks over to Rashid's car and raps on the window with his knuckle. Rashid rolls it down. The cop looks in. At roll call that afternoon, this patrolman had been cautioned against racial profiling. Yes, they were looking for Arab men, but that didn't mean they could roust anyone who looked Arab. You had to have something else, some probable cause. And they had distributed sketch artist pictures of three men made from witnesses of the neighbors of that house that had blown up in Astoria.

The cop took a long look at this guy and thought that he looked enough like one of the guys in the sketch to constitute probable cause. Besides, it was freezing out and the guy was sweating bullets. He backed away.

"Sir, please step out of the car," he said.

Rashid flung the door open violently and

began to run down West Houston Street. The cop had been a fairly good schoolboy safety not too many years ago and it only took him about twenty-five yards to catch Rashid and bring him crashing down on the untrodden snow.

Marlene is sheltering behind a wall and trying to think how many bullets she has left. She is in good position, although outgunned. One of them ought to lay down a base of fire and the others should rush her, but she thinks that this will not occur to them for some time, and then the police will be here. The main thing is that the bomb is not complete. Marlene knows a good deal about bombs and she has decided that what is on the table is a cell phone detonator and a pair of initiator charges. The main charge must be elsewhere. She gets down low and snaps her head around the corner of the door, and someone fires a burst and she shoots at the flash, and then the place explodes.

She is tossed halfway across the corridor when the wall she is leaning against blows out. The ceiling holds; she is not crushed. She does not lose consciousness, but is stunned by the magnitude of the sound. She has gone deaf. Her main problem, however, is sight. The blast from the initiator charge set off by Rashid's phone call has shattered every lightbulb in the basement, and the place is a cave, except for the dim emergency lights. These lights are dim because the air is nearly opaque with dust.

Marlene stands up and starts walking out of the basement. Her face is coated in ancient soot blown loose by the blast and stings from many small cuts. There is one on the side of the bridge of her nose that leaks blood into her good eye, and she has to keep wiping it off. She walks into the murk. After a while she sees flashlight beams ahead. Good, she thinks, the cops.

The DA's suite had been secured by every cop in the building—the DA detective's squad in its entirety and any uniforms or detectives who happened to be in the building at the time. The press had been shoved into a blocked-off hallway where they murmured and groaned like cattle in the vestibule of an abattoir. Inspector Battle was in command, of course, a duty that consisted of screaming into the phone, blaming various officers of the department for allowing this to happen, throwing a wide cordon around lower Manhattan, and attempting to insure that no additional police converged on the courthouse. On being informed that an ESU had rolled on a call some minutes ago, he demanded to be patched through to the unit commander.

He heard the explosion and stopped talking.

Everyone stopped talking, all the little groups of powerful men felt a pang of mortality. The building did not collapse; everyone pretended they had not been frightened.

The governor spoke to the warden at Auburn and explained the situation. Then he called the commander of the state police and arranged for a helicopter to be sent to the prison. An aide approached him just after he put down the phone.

"Governor, we're thinking we should go ahead with the swearing in. It shows coolness under fire. Every one of those reporters has a cell phone and if we don't talk to them pretty soon, we're going to have mobs out there. We want to play it as bomb scare, small explosion, business as usual."

The governor agreed. But when they looked for Karp, he was nowhere to be found.

Detectives Renzi and Butler of the DA squad had been sent to guard the north fire stairway entry on the eighth floor, and as usual had been told zip except not to let anyone in or out. They knew who the approaching figure was and hailed him cordially, although they did not move out of his way.

"Sorry, Butch, no one in or out," said Renzi.

"Are you guys still on the DA squad?" asked Karp.

They acknowledged that they were.

"And am I the DA?"

They looked at each other. "I guess you are, now," said Butler. "Congratulations."

"Thank you. As the DA, I'm ordering you to let me through, and I'm ordering you to follow me down to the basement."

With that, he pushed past them and through the fire door.

As he descended, Karp was thinking about something Marlene had said to him once, that the working class was so invisible to the ruling one that someone dressed in overalls and a hard hat and carrying a greasy clipboard and a couple of tools could get in nearly anywhere. And he recalled what the super, Arno Nowacki, had told him about the boiler job, and the unknown low-bid contractors. Plumbers never got security checks. Of course, that's how they did it, how they moved tons of explosive into the court-house basement in front of everyone's nose. It was as stupid, bold, and effective as 9-11.

They reached the basement, to find the main lights were out and the hallway lit dimly by the emergency lights.

Renzi grabbed his arm. "What's the story here, Butch. What're we down here for and what are we looking for?"

"They didn't tell you anything?"

"Are you kidding?"

"A bunch of terrorists have a bomb in the boiler room. They dragged it in here inside a boiler. They're threatening to blow the building unless we let one of their guys out of Auburn."

The two cops shared a look. "Ah, Butch, um, sir, I think we ought to go back where we were and leave this to the experts."

"You can do what you want," said Karp. "I need to look for my wife." Before they can say another word, he has vanished into the nearly opaque air.

Sergeant Jerome Bishop had been in this special ESU since its inception. On arriving at the courthouse, he had deployed his ten men to block all the exits and then followed his lieutenant and a team of six to find the bad guys. Bishop took the point himself. He was a big, self-confident man, an athlete, a superb shot with a spotless record, and yet he knew that some of the people on the squad still thought that he got the plum assignment because the bosses wanted a black face in there. So he took the point as often as he could, not that he needed to prove anything to assholes, but because he thought it went with the stripes.

He heard the bomb explode and flinched involuntarily, but the ceiling did not come down on them. It was inky, though, and all the ESUs turned on their lights. When the dust came pouring out they were ordered to mask up. Bishop moved cautiously forward into the cone of his light. He heard footsteps and stopped. A figure loomed in his beam, coming toward him. He told the radio net he had a possible perp in view and was ordered to engage and capture him. Bishop had an MP5. He made sure the selector was on single shot and drifted quietly to one side of the hallway.

"Freeze!" Bishop shouted. "Get down!" His shout was muffled by the mask.

The figure kept coming. Was it saying something? He couldn't tell—the sound the mask made against his ears and the net chatter in his ear bud made it hard to hear ambient sounds much softer than a gunshot or a siren. He could see now that it was a slight person dressed all in black, just as in the description the girl gave them. He shouted again for the guy to get down, get down!

Marlene, deaf, raises her hand to wipe the blood away and walks into the flashlight beam. Her eye is dazzled. She calls out, "Hello! Is that the police?"

Bishop sees the figure's hand rise, he sees the gun in it. He understands the rules of engagement. He flicks on his laser sight and the red line reaches out and touches the target's center of mass.

Karp trotted past the still-smoking boiler

room, and stepped over a mangled corpse. In the
thick dust on the floor he saw the print of high-
heeled boots. He saw that they headed toward
the boiler room and away from it. He felt a rush
of relief. He called her name. The dust is thin-
ning a little. He can see lights ahead, flashlights
and the red pencil of a targeting laser.

Bishop hears a shout from the direction of his
target. The red pencil moves. Another target has
appeared, a large man in a suit. It rushes at the
first target and takes it down. More shouts. Bishop
speaks into his radio, and orders his team forward.

"Jesus, Marlene, you could've been shot!
Didn't you hear him shouting to get down?"

She looks at him and shakes her head, points
to her ears. He realizes she can't hear anything.
But he can. Half a dozen gas-masked men in
black are surrounding them, pointing weapons.

"I'm the district attorney," says Karp.

"Get down! Get down! On your face!"

Karp and Marlene do as they are told. The
cops snap handcuffs on them. Sergeant Bishop
wonders why both of his prisoners are hysteri-
cally laughing.